Dark
of the
Moon

Dark
of the
Moon

Tess Pendergrass

Five Star • Waterville, Maine

First Edition
First Printing: December 2003

Set in 11 pt. Plantin by Elena Picard.

Printed in the United States on permanent paper.

Library of Congress Cataloging-in-Publication Data

Pendergrass, Tess.
    Dark of the moon / Tess Pendergrass.
        p. cm.
    ISBN 0-7862-5109-3 (hc : alk. paper)
    1. Police—Fiction. I. Title.
PS3566.E457D49 2003
813'.6—dc21   2002044762

Dark
of the
Moon

Acknowledgments

I want to say a heartfelt thank-you to Sergeant Ron Sligh for sharing his knowledge of the workings of a small-medium town police department and for always being willing to answer "just one more quick question." Thank you also to Amanda Gray, for being my consultant on all things medical (and never flinching at all those e-mails that began, "Now, if you wanted to kill someone . . .").

Any errors, exaggerations or downright fabrications in these areas are solely the responsibility of the author.

I also want to thank John Longshore and Katy Longshore for help with the finer points of movies and beer, Dan Landando for being my automotive guru, Michael Farrington for the necklace scene, and Marilyn Tucker for tracking down the scoop on California's seventh-grade social studies curriculum.

Chapter 1

Some people are more trouble dead than alive.

Destiny Millbrook was blissfully unaware of that truth the morning her ex-boyfriend, Alain Caine, called her from the pay phone outside the Spicy Sicilian Pizzeria.

"You're here in Hope Point?" Shock caused her to bump her elbow against her cereal bowl. She caught the bowl with her free hand just before it slid off onto the kitchen floor. Disappointment showed in the eyes of the lanky yellow Labrador retriever under the table.

"Surprised?" Alain's voice still held that teasing charm she had once found irresistible.

"Yes," she said, distinctly uncharmed, as she swiped at the spilled milk with the edge of the oversized T-shirt she'd slept in. It was due for a wash, anyway. "I am surprised. I thought you were dead."

He laughed. Alain had a light, easy laugh that went well with his light, easy approach to interpersonal relationships. "Don't sound so disappointed."

Destiny let that hang.

"I'm here for the Jasper County Arts and Crafts Fair," he plunged on, undeterred. "I think my watercolors might do well here. You could use some Southwestern sunshine in this place. I never knew this much rain fell anywhere in California."

"I've never seen any of your Southwestern paintings," Destiny reminded him. Although she had to admit that if the rain that had drenched the northern California coast for the past three days kept up much longer, he could probably sell any picture that featured more than one color.

"You've seen that first set. The Sedona series."

Destiny knocked the cereal bowl again. "Where did I see those? On the astral plane? You didn't even put an address on the one postcard you sent after you left Sacramento."

"Whoa." The word stretched into a laugh. "You're not still upset because I had to follow my muse?" He sounded almost touched.

She blew out a long breath. "No." The hurt and resentment hadn't disappeared, but they tasted old and stale, like cookies saved too long for a special occasion. "No. I'm glad to hear you've managed to keep tabs on her."

"Who?"

"Your muse." And a good thing for Alain his muse wasn't as fickle as he was. "I'll have to come by the fair and see your new work."

She might even be able to make civil conversation without wanting to disembowel him. In fact, introducing Alain to Daniel would be even more satisfactory than disembowelment . . .

She must still be half-asleep. Dragging Detective Daniel Parks away from work even to go to his own funeral would be difficult lately. Dragging him to an arts and crafts fair was pure fantasy. But Serena had mentioned wanting to go to the arts fair. She could go with her sister and do some Christmas shopping.

She shuddered. It wasn't even Thanksgiving until next week. She was not ready to think about Christmas.

"Actually, I was hoping to see you sooner than this weekend."

Destiny's trouble antennae twitched. "Why?"

"I've missed you."

A year and a half ago, she might have believed Alain meant that in a serious, relationship kind of missing. She'd come a long way since then.

"You're a beautiful woman, Des. Inside and out. Probably one of the best things that ever happened to me. Don't think it was easy to leave."

It wasn't like Alain to lay it on with a trowel. Could he actually be regretting . . . No. He'd expected her to be desperate to see him again. To greet him like a puppy left too long at the kennel. He hadn't expected to have to work for it.

"Sure," she said. "I understand. The artistic muse is a harsh taskmistress. Look, Alain—"

"I can come by now."

Destiny choked. "Now's not a good time. I'm getting ready to go to work." Or she would be, once she got off the phone.

"I can be there in a couple of minutes."

"Alain!" Something tugged on her shirt, and she tugged back. She ran a hand down to the hem, finding a damp dog nose, the rest of the dog's mouth happily chewing on the milk spots. "Fleur!"

"What?"

"Call me back tonight," Destiny said into the phone, knowing she'd regret it. But the clock on the microwave read 7:43, which meant it was really 8:19, and she had exactly sixteen minutes before she had to be out the door on her way to the Hope Point Branch of the Jasper County Library.

11

Normally Maddy wouldn't mind if she were a couple of minutes late for work, but Destiny was supposed to help her open the library building this morning, getting into the routine for Maddy's vacation next week.

"I need to ask you a favor."

She should have guessed. She couldn't even dredge up outrage. She rose to open the back door. "Out, Fleur. Outside go potty."

Fleur heaved herself up from the linoleum under the table and stared out into the downpour.

"Go on. It's almost like swimming."

Alain ignored the non sequiturs. "Are you ready for this?"

"Why not." She nudged Fleur's rear end with her slipper, and the dog hunched out into the rain.

"A friend and I were going to drive out here together. My friend knows people in Hope Point. You've got an active arts community here, you know." For a damp little nowhere town, his tone added. "Well, that didn't quite work out."

"What didn't?" Destiny dumped her soggy Grape-Nuts down the disposal. She hadn't known Grape-Nuts could get soggy.

"My friend turned out to be not as reliable as I thought. You know, these things happen."

Didn't she just. Like men who moved into your heart and your bathroom and then drove off to Arizona without a backward glance. At least Daniel hadn't skipped states on her. But he hadn't moved into her bathroom, either. She shouldn't find the idea of his old toothbrush in her toothbrush holder so appealing.

"Where's this going, Alain?" A heavy paw thumped against the back door. With her free hand, Destiny snagged a ratty old Star Wars towel off the coatrack hanging beside the doorway. She opened the door and just managed to drop the towel on the cream-colored streak plowing past. Fleur's long, deep shake only sprayed half the room. Not bad.

"I was hoping . . ."

She checked Fleur's water bowl. Fine until she came back for lunch.

"Destiny? Are you listening?"

"Yes." She wouldn't have time for a shower. She'd have to spend the whole day with bed hair. Not that it mattered much. She tried to run a hand through the frizzy mess on her head. When her disastrous impossible-to-get-wrong home perm had begun growing out, she'd gone to a salon to get it touched up. She should have opted for shaving it and starting over.

"Good. Because I really need your help. It would only be for a week and a half. From the arts and crafts fair this weekend through the Christmas Arts Fair in Shell Creek next weekend."

"What would only be a week and a half?" She started down the hall for the bedroom. The rain turned the institutional beige paint and green carpet gloomier than usual.

"I'll be on my way to Santa Cruz a week from Monday. Promise. What I'm saying is, I really need a place to stay."

"*What?*" Destiny tripped over her foot, catching herself on the doorjamb. She didn't know whether to laugh or cry. The idea of Alain's old toothbrush in her bathroom only made her tired. "You can't stay here, Alain."

"Come on, Des. You've got an extra bedroom, don't you? Or at least a couch."

"There are some cheap motels across the bay in Deepwater you might try."

13

"Destiny!" His voice slid over from wheedling to dismay. "I drove all the way here from Arizona. I haven't seen you in almost, what, two years? Three? How long has it been?"

"Sorry, Alain. Good luck. Stay dry." She lowered the phone from her ear and punched the talk button, cutting him off in mid-reminiscence.

She stood for a moment, listening to the rain on the roof. It had taken her time to recover from Alain, a drawn-out process like recovering from a bout of bronchitis. But after falling in love with Daniel, she'd come to realize that Alain's desertion had been more blessing than tragedy.

She had put Alain in her past long ago. She'd come to closure with that episode in her life. It felt good to tell him so. She wasn't worried about leaving him out in the cold.

Knowing Alain, he'd worm his way into someone's home by the time she got off work that afternoon. She might have felt less complacent in that knowledge if she'd known whose home and who was going to find him there.

Unlike Destiny, Detective Daniel Parks already knew that dead people often caused more trouble than the living. If the citizens of Hope Point expired from anything other than natural causes, he was the one who mostly ended up with the trouble.

Even so, some deaths were more troubling than others.

"She's just a kid." Daniel's friend and sometime partner, Kermit Riggs, hunched in his raincoat beside Tim Boudreaux, the county coroner. Tim was checking the lividity of the body sprawled beside the Dumpster behind the Azalea Street First Baptist Church. The church custodian had found her there barely an hour earlier.

"A kid," Kermit repeated as Tim moved the girl's long, dark brown hair away from her neck. Kermit took a ribbing

14

from his fellow officers for his own youthful looks, his painfully short crewcut and chronic clumsiness that only emphasized his gangly, almost adolescent appearance. Today, however, his blue eyes glanced up at Daniel with the premature age of those who see too much of the evil of the world.

"She looks like a high school student," Kermit said.

"Maybe college," Daniel replied. The church was only a couple of blocks from the Northwest State University campus. Still, he was afraid Kermit was right.

The girl's rain-soaked hair shielded her features as she lay sprawled facedown on the rumpled asphalt behind the church. But beneath the hair and the traces of makeup, Daniel could see the smooth skin and striking bone structure of a beautiful young woman. The custodian had closed her eyelids before calling 911, but he'd told Kermit and Graciela Martinez, the first officers on the scene, that she had brown eyes.

The rusty stain of blood that had flowed from the wound in her back merged into the dark red of her short, sleeveless sheath dress.

"Where did you find her purse?" Daniel asked.

"Next to the rhodie there," Kermit said, rising and pointing to an unruly rhododendron bush dripping over the ragged end of the asphalt. A line of cedars backed the rhododendron, edging the church property.

"Grace bagged it already. We didn't think the evidence would get any better sitting out in the rain. Like I said, it had some lipstick, a hairbrush, a packet of tissues, things like that. A prescription slip for Percocet, but there was no patient name on it. No wallet, no ID."

Daniel nodded. He would take a look at the purse and its contents back at the station. But he could trust Kermit not

15

to have overlooked anything that would have identified their body.

"The bag of marijuana wasn't inside the purse?"

Kermit shook his head. "I found that when I poked under the rhodie a bit more. The purse was latched. The baggie couldn't have fallen out of it."

Kermit didn't want the marijuana to have belonged to the victim. Daniel understood his identification with the girl, but Daniel didn't care, one way or the other. The girl didn't deserve to be dead, whatever she'd been doing for recreation.

He turned to look back toward the church's parking lot where Officer Grace Martinez was cordoning off the area with yellow crime scene tape. It wasn't strictly necessary, but Grace hated to stand around. An ambulance was backing into the lot.

"Are you almost done?" Daniel asked Tim.

"Might as well get her to the morgue." The coroner pushed himself to his feet, grunting a little as his knee popped.

"Care to take a stab at cause of death?" Daniel asked, not catching his own dark irony in time.

"Right under the seventh rib," Tim Boudreaux said, swiping moisture off his balding head. "My guess is he stabbed upward, got her heart. I'd say you're looking for a long, sharp knife. Know better after I get a closer look."

"And that's what killed her?"

"Did you see this bruising on the front of her neck?" He leaned over to roll her shoulder. Daniel nodded, though he bent down to look again. The marks reminded him of the first time he had met Destiny Millbrook. They reminded him that his first glimpse of her could have been of her corpse. That hadn't been so long ago, but he could hardly

16

imagine his life without her now. The day was dark enough without such thoughts.

"He probably held her from behind with one arm while he stabbed her with the other. From the amount of blood, she was alive at the time." Tim's broad, heavy face twisted sourly. "I'll go out on a limb and say the stab wound's your cause of death."

He waved a big hand at the crew huddling beside the waiting ambulance. Two men grabbed a stretcher from the back, and Grace lifted the crime scene tape for them.

"You got all the photographs you need?" Tim asked.

"Sylvia's been and gone," Daniel said. Kermit had taken fingerprints, too, from the Dumpster and the back door to the church social hall and any other flat surface he could find. The drizzling rain hadn't helped the process, but Daniel doubted they'd have found anything useful even with perfect weather. What they really needed was the murder weapon.

And a suspect. And an identification for the victim.

"When did she die?" Kermit asked.

"She's been here a while," Tim said. "Based on the blood and the situation of the body, I'd say she was killed right here where we found her. Last night sometime. Say between ten and midnight. I'll know more after the autopsy."

And just what was a pretty high school girl doing in this dark driveway behind First Baptist at eleven o'clock on a Wednesday night?

"Did they have a youth group meeting here last night?" Daniel asked, though he couldn't imagine the girl's skimpy red dress being proper Baptist youth group attire.

Dragging his worried gaze from the paramedics moving the body, Kermit flipped a notebook out of his pocket. It

17

caught on his thumb and tumbled to the ground. Daniel and Tim looked elsewhere as Kermit rescued it from a puddle.

"The men's Bible study group meets at seven on Wednesday nights," Kermit said, reading his notes. "The custodian is part of the group, and he says they were all out of here by eight-fifteen. He and the pastor locked the place up together and went home."

Daniel nodded. "Check that out with the pastor."

"Right." Kermit surreptitiously patted the wet notebook on his uniform slacks and then put it away. "You think this is connected with the church?"

"I doubt it." From the dress and the marijuana, he suspected underage partying and maybe a drug buy gone sour. But he never ruled anything out this early in a homicide investigation. "I'm going to have you and Grace canvass the neighborhood, see if anyone noticed anything unusual last night."

"Maybe she lived around here," Kermit said.

"Find out. I'll check missing persons when I get back to the station."

The paramedics had maneuvered the body onto their stretcher and covered her with a white sheet. With a hitch of movement, they popped the stretcher up and rolled it away toward the ambulance.

Daniel moved back to where the body had lain, taking another look at the asphalt. The weeds pushing through the cracks were already straightening themselves toward the sun. If the sun ever showed itself again.

Something glinted in one clump of weeds.

"Are we placing bets on who gets an ID first?" Tim asked. "I'm thinking this girl's had some good dental work."

"Hold that bet," Daniel said, crouching beside the weeds. He took a pen from his pocket and fished for the bit of gold that had caught his eye. A broken chain slipped off the pen tip.

"Give me a glove, Tim," he said, reaching back for the plastic medical glove the coroner handed him. It took a minute to work it on over his damp hand. He eased the necklace out of the weeds and rose to show Kermit and Tim the heart-shaped locket in his palm. Grace Martinez walked over to stand by his shoulder, her brisk efficiency as unruffled by the crime as her bobbed dark hair was by the persistent drizzle.

A rose pattern decorated the front of the locket. Daniel turned the heart over and picked away a blade of grass with his fingernails.

"For Ariel. Love, Daddy."

He flipped the catch.

"Pretty girl," Tim observed.

"Oh, hell," Grace said.

The dead girl looked up at Daniel from what was obviously a high school class photo, hair and makeup so perfect as to appear artless. She flashed a smile that looked as though it might break into laughter any moment.

The other half of the heart held another school photo. The boy didn't have Ariel's poise. With his head pulled back, his eyes wide as a startled rabbit, he wore a tie his mother had obviously picked out, and tried to look tough.

"Oh, hell," Grace repeated.

"We can call Hope Point High," Kermit suggested.

"There can't be too many students named Ariel who didn't show up for class today," Daniel agreed, glad to see Kermit was thinking like a cop, despite his distress at the murder. "If we get a hit, I'll drop by the school office. I bet

19

the vice principal knows this boy, too."

"You don't have to call the school about the girl," Grace said, her voice tight. "I know who she is."

Daniel turned to catch her gaze. "You know her?"

"Not personally, but I know of her." Grace shook her head at the knowledge. "I didn't recognize her until I connected the name with the picture. It was a few years ago—she was a kid then—but the campaign ads were all over local TV. 'Dedicated public servant, devoted father.' All the usual garbage. A clip of the candidate playing basketball in the driveway with his daughter."

Daniel's day tilted more steeply downhill. "No."

Grace nodded. "Our Jane Doe is Ariel Macaro, ex-Congressman Calvin Macaro's daughter."

Tim whistled. Kermit leaned in for another look. Daniel managed to dodge back before they knocked foreheads.

"All right," he said, holding up the locket where they all could see it. "We know who our victim is. We know her name. Let's find out why she died. Let's find out who killed her."

Chapter 2

The phone beside the computer rang, its shrill voice piercing the dim quiet of the bedroom and nearly knocking Sarah off her chair.

She gulped air to steady her heartbeat as the phone rang again. She'd become so involved in her research of Beryl Markham's pioneering aviation exploits she'd forgotten where she was, forgotten to be aware of her surroundings.

Fleur raised her cream-colored head from her paws to rest her chin on Sarah's knee.

"It's all right." Sarah scratched the dog's ears as she saved her book report file and waited for Aunt Destiny's answering machine to pick up. The message ran through and beeped, and then a nervous voice whispered across the line, "Hi, Destiny? This is Gemma Tasker, and I was just calling to—"

Sarah grabbed the phone. "Gemma? I'm here."

"Thank God," her best friend squeaked. "I don't know what message I was gonna leave if you didn't pick up. Don't forget to erase it before your aunt gets home."

"Of course I won't forget." Sarah rolled her eyes at Gemma's nerves. It made her own feel calmer. "Where are you calling from?"

"The bathroom," Gemma whispered.

Sarah glanced at the radio alarm by Aunt Destiny's bed. "Mrs. Lidsky let you out of science?"

"I told her I was on my period."

Sarah sometimes forgot how resourceful Gemma could be. Cloverbrook Middle School students weren't allowed to bring cell phones to school, but Gemma had hollowed out a ratty old paperback Webster's and lined the hole with cardboard to make a nest for her phone. Gemma's hawk-eyed grandmother knew, of course, but she considered it a safety precaution.

Sarah appreciated Mrs. Geary's practical approach to life. Much better than her own mother's annoying unconventionality. Of course, Gemma loved everything eccentric about Sarah's mom. She thought it was totally cool that Serena Davis knew so much about astrology and tarot cards and herbal teas. She believed every word of Serena's friends' claims to secret knowledge and psychic abilities.

But, if they were all so psychic, how come her mother didn't have a clue that Sarah hadn't been to school all week?

"I only have a minute," Gemma whispered. "Mrs. Lidsky'll take my hide off if I don't get back soon. What are you doing?"

"Working on my biography report."

"No, you're not." But Gemma's voice held very little hope that Sarah was actually doing something exciting and forbidden, like smoking or pretending to be a sixteen-year-old in some boy-infested Internet chat room.

"You have to read this book after I turn it in. Beryl Markham was the first person ever to fly solo nonstop east to west across the Atlantic. She grew up in Africa and raised racehorses and everything, back when women weren't supposed to be able to do stuff like that."

"Sounds more interesting than George Washington," Gemma said.

"Have you even started reading your biography yet?"

"I wouldn't mind doing it if I could read about somebody interesting. Tiffany Keegan pulled that book about Britney Spears right out of my hand."

Sarah forced herself not to sigh.

"Oh, I almost forgot," Gemma added, forgetting to whisper. "Brian Tilson asked about you at lunch."

"Really?" Sarah desperately tried to sound indifferent.

"Yeah. He said he hopes you're feeling better. And Geoff Brown said he hopes you get back from independent study soon."

"He's afraid he's going to flunk this math section if he can't look over my shoulder in class," Sarah said.

"Yeah." There was a pause. "So when are you coming back to school?"

"Maybe I won't."

"Sarah!"

She'd dreamed about it all week. "I'm learning so much more than in school. I'm already way ahead in the math and science books, and I can get all kinds of good information about history and stuff on the Internet. Maybe I'll just homeschool myself."

"You said you'd come back after we finished dissecting worms in science," Gemma wailed, but softly enough not to be heard by a stray teacher passing the seventh-grade girls' bathroom. "Today's the last day. I thought you wanted to be a scientist, anyway."

"I don't think killing worms for a bunch of seventh-grade boys to squish to gross out the girls is teaching us to become scientists," Sarah said. "It's a philosophical position."

"Well, I still don't see how you're going to be a forensic

anthropologist without dissecting stuff," Gemma said, sounding huffy. "Or how you're going to even graduate from seventh grade if you don't ever come to school. You can't have independent study forever, you know."

A crash from down the hall jerked Sarah's attention away from the telephone. Fleur's head snapped up from her knee, knocking hard against the underside of the keyboard shelf for Auntie Dess's iMac.

"And if they find out you forged that note from your mom—"

"Sh!" Sarah hissed, ears straining. Was that the click of the dead bolt on the back door? "Somebody's here."

"What?"

Fleur scrabbled up to stand beside her, the dog's ears pricking toward the kitchen. The kitchen door creaked as it scraped across a rumple in the linoleum.

Sarah gulped. If Aunt Destiny caught her here, the game was up. Her life was over. She should have been paying more attention, instead of listening to Gemma gossip. Except it was only two o'clock, and Auntie Dess had already been home for lunch to let Fleur out and she didn't get off work until six on Thursdays.

And the sound that Sarah had heard first, before the unlocking of the door, had sounded an awful lot like glass breaking. Like someone had broken the windowpane in the back door to get to the dead bolt and let themselves in.

There was a scraping sound from the kitchen, like someone dragging something across the floor. A crash as one of the kitchen chairs tumbled over. A very male curse.

Fleur began to growl, deep in her throat.

"Sarah, what's going on?" Gemma demanded.

"Someone's broken in," Sarah hissed back.

"*Broken in?* What are you talking about?"

Sarah got up from the chair, surprised to find her legs shaking. She grabbed Fleur's collar and pulled her out of the line of sight of the door.

"Somebody's broken into the house," she told Gemma, glad her voice wasn't shaking as badly as her legs. "A man. He broke the window and came in the back door. You've got to call the police."

"This is going to get ugly." Lieutenant Cyrus Tiebold, head of the Hope Point Police Department's Support Division, stood perched beside the chief's desk. His narrow frame appeared hunched like a heron's in the small office.

Flanked by Tiebold's hovering intensity and the nervous energy of the Patrol Division's Lieutenant James Marcy, Daniel felt claustrophobic. Then again, maybe it wasn't the room. He'd rather be working his cases than trapped in a meeting any day, and time wasted on the Ariel Macaro case was time given to a killer.

"It's already ugly," Chief Thomas said, his thick brows pulling his sun-weathered skin into deep creases over his broad nose. "A U.S. congressman's daughter stabbed in a dark alley over some pot. This is the most excitement the local media will have this year."

"Calvin Macaro's been retired from Congress for three or four years," Lieutenant Marcy reminded him.

"The guy 'retired' to spend more time with his daughter, get a reputation as a family man. He's active with big-time charity groups, getting his name in the news. He makes our department look like a bunch of idiots, getting his clients off." The chief's voice rumbled with exasperation as he rubbed the bridge of his nose with thick fingers before replacing his wire-rimmed glasses. "He retired from Congress right onto the short list for California's next open Senate seat. Or maybe governor. Either way, we're in for it."

"This case is the Detective Bureau's top priority," Lieutenant Tiebold said, barely flinching under the chief's of-course-it-is stare.

"It ought to go to the county's Drug Task Force," Lieutenant Marcy objected, darting in for his piece of the action. "Officers Vance and Yap have been working on the drug activity at Hope Point High for over a year. They know all the players in the teen drug scene. They've got a relationship with the sheriff's office and the other police departments in the area. They ought to get the case."

"It's a homicide," Lieutenant Tiebold said, unruffled. He shifted his weight, the better to stay loose for the attack. "Parks is a homicide detective."

"Vance and Yap would be grateful for his help in an advisory capacity," Lieutenant Marcy said.

"He got there first. It's his case."

Daniel might have felt invisible between the two parrying lieutenants, if Chief Thomas's heavy, dark eyes hadn't met his with sour humor.

"Your two cents?" the chief asked him. "You don't have two cents to offer, do you, Detective?"

"No, Chief," Daniel agreed. "Just let me do my job."

"Right."

"But, Chief—" Lieutenant Marcy edged closer to the desk.

"He's got the training and the experience," Chief Thomas said. "Vance and Yap are good cops, but they're not detectives. You know better, Lieutenant. Besides, Parks just solved that case involving Supervisor Barclay's death a couple months back. He's got a reputation. I told Calvin Macaro he'd be on this case."

"Gage Barclay wasn't even murdered!" Lieutenant

Marcy objected, adding disappointment to his general antagonism toward the Detective Bureau. "And as for experience in vice, Vance and Yap—"

"I'm sure Detective Parks would appreciate Officer Vance and Officer Yap's help, in an advisory capacity," Lieutenant Tiebold said, his sharp eyes bright with victory.

"I'll need Kermit Riggs," Daniel said. "For legwork."

Lieutenant Marcy was shaking his head. "No. Patrol Division is already spread too thin. Vance and Yap—"

"Will be continuing their drug investigations," Chief Thomas interrupted. "Parks can have Riggs."

Daniel allowed himself a silent sigh of relief. Garth Vance and Tom Yap were capable officers, but Daniel didn't want to have to worry about Vance's temper or Yap's pointed barbs in delicate situations.

"Parks can have any officer he damn well wants," the chief continued. He turned his heavy frown on both lieutenants. "Every officer in this department if that's what it takes to get this thing solved. And they're all going to cooperate. Perfectly. Am I understood?"

Marcy and Tiebold both nodded. Chief Thomas fixed his glare on Daniel. "Any resource you need. Just get it solved. Yesterday."

The intercom on the chief's desk buzzed. He punched it with emphatic force. "Yes?"

"I've got a young lady calling for Detective Parks. She says it's an emergency."

Lieutenant Marcy's thin smile barely turned up the corners of his mouth. "Don't forget to pick up the milk on your way home, Detective."

"Are you still seeing that Destiny Millbrook?" Chief Thomas asked Daniel, his own smile reluctant, but genuine.

Lieutenant Tiebold laughed, his thin, dry, heron's laugh. "I hope he is. That woman collects enough trouble to need her own private police force."

"Are we through here?" Daniel asked with forced calm.

The chief waved him off, and Daniel escaped down the hall to his own small office. He didn't like the sound of that word emergency. Destiny would not interrupt a meeting with the chief of police. She would leave a message.

As, in fact, she had done several times in the past couple of days. It wasn't like he hadn't returned the calls, leaving messages for her, too. At least the one yesterday, confirming their dinner date for tonight.

His eyes closed briefly in a spasm of guilt. He was going to have to cancel dinner.

Line three was blinking on his office telephone. He punched the button for the speakerphone. "Detective Parks speaking."

"Detective Parks?" He could barely hear the soft, high whisper. Just what he needed this afternoon. A prank call.

"Who is this?"

"Gemma." The voice swallowed and breathed. "This is Gemma Tasker, Sarah Davis's friend?"

The extravagantly freckled redhead. Pleasance Geary's granddaughter. Played catcher on Destiny's summer girls' softball team.

"Hi, Gemma." He glanced at the flat file on Ariel Macaro's death lying in the center of his desk. "What can I do for you?"

"Sarah's in trouble, Mr. Parks. I mean, Detective Parks."

"Trouble?" *Police* trouble? He quickly discarded the idea of Sarah bringing drugs or a weapon to school, but Gemma sounded scared.

28

"She thinks someone's broken into the house. She said to call you. I told her she should climb out the window, but she said she couldn't leave Fleur. I said—"

"Wait, Gemma. Where are you?"

"The bathroom."

"Where? At Sarah's house?" He started shrugging into his coat.

"At school."

"Sarah's got Fleur at school?" He checked the gun in his shoulder holster, fighting down annoyance. He didn't have time for schoolgirl escapades.

"No." Gemma's voice held all the exasperation Daniel was so carefully keeping to himself. "She's at Destiny's house."

Daniel frowned at the phone. "Why isn't she at school? Is Destiny there?"

Gemma's voice squeaked. "Detective Parks, no one's there. Sarah heard the glass breaking in the back door window, and I could hear Fleur growling, and she thought maybe the guy'd dragged a dead body into the house or something—"

Her renewed fright was infecting him. "Gemma, I'm on my way, okay?"

"Please hurry."

"I'm leaving right now." He didn't have time for this. He didn't have time to leave a homicide investigation for a questionable breaking and entering. He didn't have time to take Kermit Riggs off the homicide case to ride with him for backup. When he got hold of Sarah Davis and her overactive imagination, he was going to have a serious talk with her.

But the image of Ariel Macaro's body lying in a pool of her own blood was fresh enough in his mind to notch up his heartbeat as he headed out his office door, calling for Kermit.

Elderberry Lane appeared typically quiet for an early Thursday afternoon. The little white clapboard Destiny rented sat square in the middle of the Terrace, a neighborhood of modest homes nestled into the hill above downtown Hope Point.

Daniel eased the unmarked departmental Chevy to a stop in front of the sky-blue California bungalow next door. He saw no sign of Lars Holmgren—Destiny's elderly neighbor's sharp eyes had thwarted the last invasion of her home—and no sign of life behind the lowered blinds of Destiny's living room windows. He had half-expected Destiny's little VW Rabbit to be sitting in her driveway, explaining Sarah's intruder, but other than his beat-up bronze Chevrolet, the only other vehicle on the street was an old Westphalia van parked across the road two doors down.

"Gemma said the intruder came in through the back door," Daniel told Kermit, as they climbed out of the car. "We'll start there."

"I'd forgotten how close Destiny's house is to the university." Kermit glanced toward the north.

Daniel didn't have to ask what Kermit was thinking. The Azalea Street First Baptist Church, the scene of Ariel Macaro's recent murder, was less than half a mile from where they stood.

Adrenaline sped his steps as he and Kermit trotted across the lawn. The green and white holly bush offered good cover at the side of the house.

Daniel lifted up the back gate as he swung it open to keep it from squeaking. The yard was desolately empty, the grass shaggy and unkempt from a week of damp weather, the dried-up snow pea vines curling like skeletal fingers around their twine supports in the little garden.

Daniel and Kermit slipped along the back of the house toward the kitchen door. No sound came from inside. Fleur did not announce their coming. Which either meant their stealth had been successful or that Fleur . . .

Daniel didn't complete the thought.

He reached the end of the rear wall of the living room and, crouched low, leaned out to check the kitchen wall, set back a few feet from where he stood.

His curse didn't rise above a whisper. He glanced back at Kermit and nodded grimly. One of the small panes in the back door was gone, dark and empty against the rest of the window.

Gesturing to Kermit to cover him, Daniel unholstered his .45 and ducked across the small back walk to the other side of the kitchen door. Pushing everything from his mind except his training, refusing to imagine Sarah Davis bleeding to death on Destiny's kitchen floor, he eased forward for a quick glance through the broken windowpane.

At the sight inside, he froze, exposing himself to view and to potential enemy fire for three heartbeats too long. Then he slowly closed his eyes and returned his weapon to the shoulder holster.

He had known when Gemma called, deep in his heart, that no damsel related to Destiny Millbrook would ask for help unless she were in true distress. He should have also known that any such damsel wouldn't have the sense to wait for backup.

Chapter 3

Maddy Chance collapsed into the swivel chair next to Destiny's. "How many more hours until my plane leaves?"

"Work hours or hour hours?" Destiny asked, glancing up from the small stack of interlibrary loan requests she was sorting.

"The only ones that count," Maddy said, still draped dramatically in the chair, her flame-colored hair hanging down behind her in an artistic cascade. "Is it really only Thursday?"

"Breckenridge will still be there Saturday."

"I could be dead by Saturday." Maddy straightened up and rolled her chair over to her spot at the long, semicircular reference desk. "Or in jail. That one almost got his clock cleaned."

"The guy you just helped?" Destiny glanced up toward the mezzanine above them that circled the two-story lobby entrance. She could see the door to the county archives room from which her friend had just returned, but no sign of the tall, middle-aged man who had paused by the desk to demand assistance.

Maddy pressed the back of her hand to her forehead. "He made me ride in the elevator of doom."

"Maddy, the elevator is a little temperamental, but—"

"That thing is a death trap. Maybe it will eat him on the

way down." Maddy's face brightened at the thought, then sobered. "Watch out for the ones with the expensive suits and that distinguished touch of silver in their hair. They're stuffed shirts who think they own the world."

"Chad wears expensive suits," Destiny reminded her, forbearing to mention that Chad Geary was also a bit of a stuffed shirt. Maybe he'd never had a chance to develop his own personality growing up with an unstoppable force like Pleasance Geary for a mother. Although his niece, Gemma, lived with Pleasance, and Gemma was never dull.

Still, if Chad made Maddy happy, Destiny could overlook the way he shook out his cuffs to make the gold cufflinks flash and the fact that, as an orthodontist, he eyed her teeth with unseemly interest.

"Chad doesn't act like he's better than I am because he has a Lexus," Maddy said. " 'Dr. Royce Preston, M.D.' thinks because he's some kind of heart surgeon the rest of us should bow to his money and intellect. If he's that smart, why couldn't he figure out how to run the microfiche reader? Then he got all wigged out because I looked at the article he was reading. What do I care if he gets his kicks from meth labs exploding?"

Destiny laughed, waving the interlibrary loan requests at Maddy. "He's got to do a lot better than that to even reach the radar screen of weird."

"Mr. Dyer again?"

Destiny flipped through the stack of ILLs, all written in Edward Dyer's signature green ink. "Another scholarly work on Roswell. Two first-person accounts of alien abductions. A book by a woman he assures me is the world's leading expert on crop circles."

"I thought Mr. Dyer was the world's leading expert on crop circles."

33

"Today he was telling me about the time machine the Catholic Church has hidden in the Vatican. A Benedictine monk figured out how to gather light from past events onto film. The word among Mr. Dyer's sources is that the Pope has videos of every major event from Noah landing the Ark to Christ's crucifixion."

Maddy raised one red eyebrow. "They didn't teach me any of this stuff at St. Catherine's. Bless Mr. Dyer's heart, though. I'd go a little crazy, too, if my only son OD'd at seventeen."

Destiny's heart wrenched. Mr. Dyer might have eclectic interests, but she liked the gentle man. "I didn't know that."

"He runs a support group for teens with drug problems and their parents. He told me he wanted something positive to—"

The desk telephone rang, and Maddy reached for it. "Hello, Jasper County Library, Hope Point Branch. May I help you? She's right here."

Maddy passed the phone to Destiny with a smug grin. "Detective Daniel Parks."

"Daniel?"

"Destiny?" His terse tone choked off her surprised delight at his call. He was calling to cancel their dinner date that evening. She was *not* going to complain that she had not seen him since Sunday. She had known when she fell in love with him that he was a police officer. She had understood it wouldn't be easy. She'd thought she'd understood.

She heard him draw in a breath, but he didn't mention dinner. "Look, I've got a situation here. Can you come down to the station? There's been a break-in at your house."

"A break-in?" There was something wrong with a per-

34

son's life when her first reaction was "not again." Instead she asked, "Did he take much?"

"No. We caught the guy inside."

Destiny straightened, her heart thudding sharply. "You caught a burglar in my house? Is Fleur all right? He didn't hurt her?"

"Fleur's here with me in my office. How long do you think it will take you to get here? Fleur, leave it!"

Destiny allowed herself a relieved grin. She could imagine the havoc Fleur's tail was wreaking on Daniel's neat desk. "Did Mr. Holmgren call it in?"

"No, Sarah did. Well, Sarah called Gemma, and Gemma called me, but—"

"Sarah? My niece?"

"Apparently she was skipping school . . . What's that, Nancy?" Daniel's voice faded out.

"Daniel? You mean Sarah was in my house when the guy—"

"Destiny? I've got another call I have to take. I'll see you when you get here."

"Wait! Daniel, is Sarah there? Can I talk with her? Daniel?" Destiny stared down at the phone in her hand. He would have told her if Sarah was dead. She was sure of it. Almost.

She swiveled her chair. "Maddy—"

"Get out," Maddy ordered, snagging the stack of ILL requests from Destiny's hand. "I'll take care of Mr. Dyer. You take care of Sarah."

"Thanks." Destiny grabbed her carryall bag from under her desk and darted out the opening between the wraparound desk and the shelves of supplies and library reference works that backed their work space. The nonfiction stacks stretched behind the reference desk, below the mezzanine. Destiny hurried the opposite direction, toward the broad entrance lobby and the front doors.

Charlene Adams, the new supervisor for the Hope Point Branch of the library, waved to her from the circulation desk at the side of the entrance.

"You're leaving early?" Charlene's fox-brush auburn hair did not have a touch of gray, and the skin of her high-cheekboned face had a smooth finish that owed little to her expertly applied makeup. It was the deep crescents at the corners of her lips and the disapproving copper line of her narrow eyebrows that aged her.

"Family emergency," Destiny said, slowing briefly.

"You'll have to take it off your vacation time," Charlene warned.

Destiny managed not to laugh. Next week Maddy would be spending her vacation hours on a spur-of-the-moment rendezvous in Breckenridge with the current love of her life. Destiny was off to spend hers on a spur-of-the-moment trip to the police station.

She escaped out the glass double doors and turned for the parking lot. On the positive side, it would be the first chance she'd had to rendezvous with the love of her life in three days. On the downside, she'd probably have to kill him if he didn't do some quick explaining when she arrived.

The Hope Point police station lurked under the rear portion of City Hall like a forgotten grotto in the hill that led up to downtown. The battered lobby reminded Destiny of a nightmarish dentist's office with its flickering fluorescent bulbs, clinical green linoleum and sense of impending unpleasantness.

Nancy Dennis looked up from the reception desk with a warm smile. "Hi, Destiny. You can go right back to his office." She leaned over to unhook the latch on the swinging half door at the end of the counter.

"Thanks, Nancy."

Kermit Riggs stuck his head out the door of the officers' break room. "Hi, Des. I'll come with you. You want a cup of coffee?"

Destiny shuddered at the memory of the departmental coffee. "And I thought you were my friend."

"I'll take that as a no. Just a second." He ducked back into the break room. Destiny heard a muffled curse and the sound of hard plastic bouncing off the floor.

Kermit reappeared through the doorway, his "I ♥ Labradors" mug in his hand. The other officers had held a raffle to see who would buy Kermit an unbreakable coffee mug with a snug lid. Daniel had won, and Destiny had picked out the mug.

"Just tell me Sarah's all right," Destiny said, hurrying to keep up with Kermit's long legs down the hall.

He grinned. "She's a terrier, that one. Don't worry, she had Fleur for backup."

Destiny thought of the way Fleur threw herself on her back and exposed her tummy for petting when the UPS deliverer came by, and was not reassured.

Kermit opened the door to Daniel's office for her. Claws scrabbled on the slick gray floor, giving Destiny time to brace herself for Fleur's enthusiastic greeting. She caught a tongue across her nose, a thick otter tail thumped against her thigh, and then she heard Kermit sit down hard behind her as Fleur attacked her soul mate.

"So much for loyalty," Destiny muttered, ignoring the tangle of dog and cop as her gaze swept the cramped room, more like a cell than an office. The one window, high in the rear wall, could not compete with the institutional fluorescent lighting. A huge map of Jasper County behind the desk and a photograph of Daniel's cat, Edgar, on the desktop, were the only concessions to decorating.

Daniel had apparently escaped his office for the moment, but a smaller figure huddled in one of the metal folding chairs against the wall.

Skinny, angular, nearly as gawky and long-legged as Kermit, Sarah sat with her heels up on her seat, clutching her knees to her chest. With her oak-blond hair pulled back in a ponytail, the silver of her retainer flashing as she worried her lower lip, she looked even younger than twelve.

The green eyes that met Destiny's held none of Sarah's accustomed scientific cool.

"Sweetie, are you all right?"

Sarah shook her head and unfolded from the chair, throwing herself into Destiny's hug. For all her slenderness, she was nearly as tall as Destiny, and still growing.

"Are you hurt?"

"No." Sarah's response was muffled against Destiny's shoulder. "I'm sorry, Auntie Dess. Don't be mad at me."

"I'm not mad," Destiny assured her. "I'll be furious eventually, but right now, I'm just glad you're okay. What happened?"

Fleur's black nose pushed in between her and Sarah, and Sarah crouched down to wrap her arms around Fleur's neck. Destiny dropped into one of the battered chairs as Kermit leaned against Daniel's desk.

"I was working on your computer," Sarah explained. "I'm doing a biography report on Beryl Markham for social studies."

"Uh-huh." Destiny raised an eyebrow. "That's great, but your mom's not going to consider that points for cutting class."

"I know." Sarah hugged Fleur a little tighter at the thought of her mother's wrath. "I heard glass break in the kitchen, like someone knocked in a window. It sounded like the lock clicked and then the door opened. Fleur heard it, too, and she growled. I was going to hide in the closet with her. I knew I couldn't get her out the window with me—"

"Sarah." Destiny's chest squeezed with the thought of what could have happened to a child trapped in a closet by a criminal intruder. She had to work to find her voice again. "You should have gone out the window."

"I couldn't leave Fleur!"

"Yes, you could." Destiny met Fleur's warm brown eyes. They understood each other. Either one of them would rather be hurt than have harm come to Sarah. "You should have gotten yourself safe and trusted the police to take care of Fleur."

"You would have left Fleur alone with a burglar?" Sarah demanded, her eyes accusing.

"If I had to."

A loud snort turned their heads toward the office doorway. Detective Daniel Parks closed the door behind him. "Your aunt threw a rock the size of an orange at my head protecting that slobbering beast, Sarah, and she thought I was an armed killer. I don't know why she expects you to have any better sense."

His blue eyes met Destiny's with the wry humor that had captured her heart. She still felt the air change when he walked into a room, as if the very ions increased their charges.

It wasn't his looks, though they didn't hurt. His unruly sandy brown hair and sun-darkened skin contrasted nicely with his neat plainclothes chinos and green shirt. He filled the clothes nicely, too. But it was that steady honesty in his eyes, the humor in the set of his mouth, the way he held himself as if ready for any challenge that got to her every time.

"I don't know why I even bother to answer calls to your house anymore," Daniel said, leaning against the desk beside Kermit. "You and your relatives should hire out as your own security force. Or be thrown in protective custody for the good of the community. One or the other."

Destiny wrinkled her nose at him, then turned back to Sarah. "Go on."

Sarah rested a hand on Fleur's head. "Fleur wouldn't hide with me. The intruder was talking to himself in the kitchen, and she kept getting more and more upset. When I let go of her collar to open the closet, she charged out the bedroom door and ran down the hall.

"She started barking like crazy, and I heard the intruder yell. He sounded pretty scared, and I thought Fleur might be attacking him."

"Fleur?" Destiny looked at the Lab, whose tongue flopped out the side of her mouth as she panted. "Fleur has the killer instincts of a banana slug."

Though her dog had proven tough enough against the man who had tried to kill Destiny a few short months before. That encounter had brought out Fleur's protective instincts.

"I figured if the intruder had a gun, he would have used it," Sarah said. "I thought I'd better see what was happening, in case I should call for an ambulance. I went down the hall—"

"Tell your aunt what you took with you," Daniel interrupted.

Sarah glanced back at Destiny. "Your baseball bat."

"Tried and true," Daniel commented.

"Sarah . . ." Destiny could only thank God that Sarah was here to tell her the story.

"I didn't need it though," Sarah continued. "When I got to the kitchen, the perp was up on the kitchen table, trying to keep out of Fleur's reach."

Perp. It was Destiny's fault Sarah was spending so much time around law enforcement.

"That's how we found them," Daniel said. "Fleur pacing and growling like a rottweiler and Sarah standing guard with the bat."

Destiny closed her eyes against the image—and what might have happened. Sarah couldn't weigh more than 105 pounds. She could swing a bat, though, even if she was a pitcher.

"I could almost feel sorry for the guy," Daniel said. "I don't think I'd want those two coming after me."

"You're probably the bravest juvenile delinquent I know," Destiny grumbled, reaching over to pull Sarah's ponytail.

"I was pretty scared when I heard him break in," Sarah admitted. "But it really wasn't all that bad waiting for Detective Parks and Officer Riggs to show up. He was more scared of Fleur than we were of him. He kept wanting me to hand him the phone so he could call you, but I didn't know if it was a trick or not, so I said we could just wait for the police."

"Smart girl," Daniel agreed.

"Call me?" Destiny asked. A new chill ran up her spine. She suddenly had a very, very bad feeling . . .

"That's our next bit of business," Daniel said. With his arms crossed over his chest, he looked every bit the police interrogator. "The perp says he was in your kitchen at your invitation and that you forgot to leave

41

your key by the back door for him."

"Alain." She'd once described him to Daniel as her dead and buried love life. Unfortunately, he'd found his way back from the grave.

"That's correct. Alain Caine. You told him he could stay with you while he was here in Hope Point?" The question held no inflection at all.

"Of course not." Destiny met his gaze with a narrowed one of her own. He had to know he had no reason for jealousy. Though there was a certain satisfaction that he cared enough to feel it. "I told him to go to . . . Well, not hell, exactly, but Deepwater."

"Close enough," Sarah snorted, with the parochial pride of a preteen from a rival middle school.

Daniel's stance relaxed imperceptibly. "He was in your house without your permission?"

"He called this morning to ask if he could stay at my house while he's here for the arts shows in the area. I said no. That was the end of it." Or so she'd thought. She really should have known better.

"Do you want to press charges?"

As tempting as the thought was . . . "No."

"He broke into your house!" Sarah objected.

"And frightened Sarah," Kermit added.

"Who wasn't supposed to be there in the first place," Destiny reminded them before Sarah could get too deep into outrage. "Alain's inconvenient, but he didn't intend to steal anything or harm anyone."

"He broke the window," Daniel put in, his tone still too even.

Destiny shook her head. "Pressing charges would be more trouble than it's worth." She paused. "I don't suppose you could keep him in jail overnight, anyway?"

That brought the humor back to his eyes. "No. I'm afraid not. Sarah, on the other hand . . ."

Sarah's face took on the pinched look of a Mafia rat dumped back out on the streets of Chicago. "Do you have to tell Mom?"

Destiny stared at her. "Duh."

"I've been doing independent study," Sarah pleaded. "I was protesting the worm dissections in science. I mean, they don't have the same brain structure we do, but they're still living creatures. Why should they suffer so seventh graders can throw worm guts around for a couple of days? Anyway, Gemma says they finished today, so I could just go back to school tomorrow and Mom would never have to know—"

"Mom would never have to know what?" Serena Davis stood in the doorway of Daniel's office, one hand on her right hip, the other on the doorknob.

Even with fear and fury waging war in her eyes, her breath coming strained between clenched jaws, Destiny's sister had style. Her glossy chestnut hair fell around the collar of her white button-down shirt in gleaming waves. The shirt, unbuttoned just far enough to hint at cleavage, was set off by a turquoise teardrop necklace and tucked into perfectly creased black slacks, the slacks brushing over pointed leather boots.

She looked like she'd just walked off the floor of a modeling agency. So much for central casting, Destiny thought. Serena actually worked as a hazardous materials enforcer at Pacific Coast Community College south of Deepwater, where she also took classes in interior decorating. And Feng Shui.

"I called your mother when I called Destiny," Daniel told Sarah.

43

"If I weren't so glad to see you—" Serena unclenched her hand from the door with an effort of will. "I'm going to kill you, but you better come give me a hug first."

As Sarah obliged, Daniel met Destiny's gaze and nodded toward the door. Kermit followed the two of them past mother and daughter, and closed the door behind them as they stepped out into the hall.

"Thank you," Destiny said, glancing from Kermit to Daniel. "Thank you both."

"I'm just glad Sarah's okay," Kermit said. "And Fleur, too."

"Kerry, why don't you go collect Destiny's perp for her, and then we can get on with our real case."

As Kermit headed off toward the hallway to the holding cells, a familiar knot tightened in Destiny's stomach. She was interfering with his work again. "I'm sorry about this. I know how busy you've been."

"I agree with Kermit. I'm glad Sarah's all right." Daniel blew out a breath. "It's not safe for her to be cutting school and wandering around town."

"Thank you, Dr. Spock."

His mouth twisted down, matching hers. "It's at least a mile and a half from Serena's house to yours. Sarah's been walking that every day at seven-thirty in the morning, hiding in your shed until you leave for work, then taking the same walk home at three. Anything could happen to her, and no one would even be worried until Serena came home from work at five-thirty."

"You think I haven't thought of that?"

"She could be getting into real trouble, stealing, doing drugs—"

"Sarah?" Destiny's temper flashed. "She cut school to get out of dissecting worms. Does that sound like a drug addict to you? She doesn't even like her mother taking herbal remedies because they're not approved by the FDA. She wants to be in law enforcement when she grows up."

She didn't have to point out that Sarah practically idolized Daniel. Destiny knew it had bothered him at first that Sarah refused to call him anything but Detective Parks. It had taken him a while to understand she did it out of respect, not to distance him.

"She's at that age where kids start to rebel—"

"Being a straight A student and approaching life as a science experiment is rebelling for Sarah." Destiny raised an eyebrow to remind him of her sister.

He almost smiled, but it was gone as quickly as it came. "I got called to a murder this morning." His gaze moved down the hall as if he were afraid that if she looked in his eyes she might see what he had seen. "A teenage girl, just a few years older than Sarah. It happened not far from your neighborhood. When Gemma called and said someone had broken into your house . . ."

Destiny's irritation drained away, even before Daniel's hand found hers. His fingers felt strong and warm on her skin. He looked toward her once more.

Destiny squeezed his hand. "You know Serena's going to have Sarah under lock and key for the rest of her natural life."

"I know. I don't know how parents survive in this world. If I could get my hands on the sick scum who make it unsafe for kids to play in their own front yards . . ."

"You do," Destiny reminded him.

Daniel shook his head, his mouth curving wryly. "Those are the law's hands. My hands wouldn't stop at the cuffs on the wrists."

He slipped his fingers up to curl around her wrist and

pulled her closer. "This case is going to be bad and it's political and it's going to take a lot of legwork. But I'm glad Sarah felt she could call me for help, even if I didn't have the time to spare."

"Is that an apology?"

His eyes narrowed. "For what?"

"For getting mad because your personal life got messy and dribbled into your work."

"No." His free hand touched her jaw, and he leaned down to kiss her, a warm, firm kiss that melted away the icy insecurities that she hadn't even known were forming around her heart.

"That's not an apology, either," she noted.

"No."

"Good enough, though."

"Good." He lowered his mouth again, and she raised her own hand to his neck to pull him closer. The kiss brightened the air around her like sunshine through the clouds. Not enough to dissipate them, but enough to bring hope that the rain would not last forever.

Though in Hope Point, it sometimes felt as though it could.

Through the gentle, obscuring warmth enclosing her, she recognized the distinct sound of Kermit clearing his throat.

Reluctantly, she let go of Daniel's hand and turned to face Kermit—and the man beside him. Alain looked shorter and older than she remembered, the fine feathering of lines around his eyes burned deeper by the Arizona sun, his sandy blond hair bleached lighter.

But the dimple at the side of his self-deprecating grin was just the same.

"Destiny. You are a sight for sore eyes. Beautiful as

ever." His hazel eyes narrowed as he peered at her. "But what on earth did you do to your hair?"

Two uniformed officers pushing past Alain and Kermit rescued Destiny from the necessity of a reply. The taller, ruddier officer, shorter than Kermit, but broader, his thick neck muscled like a mastiff's, glanced at Alain, then Daniel.

"You got a suspect in the Macaro case, Detective?"

Daniel shook his head, and Destiny felt his renewed impatience. "Not yet."

"Lieutenant Marcy told us to be ready to get started on the case."

"I appreciate it, Vance, Yap." Daniel's tone betrayed none of the irritation Destiny saw flash in his eyes at the mention of Lieutenant Marcy.

The slender officer, Yap, black hair and dark eyes contrasting with the other's blond, linebacker looks, nudged his partner, Vance, with his elbow. "Down, Garth, you're interfering with the detective's love life."

Officer Vance glanced at Destiny, eyes over-wide. "Detective Parks has a love life?"

He slapped Daniel's back as Officer Yap rolled his eyes, then the two of them continued down the hall.

"Well," Alain remarked, his own eyes flaring in mock distress as he stared at Destiny. "I guess now I understand why you didn't want me staying at your house."

Chapter 4

Daniel pulled off Redwood Hill Road onto the patch of graveled shoulder spilling over the curve of the hill. He pulled the key from the ignition and listened to the Chevy sputter into silence. An aluminum gate barred the gravel driveway that swept down to the two-story redwood mansion below. There was no security box, no automatic latch. The former congressman would have to get out of his car and unlatch his gate every time he went through.

Daniel got out of the department's unmarked car and walked up to the gate. There were no hot wires on the fence that surrounded the house and its steep, wooded grounds. He saw no signs of security.

"Only in Jasper County."

He unlatched the gate and stepped through, closing it behind him. Calvin Macaro should be expecting him. From an investigatory standpoint, he preferred to surprise the people he interviewed. The sudden appearance of a police officer could throw even an accomplished liar off-guard, cause a tiny slip that unraveled a case.

But from a human perspective, Daniel was glad Chief Thomas had exercised his professional courtesy and been the one to visit Macaro that morning to break the news of the man's daughter's death.

Daniel heard the first growl just as he reached the walkway to the front door of the house. Slowly, he turned toward the sound. The long-legged elegance of the Doberman pinscher, her coat the same burnished red as the fallen redwood needles beneath her delicate feet, did not hide the determination in her dark amber eyes or the size of her teeth. That explained the lack of security at the gate.

Daniel heard the front door open behind him, but he didn't move his head. He'd never had to shoot a dog in the line of duty, partly because he knew better than to trust a dog's owner to have control of it.

"Helga!" The deep voice held a ring of authority. "Leave it. He's okay."

The dog's sharp ears twitched, and the growl stopped.

"It's all right. She won't attack."

The vibrant twitching of the dog's stub of a tail reassured him more than the words.

"Here, Helga."

The Doberman bounded forward, light as a deer, pausing to sniff at Daniel's hands before trotting up the walk to greet her master.

Daniel followed her progress toward Calvin Macaro, powerful politician, canny lawyer, and grieving father. Macaro looked older than Daniel remembered from the man's last congressional campaign, the gray hair not sleeked back, the lines uncovered by makeup, the slight paunch beneath his slate-gray silk shirt not tucked in by girdle or workouts.

"You're Detective Parks."

"That's right."

Sharp eyes examined Daniel from head to foot. "Come in, then."

Macaro waved Helga off on her rounds and walked in-

49

side, leaving Daniel to follow. The front door opened into a dim, dark-paneled hall. A desk lamp shone through the doorway to the left, and Daniel followed the light into Calvin Macaro's study.

Law books filled the glass-fronted bookcases on two sides of the room. The desk looked out past a tall redwood over a ravine down the side of Redwood Hill. Daniel guessed the view from the other side of the house, over-looking Hope Point down to the bay, would be shown off through huge windows in the living room and dining room.

Macaro rolled his black leather chair back from the desk and gestured Daniel toward a matching armchair in the corner.

"I identified her body." The words were a challenge, de-fining Macaro's fortitude and questioning Daniel's.

Daniel nodded. "Chief Thomas told me."

"Thomas is a good man."

That was also a challenge. The police chief had sup-ported Macaro's last two campaigns for Congress, as a pro-ponent of increased funding for local police forces and an opponent of legalizing marijuana, but Chief Thomas had never hidden his disapproval of lawyer Calvin Macaro's de-fense of wealthy drug defendants. Or his annoyance at how frequently Macaro got them acquitted.

"The chief has made it clear that finding your daughter's killer is the department's top priority."

Macaro grunted. "All that means is that you'll put the bastard behind bars where I can't get to him myself."

The sentiment didn't surprise Daniel, but there was something about Macaro that suggested it was more than an empty threat. Chief Thomas had filled Daniel in on Macaro's background. Raised by blue-collar, second-gener-ation immigrant parents in Chicago, he'd worked his way through college and earned a scholarship to the University of Chicago Law School. After graduation, he'd moved to San Francisco to start his own practice. His parents were dead. His wife had died of ovarian cancer when Ariel was six.

Macaro was a man accustomed to the punches life had thrown him. And he was accustomed to punching back.

Daniel pulled out his notebook. "I'm going to find the person who killed your daughter, and I intend to make sure he pays for his crime."

"Ariel was an honor student," Macaro said. For the first time, his voice betrayed him and he had to clear his throat. "Straight As. Lettered in basketball and softball. She'd just got her applications in to Stanford, UCLA, Berkeley. They'd be lucky to get her. Would have been lucky."

Macaro cleared his throat again. He lifted his hand to the desk as if expecting to find a glass of water. Daniel saw the hand was shaking. "But that was nothing compared to her spirit. She always looked on the bright side, always hoped for the best, was always willing to see the good in everyone."

The hand clenched, stopped shaking. "Even that worthless piece of trash Woodridge boy."

Macaro's dark eyes met Daniel's and any trace of weakness was gone. "He's your man, Detective. If you could call him that. Pimply little hooligan. I can't imagine what Ariel ever saw in him."

"She was dating this young man?" Daniel thought of the boy in the picture in Ariel's locket. A young, clueless tough guy, ready to take on the world. Probably much like Macaro as a teenager, though he doubted the man would ever recognize the resemblance.

"Tyler Woodridge," Macaro said, waiting for Daniel to

write it in his notebook. "A no-good punk. His family lives in some kind of trailer park. His brother's a drug dealer. I think his cousin's in jail. The whole family is trash. I thought she'd see that, get over whatever kind of pity she felt for him. That's why I let her see the son of a bitch. Until I found out he'd gotten suspended from school."

"Suspended?"

"He attacked Kyle Preston, Ariel's former boyfriend. In the hall at school. Broke the boy's nose."

"Former boyfriend?"

Macaro shook his head at Daniel's tone. "The boy's the son of Royce Preston, the heart surgeon. Best heart surgeon north of San Francisco. He fixed my ticker up well enough for me to survive that last term in Congress. Kyle's a fine young man. Smart. Polite. Everything Woodridge wasn't. Even Ariel finally saw that. She was going out to the country club with Kyle last night."

Macaro looked down at his hands, a struggle for control passing over his blunt features. "At least that's what she told me."

"She didn't go?"

"I had dinner with a client last night. When I got home, I found Helga in Ariel's bedroom. She always put the dog there when Kyle came over. We couldn't stop Helga from whizzing on his shoes."

Macaro almost smiled. "You ever see a female dog lift her leg? She's a pistol. So I put Helga out and went to bed. Didn't even think to worry until I got up this morning and Ariel wasn't home."

Daniel imagined Macaro hadn't been too pleased with Kyle Preston at that point. But something had happened to change his mind. "You talked with Kyle?"

Macaro grunted. "You're damn right. And Kyle told me

they never went out. Ariel called him last night and canceled the date, said she was going out with Tyler Woodridge. Maybe Tyler threatened her—or Kyle. Ariel and I were close. She knew she could tell me anything. But I guess parents never know everything."

Daniel could see how much the words hurt him.

"Obviously Tyler got jealous and took it out on Ariel. I should have gotten rid of that kid when I had the chance."

"We'll question young Mr. Woodridge," Daniel assured him. "You don't think Kyle Preston was the jealous type?"

"He was too well-bred not to respect Ariel's decision."

Daniel had never noticed that any amount of breeding or money dulled the basic human animal's passions, but he wasn't going to argue philosophy with Calvin Macaro.

"Mr. Macaro, do you know if your daughter ever used drugs recreationally?"

"Of course not!" Macaro snapped forward in his chair, glaring at Daniel. "How dare you? She was an athlete. She'd never mess that up with drugs."

"We found a bag of marijuana at the crime scene."

Macaro's jaw relaxed and he leaned back. "That just proves it was the Woodridge boy. I told you his brother was a dealer."

"Ariel also had a prescription for Percocet in her purse."

Macaro shrugged. "She pulled a hamstring doing wind sprints last week. She was in a lot of pain. The doctor must have prescribed it."

Daniel didn't think his doctor would prescribe him Percocet for a pulled hamstring—more likely he'd be buying over-the-counter ibuprofen. But then, he wasn't a high school basketball star.

"Mr. Macaro, can you think of anyone else who might

have wanted to harm your daughter?"

"Ariel? Of course not. She was never in trouble. Was never mean to anyone. She had friends. Not enemies."

"She was beautiful, smart, athletic. Some kids might resent that."

Macaro's eyes narrowed. "You mean like a Columbine kind of thing? Because she was popular? She had friends from all groups at that school, from the Woodridge trash to the cheerleaders to the computer geeks."

He rose, signalling the end of his patience with the interview, but Daniel had another crucial question.

"What about you, Mr. Macaro?" he asked, rising himself. "You're a powerful, wealthy man. Have you received any threats? Is there anyone who might abduct or attack your daughter to harm you?"

Daniel half-expected fireworks, but Macaro had obviously already considered that possibility.

"I've made enemies," Macaro agreed, following Daniel to the front door. "Some bitter ones. But the recent ones are all in Washington, and since I'm currently retired from public life, they have no reason to come after me."

"Your clients?" Daniel prodded, keeping his gaze locked on Macaro's. "Some of them don't have very savory reputations."

Macaro's mouth rose in a humorless smile. "But they're all very satisfied with the services I've provided them." The smile disappeared. "Tyler Woodridge is the one you want, Detective. He was the last one to see her alive. He had means, motive, and opportunity. Isn't that what you look for? Or doesn't modern police work depend on such mundane factors anymore?"

"It does," Daniel agreed. "We also still believe in gathering evidence."

Macaro's lip curled in scorn. "If you want to do your job, you'll go arrest that boy before I get hold of him. Tyler Woodridge killed my daughter. And if he didn't, he got her killed. I've got all the evidence I need to know that."

Daniel paused with his hand on the doorknob. "I'm sure I don't have to explain to you, Mr. Macaro, that interfering in a police investigation is a crime. Let us do our job. We'll find out who killed your daughter, Tyler Woodridge or not."

"We'll see."

Daniel opened the door and stepped out onto the porch. Helga stood by the porch steps, her amber eyes following his movements with all of Macaro's vigilance, but none of his hostility. Between the two, he felt more comfortable turning his back on the dog.

He walked up the drive toward the gate, his shoes crunching in the gravel drive. He understood Macaro's threats. Daniel knew he would feel the same if someone hurt someone he loved. He had felt the same, when Jake Westing had targeted Destiny for death that past summer. But he'd had his training, his experience, and his personal code of honor to hold him back.

Ostensibly retired from public life, his beloved daughter dead, Macaro had little to restrain him from executing his own revenge if he thought the police weren't handling the case to his satisfaction.

Daniel fully intended to have a little chat with Tyler Woodridge at the earliest opportunity. Meaning he would have to call Destiny to cancel dinner. But it couldn't be avoided: Whether or not Tyler Woodridge could provide the key to solving Daniel's current case, the youth was in definite danger of becoming the victim for Daniel's next one.

★ ★ ★ ★ ★

The stealthy weight of seventy pounds of yellow Labrador crinkled on plastic.

"Don't even think about it." Destiny turned to fix Fleur with a quelling glare. Fleur lifted her paw from the tarp Destiny was using to protect the threadbare hall rug, then lay back down beside it with a sigh.

Destiny dipped her brush into the can of Almond Cream Semi-Gloss on her stepladder and continued painting the top of the hall wall. "I appreciate your wanting to help. Really."

Fleur's hurt eyes clearly didn't believe her.

The doorbell rescued them both from incipient depression. Fleur danced toward the door, tail waving as she begged Destiny to hurry.

"I thought he couldn't make dinner." Destiny reached a hand to fix her hair, thought better of it just in time, and wiped the paint off her fingers onto her old jeans. She followed Fleur to the door, fumbling with the bolt. Her sister stood on the front step.

"Serena." She hoped she managed to keep the disappointment from her voice.

Fortunately, Fleur made up for her lackluster greeting. Serena pushed the dog back into the living room, focused on keeping Fleur's wet nose from marking her pale chinos.

"She's got white whiskers," Serena remarked, taking a closer look. "And what's that spot on her hip? Look at her tail!"

"That's why she's not allowed in the hall while I paint anymore," Destiny explained, shooting Fleur a look which Fleur ignored.

"You're painting? At this time of night? You can't even see in that hall after dark."

"That's why it needs painting. I've been meaning to get to it ever since I finished the living room last summer."

Serena's eyes narrowed, unconvinced, but she turned away toward the kitchen. "You do have a bottle of red wine somewhere, right?"

"Merlot. On the counter." Destiny moved back to the hall to retrieve her brush. As far as Serena was concerned, red wine was the hard stuff, and Destiny was sure Sarah's misadventure that afternoon was what had her sister hitting the bottle, but there was no point in trying to interrogate her. Serena would get to it when she was good and ready. "Fleur, stay."

Fleur pushed her nose as far over the tarp as she could reach, then plopped down, technically correct, but pleased with herself for scrunching up the plastic. Destiny rolled her eyes, but couldn't help grinning back at the dog.

Serena returned from the kitchen, setting one glass of wine beside Destiny's paint can and gripping another.

"Where's Sarah?" Destiny asked, kneeling down to edge the baseboards.

"Home." Serena leaned against the stepladder and threw back a shot of Merlot. "Jesse's there with her. I made her call David. I was tired of yelling at her. I figured it was her father's turn."

"She was out of school all week?"

"Forged my name on a permission slip. I suspect she strong-armed Gemma into impersonating me on the phone, too, but I'm not going to force her to admit that one."

Destiny glanced up to see her sister leaning away from the wooden stepladder to peer into the bathroom. "Careful! That thing's not stable. What are you doing?"

"He's not here?"

Destiny dropped her eyes back to the baseboard. Serena

might have failed to notice Sarah's truancy, but her intuition rarely let Destiny get away with anything. Destiny didn't need to give her sister any facial expression ammunition.

"He's working." She bit back the "again." "We rescheduled dinner for tomorrow night."

"I didn't mean Daniel. Alain. Kermit said you were giving him a ride back up here to his van. I thought you might have trouble getting rid of him."

That explained her sister's visit. Destiny sat back on her heels. "You came over here to check up on me."

"To back you up."

Destiny glared up at her sister. "Like hell."

Serena shrugged, lifting Destiny's wineglass off the ladder for a swig. "You dated him in the first place, Desty. You were all ready to move out to Arizona if he so much as called your name. Those Gemini types can have an irresistible charm for a fixed sign like Scorpio. I don't want you to mess things up with Daniel."

Destiny didn't have Serena's faith in astrology, but she felt a full-blown Scorpio eruption building below her rib cage. "I would never—" The words choked inside her. "How could you even say such a thing?"

"I know you wouldn't, Desty." Serena's big-sister posture eased a little. "Not even for a lot more temptation than slick old what's-his-name. And I'm sure Daniel knows it, too. But what a man knows and what his jealous instincts tell him are two different things."

The wisdom of the ages dripped from Serena's voice, honeyed with wine. "I know what a sucker you can be for a good sob story. I just wanted to make sure Alain didn't end up on your couch. Even if I knew perfectly well that's where he'd stay."

Destiny shook her head, unable to formulate an appropriately stinging reply. "Believe it or not, I've learned from my mistakes. Alain's never getting another chance to put me through hell again. And neither is anyone else."

Serena leaned toward her. "What are you talking about? You mean Daniel?"

"No." She glanced away.

"Don't give me that. I'm your big sister. I can see right through you. Besides, you're painting."

"I've painted every room in this house!"

"Yes, but the only other time I ever found you painting in the dark was when Fleur went in to have that lump on her ribs removed." Her sister's voice softened. "Desty?"

"Reenie, I don't think I can do it again. Pour my heart into another relationship just to have it fall apart because he moves on."

She felt her sister's hand brush her hair. "Don't. Just don't, Desty. I guess I shouldn't be surprised that Alain's return has brought all this up again. But Daniel's not like that. He's not going anywhere."

Not physically, Destiny thought. She glanced up at Serena. "Well, you don't need to worry about Alain. I sent him to Deepwater to look for a motel room."

"And he went?" Serena straightened in surprise. "I'm impressed. Maybe he's actually matured a little since . . . Wait." Her eyes narrowed once more. "Don't tell me you gave him money for a room."

Destiny turned back to her painting.

"Desty!"

"He said all his cash was tied up in the booth fee for the fair and that he'd pay me back by Saturday night. It was easier than arguing with him about staying here."

Serena sighed. "That, I believe. Look, when he calls you in the morning—"

"I made it clear I didn't want him to call."

Serena raised one smooth eyebrow. "When he calls you in the morning, have him call me. I can probably hook him up with someone at the fairgrounds. Maybe he can find a place to stay there."

Now it was Destiny's turn for suspicion. "Why would you do that? You never liked Alain, and he nearly scared Sarah to death this afternoon."

"I'm not doing it for Alain. I'm doing it for your peace of mind." Like a cat, Serena was more dangerous the more innocent she looked.

Destiny stood and set her paintbrush back down on the upturned lid. "All right. What's my peace of mind going to cost me?"

"I need your help with Sarah. I intend to keep a close eye on her. For the rest of her life. I want to make sure she's not in trouble."

"You know I'd do anything for Sarah."

Serena nodded. "That leads me to the favor. I've agreed to help out at the arts and crafts fair this weekend. I'll take Sarah with me. But it would be even better if you could be there, too. She likes hanging out with her Auntie Dess. It wouldn't be as bad as being spied on by her mother."

"You want me to volunteer at the fair with you?"

"It will be fun. And it's only two days. Mark needs help setting up his booth and watching the cash box, but we'll have plenty of time to shop and eat."

"Mark? Mark Banos? Jesse's brother?"

"Right. Mark." Serena's smile grew even more ingenuous.

Destiny loved Serena's boyfriend, Jesse, for the way he

treated her sister. In one short year he'd repaired much of the damage from Serena's ten troubled years of marriage to Sarah's father. But Destiny liked Jesse Banos for himself, too. He was funny, kind, and generous to a fault.

His youngest brother, Mark, shared his Greek good looks and amiable personality, but whereas Jesse was steady as a rock, Mark had all the inner fortitude of beach sand.

"Come on, Desty. Say you'll do it. It would mean a lot to me. And to Sarah. Besides, Mark's trying hard to make a new start. He could use the help."

"All right, all right." Destiny had no doubt Mark needed all the help he could get, but even if he was clean and sober—again—it was going to be a long weekend playing baby-sitter to him at the arts and . . .

She frowned. "What's Mark doing with a booth at the arts and crafts fair, anyway?" She had to laugh at Serena's carefully innocent expression. "You've got to be kidding me."

"Mark's an artist."

"Serena, he's a *tattoo* artist."

Serena smiled, the tiny smile of a cat that's just brought its paw down on an unsuspecting mouse's tail. "That's right. And you and I are going to be modeling his work."

Chapter 5

Daniel glanced up at the sprawling ranch-style house in front of him, a topaz jewel in a setting of meticulous landscaping. Despite the tall trees rising behind the house, not a redwood needle marred the trim green lawn. Daniel doubted a deer would dare nibble the rosebushes.

Unlike Calvin Macaro's quiet retreat on Redwood Hill Road, Royce Preston's home reigned in pride from its perch on a ridge crest near the north end of town, designed to be seen and admired. The distance between this house and the trailer park Daniel had just left was much farther than the three-mile drive.

Tyler Woodridge's mother had shown little concern about her son's absence, either when Daniel had visited her the night before or on his second visit that afternoon, despite the fact that Tyler had missed school for the past two days and, according to his mother, had not been home since the night of Ariel Macaro's murder.

She had invited Daniel to search her trailer, a cramped, sagging structure designed for one or two occupants, currently overflowing with the detritus of three young children, one teenager, and Mrs. Woodridge.

"The boy goes off for days at a time," she'd told him, ash from her cigarette spilling past her fingers to the floor. "Thinks he's too good for us here. He'll be eighteen in

May. That's the day he moves out for good."

"You mean after graduation?"

She'd eyed Daniel with contempt. "He's got a job over at McDonald's. Maybe they've seen him."

They hadn't. The manager was angry that Tyler had missed two shifts without calling in, though the man professed more concern than Tyler's mother had. Kermit and Grace were talking to Tyler's extended family and school friends while Daniel had moved on to his only other potential suspect thus far. Ariel's previous boyfriend, Kyle Preston.

Kyle Preston's father had shown considerably more concern about his son being questioned by police. He'd refused to allow the interview until his attorney could be present.

Daniel guessed the Buick in the driveway belonged to the lawyer. The Mercedes sedan, Lexus SUV, and BMW convertible in the open garage would belong to Dr., Mrs., and Kyle Preston, respectively.

Royce Preston opened the front door himself. Dr. Preston stood two inches taller than Daniel, his posture too stiff to be perfect. His thin lips tight with protest, he led Daniel into the living room, an uncluttered, tastefully appointed room brightened by tall front windows and a skylight in the vaulted ceiling. The only jarring note against the symphony of white carpet, mauve-toned furnishings, and dark wood trim was the two big-racked buck heads mounted on either side of the fireplace.

Daniel turned from them to where a tall, blond young man in a letterman's jacket sat on a leather sofa with a short, heavyset bulldog of a lawyer. Daniel recognized the lawyer from court.

"Bill."

"Daniel." Bill Walters flipped open the briefcase on the teak coffee table in front of him and sat back. "Kyle here has nothing to hide. I'm merely here to protect the interests of my clients. He'll answer any questions you have, as long as they pertain to the case at hand."

Daniel sat on the edge of the leather armchair closest to Kyle Preston. The boy's green eyes met his with a mixture of cocky scorn and nervous apprehension.

"I don't know anything that can help you," he stated with the belligerence of any unsure youth trying to bluster his way through his insecurities. "I didn't even see Ariel Wednesday night."

Daniel took out his notebook and flipped it to an empty page. He was in no hurry to put this teenager at his ease. "Her father said you were supposed to take her to the country club for dinner."

"She changed her mind."

"Did she tell you why?"

Kyle shrugged, uninterested in plumbing the motives of women. "She said she was going out with Tyler instead. I guess he didn't like the idea of me and Ariel being friends. Maybe he thought there was something going on."

Kyle didn't appear to mind the idea.

"You and Ariel used to be a couple."

"Last year."

An eternity when you were seventeen, though Daniel still remembered the first girl he had ever kissed. And how much it had hurt when she'd decided she preferred another boy.

"But you asked her out to dinner."

"Like I said, we were still friends." Kyle sat back on the sofa, stretching long, quarterback legs. "I called her up Wednesday night about six to tell her I was on my way. She said Tyler didn't want her to go."

"Did that bother you?"

"No." He stopped, apparently realizing Daniel would never believe that. "Not that way. It bothered me that she felt she had to do what Tyler said. I don't think she knew what she was getting into when she started going out with him. He's got issues."

"Issues?"

"Tell him about the fight, Kyle," Royce Preston said. The doctor had remained by the fireplace, still ramrod straight.

Kyle shrugged again, though he shifted uncomfortably. "It was nothing, really. I was talking to Ariel in the hall last month, and Tyler just snapped. He attacked me. They suspended him for a week, but it wasn't a big deal. I could have taken him."

"He knocked Kyle's head against a locker," Royce Preston said, outrage lacing his words. "I told the principal the boy was dangerous, but he refused to expel him. Maybe now he realizes his error."

"I drove up by the Macaros' place after I talked to Ariel," Kyle said.

Daniel's eyes snapped back to him. "You didn't tell Calvin Macaro that."

Kyle glanced away, his hands fluttering on his knees for a second before he clenched them steady. "I didn't know how much I should tell him," he said. His gaze turned back to Daniel. "I knew I could be a suspect. But Mr. Walters said to tell you everything."

"Go ahead, Kyle," the lawyer urged.

Kyle tilted his head to each side, stretching his neck. "I drove up there. I was worried maybe Ariel was in over her head. She'd never admit it, but I thought maybe she wasn't

65

going out with me because she was afraid of Tyler."

Maybe she'd had every reason to be afraid, Daniel thought. Or maybe Kyle Preston was simply taking the opportunity to get back at the boy who'd challenged his tough jock image by banging his head into a locker.

"But when I got to the house, I saw Tyler's car there. I didn't want to get in another fight. I figured I'd talk to Ariel at school on Thursday, make sure she was okay."

A flicker in the boy's eyes told Daniel that the knowledge she wasn't okay bothered him, despite his bravado.

"Where did you go after that?" Daniel asked.

"Home." The word held an insolent confidence.

"He was home with me all evening," Royce Preston interjected. "From about six-thirty until I went up to bed at eleven. His mother was out at an investment club meeting, so Kyle and I had an enjoyable evening to ourselves. Kyle did homework and then we watched the evening news."

Daniel glanced from father to son, catching Kyle's valiant attempt not to roll his eyes. He doubted Kyle's idea of an enjoyable evening was watching the news with his stiff-necked father. But when he glanced back at Royce, he caught an expression that softened the man's rigid features. A yearning so sharp it reached Daniel's heart, a yearning to find some common ground with his son, to matter to his son.

An image flashed through Daniel's memory, standing on a riverbank side by side with his own father, their fishing lines in the water connecting them despite the turmoil of adolescence.

"I think that's about all, Detective," Bill Walters spoke up from Kyle's side. "As he said, Kyle doesn't know anything that can help you."

"I just have one or two more questions," Daniel said,

keeping his gaze on Kyle. "Do you know if Ariel Macaro was using drugs?"

"That's ridiculous!" Royce Preston snapped, lunging a step closer from the fireplace. "How would Kyle know that?"

"That's definitely not an appropriate question," Bill Walters agreed, leaning forward to shut his briefcase. "I think this interview is over."

So, he could ask questions about murder, but not drugs. Interesting.

But Kyle glanced at his father and the lawyer, a scornful smile playing on his lips, before turning back to Daniel. "Ariel didn't do drugs," he said.

"We found a bag of pot at the scene."

Kyle's smirk deepened, though there was no humor in his eyes. "I didn't say Tyler didn't do them."

A very clever way of implying he did, without coming out and saying so.

"Detective?" Bill Walters stood, gesturing Daniel toward the door.

Daniel rose, too, and handed Kyle his card. "If you think of anything else, call me."

Kyle glanced at the card and stuck it in his pocket, the smile still playing at the ends of his mouth. "You bet."

Destiny lit the long white tapers she'd wedged into the sturdy silver candlesticks her grandmother had given her and settled them on her redwood burl coffee table. She'd bought the table in a fit of desperate extravagance brought on by three straight weeks of rain the previous winter, but the effect of the candlelight's reflection in the swirling polished highlights of the burl eased the remembered monetary pain.

She turned off the lights, and her comfortable, worn living room slipped into the elegance of candles and firelight. The romantic atmosphere transformed her serviceable beige stoneware and the wineglasses she'd bought at Longs Drugstore into china and crystal. More or less. And the burning oak in the fireplace almost masked the pungent odor of fresh paint from the hall.

Destiny adjusted the giant pillows she'd dug out of her closet for seating. She and Daniel might have stiff legs by the time they'd finished eating, but the ambience was worth it. If she was only going to get one evening alone with him this week, she was going to make the most of it.

The telephone rang.

"No. Don't you dare." She darted to the kitchen and grabbed the receiver. "Don't tell me. You have to cancel."

"What? How did you know?" The feminine voice at the other end of the line sharpened. "Did Chad tell Pleasance before he told me? That dirty, low-down rat. I'm going to give him a piece—"

"Maddy? Is that you?"

"Of course it's me." Her friend paused. "Who did you think it was?"

"Daniel. What's going on? What did Chad do now?"

Maddy's breath blew over the line. "He canceled our trip to Colorado next week. For a *golf* game. He got invited to play in an amateur tournament down at Pebble Beach, and he *thought I would understand.*"

"Pebble Beach is a big-time course," Destiny said halfheartedly, drawing on the sum total of her golfing knowledge.

"I'm glad I found out where his priorities are." Maddy's voice held steady, despite the hurt Destiny could hear behind it. "I just wanted to let you know that you don't have to come in early on Monday."

The doorbell rang.

"Is that Daniel?" Maddy asked.

"Just let me grab the door. I'll be right back to talk—"

"No, I'm hanging up. I'm not going to jinx your love life, too. I'm going to go take a long bath and soak Chad Geary out of my life. See you Monday."

Not that she thought Chad was good enough for Maddy, but Destiny hated to have her friend hurt again. Not the best omen for her own evening.

Destiny smoothed her skirt, a flowing gold and red print wraparound that Serena had given her for Christmas three years before. She'd never had the nerve—or the occasion— to wear it out, but it was comfortable for floor sitting. And it did show off her calves.

Everything was in place for a romantic evening. Maybe. Or maybe she looked ridiculous, lighting candles and going barefoot, like some kind of retro hippie. She should have worn blue jeans. They would have gone just as well as the skirt with her black turtleneck sweater. Of course, her comfortable jeans had muddy paw prints on them from Fleur's afternoon walk and the tight pair would cut off her femoral arteries if she tried to sit on the floor in them for more than five minutes, but—

A hesitant knock on the door brought her back to reality: she didn't have time to change. Swallowing her unexpected nervousness, she hurried to the door and swung it open.

A police detective stood on her doorstep, his sandy brown hair rumpled from restless fingers, his blue eyes distant with heavy responsibility, his body hard and unyielding in his work clothes, a slate-blue shirt and dark chocolate slacks beneath a plain brown jacket.

For a second he stood there unmoving, and she could

see the effort it took him to shake off the office he had just left. His stance relaxed; the furrow between his brows smoothed out. As he took in her outfit, she could see the spark of humor warming his eyes, along with another warmth that told her she wasn't going to care if he teased her about the skirt.

"I don't think I'm dressed for a séance," Daniel said, glancing behind her. "Candles? Have you called the power company?"

"Ambience," Destiny said tartly, standing aside for him to enter.

"Of course. Ambience. Sorry."

She didn't believe his repentance for a second, but when he put a hand on her hip and leaned in for a kiss, she decided not to be offended.

An eruption of noise from the kitchen gave her enough warning to jump out of the way of Fleur's rush toward Daniel. Yellow Lab filled the room, legs and nose everywhere. Destiny dove for the coffee table, just managing to lift the candlesticks out of the way of Fleur's whipping tail.

"Down!" Daniel ordered in a voice that froze hardened criminals in their tracks. Fleur bounced for his face, her tongue catching him from chin to forehead.

"Yuck! Fleur! Sit!" She did, and Daniel crouched down to rub her ears as her tail beat the floor ecstatically.

"Good save," he commented, as Destiny replaced the candles.

"The wineglasses weren't so lucky." She crouched down to rescue them from the carpet, along with the napkins and a knife and fork.

"At least the wineglasses weren't burning."

She snorted. "So much for ambience."

With one hand on Fleur's head to immobilize her,

Daniel cautiously got to his feet and shrugged out of his jacket. "What's ambience without a little dog hair? Dinner smells great. You didn't have to go to all this trouble. I was supposed to be feeding you tonight."

"You can make it up to me later," Destiny assured him. "And it wasn't that much trouble. You can thank the Spicy Sicilian for the aroma. Dinner's delivered."

"Anchovies on the side?" Daniel asked hopefully, settling onto one of the giant pillows. He patted a place beside him for Fleur.

"Just for you."

"You're an angel of mercy."

"I'm a saint," Destiny said, heading for the kitchen to retrieve the pizza from the oven. "And don't you forget it. I might even kiss you after you eat them."

"Is that right?"

She set the pizza on the coffee table, reserving a stern look for Fleur. "We'll see. You might want to pour me some wine."

"I might." Daniel grabbed the bottle of white zinfandel and applied the corkscrew.

Destiny settled on the pillow next to him, leaning back against the couch. "It's good to see you."

"I'm a cop." The sudden tension in his voice told her she hadn't kept the words as light as she'd intended. "This isn't just a nine-to-five job. When people start getting killed, I can't put work on hold to go out to dinner."

"I haven't seen you all week, even though nobody got killed until yesterday."

"You know what I meant." He handed her a glass of wine without looking at her, anger in the line of his jaw.

She lifted her plate for the slice of pizza he offered, but the bite she took had no flavor. "All I meant was that I'm glad to see you tonight."

He glanced at her, his eyes opaque in the firelight. "I warned you it's going to be like this sometimes."

"You did. I think I warned you I was going to love you anyway."

"You think I should have paid more attention to that part?" Maybe he didn't believe her, but his shoulders relaxed as he reached for the anchovies.

"Edgar is going to be all over you tonight," Destiny said. Daniel's cat could smell a tuna fish can opening on Mars.

Daniel grimaced in mock horror. "You're right. It's probably not safe for me to go home tonight. I have a spit kit with me. I could just crash on the couch in the officers' lounge at the station." The humor had returned to his eyes.

"You sure could." She narrowed her own at him.

"Or I could borrow your couch. Unless it's reserved for some old ex-boyfriend."

"Serena found Alain a place to stay this morning. One of Mark Banos's friends offered him a bunk in his trailer at the fairgrounds."

"So the couch is free?"

"It's about the best you can hope for, unless you start shaping up, buster."

"Mercy lodging? That's about all I deserve." He offered Fleur an anchovy, which she took delicately between her teeth and then swallowed whole. "I'm sorry about the attitude. How can I make it up to you?"

She pursed her lips, considering. "Let's see. Serena's roped me into helping Mark out at the arts and crafts fair. You could come to the fairgrounds and rescue me tomorrow afternoon. Maybe whisk me away for a romantic dinner at L'Etoile d'Esperance."

"Destiny, I can't just drop everything this weekend to go

to some craft thing—" He stopped himself. "Right. I'm probably not going to be decent company until this Ariel Macaro case is solved, and I'm not going to have much time to be any company at all. How about a romantic cup of coffee at the Banana Slug Café?"

She nodded, mollified. "That will do until you wrap this up. Then I expect L'Etoile. Do you have any suspects?"

"I can't tell you that. It's an ongoing investigation."

"I thought you might want to talk about it, get it out of your system."

"I don't discuss active cases with civilians."

Destiny sat up, throat tight as she set down her pizza. "You discussed the investigation into Supervisor Barclay's death with me."

"So far no one connected with Ariel Macaro's death has tried to strangle you or shoot you or kill your dog." He sighed heavily. "Look, it's just not good policy."

"Joe Leaphorn always used to discuss his cases with Emma before she died."

"Joe Leaphorn is a fictional character. Besides, Emma was his wife."

There was certainly nothing she could say to that. Marriage was something she and Daniel had not discussed, just as they had skirted around the issue of leaving toothbrushes at each other's houses. She kept reminding herself they hadn't even known each other three months yet. There was no need to hurry.

But then she hadn't pressed Alain for a commitment during their year-and-a-half relationship, and look how that had turned out.

She closed the pizza box to keep Fleur's nose out of it, and grabbed her plate to take it into the kitchen, but Daniel's hand on her wrist held her seated.

"I couldn't talk about cases with Tessa, either."

She glanced at Daniel from the corner of her eye, not sure what he was trying to tell her by bringing up his ex-wife. "Of course you couldn't talk about cases with Tessa. She's a defense attorney."

Daniel took the plate from her hand and set it down on the coffee table before wrapping her fingers in his. "It's not just compromising the case. I know you wouldn't share anything confidential. But it would be nice to leave it at the office for a few hours."

He pulled her over to his pillow, wrapping his arm around her shoulder. "This was a beautiful girl, Destiny, with her whole life ahead of her. From what her father and her friends have said, she was smart, funny, compassionate. No drugs, no wild partying. She was all set to go to some high-powered college to study environmental engineering. She was thinking about joining the Peace Corps. She wanted to save the world."

Destiny blew out some of the hurt she'd been hoarding. "And you have to find out why she was killed."

"Homicide investigations are bad. It's not just the victim. Ariel Macaro didn't deserve to die, but she's not hurting anymore. Her father will hurt for the rest of his life. She was all the family he had left. All his hopes for the future. He retired from Congress partly to spend more time with her before she graduated high school.

"Her friends are devastated. And scared. I can't blame them. There's no guarantee her killer won't strike again."

Destiny thought of Sarah confronting a knife-wielding serial killer with a baseball bat and a yellow Lab, and shuddered. "Do you think that's likely?"

She felt Daniel shrug. "The father thinks it was a jealous boyfriend."

"You're not so sure?"

"It doesn't look good for him. I'd hoped we'd have him in for questioning by now, but he's disappeared. We've had an APB out on him since last night, but he hasn't been home or to any of his relatives' houses." He squeezed her shoulder, his voice rumbling a little in irony. "I'm not spilling any state secrets here, just in case you were wondering. I'm sure the press will have picked up on this by now and we'll be reading all about it in the *Jasper County Register* tomorrow morning."

"I don't want state secrets." She wanted not to be shut out. "Does this kid have a history of violence? If you can tell me."

"His older brother has been in and out of the court system on drug-related charges, and one of his mother's cousins is serving time for assault. The kid himself has never been in any trouble with the law, but he did get suspended from school last month for a fight with the former boyfriend."

"He attacked the other boy at school?"

Daniel shrugged again. "That's the official story. One of the kids Kermit talked with at the high school suggested the other boy provoked him. But the former boyfriend's father is a heart surgeon, not an absentee father who forgets to send child support."

Destiny glanced up at his face. "You think the principal gave the rich kid preferential treatment?"

Daniel's lips twisted. "You sound surprised. I don't want my job to change that about you."

"Maybe this surgeon's son was just an innocent victim."

"Or maybe his father brought a high-powered lawyer over when the principal called him in after the fight. He had a lawyer there when I went over to interview Kyle this afternoon."

"Is this Kyle kid a suspect, too?"

"He was supposed to go out with Ariel that night. He was one of the last people to see her alive." Daniel shook his head. "I haven't ruled him out, even if his father swears he was home with him all evening, but he's not an official suspect. He didn't need a lawyer to answer the questions I asked about the other boy."

He shifted his weight and hugged her closer. "That's what I mean about homicides. Everyone is a suspect. Even the victim's family and closest friends. Everyone is scared. Everyone is hiding something they don't want you to know. And you have no idea if what they're hiding is important to the case or simply the fact that they have a glove compartment full of unpaid parking tickets."

"So, you were looking forward to a quiet evening of pizza."

"And you spoiled it by trying to make conversation." He grunted, bearlike. "Me tough guy. Too much talk. Not enough anchovies."

He snorted again, and nuzzled Destiny's neck. She laughed, but even as she turned to kiss him, loving the strength of his arms as he held her and the spicy whiff of his aftershave and the pepperoni from the pizza, she knew there was still a part of himself he didn't share.

He'd given her some facts on his current case in an effort to appease her, but each word had been a tightrope act. She understood. Of course he couldn't share police secrets. But some small, scared part of her couldn't help thinking of Alain and how she'd never even known he meant to leave her until he was gone. Or, maybe she had known, deep down. And now she didn't know if that was the same feeling she was getting from Daniel, or if it was just Alain's return making her paranoid.

At least his job was a better excuse for canceled dates than a golf game in Pebble Beach.

"What's wrong?" Daniel asked, pulling back from the kiss. "You look so serious."

The warmth of his concern warred with the fear in her heart. "I was just thinking that you were wrong about the anchovies, tough guy. You got plenty."

His eyebrows rose in disbelief, and he leaned in to blow in her face. She laughed again as he held her tight, preventing her from wriggling away. This time she responded wholeheartedly to his kiss, wrapping her arms behind his neck and pulling him down onto the pillow with her. His lips tasted warm and salty. She might develop a partiality for anchovies, after all.

Daniel pulled back from the kiss, his hand brushing a wild curl from her temple. She could see the echo of her awakening desire in his eyes, along with another emotion that turned his blue eyes smoky black.

"Destiny." His low voice rumbled along her nerves, all the way down into the pit of her stomach. "It's good to see you, too."

She pulled him back down, her lips brushing his just as the doorbell chimed. Fleur scrambled to her feet, her tail once more sweeping the wineglasses to the floor.

Destiny groaned, closing her eyes. "Serena."

"Or what's-his-name, the ex-boyfriend cat burglar, back for another try at your couch."

She opened her eyes and grimaced at him. "You make an interruption by Serena sound relatively good."

"Ignore it," he suggested, lowering his mouth once more. The doorbell chimed again, a sustained bingbonging that started Fleur barking in high-pitched excitement.

Destiny groaned again. "Serena with an emergency."

Daniel pulled her up with him as he rose to his feet. "Go ahead and deal with it. I'll take care of the dishes and put the pizza away."

"Right. I never argue with a man willing to wash dishes." Destiny helped him retrieve the wineglasses, glad for once of the green shag carpet and that she'd chosen white zin over merlot. She crossed to the door, steeling herself for the coming onslaught.

The man on the doorstep looked nothing like Serena, but the expression on his face reminded Destiny of her sister in emergency mode.

"Kermit!" She grabbed Fleur's collar to pull the ecstatic Lab back inside. The dog's whole body wagged, greeting her soul mate, but for once Kermit didn't bend down to play.

"I'm sorry to interrupt . . ." His gaze traveled over the pizza remains, the candles, the fire, and a rueful flush crept up his cheeks. "Really sorry."

Daniel came up beside her. "What is it, Kerry?"

"You said to let you know immediately if anything broke with the Macaro case, Detective . . ."

Destiny stifled a groan. "Detective" instead of "Daniel" meant more than an interruption. So much for a romantic evening by firelight.

"What's happened?" Daniel was already grabbing his jacket from the arm of the couch.

"Nancy just got a call from Vance and Yap. They got a line on Tyler Woodridge. He showed up at his grandparents' place. They're heading out to apprehend him."

Daniel paused, one arm in his jacket. "They were supposed to contact me before taking any action."

"I guess that's what the call to the station was for," Kermit said, though his carefully neutral expression didn't fool Destiny. He was as angry as Daniel.

"You've got the address?"

Kermit nodded.

"You're driving."

At one time, the idea of Kermit driving had terrified Destiny, but she'd learned his clumsiness disappeared behind the wheel, much as it did when he was focused on a case. Apparently that focus hadn't quite kicked in, because he tripped over the doorsill on his way out.

"I'm sorry." Daniel paused for a quick kiss before following Kermit with a more animal grace. Destiny could see the glint of the predator in his eye, though whether the prey in his sights was Tyler Woodridge or Officers Vance and Yap, she couldn't have said. "This will run late. Don't wait up. I'll call you tomorrow."

"I'll be at the arts and crafts fair . . ."

But he was already down the walk, climbing into Kermit's patrol car. The persistent drizzle diffused the streetlights, giving the scene a strange unreality. The car door slammed, and Kermit peeled away from the curb, the light on top of the cruiser strobing a warning through the night. Warning that they were heading into danger.

Destiny's hand clutched her doorknob as she watched them round the corner and disappear into the darkness. She should have told Kermit to drive carefully. She should have told Daniel she loved him. Sometimes she could forget the hazards of Daniel's job. In the mundane routine of most of his work, he was more likely to be bored to death by paperwork than shot. But sometimes the reality of the risks he faced struck her so hard just below the ribs that it knocked the breath from her.

A wet nose pressed against her free hand, and she glanced down to see Fleur gazing up at her, the dog's forehead wrinkled in concern.

"Yeah, me, too." She dug her fingers into the fur behind Fleur's right ear, glancing once more up the empty street. At least she could take comfort from the fact that Ariel's murder had involved a knifing, not a shooting. Tyler Woodridge probably didn't have a gun.

Chapter 6

"The message Nancy gave me, Vance and Yap think the kid might be armed," Kermit said, slicing off the freeway onto the second Garfield exit off-ramp at eighty miles per hour. Daniel refrained from clutching at the dashboard as the patrol car swung onto Airport Road.

"I'm surprised to hear Vance and Yap are thinking at all," Daniel muttered, watching the cypress trees lining the road whip by. Kermit took the Y fork onto Junction Road, away from the airport. "Garfield is unincorporated county land. Did they inform the sheriff's office about this apprehension?"

"Garth's impulsive," Kermit said, taking another sharp turn down a wooded country road, the Police Interceptor's high-performance suspension and V-8 engine combining for a heart-stopping ride. Daniel hoped the deer were all asleep. "But Tom usually keeps him in line. I think that's why Lieutenant Marcy partnered them together."

Kermit had more faith in James Marcy than Daniel did. Daniel had just been wondering if the lieutenant had suggested to Officers Garth Vance and Tom Yap that it would look good for the Drug Task Force to bring this particular suspect into custody on their own. No need to interrupt Detective Parks's evening.

The patrol car slowed, and Kermit turned off onto a

winding lane that dipped down to follow a narrow creek through a second-growth forest of pines and alder. Their headlights caught the bumper of another black-and-white Crown Victoria. Kermit killed the lights and engine and glided in behind Vance and Yap's car.

As Daniel and Kermit got out of the car, the momentary silence of the damp, still night was broken by a bullhorn bark of a voice that Daniel recognized immediately as Garth Vance.

"Damn it, kid, we know you're in there. Come out now, or we're coming in after you."

"The fine art of diplomacy," Daniel muttered, as he and Kermit started up the dirt driveway past Vance and Yap's patrol car. Keeping close to the brush at the side of the drive, Daniel paused at the edge of Tyler Woodridge's grandparents' lawn. More of a clearing than a lawn, he thought. The light over the trailer door showed a swath of close-cropped grass dotted with ferns and mounds of black-berry vines.

The battered seventies model Ford pickup parked beside the double-wide trailer suggested the grandparents were home, but no lights shone inside the building.

They were probably afraid to give Vance a silhouette to take a potshot at, Daniel thought darkly.

Officer Vance himself hunched behind a gnarled apple tree ten feet ahead and to the left of Daniel. The old tree hadn't been properly pruned in a decade, and its twisted, drooping limbs, a few sodden leaves still clinging damply to them, offered a screen, if not much shelter, to Garth Vance's bulky form.

Daniel turned to Kermit and mouthed, "Cover me."

He knew that some inhabitants of rural Jasper County viewed law enforcement with distrust, even those inhabitants who didn't supplement their income with a little illicit agriculture. A few delusional idiots even ran methamphetamine labs out of their homes, oblivious or indifferent to the danger of blowing themselves and their entire families to smithereens.

Still, as he crossed the yard toward the apple tree, he was less concerned about the possibility of Tyler Woodridge's grandfather getting off a load of buckshot than he was about the 9mm. in Garth Vance's hand.

"Officer Vance," he announced himself quietly, keeping his hands away from his sides as Vance whirled on him. "Detective Parks and Officer Riggs. Your backup."

Vance gestured him over with urgent jerks of his hand. "Get down," he hissed. "We've got information this creep has a gun. He knows he's looking good for the Macaro murder. He could be desperate."

Daniel crouched down beneath the apple tree's limbs and gestured toward Vance's gun. "Shouldn't you be wearing a vest?"

Vance shrugged his broad shoulders. "Restricts my aim."

In other words, Vance was too macho for a vest. Daniel fought back what could be an incipient ulcer. "What's going on here, Vance? You got an arrest warrant?"

Vance nodded. "Judge signed one this afternoon."

That was fast, given the lack of hard evidence of Tyler Woodridge's involvement in the murder, but the victim was the daughter of a former congressman.

Still, if Vance and Yap had a warrant, what was Vance doing shouting at the house from the yard? "You don't have a warrant to enter the grandparents' place."

"We didn't get word he was here until half an hour ago," Vance said. "No time to get it changed. Tom figured we could intimidate the kid into giving himself up."

Daniel glanced at the dark house. "Any luck?"

Vance caught the sarcasm. "He may be a killer, but he's still just a punk kid. We'll get him. We can wait him out if we have to."

Vance leaned forward, his free hand resting on the trunk of the tree. "Come on, kid." His bellow echoed around the small clearing. "Hiding out ain't gonna make it go away."

Daniel thought of the terrified teenager and his grandparents in the trailer, the questionable legality of Vance and Yap's apprehension techniques, the beautiful woman and candlelight he'd left behind in Hope Point to come crouch in the wet grass on a cold, wet night. He bit down on his anger. Lashing out at Garth Vance wouldn't make this go away, either.

In the absence of a good solution, what he needed was a nonlethal one. He needed a decent warrant, and cluing in the sheriff's department wouldn't be a bad idea, either.

"Where's Officer Yap?"

"Over behind the pickup. Making sure the kid doesn't climb out a back window."

"All right." He took a deep breath. "What we're going to do is this. You're going to go get Yap, and the two of you are going to go back to your patrol car and call—"

"Hey!" Vance's head snapped around, his eyes narrowed. "We're not going anywhere. This is our arrest. You can sit back and watch if you want. Otherwise you can get the hell out of our way."

"Are you telling me to go to hell, Officer?" Daniel asked, his voice deadly calm.

Even in the near darkness, he saw Vance blanch. "That's not what I said, sir. Look, Detective, we got the intel on this. We did the legwork. You can't just send us out of the way so you can make the bust."

"No one's going to be busting anything until you get the right warrant," Daniel said. "The faster you get it, the faster this gets resolved, the sooner we all get to go to bed."

Vance's face contorted in frustration. "Well, hell."

The tension in Daniel's chest eased. If he could get Vance and Yap out of the equation, maybe he could talk Tyler Woodridge into giving himself up. Or at the very least, giving up any weapon in his possession. "Go get Yap—"

But before he could finish the sentence, a sound snapped across the clearing. The click of a door latch.

Daniel and Vance both dropped lower as they watched the front door of the trailer ease open. A sneakered foot escaped from the darkness of the doorway and stepped down onto the aluminum front step, making it creak. Slowly, the rest of the foot's owner eased into view.

Unprepossessing, was Daniel's first thought. The kid was skinny enough to look taller than he was. His shoulders slouched toward each other beneath his denim jacket in defiance and fear. His dark hair hung lank over his ears. Daniel knew he was seventeen, but he still looked more boy than man, despite the attempt at a mustache across his upper lip.

"Freeze right there!" The shout came from Daniel's right. He could just make out the faint outline of Tom Yap's face peering over the hood of the old Ford pickup beside the trailer. The barrel of his Beretta glinted against the faded paint of the hood.

Tyler Woodridge turned to face him, his hands deep in the pockets of his denim jacket.

"Get your hands up, kid! Damn it, do it now!"

"Hands up!" Vance echoed, his voice catching Yap's urgency.

The young man frowned, confused, turning toward the apple tree. His foot slipped on the slick wet step, and one hand flew free as he tripped down to the gravel walkway. The other hand stuck in his pocket.

In an instant of clarity, Daniel could see how it would all play out, and his heart dropped all the way into his stomach. He opened his mouth to shout his own command, but Yap's voice snapped across the clearing like a bullet.

"Garth! He's got a gun! Stop him!"

If Daniel had stopped to think, if he had seen a cold-blooded killer standing in that doorway instead of a scared kid, he would have still been crouched in place when Vance lifted his gun. But Daniel didn't think. He was already surging forward, his forearm knocking Vance's arm skyward as the officer squeezed off his shot.

The noise temporarily deafened Daniel, but he could feel the vibration of his shout. "Cease fire!"

As the ringing of the shot faded across the clearing, he heard Kermit yelling. "Get down, kid!"

Tyler Woodridge followed Kermit's order, dropping to his face in the wet grass. Yap was shouting, too, telling Kermit to stay back, but Kermit's long legs carried him across the clearing in seconds, putting him between the teenager and Yap's line of sight.

Beside Daniel, Vance was cursing as he struggled to his feet. His breath came heavily as he clutched his gun, pointing it toward the trailer.

"Put your weapon away," Daniel ordered, waiting to be sure Vance heard and understood.

"Damn," Vance panted as he holstered his gun. "Damn, you could have got us both killed."

But Daniel heard as much terror as fury in the younger officer's voice, and he knew Vance understood exactly how close he had come to taking Tyler Woodridge's life.

Daniel crossed the clearing toward where Kermit had hefted their young suspect to his feet after a thorough frisking. Tom Yap met him there.

"No gun," Kermit said, voice tight with adrenaline and anger.

"Tyler Woodridge?" Yap said, his own breathing much calmer than Kermit's. "You're under arrest on suspicion of the murder of Ariel Macaro."

"Tyler? Are you all right? Did they hurt you?"

"What the hell do you people think you're doing?"

Daniel looked up to see Tyler's grandparents standing in the doorway of their trailer. The youth's grandfather was nearly as skinny as the boy, his grandmother heftier in the hips and shoulders than her husband. Standing in the harsh glare of the light over the door, they looked worn by life, lines dug into their faces by hard work and bitterness, but Daniel doubted they were much older than their early fifties.

Yap's voice continued behind him, reading Tyler Woodridge his rights, as Daniel swallowed his frustration and prepared to explain to these two wary people why the police were dragging their grandson away in handcuffs.

He ran a hand through his hair and took a deep breath, while he tried to remember just what that reason was. Murder. Drugs. Resisting arrest. This was going to be a long night.

Daniel lowered himself into the scarred, straight-backed wooden chair across the folding metal table from where Tyler Woodridge slouched in a matching chair. Suspicious brown eyes peered out from behind lanky locks of dark brown hair.

Daniel set down the two coffee cups he carried and slid one across the table toward the teenager. He reflected that offering a suspect the department's coffee, especially from a pot still heating on the element at midnight on a Friday night, walked a fine line between putting the suspect at ease and police brutality.

He sipped from his own cup, hoping the bitter sludge wouldn't eat through his stomach lining before the interview was over. The interrogation. They'd dragged Tyler Woodridge away in handcuffs; they could hardly expect him to be a cooperative witness at this point.

He silently cursed Vance and Yap. He'd sent them to get a warrant to search Tyler's grandparents' property. Daniel hoped they had a long, cold, wet night.

"You understand you have the right to have a lawyer present? Or your mother?"

Kermit had read the boy his rights a second time after their arrival at the station, but it never hurt to cover all the bases.

"My mother?" Tyler's laughter was bitter. "I don't need anybody. I don't need a lawyer. I didn't do anything."

"What didn't you do?"

Tyler crouched forward a little, his eyes glaring. "I know you think I killed Ariel. Why don't you just come out and ask if I done it? Huh? God."

He threw himself back in his seat, and waited. Daniel waited longer.

"I mean, how could anyone think I killed her? She was, like, better than anyone I ever met. I loved her. And she loved me, too, whether her old man liked it or not."

Daniel took another sip of his coffee, letting his face show skepticism, though all he felt was weariness. "Calvin

Macaro says you were jealous that Ariel was dating Kyle Preston."

"Oh, man." Tyler slapped a hand back against the wall in frustration. "She wasn't 'dating' him. She never could see what a true worm he was, but she was through with him. She wouldn't have dated him again if he was the last guy on earth."

Daniel raised an eyebrow. "She was supposed to go to the country club with him the night she was killed."

"Then why the hell isn't that asshole the one sitting here instead of me?" Tyler leaned forward again, throwing his hands down on the metal table. "Why aren't you asking him these questions instead of me? Because he's a doctor's kid, that's why. Because he's on the football team and is going to get a full ride to Stanford on his daddy's coattails. Same reason I got suspended from school and he got the nurse to kiss his boo-boos. 'Cause I'm just trailer trash, and who expects anything better from a kid whose father is drinking himself to death in every bar from here to Tijuana."

He snorted, and his lip curled in irony, but he didn't turn away from Daniel's skeptical gaze. Seeing the fire and the self-knowledge in those clear brown eyes, Daniel decided that Tyler Woodridge had not been a charity project for Ariel Macaro.

"You're here because Kyle Preston was home with his father all evening, because Ariel told him she was going out with you instead."

Tyler frowned and shook his head. "That's not true."

"Your car wasn't parked up at the Macaro house that night?"

He shrugged. "Yeah, I went over there to her house to convince her not to go to the country club with that jerk. But like I said, she couldn't see what a creep he was. She was worried about him. She'd heard at school that maybe he was getting into drugs. She wanted to help him out. She told me to go home, said she'd call me when she got in."

"Did she call?"

"No, man, she got *frickin' killed*." Tyler shouted the last words, nearly coming across the table at Daniel.

Daniel didn't blink. "So you didn't see Kyle Preston that night?"

Tyler's chest heaved as he breathed. He finally sat back, shaking his head. "No. I didn't see him. I left like Ariel wanted."

"Even though she was going out with your rival."

Tyler snorted again. "I trusted her, man."

"You don't look like a trusting kind of guy to me, Tyler."

The kid's lip turned scornful once more. "I don't expect you to understand. You never met her. She wouldn't cheat. She was honest, the only really honest person I ever met. She'd go ahead and tell you what was up, whether you wanted to hear it or not. Man, some girls if they dump you, you're the last to know. With Ariel, you'd be the first. That's why she wanted to talk to Kyle. She wasn't going to pass around rumors. She went right to the heart of whatever mattered."

As he talked, the sneer faded, replaced by a grief so acute, Daniel almost had to look away. The boy couldn't fake the pain that haunted his eyes.

Still, that didn't mean he hadn't killed the girl.

"Where did you go after you left Ariel?"

Tyler shrugged again. "Walking. I went to the beach. That's where me and Ariel would go when we just wanted to be quiet and be together. I had her cell phone. I was waiting for her to call."

"Nobody saw you there."

"No, man, nobody saw me."

"When did you get home?"

"I don't know."

"Would your mother know?"

Another lip curl. "Not unless she was psychic. She got home later than I did. She's got a new boyfriend. Or maybe she's back with one of the old ones."

"When did you hear about Ariel?"

"My brother Eric heard about it."

"Your brother the drug dealer?"

Tyler's eyes hardened, and he looked away. "Why am I even talking to you?"

"We found a bag of marijuana at the scene."

"Well, it wasn't Ariel's. She didn't do that stuff." Then he realized what Daniel was saying. "Screw you. You think I don't know how it looks?"

"It looks like you were hiding out, Tyler. Like you knew you'd messed up big time, and you were afraid you were going to get caught."

"Yeah? When Eric heard Ariel got killed, he heard I was being fingered for it, too. Why not? I'm no loss to anybody. Nice for her old man, too. He couldn't get rid of me while she was alive, but he'd love to see me behind bars. Whether I'm guilty or not."

Tyler's eyes sharpened and met Daniel's again, the mark of the truth teller and the calculated ploy of the practiced liar. "I'm convenient for you, too. Lots more convenient than Kyle Preston."

"Kyle Preston was with his father when Ariel was killed."

The lip curl was a snarl. "Well, maybe I was with my old man, too. If you can track him down, you could ask him."

"I'm asking you, Tyler. This state has the death penalty.

Maybe if you tell us what happened, you can convince us this wasn't premeditated murder. If you don't tell me the truth, there's nothing I can do for you."

Tyler swiped a hand across the table, sending both coffee cups flying across the room to smash against the wall. "I told you! I didn't kill her. That's the truth. You just don't want to hear it."

Daniel pushed his chair back from the table. "All right. But if you change your mind or have anything else you want to tell me, you let me know."

"Whatever."

Daniel rose, and the door to the interview room opened. Daniel nodded to Kermit, who would see that Tyler was returned to a holding cell. He exited into the corridor where Lieutenant Tiebold waited beside the one-way glass.

The lieutenant shrugged, his bony shoulders raising long, heron-wing arms. "You could have pressed harder for a confession."

Daniel shook his head. "I don't think he's ready to confess."

"It would be nice, though," Lieutenant Tiebold said, glancing into the room, where Kermit was removing the boy through the back door. "We need a conviction on this case."

Daniel ran a hand through his hair, suppressing renewed irritation at Vance and Yap. "Even a confession might not give us a conviction if we don't come up with some evidence connecting the kid to the crime. We don't even have enough to hold him."

Tiebold's eyebrows rose gracefully up his forehead. "I'd say you'd better come up with enough evidence before we have to let him back out on the street tomorrow morning."

Daniel glanced at the clock. Technically it already was morning. It wasn't going to happen. They'd have to go to

Plan B. His own personal Plan A. "We'll keep tabs on him. Take the time to gather the evidence. Get all the results from the autopsy and the crime lab. Then pick him up when we've got enough to go to the grand jury."

"One thing we don't have is time," Tiebold warned. "We need evidence tying Woodridge to the crime, and we need it now."

Daniel shook his head, staring into the now empty interview room, but seeing a murdered young woman, a frightened young man. "This kid could be telling the truth, Lieutenant. Maybe there isn't any evidence tying him to the crime because he didn't kill her."

"He killed her all right."

Daniel and Lieutenant Tiebold turned to see Garth Vance striding toward them down the hall, Tom Yap a slimmer shadow behind him. Vance held a clear evidence bag high in his right hand, inside which a jagged-edged hunting knife glinted in the fluorescent lighting.

From the smile of grim vindication that slashed across Vance's face, Daniel gathered the dark spots on the knife's grip were not mud stains.

"Give thanks for young, dumb perps," Yap said dryly.

"He killed the girl," Vance said, "and we've got all the evidence we need to convict him."

A bloody knife. As good as the proverbial smoking gun. More than Daniel could have hoped for. If the blood proved to belong to Ariel Macaro, his case was solved, nothing remaining but to tie up the loose ends. With any luck, he could go home and get some sleep. Return to the normal round of routine investigations and paperwork. Make the past week up to Destiny.

It sounded good. A gift just in time for the holiday season. He should feel grateful. Professionally satisfied. Relieved. But all he felt was a queasy discomfort in the pit of his stomach. A detective's instinct that all was not right with the world.

He hoped to heaven it was the coffee.

Chapter 7

"Whoa! You look like a biker chick." Gemma's tone said that was way cool.

"You look like a hippie." Sarah's tone said *not*.

Destiny stepped in front of the full-length mirror propped against the canvas side of Mark Banos's arts and crafts fair booth. Dark fawn-colored Celtic knots wove down her arms, a striking color against her pale skin and the white tank top she wore. A butterfly hovered just above her collarbone. A circlet of thorns wrapped around one ankle above her Chaco sandals, a sleepy dragon curled around the other.

She stretched her arms to the sides, watching the way the designs twisted and flowed. She turned her palms up, showing the roses blooming there. A smile hovered on the lips of her image in the mirror.

She might look like a hippie biker chick, but she felt like an ancient princess, decorated for a pagan ceremony that might end in either marriage or being fed to a dragon. Which, for some ancient princesses, probably amounted to much the same thing, in the end.

"What do you think?"

Destiny turned to watch her sister step out of the dressing room. Serena's arms were covered in even more intricate designs than Destiny's, a weaving of fine lines and scrollwork from her fingertips to her elbows that looked like lace gloves. Serena spun around, her hair swinging aside to reveal the Indian-inspired design running from the base of her neck to disappear into the deeply dipped back of her white sleeveless shirt.

"Whoa," Gemma said again. "Pretty cool, Mrs. Davis."

"What if it doesn't come off?" Sarah demanded. "What if you look like that forever?" Sarah's expression suggested her only recourse would be to become a nun, since she would never be able to show her face at school again.

"Henna only stains the epidermis," Mark said, from his position leaning against the display table, examining his handiwork. Sober, his dark eyes had a sharp artist's perception. "The epidermis is the outer layer of skin—"

"I know what the epidermis is," Sarah said, insulted. "What if it stains deeper?"

"It doesn't." Mark reached over to hold Serena's arm. He picked off a flake of paste he'd missed on her finger. He wasn't any taller than Serena, unlike his brother, who could rest his chin on her head. Mark's features were softer and rounder than Jesse's, too, though the brothers shared their high Greek cheekbones and thick, dark hair. Of course, Jesse had no rings through his thick, dark eyebrows. Mark had five. "Henna body art usually washes off within one to four weeks—"

"Four weeks!" Destiny squeaked. She turned on her sister. "You said a couple of days."

Serena shrugged, hazel eyes wide and innocent. "A couple of days. A couple of weeks. Something like that."

"This won't last that long," Mark said, yanking Destiny's hand away from her opposite wrist, preventing her attempt to see if the color would scrape off. "We should have left the paste on another couple of hours, but we got started late."

"I got up at six o'clock on a Saturday morning for you," Destiny reminded him. "Don't push it."

"I appreciate it," Mark assured her, with the guilelessness of those who have had their sense of irony fried by acid. "You and Serena are really helping me out. That's totally decent. And Sarah and Gemma, too."

"You sure you don't want to get one?" Serena asked, wiggling henna-ringed fingers at her daughter. "It's your one chance to have a tattoo before you turn eighteen."

"No way." Sarah backed to the far side of the tent until her legs bumped against the cash table, jiggling the change box and the brochures for the tattoo parlor where Mark worked. "I agreed to help set up and make change. That's it. Not to be some walking advertisement."

The defiant set of her chin said *you can make me be here, but you can't make me enjoy it.*

"Suit yourself," Serena said, her own eyes narrowing with annoyance.

"If I'm going to be a walking advertisement, I guess I'd better get out and walk," Destiny broke in. "We'll probably be busy here this afternoon. Maybe we should get some lunch while we can. Sarah, why don't you and Gemma come with me to carry the food?"

"I've got homework I should be doing," Sarah muttered as they stepped out of the booth into the full sunlight.

"You've got Thanksgiving vacation all next week."

"She's grounding me forever," Sarah objected, managing a credible teenage scowl. "I feel like I'm in prison."

"Tell me why you don't deserve it."

"I knew you'd take her side."

Destiny waited two beats for Sarah to look up at her.

Then she laughed. Sarah scowled harder, but couldn't keep it up.

"Fine," she huffed, throwing up her arms. "I'm your guys's slave for life."

"Your *guys's?*" Destiny asked.

"You and Serena's," Gemma explained.

Destiny stifled another laugh. "All right. What do we want to eat?"

"The food booths are down there by the livestock barns," Sarah said, leading the way.

Destiny followed the two girls, resisting the urge to rub the goose bumps on her arms, though she knew the henna had set enough not to rub off. The slanting November sun felt like a caress on her bare skin, though the air itself was crisp and cool. Not a cloud stained the slate-blue sky, though mist rose from the cow pastures beyond the county fairgrounds, the week's rain rising to meet the sun's heat.

On a day like this, Destiny remembered why she loved fall in Jasper County. The very air tasted of apple cider and pumpkin pie.

The fairgrounds' exhibition halls stood with their doors flung open, voices and footsteps ringing inside. But many of the exhibitors, like Mark, had looked toward the sky that morning and decided to set up their booths outside, on the central entrance lawn of the fairgrounds and along the walkways between the buildings. It wasn't yet noon, but already dozens of visitors wandered among the stalls, some pausing to admire a particular painting or sculpture with a critical eye, others hurrying from booth to booth with the determined myopia of holiday shoppers.

Alain had been right when he'd said Hope Point had a flourishing artistic community. Between the local artists and artisans and those like Alain who had traveled from outside the area to sell their wares, Destiny was impressed by the variety of the arts and crafts on display.

Following Sarah and Gemma toward the food trailers, she passed hand-tinted photographs, a booth of carved wooden bowls and vases, stained-glass mirrors, Japanese-inspired paintings of herons and carp, a display of brass lawn sprinklers that spun in elaborate patterns, and a booth of modern cartoon art painted on hubcaps and fenders.

"Ew," Gemma said, pausing by one of the hubcaps that showed a boa constrictor swallowing a purple-haired punk rocker whose eyes were popping out of his head.

Sarah wrinkled her nose critically. "He's put too many nerves going to the eyeball."

"Who cares?" Gemma said. "It's still gross."

"It would be grosser if you could even believe it was a real eyeball," Sarah said.

"Good observation," an amused tenor voice noted from behind them. Destiny turned to see Alain lounging in the entrance to the booth across the walkway, a cautious grin on his face. "Horror and exaggeration are more effective if you start with a decent grasp of reality. You've got an artist's eye, Miss Sarah."

Sarah shrugged, apparently unperturbed confronting Alain, even without Destiny's baseball bat in hand. "I'm not an artist. I'm a scientist."

"Maybe they're not so different as people think," Alain suggested, striding over to stand by Destiny. "Look, I wanted to apologize for scaring you the other day. I told your mother, but I wanted to tell you, too."

"I wasn't that scared. Fleur wouldn't let anyone hurt me."

"I'm sure that's true. She's quite a guard dog." Alain slanted his hazel eyes at Destiny, the old glinting charm flashing through pale lashes. "If I'd known your aunt had so many fierce protectors, I'd have found a hotel."

"Serena said one of Mark's friends took you in," Destiny said.

Alain gestured back to the booth he'd just left, a deep, canvas tent crowded with glass-topped jewelry displays and racks of batik sundresses and tie-dyed shirts. "Rollie took me in. He's got an extra bunk in his trailer. We're parked out on the other side of the racetrack."

A craggy-faced blond giant stood behind the front jewelry counter of the booth. A green and red tie-dyed bandanna barely restrained the long, corkscrewing blond hair that was echoed farther down his face by a long, corkscrewing blond beard. He almost made her own coiffure look demure. "Garcia's Creations" was printed across the orange and blue tie-dyed T-shirt stretching across his thick chest. He waved a huge hand at them.

"Rollie Garcia?" Destiny murmured, managing a meek wave for the big Viking.

"Changed it legally from Roland Halstrom," Alain said. "He's a big Grateful Dead fan."

"I guess."

"I like the body art."

She'd almost forgotten the tattoos. Alain's gaze slid over them lazily, then glanced back up, looking for a reaction.

"Mark did them," she said. "I'm his billboard."

"I wish I'd thought of that." Alain grinned at Destiny in that slow, sly way that had once set her pulse fluttering. "I think there's still room for a good sunset on your back if you want to come by my booth. I'm over in the main exhibition hall."

"We're getting lunch," Sarah said.

"The gyros place has good food," Alain said, smoothly

switching gears. "Remember that little Greek restaurant down by the river we used to go to, Des? Do you still like baklava? You should let me take you out to dinner while I'm in town. For old times' sake."

"She's busy," Sarah said, coming to stand next to Destiny. Protecting her. Destiny had to smile.

"Maybe Daniel and I can take you out for lunch next week," she offered, almost feeling guilty at the pleasure she took in turning him down.

"Detective Parks just solved a murder case," Sarah put in. "You could read about it in this morning's paper."

Alain shook his head, his eyes traveling over Destiny again. "I just never pictured your aunt with someone quite so straightlaced. I'm glad to see the tattoos. All this law enforcement could seriously cramp anyone's style."

As he turned to glance at Sarah, his gaze continued down the walkway, and his narrow face lengthened in an exaggerated frown.

"Speaking of which . . ."

Destiny turned to see two men walking toward them, one broad-shouldered and slightly red-faced from the sun, the other slender and sharper, glancing around him with quick, ironic eyes. It took her a second to place them out of uniform: the two officers who had confronted Daniel in the station the day she'd gone down to pick up Alain.

"They'd never make it undercover," Alain said, as the two men passed them to stop at Rollie Garcia's booth. "Even that big guy's ears scream, 'Cop!' I don't know what they think they're going to find, but they've been nosing around here all morning. County land isn't even their jurisdiction, is it?"

"They're probably just shopping," Sarah said. "Cops have lives, too. We'd better go get that food. Mom's going to kill me if I don't get back to help at the booth."

"I'm starved," Gemma added.

"We'll see you around," Destiny told Alain.

"Wait just a second." He fished around in the pockets of his loose canvas jacket. "I've got something for Sarah. A peace offering."

He glanced back over his shoulder toward Rollie's booth, then pulled his hand out of his pocket and held it out toward Sarah. "Rollie makes these. I thought you might like one."

Sarah reached out a slender hand to take what he offered. As she lifted it to the sunlight to get a good look, Destiny saw that it was a necklace. Probably hemp, she guessed, the natural fiber darkened to a walnut-brown and knotted expertly in some kind of intricate macrame pattern. Blue and green beads spun inside some of the knots and a small piece of polished driftwood hung from the front. Strung around the perimeter of the necklace were multicolored round tabs of candy.

"Lip Puckers," Gemma said, fingering one of the candies. "Cool."

Sarah shrugged. "I like the driftwood. It looks kind of like a dolphin." She looked up at Alain, truce in her eyes. "Thanks."

"You're welcome." He smiled his most delighted little-boy smile, and Destiny noticed that even Sarah couldn't resist smiling back.

"Come by the booth later," Alain told Sarah, though the sparkle in his eyes was for Destiny. "I want to hear your critical opinion of my paintings."

Sarah nodded. "All right." She and Gemma started down the walk to the food trailers.

Destiny smiled. "She'll give it to you, too."

"I have no doubt." Alain shook his head, flashing his grin once more. "All you Millbrook-Davis women have a way of getting a guy right where it hurts."

Destiny waved him off with a shake of her head. "Give it up, Alain. You'll survive."

Later, those words would return to pierce her heart.

Daniel passed through the front gate and glanced over the fairgrounds.

After the week he'd had, he would much rather be spending the afternoon on the sofa in his living room, the choppy Pacific stretching toward the horizon out his tall windows, Edgar purring in his lap, a book handy on the sofa arm, Destiny curled up beside him. He would forget murder and jealousy, Ariel Macaro and her father. Forget, for a moment, Tyler Woodridge, frightened and defiant in jail.

Daniel could almost hear Bruce Springsteen's gravelly croon on the stereo, almost taste the first swallow of the Lost Coast Brewery's Downtown Brown ale. He'd dreamed of such an afternoon last night, a little taste of heaven. And it could all be his if he walked out of the fairgrounds and headed his car north toward home—all except Destiny by his side.

Not even three months. He hadn't even know her for an entire football season, and already he couldn't imagine a perfect afternoon that didn't include her. Or a perfect evening that didn't contain her irrepressible energy. A perfect morning that didn't begin with her sleepy smile on the pillow beside his, her dark, coffee-with-a-hint-of-cream eyes already filling with mischief.

Daniel hadn't felt so turned inside-out about a woman in . . . Had he ever felt this way about a woman? Surely he must have felt something like this for Tessa once. He had been so certain their marriage would not go the way of the unions of so many of his colleagues and acquaintances.

He and Tessa both had the emotional scars to prove how wrong he had been. Scars that stretched and bled whenever he allowed himself to believe that things could be different with Destiny.

His job conditioned him to calculate risks, and his instincts told him the risks involved in loving again were too great. He wasn't sure his heart could survive if his relationship with Destiny self-destructed the way his marriage to Tessa had.

Yet his instincts hadn't been able to prevent his losing his heart to her in the first place.

There was certainly no other explanation for his being at the Jasper County arts and crafts fair on a beautiful autumn day other than his heart was here somewhere, among this crowd of hard-eyed shoppers and cranky children.

"At least it's not the mall," he muttered to himself, fighting his testiness and an incipient headache. He scanned the layout of booths in the open courtyard. The sign for "Body Works Body Art" stood out in hot pink and orange spray paint on a black background over a booth near the center of the courtyard.

Daniel worked his way toward it, pausing to wonder at the tin can candle holders and carved redwood wine stoppers along the way.

He spotted Mark Banos standing to the side of the tattoo booth, gesticulating enthusiastically as he spoke to a group of four younger people, all of them sporting a variety of piercings and tattoos. The African-American woman with the shaved head and elaborate black patterns on her cheeks gave her body art a sleek elegance, but the tall, skinny, blond man with the knife-through-the-heart tattoo on his arm had an amber nose stud that made Daniel want to offer him a handkerchief.

"Hey," Mark said, giving Daniel a jerky wave and a nervous grin. "Your girl's inside."

Daniel had never participated in any of Mark Banos's various run-ins with the legal authorities, but he knew he made the man uncomfortable. Identifying himself as a police officer made a lot of people nervous. That frequently came in handy on the job, but when he was off-duty it chafed him, like a shirt with a collar a half-size too small.

"Thanks." He passed around the corner of the booth before he made Mark's friends uncomfortable, too. The tall, skinny guy smelled of pot. Daniel's headache intensified.

A low, plywood counter draped in black velveteen stretched across most of the booth's front. A variety of studs and hoops filled a small display box at the end nearest the table with the cash box. The rest of the counter held books of tattoo designs, some commercial, others handmade, and photo albums of body art on real-life bodies, Mark's portfolios.

Sarah and Gemma sat behind the cash table, poring over a spread of a boy rock band in a teen magazine. Serena leaned on the counter, flipping the pages of a sample book.

She looked up and saw Daniel. "Hi, handsome. Are you in the market for a tattoo? I saw a naked mermaid in here somewhere that would look great on a nice, strong bicep like yours. Or how about 'love' and 'hate' across your knuckles? You've kind of got that Robert Mitchum charisma."

"*Mo-om.*" Sarah looked up from Gemma's magazine to give Daniel an apologetic look. "I saw *Night of the Hunter*, and you're not creepy like that at all."

"More like Harrison Ford," Gemma offered, sizing Daniel up with a critical eye. "Only not so old. Like in *Indiana Jones* or something."

"Is Destiny here?" Daniel managed to ask.

Serena smiled, that particular feline smile that made him feel as though she saw him as a very small, slow mouse. "She's just cleaning up in the back. Desty! Come out here a minute. You've got a customer."

Destiny stepped out of the dressing room, pausing as her eyes caught his. If Serena was looking for a reaction from him, Daniel supposed he didn't disappoint her. He could feel his eyes widen. A dryad. Weren't dryads the tree nymphs?

He'd never seen the point of tattoos. The human body was an aesthetic object in itself. Covering it with crude drawings of dragons and naked women struck him as graffiti, not art. At best it was unnecessary decoration. He thought he remembered Serena saying something about henna tattoos being used in Indian marriage ceremonies. Serena had enough intricate painted lace on her skin to marry a rajah.

But Destiny looked like a wood spirit. With her untamable hair and the skeptical tilt to her eyes, the warm tones of the henna against her fair skin dappling her like sunlight through the leaves, she looked as though she might disappear if he blinked, leaving behind only the hint of laughter in the breeze.

"She looks like a hippie," Sarah said.

"She looks like a biker chick," Gemma said, obviously considering that an appropriate defense.

"You look like a hippie biker chick," Daniel told her, just to see her wrinkle her nose at him. "I promised to take you out for coffee, but I don't know if hippie biker chicks drink coffee."

"Probably beer," Sarah said.

Daniel raised an eyebrow. "What brand of beer do hippies drink?"

"Organic beer."

"She looks like a Celtic priestess," Serena said, in a we-are-not-amused voice. "Very appropriate for the full moon tonight. November's moon is the Dark Moon, a time to sorrow for our losses and to move past them to renewal."

"Organic herbal tea," Sarah said, shaking her head in disgust. "I think they serve it at the Banana Slug Café."

"With organic clover honey," Daniel agreed.

"Blood," Destiny said, narrowing her eyes at both of them. "I'm pretty sure Celtic priestesses drink blood. Especially the blood of smart-mouthed heretics." She put her hands on her hips, making the looped knots on her arms dance. "I'm looking forward to that coffee, Detective. I can't wait to ruin your squeaky-clean image."

She gestured to the booth. "But do you mind waiting? We've still got an hour to go here. I'm part of the display."

"An hour." He managed to force a smile. "I suppose I can amuse myself for an hour." Maybe it wouldn't actually feel like an eternity. Maybe he'd even find a Christmas gift for his parents. He'd settle for his head not exploding. "I might need more than herbal tea afterward."

"I could compromise on some organic beer." The mischievous glint in her eyes was almost worth an hour wasted over ceramic bud vases and paintings of sand drifting against broken-down fences. "If you throw in some hot wings."

"Done. I'll just have to hope Lieutenant Marcy isn't spending his Saturday evening at the Deepwater Brewery.

He'd never let me live those tattoos down. How long do they last?"

"Too long," Sarah muttered with a dark glance at her mother's extravagant decoration.

"Like a week or two," Gemma disagreed. "And they don't hurt or anything." She pulled down the neck of her stretch-knit shirt to show the tracery of lines like a tight necklace around her throat. "I've just got to keep the paste on for a couple more hours. I think Sarah ought to get one, too. Brian Tilson would think it was cool."

Sarah gave her a disgusted look. "Like he'd even notice."

"That guy, what's-his-name, who gave you the necklace, thought Destiny looked hot." Gemma's mouth snapped shut as she glanced guiltily at Daniel.

"Alain," Sarah explained to him. "Don't worry, Destiny didn't give him the time of day."

The unexpected fury that flashed through his chest at the idea of Alain hitting on Destiny surprised him into silence. He knew what she thought of Alain. Knew she didn't want him back in her life. Yet she'd loved the man once.

"He gave you a necklace?" Serena asked.

"Yeah."

Sarah tugged a knotted hemp cord out from under her shirt and casually brought it up to her mouth to bite one of the tabs strung around it.

"Hey!" Reflexively, Daniel grabbed for the necklace, jerking it away from her teeth. The outrage in his voice rattled the booth. *"What the hell are you doing?"*

Sarah's eyes widened, green pools, as she shrank back as far as the necklace would allow. "It's just a Lip Pucker. I'm not going to choke."

"Daniel?"

He looked up at Destiny, still holding up the necklace

clenched in his fist. "Do you know what this is?" He glanced from her to Serena, his building rage increased by the incomprehension in their eyes. He looked back at Sarah and Gemma. "Do you have any idea what this is?"

The two girls blinked and said, in almost perfect unison, "A necklace?"

"Damn it. Well, thank God you don't. Sarah, take it off." He dropped the necklace to allow her to slip it over her head.

"Daniel." Destiny's eyes were angry, too, but they were angry at him. "It's just a necklace with some candy on it."

He was almost too enraged to get the words out. "The Drug Task Force has been seeing necklaces like these in area high schools. Not so elaborate as this. Usually just a cord with tablets strung along that you can bite off. Don't see much candy on them, though. These kids are stringing Ecstasy tabs so they can get a quick hit during class."

Destiny frowned. "There's nothing illegal on that necklace, is there?"

Daniel pounded the necklace in his fist against his other hand, frustrated by her response. "That's not the point. The point is that the same creep who broke into your house just gave your twelve-year-old niece a gift that associates her with drugs and the drug culture."

He glanced at Serena and saw that she, at least, understood his outrage.

"Where's his booth?" he asked her, turning toward the sunlight. "I think it's time I had a little talk with Alain Caine."

Chapter 8

Cacophony reigned in the exhibition hall, voices and footsteps bouncing off the concrete floor and high, metal-raftered ceiling with nowhere to escape.

Daniel ignored the din and its effect on his headache as he strode up the aisle with long, purposeful strides, parting the arts fair guests with no more than a grim glance. Destiny hurried behind him, though whether she was there to help him or to protect Alain from his wrath, he didn't know. Didn't much care.

Caine's booth was halfway down the right-hand aisle of the exhibition hall. Large canvases awash in Southwestern hues of ocher, slate, and rose hung from the booth's walls. Wide, shallow bowls glazed in cooling blues and greens decorated the makeshift shelves. Alain Caine sat on a folding metal chair to the side of the booth, his habitual amused smile on his face as he watched Daniel approach.

"A young woman is dead," Daniel said, the cold, hard words surprising him as much as they did Alain. "Dead because of people like you."

Alain's narrow forehead wrinkled. "I don't follow you, Detective." He looked to Destiny. "What *have* you been telling people, Des? Or did you mention that I asked you to dinner? It was just a friendly offer, Detective. Old times' sake."

Daniel tossed the necklace at him, Alain's hand not quick enough to catch it before it struck his chest. "And what about this?"

Alain's smile grew more amused. "It's a necklace. It was a gift to Sarah. I don't see that it's any business of yours."

"It becomes my business when a man with a pattern of criminal behavior starts initiating kids into drug paraphernalia."

Alain rolled his eyes. "Oh, come on, Detective. It's a candy necklace. Rollie's selling them right outside. Your cop friends have already been all over his booth. The only drugs around here are in your imagination. I don't know why you cops waste so much time rousting harmless citizens for stuff like pot and Ecstasy, anyway. There are actually dangerous criminals out there you could be going after."

Daniel didn't move, let his very stillness express the anger and disgust he felt. "You're saying marijuana and Ecstasy are harmless?"

Alain shrugged. "Hey, California's got a medical marijuana law. Pot's even good for you."

"If you don't need it for pain management? It's real good for you. It's just great for your lungs and your reflexes and your sperm count. And how about Ecstasy?" Daniel asked, voice still calm and quiet. "Is that good for you, too? Do you think it's good for children? Kids like Sarah? How about high school kids?"

"High school kids aren't children. They know what they're doing."

Daniel's fists clenched. "They know what they're doing? So it's okay when they take Ecstasy and it stops their hearts or destroys their kidneys? It's okay when they get involved in a drug culture that thrives on sex and violence? It's okay when an eighteen-year-old honor student gets brutally stabbed to death and her body gets dumped in an alley like so much garbage?"

Alain snorted and pushed himself to his feet, the amusement gone from his face. " 'Drugs don't stab people; people stab people,' " he said with careful mockery. "And I haven't stabbed anyone lately. In fact, I haven't offered anyone drugs, either. Not even Sarah. So all you've got on me is that you don't like me because I used to screw your girlfriend. Well, too bad for you that's not a jailable offense."

"Alain! Daniel!" Destiny stepped forward to intervene, but Daniel held an arm out to keep her back.

"Lucky for you, I'm a cop," Daniel said. "Though I don't think you'd be taking such cheap shots at someone who could fight back. And you wouldn't give drugs to a child, either. You'd only do just enough to cause trouble."

Alain's lip curled. "Sarah's not a child, Detective. She's making her own decisions about going to school and confronting burglars. Somebody's going to be offering her drugs soon, if they haven't already."

"And if that someone is you, I'll kill you." He didn't need to raise his voice. It was a statement of fact. "Don't go near Sarah again."

Alain forced out a laugh. "You know, Detective, you're a real pain in the ass. I don't know what you see in this guy, Des, but when you get tired of his authoritarian bullshit, you know where to find me." His hazel eyes narrowed slyly as he shot a look at Daniel. "And I know where to find you."

Daniel's hand flashed out and clutched the man's T-shirt, jerking him off-balance. Alain's eyes widened, finally registering the violence of Daniel's fury.

Daniel heard Destiny protest, but kept his eyes boring into Alain's.

"If you set one foot on Destiny's property, if you accost her in the street, if you do one thing that she could possibly object to, I will personally ensure you never bother her again." He could see all too clearly Destiny's quiet little house on her quiet little street. No alarm system. No motion sensors. Vulnerable.

"Daniel!"

"I'll make you wish you'd never been born." He shook Alain by his shirt. "Do you understand me? I don't intend to tell you twice."

"Daniel!" Destiny grabbed his right arm. "Let him go."

"Detective, hey, let go now." A masculine voice. Another hand grabbed his left shoulder, pulling him back. "Come on, now. I think the asshole's got the message."

Daniel gave Alain one last look before dropping his shirt and letting the hands pull him away.

"That's it. Back off."

Daniel's awareness expanded from his focus on Alain's eyes, and he turned toward the calming hand on his shoulder to see Tom Yap's concerned face. Garth Vance pushed forward past them, ordering Alain back into his booth. As Daniel let Tom pull him away from the confrontation and down the aisle, the officer's dark eyes regained their customary ironic humor.

"Man, I'm going to have to practice that voice you just used, Detective. You scared me, and I haven't even been introduced to your lady."

"Destiny Millbrook," Destiny said, offering Tom her hand. "Thank you for getting him out of there."

"From what I heard, that guy had it coming," Tom said.

Daniel kept walking, past the art and the junk and the

kitsch out through the front double doors into the sunlight. He knew Tom and Destiny followed him, but he couldn't look at them. He was still too angry, though the fire had died, leaving a taste like ashes in his mouth.

Destiny. Ariel Macaro. Sarah. He'd had plenty of reasons for confronting Alain Caine. But no excuse for losing his temper and threatening the man.

The sunlight sparked against his headache, and he closed his eyes.

"You really gave it to that guy, but good." Garth Vance's bluff voice intruded on his embarrassment. "I didn't think you had it in you, Detective. Good for you."

Fortunately, Garth stopped short of pounding his shoulder. Daniel opened his eyes. Garth, Tom, and Destiny stood before him in a semicircle.

"I still think Tom should have let you get a good swing in before he pulled you off," Garth said. He had on a Clint Eastwood tough-guy grin he probably practiced in front of the mirror.

"Detective Parks wouldn't have swung at him unless he swung first," Tom said, with a self-effacing twist to his wide mouth that might indicate comradely support or a cynical disdain for all human nature. It was hard to tell with Tom. "Then we'd have had to fill out an incident report. I'm on my day off."

It was even harder to gauge Destiny's reaction. She stood with her arms crossed over her chest, her mouth flattened in repressed emotion. Whatever she thought of Daniel's actions, she wasn't going to show it in front of Tom and Garth.

"You guys don't get enough of each other at the station?" he asked, deflecting his own thoughts.

"Have you seen Tom's ride?" Garth asked. "Man, he's

got a Porsche 911 convertible. Fire-engine red, 3.6-liter engine, over three hundred horses. Does zero to sixty in five seconds. The chicks can't resist a couple of law enforcement types in a car like that."

Tom's smile looked forced. "We don't spend that much time together at work. Just the big cases. You know how understaffed we are. Besides, we thought we'd come by the fair today to keep an eye on a couple of people for the Drug Task Force."

"I'm trying to convince Tom we need a party after this," Garth continued. "He's got the coolest pad. Hot tub. Wet bar. It must be nice to have rich folks."

He pounded Tom on the back with a force that made Tom grimace. Or maybe it was simply embarrassment.

"We don't want to waste our free time! And you're on your day off, too," Garth reminded Daniel, grinning even wider. "Thanks to me and Tom solving your case for you."

The reminder of Ariel's death and his late-night interview with Tyler Woodridge did not improve Daniel's pounding head.

"You two did a good job collecting and securing the evidence last night," he said, giving credit where it was due. "We wouldn't have a case without that knife."

Garth's ruddy face flushed at the praise.

"But I'm still worried." Daniel pinched his nose, trying to cut off the throbbing. He'd thought about how he'd broach this subject with Tom and Garth. After the events of the previous night, he'd expected some resentment on their part. Perhaps a moment of testosterone-charged male bonding was the best chance he was going to get.

"You got the lab tests back," Tom guessed. Kermit had said he was sharp.

"The blood matches Ariel Macaro's type. I think we can

115

assume it's hers until we get DNA confirmation, but there aren't any fingerprints, nothing to tie the knife to Tyler Woodridge."

"We found it under his grandparents' trailer!" Garth exploded.

"Yeah," Tom agreed, putting a hand on his partner's shoulder to hold him steady. "But the detective's right. It would be better to have fingerprints. I mean, what's a defense attorney going to say? Somebody could be framing the kid, right?"

"Bullshit." Garth shook his head, snorting like a bull ready to charge. "That kid's guilty. He was jealous. He knifed the girl. He tried to evade the police. He's going to jail. He oughta get a lethal injection, you ask me, forget this special circumstances crap."

"You don't think he's guilty?" Tom asked Daniel.

"He's got motive, means, and opportunity. He probably did it. But . . ." Daniel had learned over the years to trust his instincts, but he needed something besides instinct to convince Tom and Garth. "He's a bright kid. I don't understand why he'd wear gloves to commit a murder, but keep the bloody knife. Why not just throw it away?"

"Trophy," Tom suggested.

"Lots of killers do stupid things," Garth said, shrugging off the why. "That's the reason we catch them."

Both were good answers. Neither matched Daniel's impression of the frightened, defiant youth who'd been transferred to the county jail that morning. The boy whose eyes burned with an anger that could not quite hide the depth of his shock and grief at the death of the girl he'd loved.

"He's guilty," Garth stated again.

"Then let's make sure we've got the proof," Daniel said. Lying awake the night before, he had considered continuing his investigation without asking Officers Vance and Yap for help. He didn't want to waste manpower on what were only whispers of doubt in his mind. But seeing the intensity in their eyes as they frowned at him, he thought—he hoped—he'd made the right choice. They wanted this case solved as badly as he did. Even if they didn't agree with him on the perpetrator, they'd dig deep for the evidence they needed to convict the right person.

"I don't want you taking time away from your current investigations." He did not want Lieutenant Marcy to have the slightest excuse to order Vance and Yap off the Macaro case. "But you know more than anyone else at the station about the drug scene in town and at the schools. You know the kids at Hope Point High who might be linked to drugs. You have informants."

Garth was already nodding, glad to have their expertise acknowledged.

"Tyler Woodridge suggested last night that Ariel Macaro had discovered that Kyle Preston was getting involved in drugs."

Tom jerked his head up, eyebrows raised. "Mr. Squeaky-Clean? I doubt it. Consider the source. I heard Kyle Preston's got a shot at playing quarterback for Stanford. He's not going to blow that on drugs."

Daniel nodded. "I understand. But that's why I need your help. If you can do some digging without damaging the boy's reputation, we can put these accusations to rest."

"Look, Detective . . ." Tom hesitated, his eyes dark with unaccustomed gravity. "I'm sharing a confidence, but I think you need to know. Kyle Preston did have a problem, when he was living in Menlo Park. He got involved in a bad crowd. That's why his father moved his practice up here. But Kyle's been clean for the past two years. The football

117

players get random tests. You can check it out."

"He's a good kid," Garth agreed. "Tom and I set up an activities day for my nephew's Boy Scout troop. Kyle came and gave a football clinic and a crossbow demonstration."

That explained the deer heads in the Prestons' living room.

"Just make sure he's still clean. And if we can find out where that pot at the crime scene came from, that would help, too."

"Don't think you gotta look far for that," Garth said. "The older Woodridge boy."

"Can you find out for sure?"

Garth glanced at his partner, then back at Daniel, the tough-guy grin returning. "Does a wild bear crap in the woods?"

"And what will you be doing, Detective?" Tom asked, his quiet voice cutting through Garth's bravado.

"Making sure we've ruled out any other possible suspects." That was the most diplomatic way to put it. "We won't let Woodridge's attorney have a reasonable doubt to show a jury."

"Any suspects in particular?"

"That depends on what I dig up."

Tom shrugged. "Don't obsess about this, Detective. We got the right guy. It seems like an awful lot of trouble, investigating a case we've already solved, but we'll do some asking around for you."

"Enough to prove we got it right the first time," Garth added, the sharper gleam in his eyes telling Daniel the man noticed and resented the implied criticism, after all.

"We'll let you know if we come up with anything," Tom said. "As long as we're keeping our eyes open today, anyway. Can we reach you tonight if we need to?"

"I'll be home all night." Probably alone, the way the day was going.

"We'll get back to you," Tom promised, stepping away with a nod to Garth.

"Stay out of trouble. We might not be around to rescue you next time," Garth added, his teasing holding only the slightest edge of malice. He laughed, and the edge was gone. "Don't do anything I wouldn't do!"

Slapping his hand on his thigh, he followed Tom toward the food trailers.

"He obviously doesn't know you very well."

Focused on his worries about the case, Daniel had almost forgotten Destiny's presence. Maybe Tom was right. Maybe he was obsessing.

She stood apart from the group he'd formed with the other two officers, her arms still crossed, her dark eyes lasering into his. "I'd feel better if I thought you were limited to doing things only Officer Vance might do. At least then you might be predictable."

Daniel took a deep breath, forcing Ariel Macaro and Tyler Woodridge from his brain. He was off-duty, as Garth had pointed out. He had a life outside of work. Which he wouldn't have for long if he couldn't give her his full attention when she needed it.

"Destiny, I'm sorry—"

"For what?" she demanded, giving him that skeptical look that had once reminded him of Audrey Hepburn. Now it was simply pure Destiny. "For telling Alain off? He deserved it."

He could almost smile. "True."

"Then?"

"For losing my temper. For embarrassing you."

She stepped forward then, her arms untwining to reach

119

out to touch his shoulder, to brush the line of his jaw. "Apology accepted. Though I guess if you have to apologize for your temper, I should apologize for mine."

He took the hand on his shoulder in his, and squeezed, his headache eased by the simple pressure of her fingers squeezing him back. "Your temper?"

She smiled up at him. "Yes. After Alain said what he did about Sarah, I was hoping you'd pop him one right in the nose."

Sarah shifted around in her metal folding chair, pulling her feet up onto the seat and leaning over her knees to read the crumpled, stained, classroom copy of *Holes* she was supposed to finish over Thanksgiving break. But even reading couldn't whisk her away from the discomfort of the chair or the noises of the fair outside the booth or the knowledge that it was a gorgeous fall day, maybe the only sunny day they'd get all week—all month, even—and she was stuck counting change so her mother could keep an eye on her.

Why not just dump her in a cell and be done with the pretense?

She glanced over to where her mother and Aunt Destiny were helping Mark pack up his supplies. Knowing the endless afternoon was almost over didn't help. Her mother would be dragging her back over here at the crack of dawn.

"Does it look darker yet?"

Sarah's fingers clenched the sides of her book, but she looked up for the 400th time to examine the henna tattoo circling Gemma's neck.

"I think it looks darker," Gemma said, settling back into her own folding chair after yet another trip over to the mirror.

"Maybe." Sarah turned back to her book.

"Why don't you get one, Sarah? You should."

"Tattoos are stupid," Sarah said. The words bounced her chin off her knees. She couldn't believe her mother had let Mark draw all over her like that, especially since she practically got hysterical whenever Sarah wrote so much as a phone number on her palm. Like a milliliter of gel ink was going to poison her.

"You think this looks stupid?"

Guilt jolted Sarah's head back off her knees.

"No, not yours." She examined Gemma's henna necklace with a critical eye. "Yours is just enough, not too much. That reddish color looks good with your skin tones."

Gemma's anxious face relaxed slightly. "You think so?"

Sarah nodded. "Maybe if I had red hair, I'd get one, too, but it would clash with this mess." She flipped the end of her bland, dishwater ponytail with her hand.

The truth was, she'd have let Mark give her a tattoo regardless, except she'd complained about her mother's so much, she couldn't give in.

"Your hair's not that bad," Gemma said with characteristic generosity. "It's nice and thick. It could be really pretty with some highlights."

"Like my mom would let me do that."

"I'll do it for you." Gemma's eyes lit up at the prospect. "Spend the night. We'll get a kit. Grandma won't mind."

Sarah could almost see her hair floating around her shoulders, golden highlights gleaming in the sunshine. Brian Tilson standing openmouthed by the drinking fountain as she walked by. Right.

"I'm grounded for life, remember?"

"Your mom will let you come to my house over vacation," Gemma promised confidently. "At least Christmas

121

vacation. She knows my grandma's a bigger warden than she is."

"What we have here," Auntie Dess drawled from behind them, in deep, warden tones, "is a failure to communicate."

"Ha, ha."

"Don't give me that look, Sarah Constance," her aunt commanded, crouching with her hands on the backs of their chairs. "I've convinced your jailer to grant me custody of you and Gemma both on Wednesday."

Sarah sat up. "Really?"

"Don't get too excited. I'm drafting you to bake pumpkin pies for Thanksgiving. Two for us, two for the community dinner at the veterans hall."

"I don't care," Sarah said. "Just get me out of the house. You're the best, Auntie Dess. I can't believe Charlene gave you the day off."

"Maddy gave it to me, since she's not going to Colorado."

"Uncle Chad's an idiot," Gemma said.

Auntie Dess did not reply to that. "Do you want to help us with the pies, Gemma?"

"Sure, just let me check with Grandma . . . Hey!"

Sarah turned to see what had prompted Gemma's hushed exclamation. "What?"

"That guy."

Sarah knew immediately which guy she meant. A tall high school kid with autumn-wheat hair, the greenest eyes she'd ever seen, and lithe, broad shoulders had paused by the pottery booth across from them. Two other boys in Hope Point High letterman jackets lounged beside him, but he stood out like a phoenix among pigeons. He leaned across the table at the front of the booth, saying something to the high school girl manning the cash box. The girl tossed her blond hair and swallowed the gum she'd been popping with bored repetition for the past hour.

"That's Kyle Preston," Gemma whispered, her high squeak nearly loud enough to be heard at the other booth.

"Who?" Sarah asked, at the same time her aunt said, "Really?"

Sarah glanced in surprise at Auntie Dess, who was staring at the boy as if the name meant something to her.

"He's the Jaguars' star quarterback," Gemma said, rolling her eyes as if Sarah should care about high school football. "He was going with Ariel Macaro, that girl who got murdered."

"Yeah?" Sarah dropped her feet off the chair. Now *that* was interesting information.

"I thought she was dating that boy who got arrested last night," Aunt Destiny said.

Sarah stilled, caught between watching Kyle Preston flirt with the blonde in the tight T-shirt at the pottery booth and wondering at the too-casual tone of her aunt's voice.

"Tyler Woodridge," Gemma supplied.

Sarah knew that. She'd read the article in the paper. If she was going to be a forensic anthropologist or maybe a police detective, she had to keep up on the local crime scene. But Kyle Preston's name had not been in the paper. Auntie Dess must have heard it somewhere else.

"She broke up with Kyle right before homecoming," Gemma said, as if it were the gospel truth. Sarah didn't doubt it. Gemma knew all the gossip about every school in Hope Point. "He's so totally gorgeous. And a star quarterback. And he's like a champion marksman with a crossbow. And he does track. I don't know why Ariel would dump him for that Tyler kid. Tiffany Keegan said her older brother Billy said Kyle was pretty broken up about it and wanted her back."

"He doesn't look too broken up about her being murdered," Sarah said dryly, as Kyle reached over to pull the blonde's gold key pendant up from the top of her cleavage. He pretended to turn the key just above her left breast. The girl blushed and giggled, swatting at his hand.

"Ew," Sarah added.

"I don't know," Auntie Dess said. "He's working hard to look unconcerned, maybe too hard. There's a lot of tension in his shoulders. I don't know if he's as relaxed as he wants his friends to think. Do you know anything else about him, Gemma? What kind of crowd does he hang out with?"

Gemma thought about that. "Jocks, I guess, like those guys. He's smart, though. He's supposed to go to Stanford next year. I guess that's where his dad went, but you've still got to be smart to get in. He grew up down there somewhere."

"Has he ever been in any kind of trouble?"

"Like what?"

Auntie Dess shrugged with exaggerated carelessness. "I don't know. I guess I just worry about kids these days. It seems like too often they throw away bright futures on drugs and violence and stuff like that."

"Kyle Preston's not a stoner or anything," Gemma said. "Lots of kids do drugs, though."

"It only takes one bad drug experience to kill you," Auntie Dess said, in an adult voice that meant the interesting questions were over.

But Sarah wasn't worrying about the dangers of drugs. She wasn't stupid enough to mess up her brain. It was the only asset she had. Even if Gemma did somehow manage to highlight her hair.

No, she was thinking about Aunt Destiny's interest in Kyle Preston and drugs and Kyle Preston's relationship with the murdered girl, Ariel Macaro. If her aunt knew more than what they said in the paper, she must have heard something from Daniel. Which meant the police were interested in Kyle Preston. Which meant maybe he was some kind of suspect in Ariel Macaro's death.

"That's Kyle's dad," Gemma said, nodding toward a man approaching the group of football players by the pottery tent.

"How do you know?" Sarah demanded, though despite his graying brown hair and the deep lines running vertically down his cheeks, the older man was a taller, thinner version of Kyle Preston.

"He's one of Grandma's doctors," Gemma said. "He's the one who cleaned out her arteries."

"I recognize him from the library," Aunt Destiny said. "He was giving Maddy a hard time about the microfiche machine the other day."

"Kyle!" the man's voice was as thin as he was, though it held a tone of command. His lips were thin, too, tight with displeasure toward his son.

The high school quarterback pushed himself up from the pottery booth table to turn toward his father. "What are you doing here?"

For a second, Sarah thought Dr. Preston looked not just startled at the question, but uneasy. He actually stopped his forward progress toward the booth. "I'm Christmas shopping with your mother. The question is, what are *you* doing here?"

"It's a free country," Kyle said, with only a hint of nervousness under the smart remark.

Dr. Preston took a step closer, not impressed. "You've got a game tonight. You should be practicing."

"We don't have to be at the field for another half-hour,"

Kyle said, looking to his two buddies for nods of agreement. Then Kyle grinned, perfect white teeth flashing briefly at the girl across the table from him. "I just dropped by to do some Christmas shopping of my own."

"This place closes at five," Dr. Preston nodded toward the other booths where the proprietors were packing up for the day. "You're finished here. Go practice. And don't forget our appointment later."

Dr. Preston waited until his son had said a cursory good-bye to the pottery booth girl, then followed Kyle and his friends toward the front gate.

"Nice guy," Sarah muttered.

"Grandma calls him Dr. Pressed Shirt," Gemma said. "But she says he's the best heart surgeon in northern California, and that includes San Francisco."

"We're about ready to go here," Auntie Dess said, pushing off the back of Sarah's chair to rise to her feet. "Why don't you girls clean off the cash table and fold up the chairs? Maybe we can convince Mark to spend his day's income taking us all out for pizza."

"I thought you were going out with Detective Parks," Gemma said.

"Detective Parks went home," Auntie Dess said, with a reluctant twitch of humor at the corner of her mouth. "Maybe I'll take him a slice of pizza if we have some left over."

"Can we get something besides the Banana Slug Garden Supreme?" Gemma asked, slamming the cash box shut with a satisfying crash. "Mark and Mrs. Davis can have their own pizza, and we can have a different one if we get two mediums."

"Meat eater," Aunt Destiny accused.

"I don't like mushrooms," Gemma defended herself.

"You just want pepperoni."

"So do you."

"True."

Sarah laughed with them as she tucked her book in her backpack and folded up the chairs and table for the night. But her eyes followed Kyle Preston through the fairgrounds' gate. Murder, drugs, and police suspicion. And here Kyle Preston was, flirting with a new girl and trying to act like he didn't have a care in the world.

Sarah glanced around to catch Aunt Destiny also gazing toward the front gate, her eyes sharp with questions.

Chapter 9

Destiny climbed out of her old VW Rabbit and stood for a moment, breathing in the primeval smells of salt spray and cedar. The heavy moon rose behind her, streaking the walls of Daniel's low-lying house with the shadows of western red cedar and Sitka spruce. Stars shone overhead for the first time in a month, stretching away over the roof of the house toward the horizon, melting into the deep, dark emptiness of the sea.

"The Dark Moon," she whispered, feeling the silvery touch of it down her back. The designs on her arms stirred like the cedar branches in the breath of the moon.

What loss should she be mourning? What had actually happened between her and Daniel over Alain's return to her life, however brief she intended it to be? Her heart ached, sighing with the rush of the waves on the beach at the base of the cliffs far below.

The light over the front door blazed on, blinding her to the stars. The door swung open, and Daniel stood framed in the light from the living room. He stepped aside, and she walked forward, though the moonlight pulled at her like the tide.

"I didn't know if you'd want to see me tonight." He looked past her toward the car. "No Fleur?"

Destiny suppressed a surge of guilt. Fleur loved nothing

better than a walk on the beach, a treat always guaranteed after a night at Daniel's. Then again, spending the night with Sarah was also a treat. Sarah let her sleep on the bed.

"She's with Sarah and Serena."

Daniel shook his head. "Edgar will be heartbroken."

Amber eyes blinked at her from the recliner by the fireplace in the sunken living room. Edgar rose to stretch his cream-and-chocolate-colored bulk before settling once more in the chair, tucking his nose under the twitching end of his tail.

"He looks crushed," Destiny observed. She also noted the Robert Parker mystery on the table by the chair, the half-empty glass of Jim Beam beside it, the Native American flute music on the stereo weaving patterns as intricate as the Navajo rugs on the walls. "I'm interrupting your evening."

"Yes." Daniel switched off the overhead lighting, leaving the warm lamplight by the chair and the flickering of the fire. "I was hoping you would."

"Spencer's not keeping you company?" Destiny lifted the book off its face and closed it.

"Not anymore. You've lost my place."

"You should use a bookmark instead of damaging the spine like that."

"I'm not using my library voice, either. What are you going to do about it?"

Something in her stomach still curled when he grinned at her like that. She allowed herself a narrow smile in response as she crossed her arms to make the henna tattoos dance.

"You'd better watch it, buddy. You could be messing with the incarnation of a Celtic priestess here."

"I'm ready to take my chances."

He reached for her, and she stepped into his arms, so simple and easy, after all.

"I was afraid you wouldn't come," he admitted against the top of her head. "Someone called and hung up about an hour ago. I thought it was you trying to find a way to tell me to go to hell."

She huffed softly. "Trust me. If I decide to tell you to go to hell, you'll know it."

"That's one of the things I like about you."

"There are more?"

"Absolutely."

He kissed her, and doubts flashed away like fish below the sea, her heart pounding to the rhythm of the waves. He touched her neck, brushing fingertips over the butterfly there, then down her back, pulling her close. His tongue touched her lips, the bourbon sweet on his breath, and her body melted even closer in response.

She pulled back from the kiss, sucking in her ragged breath. "I thought you had a headache."

He tilted his head as though checking in. "You've worked a miraculous cure. It must be the Celtic priestess in you. I have some other aches and pains you could work on if you want."

She moved her hands up to weave her fingers into his hair. "I might have a little magic left," she agreed, stretching against the length of him. "All I need is a little firelight."

"Done." He claimed her lips with his again as he reached to switch off the lamp.

Daniel was still awake when the doorbell rang. The fire had died down to a drowsy red glow, and Destiny lay against him as he held her close beneath the throw rug on the couch.

He had thought about waking her long enough to move to the bedroom, but he hadn't wanted to disturb the magic of the night, the whisper of the fire and the distant waves mixing with the whisper of Destiny's breath as she slept. The softness of her bare skin beneath his hand. The bright cold of the stars through his tall living room windows. He felt as though his senses stretched from the heart beating beneath his fingers out into the wide unknown of the night sky.

He thought if God spoke in that moment, the words would echo through his soul.

Instead, the doorbell buzzed, a ragged, harsh sound that jerked Destiny awake.

"What?" she asked, startled.

"Doorbell," Daniel said, already working himself up off the couch behind her. "I'd better get it."

He found his jeans on the floor and threw on his shirt as he strode toward the door. He turned to check on Destiny and saw that she'd dressed as quickly as he and was heading for the kitchen to start some coffee. Anyone ringing a police detective's doorbell at—he checked the old mantel clock over the fireplace—two o'clock on a Sunday morning wasn't bringing good news.

He flicked on the porch light and checked the peephole.

"Kermit!" He swung the door open. "What's going on?"

"Detective." Kermit nodded a greeting and scraped his boots on the welcome mat. "I'm sorry to bother you. I see you've got company." He gestured toward Destiny's car.

"You're starting to make a habit of this," Daniel noted, stepping back. "You might as well come in. Destiny's making coffee."

"Thanks."

Kermit managed to maneuver the step down into the

131

living room without tripping over Edgar, who'd come down the hall from Daniel's room to wrap himself around Kermit's legs. Daniel closed his eyes and took a deep breath. Kermit's unnatural dexterity as he greeted Destiny and took a seat on one of the bar stools at the kitchen counter proved the young officer was at full alert. Daniel would be up for a while.

Daniel walked into the kitchen to lean on the counter across from Kermit. The problem must relate to Ariel Macaro's murder. That was the only open case he and Kermit were currently working together.

"What's wrong?" Destiny asked, coming up beside him. "Kermit, what's happened?"

Kermit's posture hadn't relaxed despite his perch on the stool, and his blue eyes were nearly black under pinched, fair brows.

Daniel frowned. "The dispatcher would have called if it was an emergency."

"It's not exactly an emergency," Kermit agreed, but his tone left room for doubt.

"I'll leave you two with the coffee," Destiny said, grabbing one of the mugs to put it back.

Daniel forced himself not to stop her, though it felt like old times, he, Kermit and Destiny huddled over a case. Except this wasn't Destiny's case.

Yet Kermit did call her back. "Wait, Destiny. This is something you need to hear, too."

"All right, Riggs," Daniel said. "What's going on? Spit it out."

"It's about Alain Caine."

Daniel's hands clenched on the counter. Great. The man had been in Hope Point less than a week, and already he'd been more of a pain than a bad stomach virus. "Doesn't the guy know when to quit? What's he done this time?"

"He's died," Kermit said, his professional poise crumbling as he delivered the news. "Alain Caine is dead. He's been murdered."

"Murdered?" Destiny thought she asked the question, but no sound seemed to come from her lips. Alain? Dead? The whole scene felt unreal, standing in her bare feet on Daniel's cold kitchen tiles, the overhead lighting draining all color from Kermit's and Daniel's faces. She reached for the counter to steady herself.

"Are you sure?" she asked Kermit, shaking her grip on the counter. "I mean, are you sure it was Alain?"

Kermit nodded. "The guy whose trailer he was staying in, Roland Garcia, identified him for the investigating officers, but I recognized him, too."

"And he was *murdered?*" Destiny asked. He'd only been in Hope Point for three days. Her head felt dizzy with it. She hadn't seen him in two years, hadn't ever thought she'd see him again. Hadn't wanted to. But dead? Murdered? "Deliberately?"

"Someone shot him in the chest at pretty close range," Kermit said. "It didn't seem accidental."

She could almost see the shock on Alain's face, almost feel him jerk back as the bullet struck. Dead. She shook her head. As much as he'd hurt her, as irritating as he'd been since he arrived in Hope Point, she had loved him once. Had looked into his face and thought, *This is the man I want to spend my life with.*

And close on that thought rode another, *What if it had been Daniel?* Any night while she lay sleeping, unaware of the sudden rift in the fabric of her world, Kermit or some other police officer could come to her house to tell her

Daniel had been killed in the line of duty.

Guilt burned through her that she was glad it was Alain instead of Daniel. She sent up a quick prayer for Daniel's safety, Alain's soul, and for herself.

"He was killed in Rollie Garcia's trailer?" she asked. "At the fairgrounds?"

"It looks that way," Kermit said.

"What were you doing out at the fairgrounds?" Daniel asked Kermit. "That's the sheriff's jurisdiction. What were you doing on duty, anyway?"

"Haynes was supposed to be on shift tonight, but his daughter went into the hospital with appendicitis."

"That didn't answer my question, Riggs," Daniel said. "What were you doing at the fairgrounds?"

"The sheriff's deputy who got called out to the crime scene thought it might be drug-related. He called Lieutenant Marcy to get the Drug Task Force involved, and Lieutenant Marcy called Vance and Yap. My shift—Haynes's shift—was over, so when I heard the victim's name, I went along for the ride."

"Coffee's ready," Destiny said, grabbing the carafe and pouring for the three of them. She'd made it too strong, but she didn't think drinking the whole pot would be enough to clear her brain. "I can't believe they think it was drugs," she said. "I know he was being a jerk about it today, but Alain was never into drugs. He was afraid they would interfere with his creativity."

"Did they find drugs on him?" Daniel asked.

Kermit shook his head, carefully pouring as much half-and-half into his cup as there was coffee. "No, nothing like that. I guess they were already keeping an eye on Mr. Garcia. He's had a couple of priors."

"They think the killer was after Rollie Garcia?" Destiny

sagged against the counter. "Serena found Alain a place to stay for me. It's my fault he was there."

Daniel's strong arm wrapped around her shoulder, and she let him pull her close against his side. "Of course, it's not your fault. Kermit said it was close range. Whoever shot Alain knew who he was killing."

Destiny thought of the huge Viking Alain had pointed out as Rollie Garcia, and her stomach slowed its flips. No one could mistake one man for the other. "But if the killer went there looking for drugs, and Alain got in the way . . ."

"Destiny."

She met Daniel's gaze. "What else could it have been? Alain had only been in town for three days. He didn't know anybody in Hope Point. Why would anyone kill him?"

"It might have been a robbery attempt," Daniel suggested. "If Alain did a good business today, someone might have noticed. He was selling some of those paintings for upwards of five hundred dollars."

Pain stabbed through Destiny's stomach, and she sucked in a quick breath. Alain's artwork. She hadn't had time to do more than glance at his Southwestern paintings that afternoon, but she'd known they were good. Even after he'd left for Arizona, she'd continued to use the pottery he'd given her—it had been too beautiful to smash. For all his blaming his feckless, irresponsible behavior on the demands of his "muse," his talent was real. Had been real.

And now someone had snuffed out that fragile, bright light of creative beauty. For what? A couple of hundred dollars? A thousand?

"What does the sheriff's investigator think?" she asked Kermit. "Was it robbery? Did he get any help from Officer Vance and Officer Yap? Do they have a suspect?"

"Well, sort of." Kermit shifted with uneasy tension.

"Sort of?" Daniel set his coffee cup on the counter with a thud. "What's that mean? Do they have someone in custody? Damn it, just tell me Vance didn't shoot anybody."

Kermit shook his head, and Destiny felt Daniel relax slightly beside her.

"Thank God for small favors. So do they have a theory of the crime or not? Have they applied for a proper arrest warrant? Who do they think wanted the victim dead?"

Kermit's face wrinkled with a mixture of indignation and distress, and Destiny got a very strange sensation in the pit of her stomach. "That's sort of the problem, Detective. Apparently both Vance and Yap witnessed a death threat against Alain Caine just this afternoon. The only suspect they've got is you."

Chapter 10

The lights in the officers' break room flickered with infernal deliberation, driving the lateness of the hour under Daniel's skin. The group assembled in the room stood in various uncomfortable postures, though the mismatched chairs and the green upholstered sofa were empty. As long as Chief Thomas stood, leaning a hip back against the battered coffee machine table, Daniel, Kermit, Vance, Yap, Marcy and Tiebold stood, too.

The chief's presence in the break room was unprecedented, but then so were the circumstances, and there wasn't room for all of them in the chief's office.

"Detective Parks would never kill anybody," Tom Yap was saying, his irony muted for once. "I mean, the dead guy was a jerk, okay. But if we killed every jerk we met in this line of work, the population would drop by twenty percent. We all know Detective Parks didn't do it."

"That didn't stop you from telling Deputy Pearson that Detective Parks made a death threat against the victim," Kermit pointed out. For once, Kermit's tall lankiness didn't make him look young. Braced against the door with his arms crossed over his chest, his black scowl directed at Yap and Vance, he looked positively dangerous.

"A dozen people heard him say he was going to kill the guy," Tom said. "Better Pearson heard it from me."

"He didn't say he was going to kill him," Vance said, shifting away from the wall. "He just said he was going to make him wish he'd never been born."

"He said if the guy offered drugs to a kid . . ."

"Oh, yeah." Vance stuck his hands in his pockets. "Man, this sucks. Too bad you don't have an alibi."

Kermit had already informed Daniel that the coroner, Tim Boudreaux, had given a preliminary time of death of between seven and eight o'clock that evening, though Rollie Garcia hadn't found the body until he'd returned to his trailer near midnight. Daniel had been alone at home reading his book while Destiny had been out having pizza with Serena and her family.

He thought of Destiny waiting back at his house. He'd told her to go to bed, that he'd be home soon, but he knew she wouldn't sleep. She shouldn't be alone while facing the shock of Alain's murder.

"This whole thing is ridiculous," he said.

"Of course it is," Lieutenant Marcy agreed, a little too quickly, from his perch at the chief's right side. His bright round eyes glittered with delight at Daniel's embarrassment. "But even if everyone in this room knows you're innocent, the public doesn't know. We have to err on the side of caution in these things."

"You can't remove Parks from his duties in Detective Division," Lieutenant Tiebold snapped, his long, thin body hunched in aggravation by the window. "We're short-handed as it is. There's not a shred of evidence connecting him to the crime."

"Once the sheriff's department digs deeper into the case, he'll come up with another suspect," Tom said.

"Give us the go-ahead," Garth said to Lieutenant Marcy. "Put the Drug Task Force on it. I bet you anything the murder was connected to one of Rollie Garcia's buddies, and that means drugs."

"We don't want to give anyone the idea we'd cover up for one of our own," Lieutenant Marcy demurred. "The sheriff's department will do a thorough investigation."

"Vance has a point," Chief Thomas said, his slow, deep voice hushing the rest of them. "He and Yap already have a relationship with Deputy Pearson. I'm sure he would be happy for any information they can offer him."

Daniel appreciated Garth's and Tom's eagerness, though from Lieutenant Marcy's glare, Daniel guessed the officers would pay for it later.

Chief Thomas took off his glasses and glanced down at them. The wire rims looked fragile in his big hands. "This is ridiculous. One of my detectives implicated in a murder."

He put the glasses back on and glared around the room. "Any one of you is capable of murder. I've been around long enough to know it. But—" His glare stopped at Daniel. "—I'd certainly hope you were all smarter than to shoot a guy you'd threatened to kill in front of police witnesses earlier in the day and then not even arrange to have an alibi."

Daniel's stomach relaxed a notch. He had trusted that no one in the room seriously considered him a murder suspect, but some dark place in the back of his brain had shuddered with the quicksand fear of being wrongfully accused.

"Let the sheriff's department do its job," Lieutenant Tiebold said. "If we keep our heads down, Pearson will probably have a real suspect in custody within twenty-four hours."

Chief Thomas nodded. "We'll let the sheriff handle it," he agreed. "With whatever help Vance and Yap can provide."

But his eyes when they met Daniel's held a damning

sympathy, and Daniel's stomach sank.

"Once they find a suspect, this will all blow over in a matter of days," Chief Thomas said. "But until then, I think we'd better put you on desk duty and keep you away from the press."

"Chief!" Daniel's voice was only one of a chorus of objections, but the chief waved a hand for silence.

"Lieutenant Marcy is right," he said. "It's better to err on the side of caution. The public has to know they can trust us. We'll do this by the book. Marcy will run the mandatory Internal Affairs investigation."

"But, Chief, I can do the I.A.—" Tiebold began, but the chief merely shook his head.

Lieutenant Marcy's repressed glee didn't bother Daniel. Marcy would enjoy needling him with it, but there was nothing for an Internal Affairs investigation to find. It was being chained to a desk that bothered him.

"Chief," Lieutenant Tiebold repeated, as Daniel struggled to retain his calm. "I understand your concern, but Parks isn't a serious suspect. If you put him on desk duty, it will make things look worse than they are."

"The Ariel Macaro case," Daniel said, brushing aside the question of his reputation. "You told Calvin Macaro I'd be working it. I have a commitment to solve it."

"We've got the perpetrator in custody." Lieutenant Marcy's teeth snapped sharply on the words. "I think others can take it from there."

"Tyler Woodridge is our prime suspect," Daniel said, keeping his focus on the chief so as not to give Marcy the satisfaction of his anger. "But I'm not satisfied that—"

"You can oversee the Macaro case from your desk," Chief Thomas said as he pushed himself away from the table. Coffee cups rattled. "Riggs, Vance, and Yap can tie

140

up any loose ends. That's my decision, Parks. Why don't you go home and get some sleep."

Kermit opened the door, and the chief exited, followed closely by Lieutenant Marcy. The others filed out, too, Garth Vance giving Daniel a heavy slap on the shoulder as he passed.

"Detective?" Kermit said, pausing in the doorway, but Daniel waved him out.

In the silence of the cold room, broken only by the buzzing of the overhead lights, Daniel stood quietly and breathed, letting it sink in until he believed it.

He'd been relieved of duty. Taken off an open case where the very life of the young suspect could be hanging in the balance. For however long the sheriff's investigation took, until Daniel was cleared, he was no longer a decorated, respected police detective.

He was a murder suspect.

Serena and her mother liked to say Destiny couldn't cook canned spaghetti. It wasn't true. She'd heated some Chef Boyardee for dinner just that past Wednesday night, and it had turned out fine. She didn't pretend she was an accomplished cook; she'd never had the practice. Cooking a roast or baking a chicken provided more food than she could eat in a week, and a week of pot roast was more than she cared to contemplate.

Still, she could bake. Pies, cookies, cakes—if it had a crust or contained chocolate, she could bake it. Her German chocolate pie had gotten top bids at the church pie auction the past two years. She had put Serena in an ecstatic trance with her beignets. And Daniel could not resist her chocolate–cream cheese brownies.

Pancakes were not going to defeat her.

141

Grimly, she scraped the blackened, oozing mess out of the frying pan into Daniel's kitchen garbage basket. She would clean the pan. Add more butter. Check the box again to make sure she'd added enough water to the mix.

How could she get it wrong if all she had to do was add water?

She'd wanted to have a nice breakfast waiting when Daniel returned from his walk on the beach. Not that she deceived herself into thinking he'd notice whether she put gooey, half-cooked pancakes in front of him or an elaborately prepared plate of crêpes Suzette.

She glanced toward the kitchen's side window, to see if she could see him returning up the steep path from the beach. She understood his needing time to himself, but she wasn't so sure *she* needed it. Sunlight filtered through the misty, late morning air, brightening the bristling needles of the Sitka spruce and setting the powdery dust of pancake mix dancing in the kitchen.

She sighed and turned back to the skillet. Butter. Lower the heat on the stove top. One-quarter cup of batter into the skillet.

The telephone rang, jerking her attention away from breakfast. She thought about letting the answering machine pick up, but then, it might be someone from the station calling to say a suspect had been apprehended in Alain's murder. As long as it wasn't Serena, calling to check in on her again.

Destiny had called Serena to explain why she wouldn't be helping at Mark's booth at the arts and crafts fair that morning. She'd expected the murder to shut the fair down for the day, but Serena had already called her several times to say the fair was going strong despite the rumors flying and the conspicuous police presence.

142

Destiny picked up the cordless receiver, just as she noticed she still had pancake mix all over her hand. *Great.*

"Hello?"

"Destiny? It's Maddy. Are you okay?"

Yes, rumors were flying. "What do you mean?"

"Chad went to the country club for a practice round with Calvin Macaro's law partner this morning, and he told Chad that Daniel had been put on desk duty and your old boyfriend, what's-his-name, had been killed."

Trust Maddy to come right out and say what was on her mind. "Alain was killed. The sheriff's department is looking into it. No one believes Daniel had anything to do with it."

"I should hope not. Daniel's one of the good guys. How about you? Are you doing okay? Can I bring you anything? Books? Tea? Chocolate croissants?"

Breakfast! Destiny whirled to the stove. "Damn!"

"What?"

"I burned another pancake." Holding the phone to her ear with her shoulder, she scraped the skillet yet again. "At least this one's not mushy."

"You're cooking breakfast?" The voice at the other end of the line grew even more concerned. "Where's Daniel?"

Destiny rolled her eyes as she banged the skillet into the sink and squirted it with detergent. "He's walking on the beach. I can cook pancakes, Maddy."

"Oh, right. Sounds like it's going well, too."

"If people didn't keep distracting me . . ."

But Maddy didn't laugh. "Look, if you need tomorrow off, you just go ahead and take it. Take the whole week if you need it."

Destiny shook her head, almost knocking the receiver to the floor. "Work will take my mind off things. Besides,

143

you're going to be overrun with schoolkids on break. I'll be there."

"Only if you want to," Maddy insisted. "I was going to leave you all alone at the desk this week without a second thought."

Destiny frowned. "That's right. I thought you weren't speaking to Chad the Cad."

"We talked yesterday. He took me out to L'Etoile."

Destiny had no trouble interpreting Maddy's tone. "*And?* Out with it, Miss Chance. You've obviously got something to tell me."

"Long story short? He really didn't understand how much I was looking forward to this Colorado ski trip, and he said if he'd known, he'd have given up the golf tournament in a heartbeat, even if it was a huge honor to get invited. And he said he'd take me next week instead. But not to Colorado."

"Not Colorado?" Destiny flipped her latest pancake. Perfect golden brown. She was getting the hang of it.

"Nope." Maddy paused dramatically. "Chamonix."

Destiny had to grab for the handset again. "As in *France?*"

"As in."

Destiny allowed herself a brief second of wrenching jealousy. France sounded almost far enough away to forget her troubles for the moment. "That's fantastic. I guess I'll have to find a new nickname for Dr. Geary. Chad the Rad."

"Big time."

"So you need me to work for you next week?"

"Only if you can. We don't have to go next week. Chad owes me. I'm sure I can get him to postpone it until after Christmas."

"No, you go ahead. It will take my mind off Alain, and

I'm sure the sheriff will have the case wrapped up by then."

If not, the extra work wouldn't be unwelcome, anyway. But she wouldn't think about that.

"The thing is . . ." Maddy's voice stretched. "If we left next week, I'd have another favor to ask you."

"Shoot."

"Just say no if you don't want to, I'll understand."

Destiny finally laughed. "Maddy, spit it out. Just tell your Catholic guilt I dragged it out of you."

"Puritan."

"Papist."

"Fine. Chad was feeling so guilty about making me upset that he got me the sweetest present. I mean, what a cutie. But I need someone to look after it while I'm gone."

Destiny smiled. It must be love. Chad was a handsome man, in a stiff, prim sort of way, but a "cutie"? Not so much.

"Tell me it's a diamond ring," she teased. "I could take good care of a diamond ring."

"Neither of us are ready for a ring," Maddy objected, though her wistful tone suggested otherwise. "No, this is so sweet. He came up to my door with this shoe box, and I thought, I don't know about this, maybe he's got some kind of foot fetish."

"That would bother you?" Destiny asked, thinking of her friend's extensive collection of shoes.

"Ha, ha. Well, not if he brought me Italian leather pumps. But, anyway, it wasn't shoes at all, though it does like to lick my toes."

Destiny froze with the spatula over the skillet. "Excuse me?"

"He got me a puppy!"

"A *what?*"

145

"A puppy. A long-haired dachshund puppy. I've named her Psyche."

"Psyche?"

"Chad said we should call her Cupid, but she's a girl, so it's Psyche."

Psych-o was more like it, Destiny thought, and she didn't mean the dog. This did not bode well for Maddy's shoe collection. "Maddy, what on earth gave Chad the idea that you wanted a dog? You freak out if you get *people* hair on your sofa, for heaven's sake. You once told me you didn't want to get a goldfish because it was too much responsibility."

"I like Fleur," Maddy shot back, defensive. "Even if she is big and hairy. And I'm a responsible person."

Destiny shook her head. "I know you are, but you don't get someone a puppy without asking—"

"I told him once about my old dog, Bronson, I had when I was growing up, about how smart he was and how much I still miss him. He used to come pick me up from school. Chad said it sounded like I needed another dog just like him."

"Wasn't Bronson a rottweiler?"

"A rottweiler would be a little big for my apartment, don't you think? Besides, Psyche thinks she's a rottweiler."

Suddenly, Destiny realized that the periodic noise on the line wasn't static. It was a tiny, determined growl.

"She really is too cute. She's trying to pull my sweats off. Ouch! Stop that! You're sure you won't mind watching her for a week? She's not completely potty-trained, but she's got her own crate and everything."

Mind? Wetting accidents, chewed furniture, destroyed shoes, having to get up every few hours in the middle of the night to take a puppy outside—why would she mind? When

146

she'd gotten Fleur from the Humane Society, she'd chosen an adult dog on purpose.

But this was Maddy asking for help. And though she knew exactly how much trouble a puppy could be, they stole her heart every time.

"I go home to let Fleur out every day at lunch, anyway. I'll get Sarah to help with her after school. Sarah's grounded for life; she might as well have something useful to do."

"Thank you," Maddy's voice filled with relief. "I knew I couldn't leave her at a kennel, even for Chamonix. Chad thought I was crazy, but she's just too little."

Destiny had already decided that it was Chad who was a few fruits short of a cake, but she wasn't going to deprive Maddy of a trip to France.

"I'll bring her to you next Sunday then, and I'll see you tomorrow," Maddy said. "Psyche! Not the table leg, sweetie. If you're sure you want to come in. You can call me tomorrow morning if you change your mind."

Destiny tried to work some sense out of her friend's words. "I'll be there."

That seemed good enough. "I'll see you. Hang in there. Ouch!"

And then Maddy was gone, and Destiny was back in Daniel's kitchen with pancake mix drifting through the air and the quiet hush of the ocean murmuring outside.

Alain was dead. Daniel was withdrawn and upset, as well as being an undeclared suspect in a murder investigation. She'd let down her sister and Mark by not being at the arts and crafts fair to show off her tattoos. Which still clean and bright this morning and might be so for weeks. And she'd just agreed to baby-sit a dachshund puppy for a week.

Destiny felt she was forgetting something in her litany of misery, but she was too tired to dig into her memory for it.

She heard the front door open and Daniel's steady footsteps coming up behind her in the kitchen entryway. She turned to him, glad to see the wind had brought color to his face and that his eyes sought hers only half-veiled with worry and frustration. His field coat swirled the scents of sea spray and sand toward her, and she stepped into his arms, jumping as his cold hands worked under her sweatshirt to the skin on her back.

"Are you all right?" she asked.

He nodded, with a twist to his lips that acknowledged that he wasn't, but he was better than before. "You?"

She nodded, too. Whatever she'd listed as wrong, whatever she'd forgotten, it couldn't be so bad if she and Daniel could face it together.

"I don't mean to be critical," he said, more hesitant now. "And it looks like you've been working hard in here. But is something burning?"

That's what she'd forgotten. Destiny glanced toward the stove to see smoke rising from the blackened mess in the skillet. She started to laugh, a loud, hiccuping laugh, and Daniel joined her. He pulled her into his chest and held her while she laughed and the tears ran down her cheeks.

Sarah paused by a small, round table holding a box full of Japanese-style ink paintings. She flipped through the mounted, plastic-protected renditions of bamboo and carp, redwoods and elk, trying not to show her interest in the empty space one booth down.

That had obviously been Alain Caine's booth, though he'd packed up all his artwork at the end of yesterday's selling and would never have the chance to unpack it. There was no police tape or any official presence to mark it, but those who walked by unconsciously gave the empty space a wide berth, treading gingerly, as if death were a sinkhole that might suck the unwary down from seemingly solid ground.

Sarah didn't expect to find any clues to Alain's death there, but she'd read enough of Aunt Destiny's mysteries to know that what cracked fictional homicide cases was often the unexpected. From what she'd learned from Detective Parks and Officer Riggs, what cracked real cases was mostly the average criminal's stupidity and sometimes pure luck. Either way, you had to keep your eyes and ears open to everything.

"You like any of those?"

Sarah started, looking up to see a thin, angular, young man leaning over her and the ink paintings. His dark hair was cut short at the sides, but a long lock fell over his forehead into his hazel eyes.

Sarah glanced back at the paintings, pulling out a long, narrow one. "This one of the egret." The bird's arched neck and still poise waited breathlessly against a background of half-seen reeds. "It looks like it knows we're watching it."

The young man nodded. "That's one of my favorites. The fish and cherry blossoms sell the best, but I like the birds."

"The colors are peaceful." She glanced at the signature. "Are you Sanjiro? This looks very Japanese."

The young man smiled, showing even white teeth. "And I don't? My middle name is Sanjiro, but you can call me Jon. My grandfather is Japanese. He taught me the art of Sumi-e, Japanese ink painting. I tell you what, I'll give you a deal on the egret. Half price."

Sarah glanced at the sticker on the protective plastic wrap in wary surprise. She could afford ten dollars.

Jon waved at the painting. "I like to sell my art to people who appreciate it. Besides, I don't think business is going to be so good today."

"Because of the murder."

He glanced at the empty space beside his booth. "See, you've heard about it, too."

"Did you know the man who was killed?" Sarah swallowed the sudden excitement in her throat. She'd just asked her first question in a criminal case, and it had come out completely natural.

"Naw. I mean, I spoke with him. He was a friendly guy, you know. Easy to talk to. But I didn't even know his name until the photographer the next booth down was telling me what happened this morning." Jon's mouth curved wryly as he shook his head. "He borrowed five bucks from me, though. Guess I won't ever get that back, but from what I heard, I came out lucky. He owed somebody at the fair a couple hundred."

Sarah widened her eyes, trying to look interested, but not too eager. Her mother said she looked like a hungry piranha when she was after information. "You don't know who?"

"Naw. Rumors always fly at these places. You can't believe half of them. I heard he had an old girlfriend around, too."

That was Auntie Dess. "But if he owed—"

"One of the potters, I think," the young man continued. "I guess he was supposed to be camping here with her, but she hooked back up with her ex and dumped him out in the cold. That's why he was staying with the tie-dye guy."

Not Auntie Dess. Sarah's face heated with excitement,

and apparently the young ink painter noticed, because he suddenly shut his mouth.

"I'm sorry," he said, brushing the hair from his eyes with an embarrassed gesture. "I didn't mean to upset you. You came to look at art. Grandpa says I talk too much for a painter. 'If your mouth is always moving, you're not using your eyes.'"

"That's okay," Sarah assured him. "I was just curious. I want to be an investigator when I grow up."

Sometimes being too young to have anyone take you seriously had its advantages. Jon smiled again.

"I can see you as a detective. All you need is a pipe and one of those Sherlock Holmes hats."

"I'll take the painting," Sarah said, handing him the picture of the egret. He carried it over to his cash box, and glanced down the sheet beside it for the tax as Sarah dug in her pockets for the money. She should be buying Christmas presents for her family, but she didn't think she'd want to part with the crane. Jon put the painting in a bag and handed her the change.

"Do you think she could have killed him?" she asked. She might as well get her mileage out of the kid detective thing. "His old girlfriend? Or maybe her ex?"

Jon's lower lip pushed out as he shook his head. "I heard they already have a suspect." He leaned forward, his voice lowering. "A guy came by the booth yesterday and bawled the dead guy out. I mean, this guy was serious. Told him he'd kill him if the guy messed with his girl again. I think he probably did it. But I heard they won't arrest the guy because he's a cop."

"Maybe they haven't arrested him because he didn't do it," Sarah retorted, too sharply. Her face reddened again. "I mean, just because he was upset doesn't mean he killed

151

anyone. Why would a cop kill anybody?"

Sympathy crossed the young man's angular face, and he brushed his hair back again. "I hope you keep that idealism. Maybe you'll make a difference when you're a cop. But cops get involved in bad things, too. They think they can take the law into their own hands. The ones last night were pretty rough with the tie-dye guy who owns the trailer where the guy was killed. I bet this cop killed him, and they're going to cover up for him."

"They're not!" Sarah objected, the words hot and frustrated. "Detective Parks is one of the good guys!"

Sarah bit down on her tongue, but couldn't take the words back. Jon stared at her, hazel eyes flashing between anger and confusion.

"Hey, what's going on here?"

Sarah turned to see two uniformed Hope Point PD officers push their way up to the booth, one slender and unassuming, with a hint of Asian features similar to the young painter's, the other big and broad-shouldered, his crew cut and dark sunglasses stereotyping him as law enforcement.

The shorter one examined Sarah with searching eyes. "What were you saying about Detective Parks?"

Sarah swallowed and glanced at Jon, wondering if she should apologize, or maybe give him back his painting. "I was just saying he didn't kill anybody. I know him, and I know he'd never do anything like that. He's an honorable person." Her mother had called Daniel that once, and it had seemed just the right words to describe him.

"I'm sorry," she told Jon. "I wasn't trying to trick you or anything. I just wondered if you knew who else might have killed Mr. Caine, because I know it wasn't Detective Parks."

"I know who you are," the sharp-eyed officer said,

mouth curling in a slight smile. "I saw you at the police station the other day with Detective Parks. Kermit Riggs said you cornered a burglar single-handed with a baseball bat. I wouldn't want to take you on. I'm Officer Yap, and this is Officer Vance."

Sarah struggled to keep the heat from her cheeks. She couldn't tell if Officer Yap was really impressed or if he was making fun of her.

"Look, we know Detective Parks, too," Officer Vance said, putting on that false camaraderie adults sometimes use around adolescents. "We're not going to let anybody railroad him."

"We're here to find the truth," Officer Yap interrupted, smoothly brushing over his partner's partiality. "There could be a lot of different things involved in this case. I'm sure you just want to help, but it's not safe for a young lady like yourself to get involved in a police case, especially a homicide."

"That's right," Officer Vance agreed, adjusting his shades as he glanced her way. "Leave the investigating to us, kid. We know what we're doing, and we can protect ourselves. We wouldn't want you to get hurt."

"Or to mess up the sheriff's investigation so we can't clear Detective Parks." The slight smile Officer Yap sent her was just as much a warning as Officer Vance's bluntness.

"Sure," Sarah said, biting back the urge to defend herself. She hadn't meant to get in the way. Jon the Sumi-e artist was the one who'd brought up the murder. But the officers didn't want to hear it. They'd already dismissed her and were turning back to their work.

"So," the big officer, Vance, was saying, managing to loom menacingly over the young artist, though Jon was nearly as tall as he was. "You're a font of information about this murder, are you? Were you thinking about sharing any of this with the police?"

Even from her position, backing away into the crowd, Sarah could see Jon's warm eyes hardening, his posture shrinking as he withdrew into himself.

"It's just gossip, man," he said, retreating behind his cash table, shooting a resentful glance at Sarah. "I don't know anything."

"You'd better let us be the judge of that, buddy," Vance said, leaning in again, big hands spreading on the table. "Let us in on the gossip. You don't want to be obstructing justice, right?"

Sarah scooted down the aisle that ran the length of the exhibition hall, moving out of sight of Jon's booth. She should seek out the officers after they finished talking with Jon, make sure he'd told them about the man Mr. Caine had owed money to and about his girlfriend and her ex. Any of the three of them might have had a reason to kill him. A better reason than Detective Parks, who had only been trying to protect her.

As she walked out of the exhibition hall into the sunlight, she shivered with a much deeper worry for Detective Parks than she'd felt when her mother had first told her what had happened. If Officers Vance and Yap couldn't get as much information from Jon as she had, how could she expect them to get enough information from other witnesses and potential suspects?

Some people already thought Detective Parks was guilty. In real life, murders didn't always get solved. What would happen if the sheriff's department couldn't find the real killer?

Sarah took a deep breath to steady her heartbeat. Officer

Yap and Officer Vance might not want her interfering with their investigation, and they were right. But if all she did was listen while other people talked . . .

If she hadn't been cutting school and hadn't made Gemma call the police on Mr. Caine and if she hadn't accepted that necklace from him, Detective Parks wouldn't even be in this trouble.

Sarah set her jaw and squared her shoulders. She softened her face, relaxed the "hungry piranha" look and tried tossing her hair like the high school girls did.

She was only a seventh-grader, nothing scary like those tough-guy cops. She'd just keep her eyes open for another opportunity to gather information. Regardless of Officer Vance's warning, she wasn't threatening enough to be in any danger from anyone.

Chapter 11

The intercom on Daniel's desk buzzed, causing his arm to jerk. The crumpled ball of paper he threw bounced off the edge of the dented metal garbage can and skittered across the floor. He'd grab it later; it would take up a whole ten seconds of this endless day.

He pinched the bridge of his nose with one hand as he punched the intercom with the other. He'd only been on desk duty two days, and he was already stir-crazy. He glanced at the industrial-deco clock on the wall. Make that one day and ten minutes. Only seven hours and fifty minutes left to fill.

"Detective Parks?" Nancy's voice sounded uncharacteristically apologetic, a polite fiction that she might be interrupting something important. It was about the only kindness she could offer. "The chief would like to see you."

"On my way."

He straightened his shirt and tightened his tie as he headed down the hall to Chief Thomas's office. He never wore a tie, but it seemed appropriate to being stuck at a desk all day.

The chief's door was open. Daniel paused at the threshold. The chief glanced up, his jowls drooping dourly. "Close the door."

Daniel pulled it shut and moved to stand before the

broad, dark desk. Chief Thomas did not wave him to a chair. The chief settled his paperwork and spread his big hands on the desk before looking back up at Daniel, only his eyes burning with emotion.

"What the hell is this all about with Calvin Macaro?" he demanded, his voice simmering deep in his throat.

"Macaro?" Daniel had assumed the chief wanted to see him about Alain Caine's murder, though the sheriff's department had not reported any significant progress in the case since the murder three nights before.

"I got a call from the former congressman," the chief said, leaning on the title, "the minute I walked in the door this morning. He was a little . . . miffed about the interview yesterday afternoon."

"Sir?"

The chief's caterpillar brows crawled up his forehead. "You didn't send Officers Yap and Vance to Calvin Macaro's house to gather more information for the Ariel Macaro murder investigation?"

Those few words drew a clear, unpleasant picture in Daniel's mind. Vance's blustery rudeness and Yap's sly remarks up against Calvin Macaro's prideful grief. He wondered if the officers had gotten a good look at Helga's teeth.

"I gather miffed was a euphemism, sir."

"You better damn well believe it, Detective." The chief's voice didn't rise, but the frustration in it boiled over. "Macaro is furious. He wants Vance and Yap hung from the nearest tree and your head on a platter. He claims they accused him of tampering with evidence and obstruction of justice. For God's sake, we've got the perp in custody. What were you trying to prove?"

Just when Daniel thought things couldn't get worse.

"I'm not absolutely certain we have the perp in custody,

Chief," he admitted. "Tyler Woodridge is a hot-tempered young man, but stabbing someone in the back behind a Dumpster doesn't strike me as a crime of passion. I don't like the dichotomy."

"Appreciating the symmetry of the crime isn't your job, Detective," Chief Thomas growled, with none of his usual dark humor. "Your job is to find the suspect who fits the evidence. It's the jury who decides if you've got the right guy."

"I'm worried the jury won't think so." Daniel pounced on the opening. "The evidence is all circumstantial. Tyler Woodridge is a well-spoken kid. Any halfway decent public defender is going to be able to present him as a misunderstood James Dean type. I think we need more evidence if we want a conviction. And Calvin Macaro is going to be a lot more than miffed if we don't get a conviction."

"You wanted more evidence?" The chief spoke the words with slow deliberation. "So you sent Garth Vance and Tom Yap to *harass the murdered girl's grieving father?*" His voice finally rose to low, rumbling thunder as he heaved himself to his feet. "What the hell were you thinking?"

"I asked Officers Vance and Yap to use their contacts in the teenage drug scene to come up with more information on Tyler Woodridge and any other of Ariel Macaro's acquaintances who might have had a motive for killing her." He didn't bother to spell out that he hadn't asked Vance and Yap to interview Macaro. It didn't matter. The investigation was his responsibility. "I can assure you this won't happen again."

"That is correct." Chief Thomas sank back into his chair. "It won't."

"I'll talk with Macaro. Apologize. I'll clear it up."

"No, you won't." The chief's frown relaxed from anger

to aggrieved annoyance. "I don't want you or Vance or Yap or any other damn fool in this department going anywhere near Calvin Macaro. I've calmed him down. For now. And we're going to leave it that way."

"Sir." Daniel struggled to keep his voice low and reasonable. "This is a murder investigation. I don't approve of badgering victims, but as lead investigator on this case, I can't do my job without full access to—"

"I'm pulling you from the Ariel Macaro case."

The room froze around Daniel for an instant. The light stopped flickering. The heating system hushed in the vents. He felt as if he'd just been shot in the gut, but had not yet started to bleed.

"Off the case?"

"I'm assigning it to Ben Dillon."

Now sound filled his ears. A buzzing that left him breathless. "Sir, with all respect to Detective Dillon, Ben hasn't been working this case. He doesn't know the intricacies of—"

"Then you'll apprise him of them." The chief's eyes held his. "You can't run a murder investigation from a desk, Parks."

He raised a hand to forestall Daniel's protest. "And no, I can't take you off the desk. I had hoped this Caine murder would be resolved by now, but we'll just have to give it more time. You've done the groundwork for the Macaro case. It's in good shape. Ben Dillon won't mess it up."

Chief Thomas sighed heavily. "I know this isn't easy on you, Parks. Well, tough. You're a police detective. You're, what? Not even thirty-five? You're barely out of diapers for this job. But you've been in it long enough to lose your illusions. No one ever said it would be a cakewalk. No one ever said you'd get thanked or appreciated."

Daniel nodded, unable to trust himself to speak, but taking the chief's blunt honesty as the support it was.

Chief Thomas dropped a heavy hand on the files on his desk. "Bury yourself in paperwork for the next few days, Parks. No point in brooding. Get back to work. And call off the dogs."

"Did you know the government is going to start inserting microchips into our skulls?"

Destiny didn't glance up from the computer screen where she was trying to track down the Jasper County Library system's single remaining copy of *A Fancier's Guide to Pacific Coast Marine Invertebrates*.

"Maddy, why would anyone steal a book on mollusks?"

"Like dogs, with those chips under their skin." Maddy settled into her chair in front of the computer next to Destiny's along the reference desk. "I think I'm going to get one for Psyche. She dug out under my back fence yesterday. But listen, these people chips will come with locator devices, so the government can find anyone at any time. They'll know every time we so much as walk into the bathroom."

Destiny made a note on a piece of scratch paper and looked up at Maddy. "You've been spending too much time with Mr. Dyer."

Maddy tilted her head, fixing Destiny with sharp green eyes. "Ignore the warnings at your peril," she said, in a whispery tone that sounded almost nothing like Mr. Dyer's dry, light voice. "When Big Brother comes after you, you'll have nowhere to run."

"I hope Big Brother has better things to do than keep track of my bathroom breaks."

"Charlene doesn't, though." Maddy waved her fingers

toward the circulation desk where their long-faced supervisor stood frowning toward their patron-less desk. "Try not to smile when you talk to me. She'll think we're having too much fun. On second thought, goof off while I look busy. She probably won't downsize both of us."

Destiny shook her head, swatting Maddy's hands away from her computer monitor. "It's dead today. I thought we'd be crazy this week with the schoolkids."

"It's supposed to rain tomorrow. While you're baking pumpkin pies, I'll be up to my armpits in rugrats. Special Collections is doing some inventory work this afternoon if you want to run up there and help. I think I can handle the wild workload here."

The reference desk telephone rang, and they both grabbed for it. Maddy was faster. She flashed Destiny a triumphant grin, which turned to a grimace as she listened to the caller.

"It's for you." Maddy stuck out her tongue as she passed the phone over.

Destiny tried not to laugh at Charlene's wide-eyed disapproval across the lobby. "Destiny Millbrook. May I help you?"

"Desty?"

"Serena." Destiny grimaced back at Maddy. Her sister had taken the week off work so Sarah wouldn't be home alone, and she'd already called the library four times, mostly, Destiny suspected, from boredom.

"I just got a call from Mark."

"Yeah?" Destiny's tone was not encouraging. She had worn a turtleneck to work the past two days to hide the henna tattoos from Charlene. They hadn't begun to fade yet. "I already promised I'd come to the Christmas fair in Shell Creek this weekend for him, but there is no way I'm

161

going to let him tattoo my face."

"He just ran into this guy he knows, Rollie. You know, the one Alain was staying with?"

The reminder kicked her in the ribs. A week ago, if she had heard that Alain had died in Arizona, she probably would have grieved; she had loved him once, after all. But the fact that he had come back into her life just in time to be murdered and that Daniel's job was in jeopardy because of it . . . The thought of his death had the power to send waves of nausea and grief rolling hot and cold through her body.

It was just like Alain. Even death couldn't prevent him from wreaking havoc on the lives of those around him.

Serena's voice brought Destiny back from the contemplation of the dead. "You remember Sarah saying she heard Alain had a girlfriend who dumped him right before they came out to California? Well, I guess Rollie let slip to Mark who Alain's girlfriend was. Her name is Ginger Shrieve. She's a CPA, but she does pottery in her spare time. Her ex traveled here to Jasper County with her, and they're both going to be at the Shell Creek Christmas Arts Fair on Sunday."

Destiny stifled the spark of hope that flickered in her throat. Surely if the woman or her ex-husband had killed Alain, they'd be on their way back to Arizona by now. Still, she wrote the name down. "I'll pass that along to Daniel. He can get the information to the sheriff."

"Isn't there some way he can get Kermit to check this out?"

Destiny frowned into the phone. "I don't think so. It's the sheriff's case."

"It's just that Mark said that Rollie said . . ." Serena's voice trailed off in uncharacteristic hesitation. "He said those two officers from the Drug Task Force were pigs, and he wouldn't pass any information to them, and he'd take it out on Mark if Mark told anybody."

The cold in Destiny's stomach spread. The longer this case dragged on without good leads, the harder it would be to solve, especially since most of the potential suspects would soon be scattering across the region to other Christmas season arts and crafts events.

"Don't tell Sarah I said this." Serena lowered her voice, and Destiny could picture her glancing over her shoulder to check for young spies. "But I think she might be right about one thing. Daniel may need more help than he's getting from official channels."

Destiny had been thinking the same thing. Daniel had saved her life just months ago by outwitting a ruthless criminal. She could not bear to sit idly by while another sociopath destroyed Daniel's life.

If both she and Serena were on the same wavelength, it was a sure sign that the universe was trying to tell her something. Something like, *Butt out. Disaster is imminent.*

"If we interfere in this investigation, we could get Daniel in even worse trouble," Destiny said, keeping her own voice low. She knew Maddy could hear every word, but Maddy had already proved to be the soul of discretion when would-be killers had been looking for Destiny. "We could go to jail ourselves, for obstruction of justice or something."

"I'm not talking about interfering in the investigation," her sister said, with a primness that didn't fool Destiny for a second. "I'm talking about enhancing it. I was talking with Callista—"

"Serena!"

"I didn't bring it up. She could feel the negativity

clinging to me when I went in for my tarot reading Sunday evening."

Destiny's hand ached from clutching the phone. Serena was lucky it wasn't her neck. "Serena, I really don't like the idea of you discussing this case with your—" She stopped herself from saying "nutty guru." "Your friends."

"Callista won't breathe a word," Serena said, without contrition. "Health care provider–patient confidentiality. Besides, I didn't name any names. Honestly, Desty. I only told her what she needed to know to cleanse my aura. But she did have a suggestion."

"A séance?" Destiny felt mad laughter bubbling in her throat. She could picture it now. The black candles, the incense, the eerie music. Alain's shade flirting with Callista.

Serena ignored her sarcasm. "A psychic. Callista has a friend who has worked in police investigations before. She helped find a body once where the murderer had put it in a refrigerator and buried it in his yard."

"We know where Alain's body is," Destiny reminded her, dropping her forehead to her free hand, fighting the tempting pull of hysteria.

"What if she could find out where the killer is? What could it hurt to try?"

"Other than my sanity?"

"Skeptic," Serena accused.

"Fruitcake."

"Is there a problem here?"

Destiny's head snapped up at Charlene Adams's voice. The library branch supervisor stood in front of her desk, her skin almost the same color as her neat, pale ecru suit, her thin mouth turned down even farther than normal.

"That's right, ma'am," Destiny said into the phone, pasting on a smile for Charlene. "We have several books with recipes for fruitcake. I can pull one off the shelf for you. That's right. We're open until five on Tuesdays. You're welcome."

She thumped down the receiver before Serena could muster a response.

Charlene's expression did not improve. "It doesn't look as though we need two librarians at the reference desk this afternoon."

"I think you're right," Destiny said, forcing another smile as she rose from her chair. "I'm just on my way up to Special Collections to help with their inventory. Give me a call if you need me, Maddy."

She slipped out the side of the reference desk and headed toward the elevator. No, not Maddy's "elevator of doom." With her luck this week, it would burst into flames and plummet into the basement. She turned for the stairs.

Inventory. Mind-numbing, tedious, uninspiring drudgery. Just what she needed that afternoon to forget all about death and false accusations. Forget about her niece collecting evidence and her sister consulting psychics. Forget about her own helplessness in the face of Daniel's pain. Forget about a murderer walking loose in their midst.

She paused with her foot on the bottom step of the stairs. She *had* forgotten that. With all the concern about clearing Daniel's name, she'd put out of her mind the most important fact. Daniel hadn't killed Alain. But someone had. And that someone was free and clear as long as Daniel was the chief suspect.

Which meant that anyone trying to clear Daniel's name could be ticking off a brazen, cold-blooded killer. One more reason to make certain Serena and Sarah didn't interfere in the investigation. As for herself . . .

Destiny smiled a small, grim smile. As for herself, she'd been there before.

Daniel watched the thick, black liquid pour into his coffee cup with fatalistic stoicism. Wednesday afternoon. Another agonizing day of desk-sitting was almost over. If the coffee killed him, at least he wouldn't have to return to his office on Friday.

" 'Bye, Detective Parks." Grace Martinez gave him a quick smile as she passed down the hall toward the back exit. "Happy Thanksgiving. I mean—" She hesitated. "It will get better."

"Happy Thanksgiving, Martinez," he said, waving her on. One thing he had to be thankful for: sitting desk duty made it a simple matter to get Thanksgiving off. He wouldn't have to face the earnest support of his fellow officers for the entire day tomorrow.

"Detective! I'm glad I caught you before you left."

Except for Kermit. Somehow Destiny had found out that Kermit's father was flying to Hawaii with his latest girlfriend for Thanksgiving and Kermit had no plans for the holiday.

"Green salad," Daniel said, belatedly remembering the message Destiny had passed along. "Serena said you could bring a green salad tomorrow night."

Kermit blinked, missing the coffee carafe with his first swipe and knocking the basket of sugar packets to the floor.

"Oh, right. I can do salad." Kermit folded himself to the floor to retrieve the sugar.

Serena's first suggestion had been mashed potatoes, but Destiny had feared for Kermit's fingers.

"But that's not why I was looking for you," Kermit said,

returning the sugar basket and reaching for the coffee once more.

Daniel took a discreet step back. "Why, then?"

"I found out something interesting about Kyle Preston."

Daniel's pulse picked up, but he said, "I'm no longer assigned to that case. I'm sure Ben Dillon briefed you and Vance and Yap on how he wants to run it."

"Detective Dillon seems pretty confident Tyler Woodridge is our perp," Kermit said. "He's not real interested in other ideas."

That was the impression Ben had given Daniel, as well, when Daniel had filled him in on the particulars of the case the previous afternoon. Daniel couldn't blame him.

He repeated what the chief had said to him. "We gather the evidence and the D.A.'s office presents it to the jury. They're the ones who decide on guilt or innocence."

"Yeah." Kermit's keen blue eyes never left Daniel's. "So, the more evidence they've got, the more likely they are to arrive at the correct conclusion."

Daniel sighed and risked a gulp of his coffee. "Spill it, Riggs."

"Kyle Preston has a record."

Daniel took a long moment to swallow. "You're not talking about a musical career."

"The Prestons moved up here from Menlo Park two years ago. Dr. Preston had a good practice down there. Kind of strange he'd pack up and move a couple hundred miles north to work for a small-town hospital."

"Not so strange if his son was in trouble, and the good doctor wanted to give him a fresh start," Daniel supplied, remembering something Tom Yap had said at the fairgrounds.

"Right. The record's been sealed, I guess due to Kyle

Preston's juvenile status at the time, but it's still on the books."

Daniel blew out a breath and ran his hand through his hair. "That doesn't give us anything to change the course of the investigation."

"You said Tyler told you that Ariel was worried about Kyle getting involved in drugs. If he had a prior legal problem with controlled substances, it might make it worthwhile to check a little deeper into Kyle's alibi for the night of the murder."

Exactly what Daniel had been thinking. That spoke well for Kermit's investigatory instincts, but not necessarily for the development of Kermit's career at the moment.

"That's for Ben Dillon to—"

"And another thing," Kermit interrupted, a glint in his eyes suggesting he'd saved the best for last. "Grace and I did a little digging into Tyler's brother Eric's case files. One of his busts, another dealer rolled on him in return for a deal from the D.A. The other guy was actually a bigger fish, but his attorney got most of the evidence against him thrown out on a technicality, something funny with the warrant.

"You want to know who represented the other guy in brokering the deal with the district attorney's office?" Kermit's enthusiasm couldn't wait for Daniel's reply. "Calvin Macaro."

"What's that about Calvin Macaro?"

Daniel turned with guilty speed. The police station had grown dim as the gray sky outside deepened and the department settled in for the evening routine, leaving a rare, brief moment of calm. Daniel should have noticed another officer entering the break room, but Tom Yap had quiet feet.

"Calvin Macaro helped put Tyler Woodridge's brother

168

in jail several years ago. One of those odd coincidences," Daniel explained, shrugging it off.

"Coincidence?" Tom raised his eyebrows.

"Yes." Daniel believed in coincidences. Though he also believed in examining them closely to make sure that's all they were. "Kermit's going to pass the information to Detective Dillon."

Coffee sloshed on the floor as Kermit's arms waved in rebellion. "I've got to check it out first. That's not enough to change Detective Dillon's mind about the case."

"It's not enough to change anyone's mind about the case," Daniel pointed out. "If anything, it only gives Tyler a another reason to hate Calvin Macaro. But if Ben thinks it's worth looking into any further, he'll take care of it."

"But—" Kermit's frustration robbed him of speech.

"But maybe some discreet inquiries would provide enough information to sway Detective Dillon's mind," Tom finished the thought for him.

Daniel drained the last of his coffee without tasting it. "Chief Thomas has made it clear we're not to waste department time on the matter."

Kermit glanced at his watch, then glared back at Daniel. "I'm not on department time anymore tonight."

"Riggs isn't the only one who feels like you got a raw deal being pulled from the Macaro case," Tom said. "Ben Dillon's a decent investigator, but in our minds, it's your case. I don't have anywhere I've got to be for a few hours."

"You've both got somewhere to be," Daniel growled, wiping out his cup with a paper towel and hanging it back on his peg above the coffee machine. "Off-duty. And that's where you're going to go, unless you like the idea of driving a desk. I appreciate your dedication to justice, but the both of you and Garth Vance are already in hot water with the chief because of the way I handled the case."

Tom gave an exaggerated shudder. "Both you and the chief made that clear yesterday, Detective. But don't worry about me or Garth bugging Macaro again. He's the kind of guy you might not survive pissing off twice. He said he was going to destroy your career if Tyler didn't get convicted."

"He'll have to get in line," Daniel observed dryly. "But we're talking about you, not me. And I'm not going to let you give the chief a reason to suspend you."

"Being partnered with Garth, I'm only a heartbeat away from suspension at any given time, anyway." Tom's tone left it an open question whether he was joking or not.

"I won't think much of my career if I help send an innocent kid away for life," Kermit said, with an idealism Daniel had almost forgotten.

"You're not going to feel any better if you foul up Ben's case and let a brutal murderer go free." Daniel fixed his junior officers with a fierce glare. "You've heard the old saying about too many cooks? The same goes with detectives. You two are going to keep your noses right where they belong. You tell Ben what you've learned, Kermit, and leave the rest to him.

"If there's any extracurricular investigating to be done, it will get done." He held each gaze for a moment, making sure they understood him. "But if I catch either of you going behind Ben Dillon's back on this case, I'll get you suspended myself. Is that perfectly clear?"

Tom shook his head and flashed his ironic grin. "Loud and clear. I leave it in your hands, Detective. Have a good Thanksgiving."

As Tom headed out the break room door, Daniel turned back to Kermit. "Riggs?"

Kermit shrugged, his own mouth curling up at one side.

"I knew you wouldn't sit by if it turned out the kid needs clearing. But if it turns out *you* need a little help—"

"Kermit—"

"Don't worry, I'm not going to get caught interfering." Kermit's grin broadened, then faded. "And you better not, either, Daniel."

Daniel shrugged, as uneasy with Kermit's confidence in him as with his younger friend's concern. "Don't worry about it. I'm in hot water already."

But he knew Kermit was right. If the heat got turned any higher, his water was going to boil.

Chapter 12

"Why did the turkey cross the road?" Sarah demanded, plopping down in front of the fireplace beside Destiny and Fleur, spattering them with dishwater.

"To get to the other side?" Kermit suggested, peering over his feet from his position stretched out on Serena's cushy, wall-hugger recliner.

"He was heading for the White House to get a presidential pardon," Daniel said with authority from his spot on the couch, hunched over the coffee table and Sarah's Yosemite Falls jigsaw puzzle. His grin warmed Destiny more than the fire. She hadn't seen him relax since they'd received the news of Alain's death Sunday morning.

Sarah shook her head. "He decided he'd rather get hit by a truck than have to eat tofu for Thanksgiving."

"Ho, ho." Serena reached into a bowl on the coffee table and slung a Brazil nut at her daughter. "You should count your blessings you got to eat at all."

"Even indentured servants get fed," Sarah retorted.

Her mother raised her arched brows. "I bet I could find one or two more pots that didn't fit in the dishwasher . . ."

"I thought the tofu turkey was delicious," Kermit cut in. "Just as good as regular turkey. That was the best Thanksgiving dinner I've had since I was a kid."

"The food was wonderful," Daniel agreed. "I won't

need to eat again for a week."

Serena gave her daughter a look.

"I didn't say *all* the food was bad," Sarah pointed out, uncowed. "But tofu shaped like a turkey leg still tastes like tofu. And tofu tastes like—"

"Anybody ready for pie?" Destiny asked, interrupting before the mother-daughter exchange could escalate. She suspected the forced proximity between the two over the weeklong Thanksgiving vacation would have one positive result. Sarah would be glad to get back to school on Monday.

The general chorus of groans indicated it would be a while before she needed to break out the pie, though Fleur glanced up at her with one hopeful brown eye.

"You got your share of tofu turkey," Destiny reminded her.

Fleur sighed and shifted her jaw onto Destiny's leg before drifting back to sleep.

"Maybe Detective Parks will cook the main dish for Christmas," Sarah suggested.

"Maybe," Daniel agreed, clicking a group of three pieces into Yosemite Falls. "I cook a mean Christmas goose."

His casual acceptance of the idea fluttered strangely in Destiny's heart. They hadn't even talked about Christmas, about whether or not he was going to spend the holiday with his folks in New Mexico. They hadn't talked about the future at all lately.

"Mom and Dad are talking about coming over from Sacramento for Christmas," Serena announced, curling her legs under her with feline grace. Her eyes gleamed as she purred at Daniel. "If you wouldn't mind sharing your goose with them."

Destiny shot a look at her sister, feeling the color rise in her cheeks. "I don't think we could find a goose that big."

Serena kept her gaze on Daniel, her smile widening. "I bet he could cook two geese. Our folks are sure looking forward to meeting him."

Kermit laughed. "I'd say your goose was cooked, Detective."

"You'll love Mom and Dad," Serena assured him.

"They're even crazier than Mom and Auntie Dess," Sarah put in. "Just don't ask Grandpa how he lost his pinkie finger. He's got it in a jar somewhere, and he'll get it out and show it to you."

"He will not!" Serena swung her feet to the floor with a snap. "That's just a joke he tells."

"You know," Daniel said, turning a wry smile on Destiny. "The idea of life in prison is starting to grow on me."

Sarah leaned across Fleur to tap Destiny on the shoulder. "Have you told Detective Parks about what Mark found out? About Mr. Caine's girlfriend and her ex? Did you tell him what that painter told me about Mr. Caine owing somebody money?"

Daniel's smile faded as he regarded Sarah's earnest face. "She told me, Sarah. The sheriff's department has already looked into it. The Shrieves were together all Saturday night. They haven't tracked down the rumor about the money, but few people kill their debtors before giving them a chance to repay the debt. That's not good business."

"Maybe he went to get the money, and they had a fight," Sarah said. "And of course the Shrieves would say they were together. They could be covering for each other."

Destiny reached her hand toward her niece, but Sarah jerked away. "Maybe they even killed him together. The sheriff should take them into custody and question them separately. One of them might crack."

"I thought we agreed not to bring up this topic today," Serena said, her tone brittle as she fixed her daughter with a warning look.

"But nobody's *doing* anything," Sarah protested, jumping to her feet. "This is stupid. Maybe none of the rest of you care what happens to Detective Parks, but I don't think life in prison is funny."

"That's enough," Serena said. "I don't want one more word from—"

"It's all right," Daniel said, holding up a hand to keep Sarah from running from the room. "She can't help what's on her mind. It's on my mind, too, Sarah."

Sarah crossed her arms over her chest, shrinking in anger and embarrassment, but she didn't leave.

"You ask good questions," Daniel continued. "You've got a good eye for what somebody's not telling you." He dropped the pieces of puzzle he held back onto the table. "I don't believe in discussing an ongoing investigation—" His gaze met Destiny's with another little smile that pulled at her heart. "—But I guess this isn't my investigation. I'm just a suspect. So I'll answer some of your questions if you'll remember something."

Sarah sat back down beside Fleur. "What?"

"I'm a trained police detective, and I think the sheriff's department is doing its job. Thoroughly and by the book. Okay?"

Sarah's eyes narrowed. "If *I* were investigating a crime, I wouldn't badger witnesses the way those two officers I saw were badgering Jon. He was perfectly happy to share what he knew until they started threatening him."

Daniel grimaced. "The sheriff's deputies who talked with the Shrieves didn't do any badgering," he assured her. "The Shrieves volunteered to let the deputies search their trailer, which the deputies did."

"Like they'd really have kept the murder weapon in their trailer." Sarah rolled her eyes.

Destiny noticed the cloud that crossed Daniel's face and remembered that the weapon incriminating Tyler Woodridge in the Ariel Macaro case had indeed been found beneath his grandparents' trailer. She began to understand why that bothered him.

"If they were guilty, why would they be staying in Jasper County for the Shell Creek Christmas Fair?" Serena asked. "Why not head home for Arizona?"

"Because it would make them look guilty," Sarah said, her mouth set in a stubborn line. "I bet if we did some more digging on them at the Shell Creek fair, we could find out what they're really up to."

"*We* are going to do no such thing," Daniel said, his voice stern. "Sarah, this isn't a game. This is a homicide investigation."

"Don't worry," Serena said, once more curling up on her chair. "*We* won't be going more than three feet from Mark's booth at the crafts show this weekend. *I*, on the other hand, know some of Mark's friends and I could ask some questions—"

"No, but I could," Destiny broke in. She'd dealt with the dangers of an unknown enemy before, unlike Serena. "None of them know me—"

"No, no, no." Daniel's growl brought Fleur's head up off of Destiny's knee. He glared at Serena. "Not you." Then Destiny. "Not you." Then Kermit. "And not you."

"I know how to blend in," Kermit objected. "With official law enforcement like Garth Vance on your side, maybe you need some unofficial help clearing your name."

"No!" Frustration nearly choked the word as Daniel

glared once more around the room. "I do not need your help. I do not *want* your help. I do not want anything messing up this investigation. I will be better off without your help. This is my *life*. Do you understand?"

Glancing at Kermit, Sarah, and Serena, Destiny saw the same stinging hurt she felt in her own throat. They only wanted to help because they cared about Daniel. And for all their flaws, they each had skills and contacts to offer that the sheriff's department didn't have.

But as she watched Daniel glaring down Kermit and Sarah, not letting up despite the tears Sarah tried to hide and the pain in Kermit's eyes, she realized that he'd intended his remarks to wound them. He was afraid, but not as much for his job or his freedom as for them. Unlike what she had done, he would never forget that the person they hunted was a murderer. It would not have escaped his notice that the killer would undoubtedly be willing to kill again to remain free. He would rather have every person in the room turn their backs on him than have any one of them get hurt trying to help him.

When he turned his glare on her, she glared right back. Let him think he'd infuriated her. It would make it that much easier to do whatever needed to be done at the crafts show without his interference.

The telephone rang, interrupting the strained silence.

"That's probably Jesse," Serena said, uncurling from her chair to move toward the kitchen. Serena's significant other had taken Mark with him to San Francisco to spend the holiday with their parents. Destiny knew Jesse was taking any opportunity to remove Mark from acquaintances and situations that might draw him back into drugs.

"Hold on." Serena returned from the kitchen with the cordless receiver. "It's a Lieutenant James Marcy."

"I gave the dispatcher your number as a contact number, in case they needed me tonight," Kermit said. "They should have tried the pager first, though." He checked the pager on his belt as he grabbed the handle to return his recliner to its upright position. The handle stuck. "The pager's on. The darn things. You never know if—"

The recliner handle suddenly gave way, dropping Kermit's feet to the floor with a thud and propelling him halfway out of the chair.

"It's not for you," Serena said, waving him back to forestall further disaster. "It's for Daniel."

Daniel raised his eyebrows as he stood to take the phone from Serena. "Lieutenant?"

He started toward the kitchen, but halted mid-stride in the doorway. "Where? . . . Have you run . . ." A long pause. "I see . . . Yes, I understand. Good-bye."

He slowly lowered the receiver from his ear and clicked off the talk button. "That was Lieutenant Marcy," he repeated, his words as slow as his actions. "A guy out walking his dog in the field behind the fairgrounds found a gun, a .38 Smith and Wesson. Practically out in plain view, he said. Ballistics has already matched it to the bullet that killed Alain Caine."

"Hey!" Kermit said, managing to work free of his chair. "That's a break."

"It's about time," Sarah said. "Did they get fingerprints off of it? Maybe they can get the guy now. If they're not too clueless."

"No fingerprints," Daniel said, turning back to them. His face looked blank and pale, as if all expression had been bleached away, but there was something in his eyes as he stared at the phone that made Destiny's stomach lurch. "But they ran the serial number and came up with a match."

"Who does it belong to?" Sarah demanded. "The Shrieves, I bet."

Daniel shook his head. "It was originally registered to a man by the name of Floyd Elgar."

Sarah grinned. "Gotcha!"

"That name sounds familiar," Kermit said.

"Floyd Elgar was arrested four years ago for the attempted murder of his wife and her boyfriend. It would have been murder, but Mr. Elgar wasn't a very good shot."

"Why's he out of jail already?" Sarah demanded.

"He's not." Daniel's voice sounded dead in Destiny's ears. "He's in San Quentin. His gun was stolen from the police evidence locker sometime after his trial." Daniel looked up from the telephone receiver in his hand. "I was the arresting officer in that case."

The darkness inside the cab of Daniel's battered Toyota pickup felt more impenetrable than the night outside, where the moon managed a pale glow through the seams in the clouds. Destiny clutched the cardboard box packed with leftovers in her lap, but the holiday scents of sweet potatoes and pumpkin and cranberry tasted heavy and sad. Daniel had the heat blowing hard, but Destiny thought she had never felt so cold.

"The evidence room clerk," she said. "The one you said was fired a couple of years ago for stealing drugs from evidence. Kermit's right. He must have stolen the gun, too. Could he have a grudge against you for—"

"He moved to L.A.," Daniel said, cold and clipped. "Maybe he sold the gun for drugs before he left. I don't know. It doesn't really matter."

"So it just circulated in the drug community until someone killed Alain with it?" Destiny breathed in, muffling her frustration. "I know you believe in coincidence. But . . ."

"But what?" He glanced at her then, eyes black as the night. "If it's not a coincidence, then what? At the time I had access to that gun. I had a dispute with Alain Caine the day he died. I don't have an alibi."

"You didn't kill Alain."

He flicked another hard glance at her. "You sure?"

She glared back. "Yes."

"Well, isn't that nice." He swung the truck hard onto Elderberry Lane. "But Lieutenant Marcy isn't sure. The sheriff's department isn't sure. The chief won't be sure. The men and women I work with won't be sure. And the general public sure as hell won't be sure."

"Which is exactly why those of us who *are* sure have to figure out what the hell is really going on here!" She tried to take another deep breath, but her stomach was too tight. "I know you're upset, but you have to help us help you."

"I told you I don't want your help!" He slammed his hands on the steering wheel as the truck jerked to a stop in front of Destiny's house. Destiny heard Fleur scrambling to her feet in the truck bed behind them.

"Daniel, if the sheriff's department is convinced you're guilty, they're going to stop looking for other suspects."

The jagged sound that burst from his throat couldn't be called laughter. "You think I don't know that?"

"Then you've got to provide them another suspect if you can. Can you think of anyone who might have a grudge against you? Somebody you put away on a drug charge who might want to destroy your career by framing you for murder?"

He merely stared at her, and even Destiny could hear how ridiculous the idea sounded. Few criminals had the creativity or the patience to plan something so elaborate, and it seemed nearly impossible that a criminal could have connected Alain to Daniel, known Daniel would not have an alibi, and then murdered one man purely to wreak revenge on another.

A soft, eager whine reached Destiny through the back window connecting the truck cab and camper shell.

"Let's talk about it inside," she suggested, wrestling the door open.

"I'm not coming in."

She turned on him, prepared to shout or cry or argue until she broke through the cold, black wall he'd thrown up around himself, but the sudden weariness and despair she saw in his eyes stole the words away.

"This is going to be bad, Destiny. I don't want you involved."

"Well, isn't that nice," she repeated back to him. "But it's a little late for that. I was the one who dated Alain. He broke into my house. He gave that necklace to my niece. Heck, if it weren't for you, I'd probably be the sheriff's prime suspect."

Daniel's lip twitched. "You don't want to confess to anything, do you? I could find you a good lawyer. Of course, the judge might have some trouble overlooking your alibi."

"Maybe you could find me a bad lawyer." She reached over to touch his arm. "You know, it's time for you to get one."

He grimaced. "If they arrest me, that's soon enough. They still don't have a case."

"Call your lawyer, Daniel, before you get arrested. She needs to know what she'll be up against in a worst-case scenario."

He raised an eyebrow. "You mean Tessa? I don't think

181

hiring my ex-wife to defend me against a murder charge is such a great plan."

Destiny didn't like it all that much, either, but she liked the idea of Daniel being indicted for murder a lot less. "She's the best defense lawyer in Jasper County; you've said that yourself."

Daniel sighed, running a hand through his already rumpled hair. "I'll think about it when the time comes, all right? I can't think about it tonight. I need to get some sleep."

The whine from the back of the truck came again, louder this time.

"Fleur wants her beauty sleep, too," he said,

"Fleur wants her bedtime cookie," Destiny muttered, shooting a dark glance through the truck's back window. "As if she didn't get enough treats from all you softies at Serena's tonight."

Daniel's hand brushed the side of her cheek, though he pulled back as she turned. "Your belief in me means a great deal," he said, his voice soft and low. "But we've only known each other a few months. You don't owe me anything. I don't want this ugliness to touch you."

He opened his door and slipped out, moving behind the truck to open the back for Fleur. Destiny climbed out with the box of food, barely avoiding being bowled over by the lanky bundle of yellow enthusiasm leaping to the street. Doing an impromptu two-step with the dog, she followed Daniel back to the driver's side door.

She couldn't stop him from getting back in, but she angled the box so he couldn't shut the door.

"It's not a matter of owing you anything," she said, looking up into his face, as familiar as her own heart after just three months, as unfathomable as the workings of that same heart. "I love you. What touches you will always touch me."

"I love you, too." His words touched her as gently as the faint glow of the moon, even as he eased the box back and shut his door. "That's why I can't allow that to happen."

The truck's engine roared to life, and Destiny had to move away to call Fleur onto the sidewalk as Daniel put the truck in gear.

Daniel's despair weighed on her like the heavy clouds above the town as she watched him drive away into the night. Fleur leaned against her thigh, watching, too.

"Jerk."

The Lab glanced up at Destiny, forehead wrinkled in query. Destiny turned toward the house, waving Fleur ahead.

"Not that I wouldn't be a jerk, too, if I were about to lose my job and get indicted for a murder I didn't commit. But this noble 'for your own good' crap just ticks me off."

Fleur's tail waved in agreement as she led Destiny up to the front door.

"I mean—" Destiny had to stop her dialogue with the dog to hold her purse in her teeth while she dug out her keys. Despite Fleur's thoughtful consideration of her words, she didn't dare set down a box of food-filled plastic storage containers and foil-wrapped goodies under the dog's nose. Dropping the purse into the box and turning the key in the lock, she continued, "I mean, if you really love someone and want what's best for them, shouldn't you allow them to make their own decisions?"

Fleur ran ahead to sit by the kitchen counter, giving Destiny a quizzical look.

"What decisions? I haven't decided yet," Destiny said, transferring the contents of her box to the fridge. "But I'm not going to turn my back on him, just because he thinks it would be better for me. And I'm not going to give up on clearing his name just because it might upset the sheriff."

She shut the refrigerator door, suddenly aware of the deep silence in the house, of the darkness barely dispelled by the kitchen light over her head, of the cold aloneness deep in her bones.

"I don't know what I'm going to do, Fleur," she admitted, crouching down to brush back the dog's ears.

Fleur whined softly.

"Oh, sorry. You want your cookie." But before Destiny could stand, Fleur leaned forward to rest her chin on Destiny's shoulder. Destiny wrapped her arms around the dog and hugged her tight.

"I don't know what I'm going to do," she whispered into Fleur's neck. "Pray." That was all she could do for tonight. "God will have to be working on this one, Fleur. Because it sure doesn't look good."

Chapter 13

Destiny adjusted the scoop neckline of her T-shirt to show off the butterfly that still fluttered with her pulse just above her collarbone. The short sleeves showed most of the Celtic knots down her arms, and she hadn't worn socks, so the tattoos at her ankles peeked between her low sneakers and the hem of her jeans.

She glanced at the eyes looking back at her from the bathroom mirror and saw nothing but determination. She was no hippie biker chick today. She was a warrior.

"Maybe a warrior princess? Do I look like Xena, Fleur?"

Fleur glanced up from her spot by the bathroom door, then heaved herself to her feet and padded away down the hall.

"Great. Thanks a lot," Destiny called after her. She glanced back at the mirror. Not that Fleur was wrong. Xena had bigger muscles and much tamer hair. That was all right. If the artists and artisans at the Shell Creek Christmas Fair didn't notice she was a warrior, she'd have an edge on them when she went in for the kill.

For the first time, the determination in her eyes slipped, revealing the shadows behind it.

In the three days since Thanksgiving, Daniel had not been indicted nor fired from his job. But the only reason she knew that was from talking to Kermit. Daniel hadn't so much as returned her calls. She'd driven up to his house the previous afternoon, only to find his old truck gone. Kermit had called her last night to assure her Daniel had returned home, but apparently he wouldn't talk with Kermit, either.

Destiny straightened her spine and gave herself her best warrior glare. If Daniel had given up, then clearing his name depended on the rest of them. She, for one, had no intention of giving up. Her past had indirectly gotten Daniel into this mess. It was up to her to get him out. Starting today.

Someone at the Christmas fair had to know something. If she dug deep enough, she would find out who and what.

A muffled woof from the living room brought her attention back from thoughts of murder as the doorbell chimed. Destiny hurried down the hall to the front door where Fleur waited in gleeful anticipation.

"Sit!"

Fleur sat, though her expression indicated she didn't for a moment believe that any human in their right mind wouldn't want to be greeted by seventy-five pounds of bouncing yellow Labrador.

Destiny swung open the door, immediately stepping back as a frowning giant loomed toward her through the doorway. She managed to suppress a squeak of fear as her jangled nerves rattled through her body before settling back to a slow hum.

"Chad." She always forgot how tall Maddy's boyfriend, Chad Geary, really was. Somehow his personality didn't seem big enough to fill a six-foot-three frame. "I wasn't expecting you."

"Who *were* you expecting?" he asked, noting the hand she held to her chest to keep her heart inside. "Jack the Ripper?"

186

Before she could reply, he turned his weak tea–colored eyes on Fleur. "Don't let her jump on me. These are tailored pants."

Destiny gamely clamped down her thought that Jack the Ripper might be more amusing company. She turned to remind Fleur to sit. But although Fleur had risen to her feet, the dog was showing no interest in their visitor whatsoever. Her thick, otter tail quivered behind her as she stared intently at the open door.

"Destiny?" Maddy's voice floated ahead of her as a small, sturdy cat carrier banged against Destiny's door frame. Maddy followed behind, a bag of premium dog food squeezed under the arm that held the cat carrier, her other arm clutched to her chest. "Meet Psyche!"

A tiny black nose stuck up over the arm of Maddy's stylish blue wool coat, followed by a dark caramel-colored muzzle and bright black eyes. Long, blond-streaked ears perked up to dwarf the narrow head as the black eyes focused on Fleur.

Fleur took a cautious step forward. The sudden, sharp, deafening outpouring of noise from the creature in Maddy's arms knocked Destiny and Fleur back on their heels. Tiny feet scrabbled on Maddy's coat as the beast manifested its intention to fly through the air and take Fleur to the mat.

"Chad?" Maddy pleaded, trying to hold onto the squirming puppy, but it was Destiny who rushed forward to grab the carrier and dog food bag. "She's never seen a dog as big as Fleur," Maddy said, raising her voice to be heard over the racket.

"Fleur's wonderful with puppies," Destiny assured her, though she could see the same trepidation in Fleur's eyes as she felt in her own. "I'm sure they'll get along once Psyche gets used to her."

"Put her down and let them get acquainted, Madelyn," Chad suggested. "She's ruining your coat."

"No, I—" Maddy started to object, but Psyche's long, whipcord body jackknifed in her arms, and she barely managed to hang on long enough to break the puppy's tumble to Destiny's carpet.

Psyche slipped through her grabbing hands, heading straight for Fleur. Fleur's eyes widened, and her tail and legs stiffened as the creature charged. The dachshund skidded to a stop just inches from Fleur's feet, her own front feet lifting off the ground in excitement at each piercing yap.

Slowly, Fleur lowered her nose, her nostrils flaring as she took in Psyche's scent. Psyche flattened herself to the ground—not a difficult maneuver for an animal with such short legs—and pulled her ears back in sudden consternation. Then, with the boldness of a heart that knows no fear, she jumped at Fleur's face.

Fleur leapt back, and Psyche followed, emboldened by the retreat. Fleur turned to take refuge behind Destiny, and Psyche gave chase, her short legs flying as Fleur made a slow, stately flight around the humans.

Reassured that the little puppy was a threat to nothing but Fleur's dignity, Destiny looked back up at Chad and Maddy. "I wasn't expecting you until tonight."

"I know. I'm so sorry," Maddy said, reaching again for Psyche, who darted just out of reach, then continued her enthusiastic pursuit of Fleur. "Chad's travel agent called this morning to say he could get us on an earlier flight. I would have dropped her off at the kennel for you to pick up this afternoon, but they're not open on Sunday—"

"Destiny doesn't mind," Chad assured her. "She's used to this. One more dog won't make any difference."

188

Once more Destiny saw her own thoughts perfectly echoed in Fleur's troubled eyes.

"Psyche isn't a dog," Maddy reminded him. "She's a puppy. That's a lot more trouble than Fleur."

"It normally wouldn't be any trouble at all," Destiny said, stretching the truth slightly for Maddy's sake. "But I'm due up in Shell Creek in half an hour for the Christmas arts fair."

"You're going to wear that?" Chad asked, indicating her T-shirt and sneakers. "Women and shopping. It's not like the mall up there, you know. They get a sea breeze. You'll freeze to death."

"I'm not going shopping," Destiny said, reining in her annoyance. "I'm spending all afternoon helping Mark Banos with his henna tattoo booth. I promised Serena I'd be there."

"Just put Psyche in her crate," Chad said, pointing to the cat carrier in Destiny's hand. "It's got a bed and everything. She likes it in there, and it will keep her out of your shoes."

"She can't stay in a crate all day," Destiny and Maddy objected in chorus.

"She's just a puppy," Maddy said, as Destiny explained, "She has to get out to pee."

"Speaking of which . . ." Chad warned.

Destiny turned just in time to see Psyche rising from a squat to resume her chase after Fleur.

"No!" Maddy wailed, lunging wildly after the puppy. After a mad scrabble on the floor, she rose with Psyche wiggling and yapping in her arms.

"She's just excited," Destiny said, setting the crate on the coffee table and heading for the kitchen counter to grab a handful of paper towels, hoping she hadn't just heard

Chad mutter, "She's always excited."

"Here let me do that," Maddy commanded, grabbing the paper towels from Destiny and thrusting Psyche into her hands. "I told you we can't just drop by and dump Psyche on Destiny unexpectedly like this, Chad. We'll just take the later flight. It's no big deal."

"But we're packed." Chad's voice rose in animation. "We're on our way to the airport. Do you want to go to Chamonix or not?"

"It's all right," Destiny interrupted, seeing the color rise in Maddy's cheeks. "You guys go ahead to the airport. I'll take Psyche with me to the Christmas fair."

Maddy and Chad both turned to look at her as though she were nuts, which was undoubtedly true, but at least she'd prevented the imminent explosion.

"You said Psyche likes her crate," she explained, looking down at the small, silky-haired beast panting heavily in her arms. Psyche still stared in fascination at Fleur, but she appeared to have worn out her vocal cords for the moment. "I can keep her in the booth with me and take her out every hour or so for some exercise. She has a leash?"

Maddy nodded, turning to the coffee table to open the crate. She pulled out a slender copper-colored leash that matched the dainty copper-colored collar on Psyche's neck.

"I put her toys in there, too," Maddy said. "She loves her tug rope. And I've taped her vet's name and number to the side of the crate here."

"Then we're all set," Destiny said, ignoring Fleur's look of reproach at her betrayal. "You two go on to the airport. Have a great time. Don't worry about Psyche. We'll be fine."

"See?" Chad said, striding toward the door. "They'll be fine. Let's go."

Maddy paused beside Destiny, reaching for Psyche. She lifted the tiny terror up to nose level, her green eyes softening. "You be a good girl, Psyche. Be a good puppy. I wish I could take you with me, but I'll bring you back something special from France."

A tiny pink tongue flicked out to curl around Maddy's nose, while the puppy's tail whipped frantically, and for one second Destiny understood why Maddy had fallen in love with the dog.

"We'll be fine," Destiny assured her again, more gently this time. "Go. Have a good time."

"I didn't even want a dog," Maddy said, reluctantly handing her back. "Now I'd almost rather stay home than spend a week in Chamonix without her."

"I know what you mean," Destiny said, glancing at Fleur. Her lanky, sheddy, occasionally drooly and even smelly companion had saved her confidence and self-esteem after her breakup with Alain, and more recently Fleur had even saved her life. What was a week of skiing and croissants compared to that? On the other hand: "There's no way you're giving up a chance to go to France. I'd have to have you committed. Psyche will be perfectly happy playing with Fleur all week."

A horn blared outside.

"I think Chad's getting impatient."

Maddy leaned over to give Psyche one last kiss. "He's just jealous."

"I can tell."

Maddy hurried to the door, as if she needed to build up enough speed to escape Psyche's orbit. But as she dashed out, she paused with a hand on the door frame. "I'll call to check up on her!"

"From France?"

But Maddy was gone, the door slamming shut behind her. Immediately, Psyche began to cry, a high, piercing whimper that cut through Destiny's heart. And her nerves.

With a huge sigh, Fleur stood up and left the room.

"Thanks for the support!" Destiny called after her as Psyche began to yip, each burst of pitiful noise bouncing the puppy's small body against Destiny's chest.

Destiny sucked back the sense of helplessness that surged up her throat. What had happened to the warrior princess? A puppy was nothing compared to murder and false accusations.

She bent down and set the little dachshund on her feet. "Come on, Psycho—er, Psyche. Let's go outside and see if you have to go potty again."

Perhaps she should not have mentioned the word potty. She headed for the kitchen to grab the paper towels. She'd have to remember to bring the roll with her to the Christmas fair.

The sun warmed her shoulders despite the damp bite of the breeze off the ocean. Light dazzled on the waves breaking on the beach of Shell Creek cove at the base of the low cliffs. Sharp seagull voices cut through the hush-crash of the waves, and Destiny thought she could hear the bark of sea lions from the rocks thrusting up through the sea at the mouth of the cove and from Cypress Head, just to the south between the cove and Shell Creek harbor.

Nearer at hand, the noise of human voices mingled with the rhythm of axes hewing wood at the redwood burl carving demonstration. White canvas-sided booths dotted Shell Creek Park, the green expanse of the park picnic grounds spreading in a long, wide strip between Seabreak Drive and the cliff's edge, bounded on the south by the narrow parking lot and on the north by a trail-threaded wood that stretched along the coastline.

Shell Creek's annual one-day crafts show was smaller and less formal than the county arts and crafts fair, though many of the exhibitors from the county show had remained to attend this one. A number of booths offered more touristy items than the arts fair, the redwood burl key chains and driftwood wind chimes that local Shell Creek artisans sold in the old harbor town's shops all year. Sea-inspired jewelry and seashell decorations also appeared to be well-represented.

Destiny's eye caught the bright turquoise and hot pink swirls of color from Rollie Garcia's booth of batiks and tie-dyes near the park rest rooms by the trees. Destiny hadn't expected the big Viking to show. Not after having a man murdered in his trailer barely a week before. Then again, maybe he had to be there. Maybe selling his garments and jewelry composed his entire livelihood.

Unless the Drug Task Force was right about his extra-legal activities. Just one of the things she wanted to discover today.

Destiny hefted Psyche's crate out of the back of her Rabbit, and turned to make her way toward the hulking cypress tree at the far end of the park, near the path down to the beach. Serena had told her Mark intended to set up his booth near the ancient tree.

As she neared the "Body Works Body Art" booth, she saw Mark nearby, chatting with a middle-aged couple sporting nearly identical gray ponytails, though the man also wore a neatly trimmed beard and mustache. The two laughed as Mark emphasized an anecdote with broad hand waving, spraying cigarette ash across the grass.

Destiny waved as he glanced up. His wide grin faded and

he dropped the cigarette, focusing his attention on the butt as he ground it into the grass with the toe of his biking boots.

Destiny glanced down at the carrier in her hand. If he didn't like Psyche's presence now, she could just imagine how he was going to react when the puppy got comfortable and started yapping. She ducked into the canvas-sided booth to find Sarah alone at the cash table, smooth, dark blond hair falling across her face as she hunched over her seventh-grade social studies book.

"Back to school tomorrow?" Destiny asked, settling the dog carrier down on the table.

"It's stupid," Sarah muttered, slamming the book closed. "I've already learned all the math we're going to do before Christmas break, I've finished my biography report and I've read the history stuff twice this week. Why should I have to waste my time . . ." Her voice trailed off as she looked up. "What is that?"

"*That* is Psyche."

Sarah was already reaching for the latch to the carrier.

"Careful—" Destiny tried to warn her, but Sarah had the door open, and Psyche streaked out, skidding right off the edge of the table into Sarah's lap. For a moment, girl and dog looked equally startled. Then Sarah lifted the puppy up to her face, and Psyche's tongue flashed out.

"Ugh!" Sarah gasped, laughing. "She stuck her tongue up my nose! She's adorable. When did you get her? What does Fleur think? Why didn't you tell me you were getting a puppy?"

"I'm not," Destiny said. "She's Maddy's. I agreed to watch her for a week. Maddy dropped her off early, so I had to bring her with me. I'm going to walk her in between customers. She's got the bladder of a flea."

"I'll walk her for you," Sarah volunteered, unhooking Psyche's leash from the carrier door and fixing it to the dog's collar. She set the little dachshund on the grass, and Psyche leaped at Sarah's sneakers, sinking her teeth into the laces and jerking them back and forth with short, fierce growls.

Sarah gently unhooked the needle-sharp teeth from her shoes and headed out of the booth, Psyche barking excitedly at her heels.

"Destiny?"

Mark stood in front of the cash table, hands tucked under his armpits below his muscle shirt. His liquid dark eyes didn't quite meet hers. "I didn't think you were going to come today, what with Daniel and all . . ."

"I made it." Destiny twisted her arms to show off the henna tattoos. "I'm ready to advertise your artistic talent."

"Yeah, um, I don't know." Mark's eyes wandered around the booth. "I mean, if that's such a good idea."

Destiny followed his eyes to the cash table and grabbed for the dog carrier. "Sorry about this," she said. "I didn't know I'd have Psyche today. But I won't let her chase anyone off. She's so cute, she'll probably be bringing the customers in. And she's just a little puppy. She'll probably sleep most of the afternoon, anyway."

Lightning did not strike her dead on the spot, so maybe it was even true.

"Puppy?" Mark asked, eyes finally focusing on the carrier as Destiny stashed it under the table. "Oh, that's okay."

Destiny straightened to scrutinize his face, afraid to check his pupils, but unable to stop herself from doing so. They looked normal to her, though that didn't necessarily mean he was sober. "Mark? Are you all right?"

He finally looked at her then, his round, open face uncomfortable with evasion. "Huh? Oh, yeah. Look, Destiny, you don't have to be here today. Serena just went over to the rest rooms. She'll be back any minute. You could just go home and relax."

Destiny felt her eyebrows knit together like Daniel's did when he was confused. "I'm fine here, Mark. I don't mind helping you out."

"Uh-huh." He still stared at her. "That's nice. I mean, I appreciate it and all. But I don't think I need your help. I mean, I'm not sure it would be helpful to have you here. I mean, with your connection to Daniel."

Destiny felt goose bumps creep up the tattoos on her arms. "What do you mean?"

"You know." He shrugged, seeming to hope if he stared at her long enough, she'd get his meaning without his having to express it.

"No, Mark, I don't." Though her raised voice indicated maybe she did.

"It's like, you're with law enforcement, you know?" He shrugged again, helplessly. "I know Daniel wouldn't kill anybody, but some people around here think he did. And, you know, with the cops coming around and asking everybody questions all the time . . ."

"I see. It might be better for your business if I didn't hang around here."

She couldn't keep the hurt and anger from her voice, but all she saw in Mark's eyes was relief. She swallowed hard, wondering if this was a taste of what Daniel had been facing all week. Another incentive to dig into the rumors flying among the vendors. "Do you mind if I leave Psyche with Sarah here at the booth for awhile? I'd like to do some shopping."

"No problem," he assured her with eager generosity.

"Leave her here as long as you need to. Thanks for not getting mad. It's not you. It's just, you know, people are kind of nervous."

Mark certainly looked nervous. The green and blue snake tattoo coiled around his upper right arm was twitching.

"Tell Sarah I'll be back for Psyche in an hour or so." As Destiny brushed past Mark out into the watery autumn sunlight, she imagined that some of his friends might be nervous, too. Friends like Rollie Garcia, perhaps. Friends from Mark's old life of drugs and petty crime.

She missed a step, glancing back to catch Mark watching her walk away, a shadow of fear in his eyes.

She hoped it was his old life.

"Sarah? Sarah! Didn't you notice we had a customer?"

Jerked back from feudal Japan, Sarah glanced up from her folding chair to meet her mother's exasperated expression.

"This is so stupid," she said, pointing to her social studies book and ignoring the comment about the customer Mark had just led into the privacy of the back of the booth. "They don't tell you enough about anything. Like the samurai and stuff. They don't even mention ninjas. Do you know anything about ninjas? I bet Mrs. Cannon doesn't. She doesn't care about history. She just wants us to memorize dates so we can pass the state tests."

"Do you really want to be reminding me about your bad attitude toward school?"

Sarah shrugged, tilting her chin higher. "It doesn't matter what I say. I've got to get on the bus in the morning, anyway."

Her mother's eyebrows rose. "Who said anything about

the bus? You're got your own private limousine service, sister. I'm driving you to school."

Sarah's mouth dropped open in outrage. *"Driving* me? What, you think I'm going to ditch again, after this week of hell? You don't trust me."

Her mother snorted. "I did trust you. Until you proved I couldn't. It takes a lot longer to rebuild trust than it does to lose it. And I don't see you working very hard at it."

"What's this, then?" Sarah slammed her textbook on the table in front of her, making the cash box rattle. "I've done all my homework for the rest of the year, practically. I've been your stupid slave all week. What more do you want?"

"Maybe a little maturity to go with all those IQ points? You don't let a three-year-old cross the road by herself, no matter how smart she is." Her mother smiled, as though she'd made an irrefutable argument.

Sarah just shook her head and looked away. How could she prove her maturity if she always got treated like a three-year-old? In four years she'd be a legal adult. Shouldn't she be practicing?

The flashy red and black of a Hope Point High letterman's jacket caught her eye passing the booth. She'd only seen Kyle Preston once before, but she would recognize those broad shoulders and that chiseled profile anywhere. His wheat-colored hair was almost the same color as hers, but it made him look like Brad Pitt or something, while it just made her fade out of sight.

The high school senior paused, scanning the park before him. Seeing what he was searching for, he stalked across the picnic area, his expression intent.

Mark's booth stood on a slight rise near the cliff's edge, so Sarah could watch Kyle's progress through the crafts show. Gemma was right. He was gorgeous. A lot more gorgeous than the picture of Tyler Woodridge that the *Jasper County Register* had run. But maybe that was part of why Ariel Macaro had stopped going out with Kyle. He looked like he appreciated his own talent and good looks more than anyone else could.

Arrogant, Sarah decided, wondering if Auntie Dess could be right about Kyle Preston's being more insecure than he looked. She didn't see any evidence of it watching him push through the other Christmas fair patrons as though he were royalty they should part before, a prince deigning to gift the lowly arts and crafts crowd with his presence.

What *was* a high school football hero doing at a crafts show for the second week in a row, anyway? Without his entourage of hulking linemen?

Her eyes narrowed as she watched him slow his pace, shooting quick glances around him, as though to see if anyone were watching. He was too impatient to be devious, though. His pace slowed further, but his direction never faltered. He was heading straight for the psychedelic colors of Rollie Garcia's booth.

"Sarah?" Her mother's voice interrupted her concentration. "Have you seen my sweater?"

"No." Sarah leaned sideways to keep her eyes on Kyle Preston, but she no longer had a clear line of sight. She'd never know what took him to Rollie Garcia if she watched from afar. She glanced at her mother. "I think you left your sweater in the car. I'll run and get it."

She jumped to her feet, knocking her metal chair back. A surprised, sleepy yip sounded from the dog carrier at her feet.

"And I'll take Psyche for a walk, too," she said, gathering the puppy from the confines of the carrier.

Her mother's eyebrows rose once more. "Don't tell me

you took that maturity lecture to heart, young lady."

Sarah shot her a grimace. Compliance would only arouse suspicion. "Sure, Mom. Whatever. We'll be back when Psyche's bladder is empty."

That ought to give her plenty of time for a tour of the park. And if a trip to the rest rooms for herself brought her right up beside Rollie Garcia's tie-dye booth . . . Well, she couldn't help that, could she?

Chapter 14

Finding Ginger Shrieve's pottery booth took Destiny less time than the detour to her Rabbit to pick up her jacket. There was an upside to Mark's decision not to use her as a billboard, Destiny had to admit as she hugged the cozy midnight-blue fleece across her chest. Chad Geary had been right about the cool sea breeze.

She edged into the warmer sunlight, out of the shade of the spruce, redwoods, and alder lining the north edge of the picnic area, her eyes on the large, open-sided booth displaying a muted rainbow of bowls, mugs, and vases a few yards away. Sturdy, finished wood shelves showed the pottery to advantage, and the brochures displayed in a rack on the top front shelf were glossy, professional productions.

Destiny had learned a little about pottery during her relationship with Alain, enough to judge that Ginger Shrieve's pieces showed decent workmanship, even a little flair. But she suspected that the superior quality of their presentation owed more to the artist's day job as a CPA than from craft fair income.

The potter took as much care showcasing herself as she did her wares. Her permed blond hair was pulled back in a graceful twist, loose curls framing a face so carefully made up as to appear natural. Likewise, her faded blue jeans and billowy, powder-blue blouse artlessly displayed her curves.

Her laughter, however, was loud and genuine as she counted out change for a slender, elderly man purchasing a tiny blue bud vase. Destiny waited for the man to walk away before approaching the booth.

"Ginger Shrieve?" she asked, as the woman bent to pull a bottle of mineral water from beneath her table. Up close, Destiny could see fine lines radiating from the woman's mouth and eyes, see a sharpness in her features suggesting she was a good ten years older than Destiny had taken her for.

The woman raised an eyebrow as she drank from the bottle. She set her water down before replying. "That's me. Can I help you? I'm offering a sale on spoon rests today." She gestured to a shelf of shallow disks in a variety of brightly swirled colors. "Two for one."

Destiny wondered if Miss Manners had a rule for such encounters. "Mrs. Shrieve, my name is Destiny Millbrook. I wondered if I could talk with you about—"

But the woman's sky-blue eyes had already narrowed at Destiny's name. "You want to talk about Alain Caine."

Far better for a detective to have limp, dishwater hair than fiery curls or a midnight-black waterfall down her back, Sarah decided, slipping up beside a rack of sky-blue and deep plum batik sundresses.

None of the passing crafts show patrons gave her a second glance, even with Psyche dancing around her heels. She might as well have been invisible to the two people standing just inside the booth.

Rollie Garcia's bright yellow and green tie-dye shirt stretched tight across his huge chest, his hefty frame over-shadowing Kyle Preston's athletic build, but even so, he appeared to Sarah to have shrunk since the weekend before.

The friendly grin had fled, hiding his wide mouth beneath his brush of a mustache. He stood with shoulders hunched, arms hugged tight across his stomach, no wild gestures or loud laughter to increase his size.

He was shaking his head at whatever Kyle was telling him, his blond mane swishing around his jaws. Sarah could hear the intensity in Kyle's hissed voice as he thrust a small packet at the other man, but she couldn't catch the words. She'd have to get closer.

She glanced down at Psyche, who was sitting quietly beside her, the puppy's long tongue hanging out one side of her jaw as she panted. Sarah scooped her up, and, unzipping her sweatshirt halfway, she tucked the little dog inside. Now she could move.

If she slipped around the rack of sundresses, she might be able to hear Kyle and Rollie's conversation.

She was just edging sideways when a heavy hand fell on her shoulder.

"That's right. I wanted to talk with you about Alain." Destiny had expected any reaction from hostility to anger to nervous discomfort, but Ginger Shrieve merely crossed her arms under her imposing cleavage and gave Destiny a thorough once-over.

"I thought you'd be cuter," she said, meeting Destiny's eyes with her own level gaze. "The way Alain talked about you. He'd get all nostalgic about the girl he left behind in California. So pretty and full of life. But too young to understand his artistic soul."

"He was only six months older than I am!" Destiny objected, disgusted by how quickly Alain could irritate her even from the grave.

Ginger laughed, hearty and loud, as she pulled out her

chair and dropped into it. "I always suspected the problem with his California girl was Alain's maturity level, not yours. Even when I thought you were a nineteen-year-old ingenue. I can't say I liked you much, either way. I'll never see thirty or a size six again."

Destiny snorted. "Alain had a knack for making people feel like they didn't quite measure up to his ideals. I didn't have enough of a figure. Not to mention I was too practical and I didn't believe in him enough."

"That mean you didn't trust him with your credit card?"

"You got it."

"Smart girl." Ginger pointed a black leather-booted toe across the booth. "There's another chair there, if you want to take a seat. My husband's supposed to be keeping me company, but he ran out of cigarettes."

Destiny sat in the sagging director's chair she indicated. "I'm trying to figure out how Alain got caught up in something that got him murdered." The truth was all she had. "I don't have any right to ask you personal questions, but I would appreciate your help."

Ginger took another long sip of mineral water, once more looking Destiny up and down. "I heard your current squeeze is the cop they've fingered for killing him. It'd be a lot better for you if the police thought Alain might have been killed by somebody else's jealous man. Hey, I don't blame you, honey, but I can't help you there. Buzz was with me all that night."

"Alain said he was supposed to have a ride out here with a friend, but the friend turned out to be unreliable."

Ginger shook her head, letting out a soft whistle through her teeth. "Alain broke it off with me three months ago. He needed 'more freedom for his art to thrive.' Not long after Alain dumped me, Buzz came back around to see if we could patch things up. I guess he found out living alone was pretty damn lonely. I thought so, too. Maybe we both did some growing up, because it's turning out we like each other even better than we used to. There was never any chance Alain was shacking up with me for this little trip."

"Alain wasn't too good at taking no for an answer."

"That was his problem, not mine."

"Alain's problems tended to shift onto other people," Destiny said, thinking of Sarah and her baseball bat.

"Is that why your boyfriend went looking for him the afternoon before he died?" Ginger's eyes were clear, but hard.

"That's why," Destiny agreed, equally direct. "And I bet Buzz wasn't any happier about him hanging around than Daniel was."

"Ha." Ginger's snort was almost amused. "You got that right. But you've never seen Buzz, have you? His neck's bigger around than Alain's head. If Alain had pissed him off bad enough, he'd have picked him up and snapped him like a twig. He wouldn't need a gun."

Destiny chewed her lip, trying to decide how much to say. "Listen, I believe you. Shooting a guy through a pillow doesn't sound like a crime of passion to me. I'm not asking you to tell me Buzz slipped out at seven o'clock and returned smelling like gunpowder. I'm just asking you to help me understand what was going on with Alain that weekend. You know a lot more about Alain's relationships with the other people at the fair than I do."

Ginger kept her eyes on Destiny, though her French-manicured finger flicked the pop-up cap of her water bottle up and down. "Look, I wasn't too happy with Alain the day he died. He came by my booth that afternoon, laying on the charm. When Buzz showed up, Alain needled him. I don't need that kind of stress. I told Alain to get out of my life but good, and stay out. And at the time, I would have been happy to never lay eyes on him again. But that doesn't mean I'm glad he's dead. He didn't deserve what happened to him. I have no intention of helping whoever killed him get away with it."

"Neither do I," Destiny promised, her desperation edging her voice. "Daniel did not kill Alain, Ginger. I know that, just as surely as you know Buzz didn't do it. But someone did. And even if Daniel wasn't involved, I'd still want to see the killer brought to justice. I loved Alain once, too."

Ginger sighed and leaned farther back in her chair. "Like I said, I don't blame you for wanting to help out your man. But there's really nothing I can tell you. Alain was his usual self last weekend, into everything, meeting everybody. And everybody liked him. You know him. Knew him. You can't help but like him until you need to rely on him for something. I don't see how he could have had time to goad anyone into killing him."

"He didn't try to borrow money from you? I heard he already owed somebody at the fair a couple hundred dollars."

"You didn't hear it right." Ginger flicked the water bottle cap shut and set it aside, her face settling into tired lines. "You know, I'd almost forgotten about that. I tried to tell one of the deputies, but he was too interested in seeing if I had an M16 hidden in my shampoo bottles."

"Alain told you something?" Destiny's hands clenched in her lap, and she realized how little hope she'd actually had for this interview. It was easier not to hope than to be disappointed again. But the chagrin on Ginger's face over her loose tongue shot adrenaline up Destiny's nerves. "What do you know?"

★ ★ ★ ★ ★

Sarah jumped, nearly crashing through the rack of dresses in front of her. The hand on her shoulder pulled her back, away from the booth.

"Still snooping around?"

She spun, her heart pounding hard against her throat, as she came face to face with the Japanese ink-painting artist she'd met the weekend before. He was taller than she'd remembered, fooled by his slenderness. This close, she had to tilt her head back to look into his face.

"Jon," she said, only squeaking a little. "You scared me."

His hazel eyes regarded her flatly. "The dead guy, he was a friend of that Garcia fellow, wasn't he? How long have you been spying here?"

"Shh!" Sarah stepped around him, turning him away from Rollie's booth. "I'm not spying."

"Really? So you wouldn't mind if I called him over here to say hi?"

Sarah grabbed his arm. "No! Stop it. This isn't any of your business."

Jon snorted. "Well, that's the pot calling the kettle black. I thought your police friends told you to leave the investigating to them."

"Maybe you haven't noticed, but they're not doing such a great job," Sarah shot back.

"I heard they found the murder weapon. A police piece. Doesn't sound too good for your friend." He tilted his head in challenge.

"They didn't even know about Mr. Caine's old girlfriend until I heard about her from you," Sarah said, a challenge of her own. An investigator had to remain cool. "I'm just wondering what else they haven't heard because people like you don't care if a police officer loses his job and his reputation because of a false accusation."

Jon's eyes narrowed as he stared down at her. "Maybe they'd hear more if they gave up the strong-arm tactics. People are scared. I mean, if one policeman can get away with killing a guy, what about the rest of them? Why should we talk?"

"Because Detective Parks didn't kill anybody." The exasperation in her voice brought a sleepy yip from Psyche.

"What's that?" Jon asked, taking a quick step back before peering at her sweatshirt. "A rat?"

"A dog," Sarah corrected, as Psyche stuck a caramel-colored snout out over her zipper. "She's just a puppy."

Psyche eyed Jon for a moment, decided he wasn't worth the effort, and sagged back into sleep.

For the first time, Jon's face relaxed. His wide, thin lips almost slipped into a smile. "Protector of the innocent. Champion of justice. Bane to the rest of us." He regarded her for a long moment, biting his lower lip. "Look, I'm not really mad at you for last week. You're okay. Or maybe I just want to think that because you bought one of my paintings."

"I really did like the painting. I've got it up in my room," she told him.

He did smile finally, and Sarah couldn't help her mouth twitching in return. That little smile even made him kind of cute, for an older guy. He might be only nineteen or twenty. In six years, that wouldn't be such a big age gap.

She grimaced. She was starting to sound like Gemma. Pretty dumb for a professional investigator.

"I did some more egrets this week," Jon told her. "One black-and-white one you might like. Sumi-e artists like to say that black ink can create all the colors of the rainbow."

"I looked it up on the Internet," Sarah said. "One site said that the Japanese verb for painting is the same as for writing."

Jon's smile curled a little higher. "You certainly do your research. Ink painting came from the art of writing."

"You know how to write Japanese characters?"

"Sure."

Sarah shook her head. "See, that's so much more interesting than what we're learning in social studies."

Jon's snort of laughter caught her off-guard. "Sarah, how old are you?"

"Thirteen." Well, almost.

"You're a pretty smart girl, but not very street-smart. Look, I don't want to see you get into trouble, okay? That's what I wanted to tell you. You don't want to be sneaking around Rollie Garcia and guys like him. You could get hurt."

A sudden freshening of the breeze off the ocean chilled Sarah through her sweatshirt. "Are you trying to scare me?"

"No, I . . ." Jon frowned at her. "Yeah, I guess I am. I'm just a local artist, and I don't know all these people, but I keep my ears open, and it seems like a lot of folks are pretty nervous. It's nothing for a kid like you to get involved in."

"I'm not a kid." Sarah snapped her mouth shut. Saying that made her sound just like one. What did she care if he thought she was a kid, anyway?

But Jon didn't laugh at her. "Okay, it's nothing for a young lady like you to get involved in. Look, I've got to get back to my booth. My sister spelled me so I could get some lunch, but she's got a kayaking class down at the cove this afternoon. Just promise me you'll stay out of Rollie Garcia's way."

His stubborn expression said he wasn't going to leave

209

her alone until she agreed.

Sarah sighed. "All right. I promise." She had always intended to keep out of Rollie Garcia's way, anyway. That's what hiding behind the sundresses and blending in with the crowd was for. "Anybody else you think I should be staying away from?"

She couldn't have come up with such an innocently sneaky question if she'd been trying. But her burst of exasperation brought forth a similar response from Jon.

"As a matter of fact," he said. "How about anybody who had anything to do with the dead guy?"

"Like who?"

"Like his ex-girlfriend and her bruiser husband? Like the guy he borrowed all that money from?"

"You don't even know who they are," Sarah reminded him.

"Don't I?"

"Who did Alain borrow money from?" Destiny pressed, not allowing Ginger to retreat. "I know he was strapped when he reached Hope Point."

But Ginger was shaking her head. "By the time he came by my booth, he'd sold a bunch of pottery and one of his bigger paintings. He said he'd already made enough cash to pay for the trip from Arizona and have some left over, and he was planning to see if he could find a room to rent for the week in between the shows so he didn't have to stay in the trailer he was crashing in."

"Rollie Garcia's trailer."

"He's the batik fellow, right?" Ginger's gaze drifted toward the rest rooms, though Garcia's Creations were hidden by an intervening booth. "I can't remember exactly what Alain said about staying there. Interesting, or something. No. Fascinating. With that little eyebrow thing like Mr. Spock."

"Drugs?" Destiny asked, a strange taste of excitement and remorse mixing in her mouth.

Ginger lifted both hands, palms out. "I didn't say that. Alain wasn't into drugs, but he didn't care much if other people did them. That wouldn't have intrigued him so much. But I think drugs must have come into play somewhere. He did have someone else's cash on him, but he hadn't borrowed it for himself. Maybe making a transaction for this other guy. The kind of transaction where the guy couldn't go to the police after Alain's death and ask for the money back, if you see what I mean."

"And you didn't tell this to the sheriff's department?"

Ginger straightened, her eyes sparking. "I told you, I tried. They were just disappointed they couldn't pin the murder on Buzz. Besides, it was only about fifty or a hundred dollars. And it's not like Alain was planning to cheat the fellow. He was just hoping for a favor back."

Destiny's nails dug into her palms. She wanted to strangle Ginger for not ensuring this information got police attention, but on the other hand, she knew it wasn't Ginger's fault. There wasn't anything in what Ginger had said that would exonerate Daniel. Rumors and suppositions weren't evidence. And a hundred dollars, even a hundred dollars' worth of illegal drugs, wasn't much of a motive for murder.

"Do you know who he was holding the money for?" she asked.

Ginger turned to reach for her water bottle. Her hand knocked against it, and it tumbled to the ground by her feet.

"I don't know," she said, fumbling with the bottle, finally bringing it up to her lap. But she never looked back at Destiny.

"Please, Ginger." Destiny leaned forward out of her chair. "I'm not looking to get anyone in trouble. But I need to talk with anyone who talked with Alain that day. This could be important."

"I said I don't know." The blue eyes flashed again; the full mouth thinned in defiance.

Destiny's own frustration propelled her to her feet. "I know what you said. You lied."

Ginger rose, too. "I don't care what you think. I don't have to tell you a damn thing."

"Maybe you'll change your mind when you're talking to the police." Destiny regretted the threat the minute it left her mouth. Intimidation only entrenched Ginger further into her position.

"I think you'd better leave."

Destiny clasped her hands together to stop them from shaking. "Please. You have to help me. This is about a man's life—"

A wild, high-pitched yapping from behind her turned Destiny's head toward the woods. But it was the desperate scream that followed that chilled her blood.

"Sarah!" The name burst from her lungs. "That's my niece!"

Chapter 15

By the time Jon had watched her walk almost to the parking lot and she had circled around half the other crafts displays to reach the Garcia's Creations booth from behind, Kyle Preston was gone. Sarah wasn't surprised, but the disappointment at finding Rollie Garcia locked in conversation with a total stranger lodged deep in her stomach, next to the uneasy lump left by what Jon had told her about the people who had known Mr. Caine.

Standing at the back of the booth, peering in through the loose joining of the rear and side canvas panels at the corner support pole, she had a perfect listening post, if only Kyle had stuck around a little longer. She could hear almost every word the wiry, balding little man was saying to Rollie Garcia, even though his voice was pitched low.

"It's for this toothache I got," the man was saying, his voice a thin, annoying whine. He wiped a hand over his bare head, which was sweating despite the cool breeze. "Come on, man. A little Vicodin or something? You gotta help me out here. I'm dying."

"You got a toothache, go to your dentist," Rollie growled. Their profiles were turned to Sarah, and she could see the tension in the big man's jaw, despite his thick blond beard.

"Come on, Rollie. Don't do this to me. I know it took

me a while to pay you last time, but I did pay, didn't I? And I've got the cash on me. Right here." The man started to dig a wallet out of the back pocket of his wrinkled chinos, but Rollie knocked his hand away.

"You idiot! What the hell do you think you're doing, flashing cash around?"

The man's pencil-thin eyebrows rose, and his chuckle stuck nervously in his nose. "You are selling T-shirts, right?"

Rollie wiped a hand across his mouth and shook his head, moving away toward the front of the booth. "Screw you, Waller."

Sarah pulled back from her spy hole for a quick look around. No one was watching her, but someone would notice if she stayed there much longer. She couldn't walk away, though. Whatever that man Waller wanted to buy from Rollie Garcia, it wasn't a T-shirt.

Moving as casually as she could, she followed the back of the booth and turned the corner closest to the edge of the forest that stretched north from the picnic area. Hidden from the rest of the fair by the booth and closed in by the trees, she crouched down, careful not to jostle Psyche, sound asleep in her sweatshirt. The canvas ended about a foot above the grass. If she leaned forward a little, she could see the men's shoes, Waller's sockless penny loafers and Rollie's worn-out sandals. Even the big man's feet were hairy.

"I'm not selling anything but clothing and jewelry, Waller," Rollie insisted, his voice rumbling from his big chest despite his attempt to keep it low.

"That's not what I heard."

"Yeah? Well, maybe you need a hearing aid. Did you hear that a guy got himself whacked in my trailer last weekend?"

Sarah's heart was pounding so hard, she missed Waller's reply. She took a deep breath and held it, trying to calm her pulse.

"That's right, and the cops have been up my butt all week," Rollie continued, his voice rising. "They probably saw you come in here, did you think of that? I don't need this headache. I'm keeping my nose clean. That guy bled all over my floor, man. I don't plan to be next."

"Don't bullshit me, Roland." Waller's voice got thinner and higher than Sarah had thought possible. "I've got eyes, too. I know you've got what I want. Where'd you stash it? In your cash drawer? How about this bag under your chair?"

The sudden clatter of a folding metal chair coming at her sent Sarah scrambling backwards. She saw the imprint of an elbow stretch out the side of the booth, heard a thump and a curse, saw papers, chocolate bar wrappers, and rolls of change scatter on the ground around the staggering feet of the men.

Judging from the movement of the penny loafers, Waller was quick. But he was no match for Rollie's size. Waller's rear end struck the grass inside the booth hard, and Rollie's big hands scooped up the detritus Waller had dumped from his bag.

As the two men rose to their feet, their voices still intense, but too low for Sarah to understand, she saw that Rollie had missed a scrap of paper that had nearly blown out of the booth in the scuffle. It was just a small, rectangular scrap, but it had writing on it.

She glanced around again, but she was well out of sight of the rest of the crafts show patrons. The paper scrap probably wasn't a clue, but she couldn't walk away empty-handed. Detective Parks always said breaking a case was ninety percent sweat and ten percent pure luck.

She edged back toward the booth wall. She could no longer see Rollie or Waller's shoes. They must have moved over to the other side of the booth.

Now was her chance.

She reached out and grabbed the scrap of paper, rising quickly to her feet, her heart thudding heavily in her throat. Flattening out the paper, actually two copies of the same thing stuck together, she saw it was printed with a pattern of pink hatch marks and had an almost unintelligible scrawl of words and numbers in the center.

Four wigs? No, mgs. Milligrams. She glanced at the printing on the top left of the note. Jasper County Heart Specialists. Dr. Royce Preston. A phone number. This was a prescription. For—she peered at the scrawl—Dilaudid. From Kyle Preston's father. Was that what Kyle had been talking with Rollie about?

She struggled with her disappointment. She had assumed that solving the connection between Kyle and Rollie would somehow relate to Detective Parks's predicament. Rollie was connected to Mr. Caine's murder. Kyle was connected to Ariel Macaro's murder. Detective Parks was connected to both, so any connection between the two must be related to him, too.

Then again, Detective Parks always said he believed in coincidences, especially in a small town.

"What do you think you're doing?"

Sarah whirled, furious with herself for getting ambushed twice in one day. The fury froze, a shard of ice in her chest, as she had to take a step back to look all the way up into the face of the man confronting her. A face whose red anger could not be hidden by its thick yellow beard.

Sarah's voice shrank inside her. "I . . ."

"Where did you get that?" Rollie Garcia's eyes, wide with emotion, moved from her face to the paper in her hand. "Give it to me!"

She tried to move her hand, but his was faster. The thick fingers, chapped from his work, crushed hers for an instant before he jerked the prescription from her grasp.

"I saw it blow out of your booth," Sarah said, the almost plausible words tumbling out. "I didn't want you to lose it."

The color left the big man's face as he stared at the piece of paper in his hand. His fist clenched around it, crumpling it, before he stuffed it in a pocket of his cargo shorts.

"I saw it was from Dr. Preston," she said, the ordinariness of her find reassuring her. "I thought it might be important for you to get it back, for your heart."

She half-feared his heart might be failing him right there beside his booth, his color kept changing so rapidly.

"That's right," he said. "I have congestive heart failure."

Sarah nodded. "I'm glad you've got it back, then. I'd better get going. I'm supposed to be running Mark's cash box."

She stepped sideways to bypass him, but he stepped with her, blocking her way.

"Mark? Mark who? Mark Banos?"

She nodded, shrugging with her best innocent-kid look. "I'm helping out in his booth for the day. He's expecting me back, so—"

"Just what the hell are you doing here? Did Mark tell you to spy on me? How long have you been snooping around?"

The words pelted at her, Rollie's eyes fixed on her with the same intensity as his questions, but his voice broke with more dread than rage.

"I was just coming back from the rest rooms," Sarah

said, gesturing over her shoulder to the nearby wooden building. "That's all."

"Like hell. What were you doing grabbing my stuff? I saw your hand come into the tent. Were you spying on me?" He aimed a finger at her, and she saw that it was shaking. Almost as much as her knees shook.

She took a quick breath, trying not to give voice to her fear. She was at a public event. He couldn't hurt her. But his eyes looked wilder by the minute, like a feral cat beginning to realize it has walked into a trap. And she didn't know why.

"I was just walking by," she insisted. "I didn't hear anything."

"Just like you didn't steal anything?" He pulled the prescription out of his pocket to wave it at her before thrusting it back in place. "What else did you take? You little brat. You can tell Mark Banos to kiss my ass."

He took a step closer, looming over her. "I'm not going to be next on the list because he thinks he's hot stuff, Mr. Clean and Sober with the big-shot police detective friends. That cop's going down, getting taken out, and Mark'd better be careful or he'll be next. Us nobodies are easy to dispose of next to a cop. But it's not going to be me. I'll show them what happens to people who mess with Roland Halstrom."

He slammed his fist into his palm inches from her nose. Something in his eyes told Sarah he was working himself up to hit her next, no matter how many people were nearby.

"Tell me what you heard, you little snot."

Sarah threw herself backwards, slipping on the grass as she turned. Three steps would take her around the back of the booth, back into the sight of the crafts show attendees beyond. She opened her mouth to scream, but a huge hand

218

slapped down over her face and another wrapped across her chest, pinning her arms.

With a suddenness that wrenched her breath away, she was being thrust into the forest looming beside the booth, leafless fall brush catching at her hair as Rollie stumbled into the cool, dark shade of the spruce and redwoods, skidding down a root-studded embankment for a dizzy moment before hitting the trail toward a log-choked gully. The creek below rushed toward the ocean mere hundreds of yards away, but the primeval trees and damp banks sucked the sound from the air, stripping the ocean nearby and the crowds above from Sarah's reality.

A reality that Detective Parks, Officers Vance and Yap, her mother, and Jon had all warned her about and that she had never once believed in. The reality that she was being dragged into the woods by a man who outweighed her by probably 150 pounds, who might be on drugs, was terrifyingly angry, and, worse, simply terrified.

She wanted to tell him she didn't know anything, didn't plan to tell anyone anything, didn't care what he did as long as he let her go. As long as he didn't break her neck with one jerk of his arm and throw her body into the gully. As long as he didn't stab her through the heart from behind as someone had done to Ariel Macaro.

The thought of Ariel's death, of what it would do to Aunt Destiny and her mother to search the woods for her and find her murdered body, the thought that Rollie might get away with it as someone was getting away with Alain Caine's murder, melted the icy panic that had frozen her limbs since he'd grabbed her.

Detective Parks had told her one of the best self-defense tactics was a piercing scream. But that was only if you could get a scream out. Sarah whipped her head from side to side beneath her captor's hand. She tried to bite him, but couldn't get purchase with her teeth. She kicked at his bare shins with her sneakers, jabbed his stomach with her elbows.

"Stop it, you little brat. Don't make me hurt you."

His fingers slipped on her face, and for a second she thought he was going to move his hand away from her mouth, but instead his thumb and forefinger pinched together across her nose, cutting off her air.

"Calm down, or you'll suffocate. I just want to make sure you don't screw me over. And I'll do it. One way or the other. Don't think I won't. Just tell me what you know, and I'll let you go."

Sarah bucked against his hold, his hand a vacuum against her mouth. Tree trunks danced around her. Her vision darkened as her lungs strained for air.

Rollie lurched sideways on the uneven footing of the path, swinging her around to bump hard into a redwood tree, the shaggy bark scraping the left side of her face, her stomach banging against the trunk as Rollie struggled to regain his balance.

Her stomach fluttered and writhed as though it was leaving her body. Sarah thought she was about to lose consciousness. Until the writhing lump dug its tiny feet into her gut and thrust a protesting snout up out of her sweatshirt.

At the sudden explosion of vexed yapping, Rollie's hand slipped, giving Sarah a blessed gasp of air. When Psyche lunged upward to dig her needle-sharp baby teeth into the fleshy part of the hairy arm draped across Sarah's chest, Rollie let go of Sarah's mouth altogether, jerking away from her with a startled cry.

Clutching Psyche to her chest, Sarah crashed into the

brush up the bank, putting Detective Parks's advice about shrieking to good use.

Destiny reached the trees without ever knowing how she left Ginger Shrieve's booth.

"Sarah! Sarah!"

She crashed into the woods along the first narrow footpath she came to, following Psyche's unabated yipping and Sarah's frantic voice.

"Help! Fire!" Sarah shouted the words she'd been taught were most likely to elicit help from casual bystanders. Code words for kidnapping, rape, murder.

Destiny plunged off the path, through a tangle of huckleberry bushes.

"We're coming," she shouted back, having no idea whether or not Ginger followed or had sent anyone after her. "Police! Hold on."

And then she saw the blond hair, scrambling up the bank ahead of her through a thick barrier of fiddlehead ferns. She reached Sarah just in time to help haul the girl to her feet, pulling Sarah into a protective embrace, even as she looked beyond her for pursuers.

She could hear Sarah's harsh, sobbing breath, Psyche's frantic barking, thin shouts from behind her. Her straining ears might have caught the faint pounding of feet receding into the forest, but she could not be sure.

"He dragged me into the woods," Sarah gasped, looking back behind her. "He was so big. I couldn't get away."

"What happened?" Destiny asked, pulling her back toward the open park. The priorities of reaching safety, reassuring Sarah, and not contaminating the crime scene crowded together in her head. That's what she got for dating a cop.

221

"He was acting crazy," Sarah said, her overburdened lungs settling into an intermittent hiccup. "I thought he was going to kill me. But Killer here got me free."

Sarah shrugged out of Destiny's hold to pull Psyche from the front of her sweatshirt, bringing the puppy close so Psyche could swipe Sarah's nose with her tongue. "Oh, you're such a good girl, such a brave little girl."

Destiny threw an arm around her niece's shoulders. She couldn't tell if Sarah was shaking; her own arm was shaking too hard. "I was just thinking the same thing about you. My God, sweetie. What happened? Did he grab you coming out of the rest rooms or something? Did you get a good look at him? Could you describe him for the police?"

"Destiny?" Ginger Shrieve's vibrant alto cut through the muffling trees. Destiny caught a glimpse of curly blond hair and a looming shape behind it she assumed to be Ginger's husband, Buzz.

"Over here!" she called back.

"Auntie Dess?" Sarah's urgent voice brought her back to her niece. "Of course, I recognized him. The guy who grabbed me was Rollie Garcia."

The late afternoon sunlight swept off the ocean as uncompromisingly as the breeze. Destiny had to shield her eyes from the shards of brilliance, even as she hunched beside Serena's blue Subaru Outback in a fruitless attempt to get out of the wind.

Sarah sat sideways in the front passenger seat. Serena had dug a thick, woven blanket out of the back of the station wagon and wrapped it around Sarah's shoulders, but Sarah hardly seemed to notice her own goose bumps as she repeated her story once more for Officer George.

Shell Creek's single patrol officer was scribbling tiny,

222

crabbed notes in a battered black pocket notebook.

"And he had no idea you had a dog in your sweatshirt?" Officer George's narrow shoulders shook with his disbelieving bark of laughter. "I wish I could have seen his face. Foiled by a wiener dog!"

"Psyche is a hero," Sarah said sternly, stroking the puppy who sat, under protest, in the girl's lap. Psyche obviously would have preferred dashing around everyone's ankles, but she'd already tried to sever Officer George's Achilles tendon.

"She is a hero," Officer George agreed, his face, heavily lined by sea and sun, settling into a more serious mood. "And you are a very lucky young lady."

Destiny watched a shadow pass across Sarah's face, the shadow of knowing that her world was not safe in the way she had believed it to be just that morning.

"I know I'm lucky," Sarah said, for the moment fully contrite. "Killer here probably saved my life."

Serena stood to the right of the open car door, her hand moving to hover just over her daughter's hair, the horror of what might have happened clearly etched in her face.

"I don't know why he went so crazy," Sarah continued. "I didn't even hear anything useful."

"If this character has drug-related priors, he could be looking at three strikes," Officer George explained. "That's a pretty good reason not to get caught."

"He told that guy Waller that he didn't have whatever it was he was looking for," Sarah said.

"He still might have had something he wouldn't have wanted the police to find if you'd given us probable cause to search his booth."

"But you *didn't* find anything," Sarah reminded him.

After calling the sheriff's department, who had called in

their volunteer posse to help track the suspect through the Shell Creek Park forest, Shell Creek Police Chief Bartholomew had coordinated the manhunt, while Officer George searched Rollie Garcia's booth for clues to where he might run and what he might be running from.

So far, both efforts had proven fruitless. Even the bag Sarah had seen in Rollie's booth was gone.

"Is there anything else you can think of?" Officer George asked, glancing around to include Serena and Destiny. "Anything that might help us find this man? Is there any possible reason he might have wanted to hurt Sarah in particular, besides discovering her spying on him?"

Destiny saw Sarah's mouth open to object to the word "spying," but a disapproving look from her mother kept her quiet.

"After this incident, I can't believe Rollie Garcia was only an innocent bystander in Alain Caine's murder last week," Destiny said. Officer George had already promised to share the results of his investigation with the sheriff's department, but she wasn't sure he realized all the implications of what Sarah had told them.

"He obviously has something to hide," she continued. "Something worth terrifying a young girl for, possibly killing for. And what he said to Sarah about Daniel—Detective Parks—getting taken down; it sounds like Rollie thinks Daniel was set up for Alain's murder."

"We'll see what Deputy Pearson thinks," Officer George promised, sympathetic, but unwilling to intrude on another department's problems. "I'm sure he'll contact you if he needs more information. With any luck, we'll have Mr. Garcia in custody by this evening, and Deputy Pearson can get some answers from him directly."

He closed his notebook, carefully tucking both it and his

pen into his pocket. "I think that's all we need at this time. We know how to get in touch with you if we have any other questions. Unless there's anything else you've thought of that you want to tell us, Miss Davis? Now that you've had a chance to recover a little."

Sarah shook her head as she cuddled Psyche closer to her chest. "No, sir. I don't have anything else I want to tell you."

Her odd repetition of the phrasing caught Destiny's attention, but Officer George was gesturing for Destiny to follow him a few feet away as Serena got Sarah ready to leave for home.

"You know that a high school girl was murdered down to Hope Point less than two weeks ago," the officer said, the lines in his face shifting somberly. "And this attack on Sarah probably should have ended a lot worse than it did. We don't get much crime up here in Shell Creek, and we sure don't like it when the crimes are against kids. I hope we catch this Garcia fellow. I know we'll do all we can, and so will the sheriff's posse. But if I were you and your sister, I'd keep that niece of yours confined to quarters for awhile."

Destiny thought of the anguished fear that still haunted Serena's eyes, despite the two hours that had passed since Sarah's attack. "I don't think that's going to be a problem for the next few weeks."

"I was thinking years," Officer George observed, sending a glance back at Sarah. "That one's too clever for her own good."

Destiny matched his rueful smile, but as she watched Officer George walk back across the park, the crafts booths collapsing around him like snowy egrets preparing to fly back to their roosts for the night, Destiny felt the shadows of the day settling in around her.

She'd learned the tenuousness of her own life with gut-wrenching suddenness that September when a stranger had tried to strangle her for no better motivation than his own greed. It was a world-altering knowledge, having her own mortality shown up for the insubstantial wisp of breath that it was. Yet good had somehow come of it, too. The need to notice each moment of grace that touched her life. The need to take the risk of loving other people.

A risk which her own mortality could never make as sharp as the sudden reminder that her loved ones were mortal, too. If anything had happened to Sarah . . . And it would have been her fault for getting Sarah involved in this situation, the result of a series of bad decisions going all the way back to dating Alain Caine in the first place. She was apparently going to be paying for that one forever.

"This is all your fault."

She turned, startled at the echo of her thoughts, to see Daniel striding toward her across the long, narrow parking lot. She hadn't seen him since Thanksgiving, and though that had only been three days before, it felt as great a separation as if they hadn't spoken in years.

Somehow, in that short amount of time, she'd forgotten the permanent disarray of his sandy brown hair, the way that slate-colored shirt he wore sharpened the blue of his eyes, the way her heart caught painfully at how much she loved him.

He looked as if he hadn't slept in years, the sun-wrinkles etched deeper into his face, his mouth dragged down by care.

Only his eyes looked bright, yet they held no warmth as he closed on her.

"What's my fault?" she asked, her voice sharper than she

intended, with relief at seeing him and hurt that he hadn't so much as called.

"Sarah could have been killed," he said, stopping a mere foot from her. "I told you to stay out of this, and you ignored me, and look what happened."

Destiny straightened, a trickle of anger seeping down her throat. "I never would have let Sarah do something so dangerous as spy on Rollie Garcia, and you know it."

"Do I?" He tilted his head in skepticism. "When Kermit called to tell me about Garcia's attack on Sarah, he also mentioned that the sheriff's deputy he talked to said Ginger and Buzz Shrieve were involved in her rescue. Tell me you've never met Ginger and Buzz Shrieve. Tell me you weren't asking them questions about last weekend."

"I stopped to talk with Ginger Shrieve," Destiny said, hands on her hips. "I wasn't spying. I told her up front who I was, and we talked about Alain and what happened last weekend. There's nothing wrong with that."

"Yes, there is something wrong. It's none of your business."

Destiny's fingers dug into her hip bones. "What the hell do you mean, it's none of my business?" If her fierce tone startled her, it obviously startled Daniel more. "Alain might be just another body to you, but he was a person to me, Detective. This isn't *your* case that I'm interfering with. This is a murder that's interfered with me. A friend of mine is dead, and another friend is a suspect in his death, and another man involved just attacked my niece."

Daniel opened his mouth, but she didn't slow down. "You can go ahead and withdraw from the world, seclude yourself in your little retreat down the road, pretend none of this hurts anybody but you, but I don't have that luxury. I have other people to think about."

She knew the words were unfair. She didn't care. She didn't care if he yelled back, if he cursed at her, if he kicked one of the nearby cars. If he fought back, she could keep fighting.

But instead his face went still, his mouth thinning, his eyes shuttering the emotions within. "Are you thinking of other people? Are you thinking at all? Are you thinking that Sarah could have been killed? Were you thinking that Ginger Shrieve might have complained to the sheriff that you were harassing her? That it might be brought up if the case goes to trial? What if Buzz Shrieve had taken exception to your questioning his wife, and he'd dragged *you* out into the woods? Did you think about what that would have done to . . . to those who care about you?"

He shook his head, teeth clenching against the words. "If you were thinking at all, you would have stayed home."

Destiny nodded, eyes wide against angry tears. "You're right. If I were thinking about how I shouldn't care how indifferent the official investigation has been, and how you'd just as soon I give up, then I probably would have stayed home."

She sucked in her breath and lowered her voice, though none of the artisans packing up their wares appeared to be paying them any attention. "But since I didn't stay home, I did find out a few things. And so did Sarah. This ought to convince Deputy Pearson to put Rollie Garcia at the head of his suspect list in Alain's murder."

Exasperation cracked the hard shell of Daniel's expression. "What, you think they're going to catch Garcia and he's going to confess to murder? He's got an alibi, for heaven's sake. Twenty or thirty people saw him at a party that night. Besides, there's nothing to connect his attack on Sarah with Alain's death. A murder suspect on administrative leave is worth two in the bush."

"Daniel—"

"At least when he was here, the police could keep an eye on him. Yap and Vance have been looking into his activities in the area. Maybe they would have found something important. If he hadn't run."

And they were back to its being all her fault. She could see the accusation in his eyes.

His mouth twitched with irony. "Thanks for the help. How foolish of me to tell you to stay out of it."

He turned and walked away.

Chapter 16

The split lengths of seasoned oak clattered in the still afternoon air as Daniel arranged another armload on the woodpile along the side of his house. Between central heating and the probability of spending the next twenty years to life in prison, he figured buying a half-cord of wood could be considered extravagant. But the work of driving up into the mountains to buy it, loading it into the truck, and unloading it once more had consumed much of the day—what was it now, Wednesday?—and the ache in his arms felt healthy and good.

It helped him ignore the empty ache in his chest.

As he walked back to his truck for what could be the last armload if he didn't mind risking a debilitating back injury, which, at the moment, seemed the least of his worries, another pickup rumbled down his road and swung into his driveway. The mammoth, champagne-colored, extended-cab Dodge made his old Toyota look like a Tonka toy.

The two girls in the backseat were equally dwarfed by the truck's dimensions, but the six-foot, sixty-five-year-old grandmother at the wheel looked right at home.

Her window hushed down as Daniel walked over.

"Pleasance," he said, pulling his work glove off his right hand to take the one she offered through the window. "This is a surprise."

He didn't want to offend Pleasance Geary, or the two girls, her granddaughter, Gemma, and Gemma's best friend, Sarah. But if Destiny had prompted this visit as a tactic—

"It's a surprise to me, too," Pleasance agreed. "I'm not one to let children take themselves too seriously, but our girl Sarah has convinced me she really does need to see you. Gemma and I'll go on into town and have some chowder at the Dockside. We'll be back in half an hour or so."

"Wait! What are you—"

But Sarah was already climbing out of the backseat, her legs coltish on the long jump to the ground.

"Just make sure she's here when I get back," Pleasance commanded, throwing the truck into reverse. "I don't like going behind a parent's back, and if Sarah gives me any reason to regret it, I'm going to make sure she's sorrier than I am. You hear me, young lady?"

Sarah nodded, properly solemn. As the truck backed out of the drive, briefly threatening the little Honda Civic parked in the driveway across the road, Gemma sent Sarah a short wave, and Sarah watched the truck bounce down the poorly paved road toward Shell Creek.

As the roar of the diesel engine faded, the customary hushed silence returned to Daniel's property, the hush at the end of a dead-end road above the sea. He knew he would regret breaking the silence, but he couldn't very well leave Sarah standing in his driveway until Pleasance returned.

Though the thought tempted him.

"Here," he said instead, thrusting his gloves at her and then handing her a pile of firewood when she'd pulled them on. He hefted the remaining logs and followed her to the woodpile, where they spent a few more silent moments arranging the wood and covering it with a tarp.

"Come on inside," Daniel said, leading the way around to the front door. He could clean out the truck bed later. "I'm going to get a cup of coffee. Do you want some?"

"Sure."

They both knew Serena wouldn't approve of Sarah polluting her body with caffeine, but then, Sarah wasn't supposed to be there at all.

Sarah followed Daniel into the kitchen and he gestured her to take a seat at the kitchen table while he poured the coffee. He mixed a healthy dose of milk and sugar into Sarah's, then joined her at the table.

Edgar had already found Sarah's lap. He made a ridiculous picture, trying not to let any part of his furry bulk slide off Sarah's skinny legs. His fierce, amber eyes chastised Daniel for ignoring him for so long that he had to stoop to such indignity for a friendly pat.

"You're wasting your time," Daniel said to both the cat and the girl. "You're in enough trouble, Sarah, without lying to your mother."

"I have to tell you something," Sarah said, her clear green eyes meeting his. "If you think I should tell Mom, I will, but I wanted to tell you first."

"If this has anything to do with your aunt—"

"No. I haven't told her, either."

Against his better judgment, Daniel found himself curious. "Go ahead then. Shoot."

"It's about the other day, at the Christmas fair."

"When Garcia attacked you?" His hand clenched around his cup in sudden apprehension that Sarah might have suffered more than she'd told her rescuers, but she was shaking her head.

"Before that. When I found his prescription and he grabbed it from me."

"When you were spying." Somehow his fierce scowl failed to discourage her.

"And before that, when this guy I knew there was telling me that Rollie Garcia might be dangerous."

"What guy?" Daniel demanded, for a brief second understanding how a protective uncle would feel. He brushed the thought away. "And why the hell didn't you listen to him?"

"He's a painter, a local artist," Sarah said, apparently deciding the second question was rhetorical. "The one I talked to the day after Mr. Caine died? All he said about Rollie Garcia was to stay away from him, nothing useful. But you remember how he said some guy at the first fair had loaned Mr. Caine a lot of money?"

"I remember." Kermit had told him that Destiny said Ginger Shrieve had said much the same thing. Daniel hadn't wanted to talk with Kermit any more than he wanted to talk with Destiny, but Kermit had the advantage of a badge. Why either one of them thought the information was interesting, he didn't know. "A hundred dollars, two hundred dollars. I know it seems like a lot to you, but it's not worth killing anyone over."

"I hope not," Sarah said, her eyes clouding. "I didn't want to worry Mom or Auntie Dess or get anyone else in trouble. And I thought if I went to the police station those officers Vance and Yap would just laugh at me. So I waited until I could talk with you. Jon told me something about that money."

Daniel didn't know whether to smile or sigh. "Anything Jon told you is hearsay, Sarah, which means—"

"I know what hearsay is," Sarah said, suddenly sharp,

hurt at his treating her like a kid. "And I know it's not admissible in court. And like you said, it's probably not important to the case. But it might still be important."

Daniel pulled himself back from his own frustration to nod. It obviously was important to Sarah. "What did Jon tell you about the money?"

"He told me who gave it to Mr. Caine," Sarah said. Edgar grunted in protest as she leaned forward over him to tell Daniel, "It was Mark."

"Mark?" Daniel asked, taking a moment for the information to click, for the puzzle piece to fall into place to explain Sarah's uneasiness, to explain her visit to him that afternoon. "You mean Mark *Banos?*"

Destiny glanced at the clock for possibly the hundredth time that afternoon. Only four hours, forty-eight minutes and fifteen seconds until the library closed. She was glad that the Hope Point Branch of the Jasper County Library could stay open late two nights a week—not a simple feat based on their severely squeezed budget. But she'd be happy when Maddy got home next week to take one of the late shifts.

At least she had only forty-eight minutes—and nine seconds—until she could escape for a quick dinner at home. Not that anything would be better at home. Except Fleur would be there to keep her company.

Then again, so would Psyche. Destiny's lips twitched against her will. Even knowing Psyche would pee all over the floor as soon as Destiny let her out of the bathroom, even knowing the little dog would somehow destroy yet another shoe before the evening was over and that she'd chase Fleur around the kitchen table, yapping relentlessly, while Destiny ate dinner, Destiny couldn't help but smile.

Part of it was the fact that Psyche had saved Sarah's life. Part of it was that despite her yapping, incontinent, destructive behavior, there was something about her . . . No, all right. All of it was the fact that Psyche had saved Sarah's life.

The telephone on her desk rang, and she grabbed for it. Helping library patrons find the information they needed was always the best part of her job, but this week it was the only thing that could drag her mind away from her own troubles.

"Call for you." The curt voice in her receiver turned Destiny's head toward the circulation desk. Charlene, the branch supervisor, stared back at her, her lips tight with disapproval as she spoke into her phone. "Personal business."

"Thank you," Destiny said, resisting the urge to argue. It couldn't be too personal. Serena and Daniel both knew the direct number to her extension. Not that Daniel would call. And she'd already told Serena not to call her at work again that week unless it was an emergency.

And then she'd had to explain that her refusal to drive up to Daniel's house and walk in on him unannounced was *not* an emergency.

"But this is your *life*, Desty," Serena had pleaded. "I can't stand by while you let the best thing that's ever happened to you slip right out of your hands."

"Let it?" Destiny had burst out, with all the quiet intensity a library atmosphere would allow. "I've tried calling. I've even asked Kermit to ask him to call me. What am I supposed to do, Reenie? Climb down the chimney and chain myself to the fireplace until he talks to me?"

"Chaining yourself to the bed might be more effective," Serena had drawled.

Destiny had hung up.

She loved Daniel. But she couldn't make him love her enough to let her in.

"Hello?" The tentative voice brought her back to her current phone call. Personal business, Charlene had said, but she didn't recognize the caller.

"Destiny Millbrook," she said automatically. "Jasper County Library, Hope Point Branch. How may I help you?"

"Destiny? This is Ginger Shrieve."

Destiny blinked at her receiver. "Ginger? Where are you? I thought you and Buzz drove back to Sedona."

"We did." The line hummed quietly for a second. "I just haven't been able to sleep well since we got back. I keep thinking about your niece, about that Garcia fellow attacking her. Have they caught him yet?"

"No, not yet."

Rollie Garcia had disappeared into the woods north of Shell Creek Park and never resurfaced. He'd made no attempt to recover his belongings from his trailer, still parked at the Jasper County Fairgrounds. He'd contacted none of his known associates.

"But Sarah is going to be fine," she assured Ginger. "The police don't think he has any reason to try to hurt her again, but we're all keeping a close eye on her."

And for once Sarah wasn't complaining about it, either. Destiny thought she'd even begun to understand some of her mother's protectiveness.

"I'm glad to hear that," Ginger said, a little of her accustomed spirit returning to her voice. "It's been bothering me since we left. Her getting attacked because of looking into Alain's murder and all. It's made me wonder . . . Maybe there's something to what you said. Maybe your guy didn't kill him, after all, and there's somebody out there who might be able to help find out who did."

"Somebody has to know something," Destiny said, more from habit than hope. The murderer knew, but he—or she—wasn't likely to be telling anyone.

"Right. And I just thought, well, it's been weighing on my conscience, what you said about me lying about not knowing who Alain was holding that money for. Mind you, I still don't want to get anybody in trouble unnecessarily. But you're right, Alain told me who it was. And I guess I should tell you. It was that fellow who does the tattoos."

Destiny frowned, running through the arts and crafts fair booths in her mind. She hadn't noticed anyone else offering tattoos. She'd thought encouraging Mark to offer temporary tattoos—more or less temporary; she still had to wear a turtleneck to work—at the fair was an ingenious, original idea on Serena's part.

Surely if someone besides Mark had been giving henna tattoos, she would have noticed—

Oh, hell. She *would* have noticed. "You're talking about Mark Banos, the Body Works Body Art booth."

"Alain thought it was pretty funny, that your detective was all over him about a candy necklace, and there you were doing advertising for a fellow who wanted Alain's help with this not so legal 'transaction.' "

Alain would have found that highly amusing, Destiny had no doubt. But the anger beginning to build inside her didn't have room for Alain.

"I only kept it from you, because I honestly didn't think it was important," Ginger continued.

And maybe because she'd thought it better to have Daniel firmly under suspicion than to have the investigation continue fishing where it might once more hook into Buzz Shrieve. But that didn't matter much at the moment.

"Thanks for telling me this, Ginger," Destiny said,

struggling to keep her voice calm, despite the grim anger in her jaw. The information probably wouldn't lead to Alain's killer. She didn't even know whether to hope it did or not. But it was certainly something Mark's brother, Jesse, her sister's fiancé, ought to know.

"I don't want to get him in any trouble," Ginger repeated. "This is just what Alain told me."

"I understand," Destiny assured her. "It doesn't sound like he's done anything to be prosecuted for."

She didn't add that the police were the least of Mark Banos's worries at the moment. Fortunately for Mr. Banos, she wasn't licensed to carry a concealed weapon.

As she got off the phone with Ginger, she glanced once more at the clock. Time to take an early dinner.

Daniel squeezed his medium-sized truck into a compact-sized space on the street by sheer force of will. How a place the size of Hope Point could have a downtown parking crisis, he would never understand. Of course, there were plenty of spots available two blocks from downtown, but the less time he spent visible on the street, the better. He was glad of the somber low clouds and early December nightfall.

The eye-catching, Day-Glo splashes on the black Body Works Body Art sign were barely visible in the gloom along narrow Tenth Street, really little more than an alley between the block-length buildings on either side. The tattoo parlor's front windows were curtained in black to offer privacy to clients, but light spilled through the glazed window on the door, and the hand-lettered sign hanging from the knob read "OPEN."

Sheer boiling irritation had brought him this far without pausing to consider a sensible course of action. As a police officer, he knew better than to act on emotion, especially when confronting an uncooperative witness. Then again, he no longer carried a badge.

The door knocked back against the inside wall with a satisfying bang as he strode into the store. The front part of the parlor was narrow and cramped, a few chairs arranged beside small end tables for clients looking at tattoo designs or waiting for those being tattooed. The long counter divided the entrance from the open space in back where clients were tattooed, black drapes on runners available for privacy if the tattoo or piercing required it. Daniel smelled something that might have been pain sweat, mixed with the incense burning at the end of the counter.

An older man in a Harley-Davidson jacket leaned on the counter a few feet from Daniel, talking with Mark, who was cleaning the counter in a desultory fashion while he chatted. He glanced up at Daniel, and the cheerful greeting died on his lips.

"Oh. Hey."

"We need to have a chat," Daniel said. He might not be allowed a gun at the moment, but nobody said he couldn't use the voice. "Privately."

The guy in the Harley jacket shot Mark a questioning look. Mark nodded, though his face sagged. "It's okay."

The older man shrugged, giving Daniel a long look as he passed toward the door.

"What can I do for you?" Mark asked, trying for casual.

The front door slammed into the wall again, signalling a new intruder. "Mark Banos, you lying, worthless piece of—"

She slammed the door shut behind her, cutting off her words. Her eyes shone almost incandescent with righteous fury, her dark, nearly mahogany hair wild from the humidity.

An avenging angel would look just like that, Daniel thought, terrifying and beautiful all at once. Then she saw him, and the force of her wrath turned briefly from Mark.

"What are *you* doing here?"

"I was about to call Mark a lying, worthless piece of something or other, but you beat me to it," he said, knowing he couldn't afford the humor, knowing he shouldn't be glad to see her, unable to convince his heart of that.

"What are you mad at me for?" Mark demanded, foolishly refocusing them both. He took a step back as Destiny stalked up to the counter, laying her hands carefully palm down on top.

"I will get to you in a minute," she promised, the low, fierce hum in her voice backing Mark up yet another step. She turned to Daniel. "Why are you here?" she repeated, in the same low growl.

"I was thinking about a tattoo," he said, risking life and limb, but unable to stop himself. "Don't let me interfere with your business."

The look she gave him told him just how far beneath contempt he was, but at least he wasn't Mark. The man's face looked almost ghostly pale beneath his halo of dark curls when Destiny turned her glare on him.

"Fine," she said, her voice feral as a stalking cat's. "I don't really care who hears this. I just wanted to come to you directly, Mark, before I go to the police. What kind of drugs were you planning to buy from Rollie Garcia when you gave Alain that money?"

"What?" Mark asked, his shock at the question not quite enough to pass for righteous indignation. "What are you talking about? Who told you that?"

"Did you think Alain wouldn't tell anybody?" Disgust

dripped from every word. "He probably told half the people at that fair, just to make sure it would get back to me. He'd be having a good laugh right now. If he weren't dead."

Mark's hands jerked and twitched at his sides. "That's a lie. Somebody who doesn't like me." He looked at Daniel. "I don't have to talk to you. You're not even an acting cop."

Daniel nodded, leaning against the wall. "That's right. I'm not. I'm a suspected murderer." He grinned without humor. "I wouldn't expect any Miranda warning."

Mark's face wrinkled. "She's probably making it up to protect you. She doesn't have any witnesses—"

"I do," Destiny said quietly, the anger ebbing from her voice as disappointment filled it. "A woman who doesn't even know you and has no reason to dislike you. She even lied to protect you, but she decided after Rollie Garcia attacked Sarah that maybe that wasn't such a good idea."

Mark shook his head, eyes skipping back to Daniel. "You don't believe this crap, right?"

"I heard the same thing, Mark," he said, careful to keep his voice neutral, letting Destiny play bad cop. "I came by to give you a chance to explain. To tell the truth. You can see how it looks." He gestured to indicate Destiny's reaction. "You give money to a guy to buy drugs for you from an acquaintance from your wilder days. The guy turns up dead in the acquaintance's trailer. The acquaintance attacks a girl, the daughter of your brother's fiancée. And through all of this, you don't say anything."

Daniel shook his head. "It doesn't look good, Mark."

"*Man.*" Mark spun and slapped a palm against the wall. "Why do you think I didn't say anything? I knew what it would look like. Shit. And I didn't even know anything that would help you, man. I swear I would have come forward if I had."

"Sure," Destiny snarled. "We believe you. A drug addict and a liar."

"I wasn't buying drugs," Mark said, coming up to the counter. "I'm clean. I swear. I just needed something for my bursitis." He clutched at his right shoulder, wincing for emphasis. "I mean, the tattoo business is my livelihood. If I can't do that, I'm on the street. But all those doctors at the clinic know about my history. All the doc would say is take over-the-counter painkillers."

He waited for them to sympathize, realized it wasn't going to happen, and continued. "And I did, man. I was popping that ibuprofen like candy. And then Serena tells me I could be permanently damaging my liver."

Daniel saw Destiny's fingers dig into the counter.

"If you even think about blaming this on my sister, who has given you every chance in the world to—"

"No, no." Mark backed off again. "But I was taking that stuff right and left, and it wasn't doing it for me, like, at all. I heard that Rollie could get you some stuff if you couldn't get it from your doctor. Not illegal stuff," he added hastily. "He could get you a prescription. All I wanted was a supply of Tylenol 4s. For my bursitis."

He shrugged. "I helped Serena hook Alain up with Rollie for a place to stay. I thought maybe Alain would help me out, buy the stuff for me. He was cool with it. No big deal."

Before Destiny could respond to that, Daniel stepped in again. "Why didn't you go directly to Rollie? Why give the money to a guy you hardly even knew?"

"Hey, he was a friend of Destiny's, right?" Mark's guileless eyes widened. "And if I went to Rollie, he would have given me a hard time. He always said I couldn't get clean, and then when I did, he made fun of me. I was afraid he'd tell people and get me in trouble."

"So you gave Alain the money so Rollie wouldn't blow the whole situation out of proportion," Daniel said, as if it were the most natural thing in the world. He moved up beside Destiny along the counter, lowering his voice so that Mark had to edge closer to hear. "That's all well and good, Mark, but that doesn't explain why you went to Rollie Garcia after Alain died to get your money back."

It was just a guess, from what Sarah had told him of what Rollie Garcia had said, but Mark jumped as if Daniel had tried to strike him.

"Who told you that?" he said, although even he seemed to recognize the futility of the phrase. His mouth drooped into a sulk. "A hundred bucks is a lot of money," he said. "The cops didn't find that much on Alain's body. I figured he must have given it to Rollie already, and when he died, Rollie just decided he could keep it. I didn't think that was fair."

"So you went to see Rollie," Destiny said.

"I told him if he didn't want to pay me back, he could just give me the scrips he owed me, but he freaked on me." Mark grimaced at the memory. "I mean, wow. It was just totally unlike him. He could be a pain with the teasing, but I never saw him hurt anybody. He was like, 'I don't know what you're talking about, but if I did, I'd rip you a new asshole.' Stuff like that."

Mark shuddered dramatically. "I told him, yeah, whatever. I mean, he was a big dude. I didn't want to mess with him. Even for a hundred bucks." His eyes locked on Daniel's, brightening with a sudden idea. "That's why I didn't come to you, man. I mean, I was scared he'd come after me."

Destiny snorted. "Bull."

"No way," Mark assured her, leaning forward earnestly. "The dude was scary when he was mad. I mean, look what he did to Sarah."

"That's true," Daniel said, letting his voice harden. "Look at that. You know why he attacked Sarah?"

Mark blinked. "Because she was spying on him."

"Because he thought you sent her to spy on him."

"*What?*" Destiny and Mark demanded as one.

"Who told you that?" Mark asked again, but this time only in the plaintive hope it wasn't true.

"He thought you were still trying to get your money back," Daniel continued. "And he said you'd better watch out, or you'd end up like Alain Caine."

"Geez, I never told her to talk to Rollie," Mark said, turning a pleading eye on Destiny. "You know I love Sarah like she's my niece. She's a great kid. I'd never do anything to put her in danger."

"Like leaving Rollie Garcia out on the street where he might come after her again?" Daniel asked, quiet and low. "Or maybe after you? Are you sure you don't have any idea where he's hiding? How many people are going to know you talked to me and Destiny? You're sure nobody's going to tell Rollie?"

"Hey, man, that's not right." Mark danced back, then up to the counter again, renewed agitation bouncing out through the soles of his feet. "You can't tell anybody I talked to you. I just did it because you're like family, right?"

"Family?" Destiny slammed her palms on the counter. "Like the Manson family, maybe. How can you think you can lie to the police and to the people who care about you and put children in danger and not face any consequences for it?"

Daniel raised an eyebrow. "I can't order her not to repeat all of this to anybody, Mark. But if you tell us where Rollie Garcia is, the police will pick him up. You'll be safe."

But Mark was shaking his head, a motion that got harder and faster until he almost lost his balance and had to stop. "No, man. I don't know where he is. But I don't think it's anywhere he's going to come get me from, man. You can't do this to me. Shit."

He slapped his thighs, eyes jerking around the back area of the shop as if looking for a hole to jump into.

"Daniel's been suspended from his job on suspicion of a crime he didn't commit, and the whole time you were hiding information, and *we* can't do this to *you?*" Destiny's voice held no mercy. "If you really don't know where Garcia is, maybe you'd better find somebody who can tell you."

"You don't understand," Mark said, almost wailing. "I don't want to know where he is. I'm sure as hell not going looking for anybody who does. Because wherever he is, it might not be so great, right? And I don't want to run into whoever put him there."

"What are you talking about?" Destiny demanded.

But Daniel's muscles tensed as Mark's sudden anxiety came into clearer focus. "You think something's happened to him?"

Mark stopped moving and stared at him as if he were an idiot. "The dude's like six-four. He's a bear. He stands out. I mean, where's he going to hide? Somebody took him out, man."

"You think somebody killed him?" Destiny asked, her tone incredulous. "Why? He was the one threatening people. Maybe he was even the one who killed Alain."

"He had an alibi," Daniel reminded her.

245

"A party? He could have slipped away for half an hour without anyone noticing."

Maybe. But Daniel knew how thoroughly Vance and Yap must have dug into Rollie Garcia's alibi. A drifting peddler known to be a former drug dealer made a satisfying suspect. If they or the sheriff's department had found a hole in Garcia's alibi, they would have brought him in for questioning.

"Man, he didn't kill anybody," Mark said, disgust slowing his nervous twitching. "Not in his own trailer. I mean, that was his home. You don't off somebody in your living room."

Daniel knew that wasn't strictly accurate, but he let Mark continue.

"Besides, Rollie could be a little high-strung, but he never hurt anybody."

"He dragged Sarah into the woods," Destiny reminded him. "You said he threatened you."

"He did," Mark agreed, as if she'd just made his point for him. "He freaked on me, man. I'd never seen him like that, even on acid. It was like he was jumping at his own shadow. He was scared shitless."

"Why?"

"Because he knew something." Mark rolled his eyes at having to explain it. "He must have known who popped Alain. And whoever it was knew he knew. And if he thought Rollie might even think about giving him up, he'd pop Rollie, too. And after Rollie got fingered for grabbing Sarah, the guy knew if Rollie got picked up, he'd roll to get a deal or something."

"If he knew something, why didn't he tell the police?" Destiny demanded.

"Like they're going to protect an ex-con?" Mark's hands

waved again. "Like they'd protect me? I don't even know who this killer is, and he could be waiting for me out in the alley tonight when I lock up."

Destiny leaned toward him, her voice earnest. "If he were arrested—"

"They haven't arrested *him*." Mark gestured toward Daniel. "What if Daniel really did it? He could be going around killing us one by one. I could be next. And then who's going to protect you?

"That's right," Mark continued, before she could answer. "Nobody. Rollie said he wasn't going to be next, but he was. Well, I'm not going to be next on the list. I know how to protect myself."

He jerked forward, reaching under the counter, and Daniel suddenly realized how alone they were in this small, dark shop on this small, dark side street, alone with a frightened man who might be on drugs or even be a killer. Or, worse, who might be exactly what he said he was, a frightened man with reason to believe Daniel might want him dead.

The one person Daniel loved most in the world stood between him and Mark's crackling nerves. And Daniel's gun was in a police weapons locker five blocks away in the Hope Point police station.

Chapter 17

There was no time to think. Daniel lunged forward in the same instant Destiny did, each locking a hand on Mark's Metallica T-shirt. The force of their combined pull backwards yanked him halfway across the counter.

His arms flew forward to steady himself. The object in his right hand clattered on the counter and spun across it, falling to the floor at Destiny's feet.

"Pepper spray," Daniel noted, not letting go of Mark's shirt.

Destiny nodded, the color that had drained from her face rushing back.

"Maybe we overreacted," Daniel continued.

"Maybe," she agreed.

"It's legal, man!" Mark wailed from his position sprawled across the counter. "I even took a self-defense class to learn how to use it, like in case I get robbed. I just wanted to take it home with me, maybe get to my car without getting nailed."

"I think we can let him go," Daniel suggested.

Destiny nodded, and they both released his shirt. Mark slid back until his feet hit the floor behind the counter. Daniel retrieved the pepper spray from the floor. Mark raised an arm to cover his eyes, but, after a moment, reached over to take the canister from Daniel.

"Whoa, man."

"Sorry about that," Daniel said.

"Not that sorry," Destiny muttered, brushing her hands on her pants. "How are we supposed to trust you, Mark? Getting messed up with drugs again? You let down everybody who believes in you."

"I'm not messed up in drugs again, I swear," Mark said.

Daniel guessed he'd sworn the same oath before, probably sworn it while high. But there was a remorse in his wide eyes that didn't fit with the glib outrage of a liar.

"Hey, after what happened to Alain, I was going to go back on the ibuprofen, but Serena, when I told her I was still hurting, she like turned me on to some herbal stuff. Like these ginger capsules, you know? And vitamin E and selenium are supposed to be good for inflammation."

"Maybe some physical therapy?" Destiny suggested, though her obvious skepticism of his sincerity didn't soften.

"I'm thinking, like, a bulletproof vest," Mark said, shifting the pepper spray to his left hand as he dug a key ring out of his pocket. His feet bounced a little. "You guys won't spread around what I told you, right? Rollie's been around the block a few times. I mean, if he was scared . . ."

"I don't think your name will have to come up," Daniel told him. "As long as what you've said is true."

"It is. I swear, man."

"I'm not going to hide this from Serena and Jesse," Destiny warned him.

"Yeah, like, I know. At least if Jesse kills me, my folks'll know what happened to me." Mark shuddered again. "Two guys dead, man. Rollie always called us nobodies, you know, us guys who've had brushes with the law. Who knows how many more murders this guy can get away with? I mean, look at that senator's daughter or whatever. They caught that guy in days."

Three murders in two weeks, an all-time record in Hope Point. Two murders in two weeks, Daniel amended his thoughts. Rollie Garcia was more than likely still breathing. Mark obviously had a penchant for melodrama. But Sarah had also said that Rollie Garcia was afraid. Afraid enough that even a girl in fear for her own life could see it.

"Can I lock up now?" Mark asked.

"Sure," Daniel agreed. Then, tugged to some kind of sympathy for the man, or maybe just by the need to feel useful again, he added, "Do you want me to walk you to your car?"

Mark's eyes flashed wide. "No way, man. I mean, the less time I spend around you the better. No offense."

"None taken." Daniel almost smiled.

Mark pushed through the swinging door at the end of the counter, keeping his distance as Daniel and Destiny left the shop. The key turned hastily behind them.

The clouds had drifted lower, the waterlogged air diffusing the oranges and yellows of the street lamps into a pervasive half-light, like the set of a local theater production. Except that the dangers Daniel imagined in the shadowed doorways and darkened alleys weren't wielding plastic knives and cap guns.

Somehow the dread and shame of being falsely accused had distracted him from the truth that the real killer still walked free.

He watched Destiny turn up the collar of her wool coat, knowing her hands would be cold, wanting to take them in his and hold them until the warmth coursed between him and her again. But, as Mark had pointed out, as long as the killer needed Daniel isolated and under suspicion, the less time anyone spent around him the better.

No matter how good it had felt to stand beside her again and work as a team.

"Destiny." His voice was huskier than it should have been. "You shouldn't have come here tonight. When you found out Mark was lying, you should have called—" Not him. He was a murder suspect, and he wasn't answering her calls, anyway. "—You should have called Kermit. Mark could have been involved in Alain's death. He still could be."

Something about the expectant hush of the night, the sudden rush of life through his veins at what he'd learned from Mark, what he felt for Destiny, almost made him reach for her. But he was a better cop than that.

"You can't be around this case, Destiny. You can't be around me. It's too dangerous."

She turned toward him, her dark eyes burning with a deep, steady fire. "You don't want my help."

"It's too dangerous," he repeated.

"When I was in trouble, you helped me, a stranger. You took me into your house. You faced down Jake Westing's gun. You walked through fire. Literally."

"It was my job. It's what I'm trained to do."

Her skeptical eyebrows tilted. "So now that you're not on active duty, if someone attacked me walking back to my car tonight, you'd just stand by?"

"That doesn't even deserve a—"

"If I were drowning, you wouldn't jump into the river to save me? If my house burned down, you wouldn't take me in? If I broke my ankle, you wouldn't let me lean on you? If my parents got injured in a skiing accident, and I had to go to Sacramento to help them out for a month, you wouldn't take Fleur for me?"

"For a whole month?"

Her eyes only got fiercer. "If our places were reversed, Daniel, and I was accused of murder, and I told you I didn't want your help, what would you do?"

"It's not the same." He knew she had to see that. "Investigating crime is my job." *Was* his job. "I'm trained to defend myself. I have trained backup. I—"

"I'm not talking about the damn investigation." Her voice crackled with electric intensity. "I'm talking about support. I'm talking about someone to talk to. About someone to hold you when you don't know what to do next. About someone to help with the cooking and cleaning—"

"Cooking and cleaning? You?" But her hurt, or his own, fractured the teasing.

"It's okay for me to need help." She nodded, confirming it to herself. "That's okay. But it's not okay for you. You think you love me enough to stand by me, but you won't let me love you that much. You're not sparing me pain by pushing me away. Me or Kermit or any of your friends. You're not being selfless. Just selfish. Or cowardly."

She turned as if to walk away, then whirled around once more, and he could see the tears shining in her eyes.

"Is that unfair to say?" she demanded. "Because you're hurting? Because you're trying to be noble? Well, I'll tell you what, love isn't about being noble. It's about sticking it out through the hard times. It's about sharing the fear and the waiting and even the danger, because if you don't, how can it really be love?"

She bit her lower lip, shaking her head at him. "Didn't you learn anything from your divorce? Because I learned a lot from Alain leaving me. I learned a lot about trust. I trust you, Daniel. I know you'd never just walk out to follow your muse. I know you didn't kill Alain. But I need more than that.

252

"I need to know that you trust me."

"You don't understand." His voice sounded cold, even in his own ears, but he felt cold, all the way to his heart. "How can I trust you, when I repeatedly asked you not to interfere in this case, and here you are again tonight, coming to talk to Mark without a word to anyone. Without even a second thought."

"That had nothing to do with you," she said. "That had to do with Mark's drug problem. Which is a family problem. And that—" She gave him a bitter half-smile. "—That's none of your business."

She spun around and strode away.

Daniel watched her, across H Street, up another half-block to her car. He watched her rear lights flicker on, watched her drive away. He stood there for a long moment before stuffing his hands into the pockets of his field coat and turning down the street toward his own waiting truck.

Anger boiled in his stomach, firing the emptiness inside him. Anger at Destiny's anger, anger at Mark's lying, at Alain Caine's killer, at the lack of progress in the police investigation, at fate. But mostly at himself.

If he lost his job, if he lost his freedom, if he lost Destiny . . . Then the killer had won. And he would have let it happen.

It was time to stop asking questions and start getting some answers. At least their little chat with Mark had given him a new angle to explore.

Mark Banos had asked Alain Caine to buy prescription drugs for him from Rollie Garcia. Rollie Garcia had been seen arguing with young Kyle Preston less than a quarter-hour before Sarah Davis found a prescription for Dilaudid on a prescription pad from Royce Preston's office in Rollie Garcia's possession. Kyle Preston was on Daniel's personal list of potential suspects in the murder of Ariel Macaro, despite Kyle's father's giving him a dubious alibi.

And at the scene of Ariel Macaro's murder, Kermit Riggs had found a prescription for Percocet that her father could not explain.

Daniel believed in coincidence, but it was time to make sure that's all this was. Time to step on the toes of the Macaros and the Prestons. Before anyone else got hurt.

"Excuse me."

The words were a command rather than a request. Destiny looked up across her desk into a pair of green-flecked granite eyes. She recognized the thin, disapproving lips and sharp, pincher-like eyebrows that went with them, but it took her a moment to remember from where.

"I require help with the microfiche machines," he said, the words impatient and precise as he settled his leather briefcase on her desk. "I was told the main reference librarian is out for the week, and you are filling in for her."

Ah, yes, Maddy's problem patron. Dr. Royce Preston, the heart surgeon. Dr. Pressed Shirt, Gemma had said her grandmother called him. Father to Kyle Preston, local golden boy and potential murder suspect.

"The woman at the checkout desk said you might be capable of assisting me."

Destiny guessed Kyle must have inherited his looks and people skills from his mother.

"I'd be happy to help you," she said. Dr. Preston looked taken aback by her enthusiasm. He couldn't know that only the previous evening she'd discovered her sister's future brother-in-law had attempted to buy prescription painkillers from a violence-prone drug offender to whom Dr. Preston had prescribed Dilaudid. From the quick research she'd done on the Internet the night before, she'd love to ask Dr. Preston why he would prescribe an opiate derivative for a patient with congestive heart failure.

She'd also love to ask him if his son had really been at home on the night Ariel Macaro was murdered, whether the doctor had ever met a man named Alain Caine, and, just for good measure, did he think Calvin Macaro had any shady associates from the crime world who might . . .

She cut off her thoughts with a snap. *It's not any of your business.* Daniel had made that perfectly clear. He didn't want her help, didn't want her involved, didn't want her. And didn't trust her to have the sense to accept it. The memory ground in her stomach like broken glass as she followed Dr. Royce Preston's imperious gait to the elevator.

She stepped into the cage without trepidation. The fear of crashing elevators had lost its power in the face of the current reality of her life.

Part of her understood Daniel's reaction to the collapse of his career and possibly his life. His whole sense of himself was wrapped in his identity as a man in control, helping others find justice, protecting the helpless. He wasn't supposed to be the helpless one.

Her heart ached for him, alone and in trouble, with no progress in his case, no sign of Rollie Garcia, and the D.A.'s office beginning to sound impatient with the sheriff's investigation.

But he wasn't the only one hurting.

"I need copies of the *Jasper County Register* for the past six months," Royce Preston stated, striding across the mezzanine and through the glass doors into the county archives room. He stopped at the scarred wooden table holding the library's four microfiche machines and awkwardly folded his long legs into the chair in front of the machine farthest from the door.

"Do you want me to show you how to find the materials you need?" Destiny asked, pausing on her way to the microfiche files.

"I don't have time to waste on filing. I have a surgery at eleven." Dr. Preston lifted his briefcase to the table beside the microfiche reader, swiftly spinning the numbers on the combination lock. He glanced up. "The past six months, back to June fifth. I've already done the four years before that."

Destiny continued to the microfiche file cabinets, contemplating the nature of time and its wasting, and how little of her own she wanted to waste on thoughtless, arrogant, self-satisfied . . . She slowed her breathing and pulled two years' worth of the *Jasper County Register*. She could have insisted Dr. Preston do this himself. But then she wouldn't have the chance to find out why he considered studying the paper a worthwhile use of his precious time.

The *Register* was the county's only daily paper, but even including the predictable weather forecast (foggy with a chance of rain, rain with the possibility of fog developing later) and a thorough rundown of the local high school sports scores, the paper rarely had enough news to fill more than two sections of newsprint. Six months of the paper on microfiche was still not an unwieldy pile of cards.

Destiny settled the stack of four-by-six microfiche cards on the table beside Dr. Preston. "Here you go."

Without glancing up, he lifted the first card in a long, bony hand, checking the title and dates. He pulled it from its protective plastic sleeve, set it back down and pulled a notepad from his briefcase.

Apparently Destiny had disappeared from his consciousness. She could probably stand behind him and read the paper over his shoulder without his ever noticing. And waste another ten minutes finding out all of Kyle Preston's football statistics.

She stifled a sigh as she glanced toward the microfiche files. She could straighten them and then stop by Dr. Preston's machine again before heading back down to her desk.

"I believe I asked for your help." Dr. Preston's sharp tone turned her back to meet his granite eyes.

"Do you need more dates?" No wonder Maddy had wanted to clean his clock.

"Not if you brought me what I asked for." His tone said it was highly unlikely she'd gotten it right, but he was giving her the benefit of the doubt. "I need the machine set up."

Destiny blinked. The microfiche reader might look like a big, bulky, eighties-style computer monitor, but it was almost defiantly low-tech. All the machine did was backlight the microfiche film and magnify the text printed on it, displaying the results on the screen. "There's not really any setup. You turn on this switch here—"

"I don't require a play-by-play."

As she reached for the power switch, the absurdity of the situation suddenly overrode her irritation, and she had to choke down a rumble of laughter. The great doctor didn't know how to work a microfiche machine. Learning would require being instructed by a mere librarian. Therefore, it was beneath his dignity to learn.

She wondered how many other things his dignity prevented him from doing in his life, and she almost felt sorry for him. Then she thought of what his receptionists and nurses must put up with from him, and the pity faded away.

"There you go," she said, settling the microfiche card

into the tray and using the knobs to center the paper's headline for June fifth on the screen in front of him. "What section of the paper are you looking for?"

"I can find it." He waved her away. "I'll call you when I need you again."

Destiny smiled grimly at the back of his head as she stood. He could call all he wanted, but she'd be back down at her desk, helping patrons who actually needed help.

"Ms. Millbrook!" The dry, eager voice turned her toward the entrance to the archives room. Dark eyes shone warmly behind large, round glasses on a round, balding head as a short, spare man hurried over to greet her.

"Mr. Dyer." Precisely the break she needed from Dr. Pressed Shirt. "What are you looking for today? More information on the Kennedy assassinations?"

"Mars," he said, eyes bright with excitement. "And terraforming. The way we're destroying the world we live in, we should be making contingency plans for after Earth becomes completely uninhabitable."

"Hydrogen-powered cars," Destiny suggested.

"And solar energy," Mr. Dyer agreed.

"There's a catalog station over here, let's see what we can do to get you started—"

"Edward?" Dr. Preston's voice interrupted her.

"Royce! Hello." Mr. Dyer turned the full force of his V-shaped smile on the heart surgeon, reaching out with both hands to shake Dr. Preston's. "It's so good to see you."

"You, too," Dr. Preston said, actually looking pleased, though he quickly pulled his hand back, resting it on the microfiche controls. "I'm just doing some research before I have to be at the hospital this morning. If I have time to get anything done, after getting this ridiculous machine set up."

He glanced darkly at Destiny.

"Microfiche." Mr. Dyer nodded his head sagely. "Technology is wonderful, but there's nothing like real paper. Something you can hold in your hand."

"These machines are infernal. And half the time there's no one around to help you with them."

Before Destiny could respond to that, Mr. Dyer jumped in. "Why don't you let me give you a hand? I'm used to research with all sorts of media."

Dr. Preston glanced down at his notepad, then at the microfiche reader screen. "I couldn't ask you to do that. The library has staff."

"I love searching through old newspapers," Mr. Dyer said, taking the seat next to him. "And having something useful to do. We'll make quick work of it, and let Ms. Millbrook get back to hers."

He flashed Destiny a conspiratorial smile, and she grinned back in gratitude.

"I'll come back and check on you," she promised. "You're in good hands with Mr. Dyer, Dr. Preston. You're lucky to have his help. It's nice to have friends like that."

Dr. Preston's face lengthened with his frown as he glanced away from Mr. Dyer. "We have a nodding acquaintance. Hope Point is a very small town. You quickly meet anyone of any consequence."

She had managed to swallow all of his swipes at her, but his sudden embarrassment at his association with Mr. Dyer pushed her one step too far. "That's why I find it so interesting that I've never met you before, Dr. Preston, since we know so many of the same people. Mr. Dyer, for instance, and Pleasance Geary, Detective Daniel Parks and . . . Rollie Garcia."

She gave him a second to register the name. "It must

have been a bit of a shock to hear a patient of yours was a fugitive from the law."

Dr. Preston's thin lips disappeared. "He was not a patient of mine."

"You wrote him a prescription for a rather powerful painkiller."

A spot of color rose on the crest of each cheekbone. "He came to see me on the recommendation of his regular doctor in the Bay Area. I was doing a favor for an old colleague."

His eyes, once more hard as stone, showed only offense at her question. And yet, he had answered it. A tendril of excitement curled in her stomach. Prominent heart surgeons didn't answer impertinent questions. But men trying to hide something did.

"Was it Rollie Garcia you went to meet at the county arts and crafts fair a couple of weeks ago? I saw you and your son at the fairgrounds. I guess your son knew Mr. Garcia, too?"

"My son did *not* know that man." Dr. Preston's hand curled into a fist on his briefcase. "As I explained to the police after that Garcia fellow disappeared, my son was seen in his booth up at Shell Creek because he was haggling over the price of a T-shirt. That was the only contact they had."

She caught an anxious look from Mr. Dyer, asking her to drop it, but she could feel the fish nibbling at the end of her line.

"So neither of you met with Mr. Garcia on the night of that first crafts fair, the night the artist from Arizona was killed in Garcia's trailer?"

Her words broke him out of his defensive position, and he sat up straight as a rake. "What are you implying? If you mean to suggest either myself or my son had anything to do

260

with the tawdry, pathetic events of that evening, I assure you I have a very good lawyer who would love to sink his teeth into a defamation of character suit."

She had no doubt of that. But the threat seemed excessive. Unless the important thing was not getting her to leave him alone, but convincing her to keep her mouth shut.

"The man who was killed that night was a talented artist with no criminal record." She found herself struggling to keep her voice level. "You may find his death tawdry and pathetic, but I consider it tragic. The police consider it a felony murder case. Have they asked you where you were that night, Doctor?"

"My whereabouts on that night are none of your business!"

He'd finally told her off, but from the flash of panic in his eyes, she knew it was only because she'd reached the point where he didn't have an answer prepared. Unfortunately, she didn't have a follow-up prepared, either. The question had been a cheap shot. She'd never expected him to resist answering it. Never remotely considered him a suspect in Alain's death.

Not in her wildest imaginings. And she'd had a few of those.

"True, it's none of my business, but the police might be interested," she said, nearly wincing at the lameness of the warning.

"As your superiors here at the library might be interested in your rude and disrespectful treatment of a pillar of this community."

"Royce, you and I had better get working on that research, if you've got surgery in a few hours," Mr. Dyer said, verbally inserting himself between them. He gave Destiny a strangely sorrowful, but stern look. "We'll call you if we need assistance, Ms. Millbrook."

She could face down Dr. Preston's intimidating arrogance, his imperious orders and sniping threats, but Mr. Dyer's quiet disapproval loosened the knots of anger and suspicion that had bound her actions for what seemed a very long time.

"I'll be downstairs."

As she walked toward the door, she heard Dr. Preston's thin voice, "That woman has no right to question me. I won't put up with such rudeness. She shouldn't be working with—"

"She's hurting, too," Mr. Dyer's softer words cut through the heart surgeon's shrill tones. "We all hurt for the ones we love."

She tried not to picture Daniel as she'd seen him the night before, the tough cop exterior impenetrable to her, by love or by anger.

She knew him well enough, though, to have seen the sudden speculation in his eyes when Mark had spoken of buying prescription drugs. Maybe he hadn't withdrawn as far as he thought he had. Maybe that spark would even be enough to drag him out of his isolation in order to check Mark's story out.

She hoped he was having better luck than she was.

"Hope Point Police Department. Nancy Dennis speaking."

Daniel's throat tightened. After all his years on the force, he did not want to hear the change in Nancy's voice when he said his name. Better to sit alone in his house, allow all his colleagues to pretend he had gone on vacation or died.

He remembered Destiny's voice the night before, accusing him of cowardice.

"Nancy, this is Daniel Parks."

"Detective Parks!" Her voice rose in excitement, then faltered, and he realized she wasn't sure if she should be addressing him that way. She hurried on. "What can I do for you?"

"Is Kermit there?"

"He's on patrol. Would you like me to have him call you when he gets a chance?"

Yes, he would like that. He knew exactly where Kermit stood: firmly behind him, even when Daniel asked him to back off. But he couldn't wait that long.

"I'll take Vance or Yap, if they're around."

"I saw Tom in the break room a few minutes ago. Let me see if I can catch him for you."

A few moments later, Tom Yap's voice sounded in his ear. Daniel could picture the ironic light in his eyes as he spoke. "Detective Parks?"

"Tom. I don't want to take up your time. I just have a quick question." Now to ask it without stepping on anyone's toes. "I was thinking about the Ariel Macaro case, and I remembered that prescription Kermit found."

"Prescription?"

"The one for Percocet. Her father said it might be for a pulled hamstring, but I got to thinking about it, and Percocet seems over-the-top for a sports injury. I wondered if anyone had checked with the prescribing doctor."

Silence stretched over the line. "I haven't heard anything about a prescription."

"It probably didn't seem important," Daniel admitted. It had caught his eye at the time of the murder, but he, too, had forgotten about it in the rush to arrest Tyler Woodridge. There was no reason for Ben Dillon or the other officers to think anything of it. "It probably *isn't* important.

But I've come across some coincidental information, and I think it would be worth a ten-minute phone call to the doctor. Do you mind going down to the evidence locker and digging up the doctor's name and number?"

"It's not that I'd mind, Detective, but—"

"I know I'm not on the case," Daniel said, swallowing the bitter taste of it. "I won't call the doctor myself. I just want to have the name to give to Ben when I pass along my information."

"No, it's not that," Tom assured him, apologetic. "Please. It's not that at all. It's just that it's not going to do me any good to go to the evidence locker. Detective Dillon has had me and Garth go over that stuff a hundred times, looking for something to connect Tyler Woodridge to the murder scene."

"So you know the doctor's name?" He bit back his eagerness. As he'd already told Tom, it was probably nothing . . .

"No. That's not what I'm saying. I mean there is no prescription of any kind among Ariel Macaro's effects."

Chapter 18

"I can't believe I didn't see them there." The short, round-faced woman gestured helplessly at the shelf of Anne Perry mysteries Destiny had led her to. "I'm so sorry to bother you."

"That's what I'm here for," Destiny assured her. "And if you have any trouble finding anything else, just come get me."

"Thank you so much." The woman sat down on a rolling stool in front of the shelf and pulled a pile of books onto her lap.

Destiny left her to it and headed for the elevator, her day brightened by the positive encounter. It didn't matter that she had to ride up to the second floor to show someone a long shelf of hard-to-miss books. What mattered was that she'd helped someone out. Which far outweighed the occasional negative experience of coping with an obnoxious patron like Royce Preston.

As she stepped into the elevator, her finger hesitated on the lobby button. She did not have any desire to embarrass herself or Mr. Dyer any further, but she couldn't get Dr. Preston's evasiveness about the arts and crafts fair out of her mind. She *had* promised to check on the two men's progress with the microfiche machine.

She pressed M before she could change her mind. The

elevator rocked and jolted to a stop at the mezzanine. She hopped out before it changed its mind about allowing her to escape, nearly knocking into the patron charging in past her.

"Dr. Preston, did you find—"

The doors creaked closed, and he was gone. Almost as relieved as she was disappointed, Destiny continued on into the archives room. She found Mr. Dyer amid a pile of microfiche cards, peering shortsightedly at the dates on the labels, trying to put them back in order.

"He left you to clean up his mess?" Destiny asked in disbelief, picking up a card that had fallen to the floor.

Mr. Dyer glanced up. "The hospital paged. A patient in cardiac arrest."

Destiny grimaced in shame. "Consider me properly chastened."

"I know Royce's manner is abrasive," Mr. Dyer said, straightening his small pile. "But he does have a lot on his mind. He's faced his own share of trouble in his life. If you met him under other circumstances, you'd find he has a surprising capacity for compassion."

Destiny suspected Mr. Dyer's own capacity for compassion colored his impressions of others, but she nodded noncommittally.

She pulled a card out from under the corner of the microfiche machine and a piece of lined yellow paper came with it. In a neat row down the left side of the paper was a list of dates, day of the week, month, day, and year, each followed by an almost illegible scrawl which might have indicated names. The last few sets of dates and names were written in green ink.

"Is this yours?"

Mr. Dyer looked at the paper. "Royce's," he said.

"Court cases. Those are the ones we found today. I took some notes for him."

"Court cases?"

"That's what he was looking for in the paper. He was keeping a list of the lawyers and police witnesses, but I guess he took that with him."

Destiny peered under the machine. She found an old cough drop wrapper, but no more paper. "I wonder what he was looking for?"

"He wasn't ready to divulge that information," Mr. Dyer said, a glint in his eye as he lowered his voice. "I got the feeling he didn't want to put me in danger."

Destiny managed to suppress her smile. "A conspiracy?"

"Anyone with power can be tempted to abuse it." Mr. Dyer chided her skepticism. "You don't need a congressional subcommittee to have a conspiracy. Although a congressman's involvement gives you a heads up."

Destiny thought of the circumstantial evidence against Daniel—his fight with Alain, his lack of an alibi, the gun stolen from the police evidence locker. She could laugh at Mr. Dyer's ability to see evidence of a conspiracy in a list of court cases, but she could also understand the human need to make connections, to find meaning in random events.

The longer it took to clear Daniel of Alain's murder, the more the word *framed* popped up in her head. Though who could possibly benefit from Daniel's going to prison for murder?

The real murderer, for one.

"I take it there's no new information in the case against your detective?" Mr Dyer asked, as if reading her mind.

Given his interest in psychic phenomena, the thought unsettled her, though it didn't surprise her he knew about Daniel's predicament. He was as well-informed about local events as he was about those on the astral plane.

"No," she admitted. "Not that I know of."

"It must be very hard on you. I can see how troubled you are."

Destiny felt her cheeks redden, thinking of her earlier behavior toward Dr. Preston.

"And it must be very hard on your young man."

"Yes."

Mr. Dyer nodded. "It has always seemed strange to me how many of these trials strike us at this time of year, when we are so determined that everyone must be happy."

"You mean Christmastime." Destiny suddenly realized it was, indeed, the first week of December. She'd bought some books and an Oakland A's sweatshirt for Sarah in October, but she didn't have presents for anyone else yet. Hadn't sent any Christmas cards. Hadn't even noticed the Christmas jingles that must already be playing in Safeway and Longs and the Hope Point Co-Op.

"My son died on December eighteenth, ten years ago," Mr. Dyer said, his eyes serene as ever, though they drifted toward the past. "I remember telling someone that you'd expect God to keep such things from happening at Christmas. You hear so many stories of Christmas miracles. And my friend reminded me that the promise of Christmas isn't that God won't let anything bad happen to us, it's that he will be there through the bad as well as the good."

Something twisted in Destiny's heart. "Thank you for reminding me."

"It is an important message to pass along," Mr. Dyer said. "You may not be able to change your outer circumstances, but you can face them with love and peace. Your detective needs to hear it."

Destiny's hand clenched involuntarily around the paper

she held. "I don't know if he'll be willing to listen to anything I have to say until this case is cleared up."

If then.

She gestured with the crumpled piece of notebook paper. "And how is it going to be cleared up if no one is willing to step forward and tell the truth?" She thought of Mark, and frustration sharpened her voice. "Everyone thinks they have a good reason for lying or simply keeping quiet, but the person who is going to pay the price is an innocent man. Take Dr. Preston. What would it have hurt him to tell me where he was the night Alain Caine was killed?"

He had been so strangely willing to answer all her questions but that one. As though he'd had answers prepared to cover just such a line of questioning, but had never expected to have to provide an alibi for his own whereabouts.

"What possible reason could he have for murdering an out-of-state artist?" she asked out loud. "But getting so defensive at the question makes him look guilty. Guilty of something. It makes me think the sheriff's department ought to find out where he was that night."

Mr. Dyer shook his head. "No. There has been enough pain caused by this murder. I know where Royce was that night."

"What? Where?"

Mr. Dyer's face clouded with sorrow. "I can't tell you."

They stood for a moment, staring at each other, before Destiny heard her name being called. She turned to see Charlene frowning at her from the doorway to the archives room.

"There's a line at your desk," Charlene said.

Five minutes earlier, Charlene's curt tone might have nudged Destiny into responding in kind. But Mr. Dyer's comments about love and peace must have pierced the angry guard around her heart. At least enough to recognize that Charlene's chronic hostility came from deep inside Charlene, not from anything she herself had done.

If her own personal troubles could drive her to accuse a heart surgeon of murder and to accost Mark Banos by calling him a lying, worthless, piece of . . . She cringed at the thought. Perhaps Charlene's problems matched her own.

Although she doubted any of Charlene's ex-boyfriends had gotten themselves murdered lately. She doubted they would dare.

She met Charlene's belligerent gaze with as much compassion as she could muster. "Thanks for taking the time to come up and let me know. I'll be right there, as soon as I finish helping Mr. Dyer with the microfiche."

Charlene's eyes narrowed. "With Madelyn gone, you can't afford to take so much time with each patron."

Especially not the crazy ones, Destiny heard the unspoken message clearly. She tried on Mr. Dyer's calm little smile. There were advantages to crazy. "Thank goodness Maddy's coming home tomorrow. Don't worry. I'll hurry."

Charlene's frown pursed her lips into the shape of a pale mauve sea anemone. "Do so." She backed out of the doorway and disappeared.

"I can finish this up," Mr. Dyer said, taking Destiny's stack of cards and adding it to his own. "I've gotten pretty good at filing over the years."

"Thank you so much. That would be great." Destiny offered him the crumpled piece of yellow paper she still held in her hand. "Do you want to give this back to Dr. Preston?"

Mr. Dyer waved it away. "You keep it. He might come back to the library looking for it. And it might be good for someone else to have a list of those cases, if anything happens to Royce."

She almost laughed at his joke, until she saw he didn't mean it as one.

"Don't tell anyone else about this list," he warned, tapping the paper in her hand with his finger. He sighed and shook his head, the conspiratorial zeal fading from his eyes. "Royce thinks he can protect his son. I don't know how to tell him we can't control the fate of others."

He smiled suddenly at her, though the sorrow still lingered behind his dark eyes. "That never stops us from trying, though, does it? You go on and don't worry about these microfiche cards. They'll be in good order when you need them. And don't forget to share that good heart of yours with your detective."

The telephone rang, jerking Daniel away from his impatient pacing through the kitchen to the dining room and back. He dashed for the phone, nearly tumbling over Edgar, who howled his outrage before padding off toward the bedroom in a huff.

"Kermit?"

"Here."

Kermit's terse tone told him the bad news, but Daniel asked anyway. "No prescription?"

"Not in the evidence locker, not on the list of Ariel's personal effects."

So Tom hadn't simply been blowing him off as a nuisance by refusing to go look for the prescription. It really wasn't there.

"What about the rest of the things on your list?" Daniel asked.

He could hear the flap of Kermit's notebook over the

phone as it dropped to the floor. A brief scuffle. Kermit returned to the line. "It all checks out. Not that there was much there to begin with, but even the loose stick of gum was still in her purse."

"You're sure the prescription got put in with the rest of the evidence?"

"I'm sure."

"I know how competent you are, Kerry. But it would be easy to lose a scrap of paper in a breeze in a parking lot. Easier than inside a police station." In so many ways.

"I'm sure," Kermit repeated. Then, "It's not the first time this has ever happened."

Daniel thought of the gun that had killed Alain Caine. An unfilled prescription seemed unimportant in comparison. But in the paradoxical way his instincts sometimes worked, the harder the prescription was to find, the more important it felt.

"The prescription was for Percocet?" he asked, taking Kermit back to his notes, back to that day behind the Baptist church.

Another rustle of paper. "That's right. I didn't write down the dosage or amount."

Why should he? All of that would be in the evidence locker in the unlikely event it turned out to be important. "That's all right. Do you remember the name of the doctor who wrote the prescription?"

He could hear Kermit's frustration in the silence over the line.

"Take your time. The doctor's name, probably the clinic, would be printed somewhere on the prescription."

"She was dead. She'd been stabbed to death."

"That's all any of us were concerned with," Daniel said. Under normal circumstances, he would simply call Ariel's father and ask for the name of her doctor. But these were not normal circumstances, and Calvin Macaro wasn't likely to give him the time of day. He couldn't get Kermit in trouble by having him call the ex-congressman. It probably wasn't even important. And yet.

"I know I glanced at it. But I just can't . . . Wait." Kermit's notebook slapped rhythmically against the wall as he thought. "That's right. It reminded me of a shoe. Reebok. Adidas . . . Abatas. That was it. Dr. Abatas."

Daniel blew out his breath in relief and appreciation for Kermit's memory. "I believe it's time I gave Dr. Abatas a call."

"Detective—" Kermit cut himself off. "Just be careful."

"Don't worry," Daniel assured him. He laughed without humor. "What could go wrong?"

"Sure you can't come over tomorrow?" Gemma asked, as she and Sarah hurried down the Cloverbrook Middle School hallway toward the waiting buses. "Grandma said we could have pizza and ice cream after the game. Hope Point High will win the county title if they win this game and Deepwater loses to Cantorville."

Sarah glanced toward where Gemma's grandmother waited in her huge diesel pickup, and a flash of midnight blue beside it caught her eye.

"I don't think so," she said, jerking her head toward the Subaru parked behind the Dodge truck. "I guess my mom doesn't even trust me to ride the bus anymore. I think she's looking into getting one of those home monitoring systems like they put on convicts, the things you wear on your ankles."

Gemma scrunched her nose, her freckles clumping. "Wow. Good luck."

Sarah doubted anything less than divine intervention could rescue her now, but she waved to Gemma and tromped over to climb into the passenger's seat of the Subaru.

"You're supposed to be at work," she said, slamming the door just a little too hard. "Don't tell me you're playing hooky. It must run in the family."

She felt ashamed of the words, even as they left her mouth, but to pick her up at school like a truant who couldn't even be trusted to ride the bus home . . . Her defensive inner monologue slowed as she realized her mother wasn't responding. She glanced over and saw the tension lines radiating from her mother's mouth as Serena steered the station wagon out onto the road. Sarah had never noticed those wrinkles, or the ones around her mother's eyes.

"What's wrong?" she asked. "Did something happen?"

Serena glanced at her. "I got out of work early to be there when Jesse went to talk to Mark."

A wave of guilt washed over Sarah, though she knew she'd had to tell Detective Parks about Mark. "Aunt Destiny said Mark just wanted some pain medication for his shoulder," she offered.

"Tylenol 4s would certainly stop the pain," Serena said. "Even if I'd broken his head open for betraying Jesse that way. And me and Destiny and Daniel."

She stopped at a stop sign, and turned to look directly at Sarah. "Mark can't take medication like that, Sarah. T-4s contain codeine. They're serious pain relievers. Not for bursitis. Especially not for someone as susceptible to chemical dependency as Mark is."

"You think he just wanted to get high?"

Serena sighed heavily as she turned onto their street. "I don't know. I think he really wanted to stop the pain. But something in him couldn't just stop at what his doctor was willing to prescribe for him."

"But he didn't get it," Sarah reminded her, hearing the thin sound of hope in her own voice. "He didn't take any."

"This time."

Sarah pulled her feet up onto her seat and rested her chin on her knees. She remembered when Mark had gone into rehab, Jesse repeating over and over for them not to expect too much, quoting statistics on addiction recovery and relapse. Even when Mark had come back, Jesse had warned them not to get their hopes up. But Sarah had seen the hope shining bright in Jesse's dark eyes.

The Subaru pulled into the driveway of their house, and Serena turned off the ignition. They sat for a moment in silence as the engine died.

"I worry about you, Sarah." Her mother stared out the windshield. "When you skip school. When I don't know where you are or who you're with. It's not because I don't trust you or I doubt your intelligence. I brag about you to my friends, how responsible you are, how smart you are."

She turned to look at Sarah. "I worry because I'm your mother, and I love you. I worry because Mark's parents loved him, and he had an older brother to look out for him, and he still got involved in drugs, and that may hurt him for the rest of his life.

"When you move out on your own in a few years, you're going to have to make all these decisions for yourself. But as long as you're living with me, I'm going to protect you as much as I can. It's my job."

Her mother's wry smile unknotted the resentment Sarah had been holding in for two weeks. Or more. And maybe it even eased the fear that because she'd cut school, her mother didn't love her quite as much as she had before.

"I'm sorry, Mom. I'm sorry I worried you. But I'm not doing drugs."

"I know, baby." Serena reached across the seat and pulled her into a hug made awkward by seat belts, but comforting nonetheless. "And I know you're bored in school, but it's still important that you go. It's up to you to learn as much as you can there."

Sarah couldn't hold back a smile. "Then you'll be glad to hear what I did this week."

Serena's eyes narrowed. "Uh-oh. Do I really want to know?"

"I told Mrs. Cannon I thought we'd learn more about Japan if we had a hands-on experience with Japanese culture. I gave her Jon Matthews's phone number, the Sumi-e artist I met? I had his card with my egret painting. Mrs. Cannon called him, and he's going to come next week to give us an ink painting demonstration and lesson. And his grandfather is bringing a real samurai sword and his mother is going to conduct a tea ceremony for our class."

And because things were starting to get right between her and her mother, Sarah let slip the best news of all. "Brian Tilson said I was the coolest thing to happen to Mrs. Cannon's class in twenty years."

Serena shook her head, though her eyes laughed. "Incorrigible, that's what you are. And just for Brian Tilson's information, you're not allowed to date until you're thirty-five."

"Thirty-*five*," Sarah wailed, in exaggerated horror. "I might as well be dead."

"Ha, ha." Her almost-thirty-three-year-old mother pulled her ponytail. "Very funny." She hugged Sarah again. "I love you."

"I love you, too, Mom."

"Just don't do anything too crazy for awhile, okay? I'd hate for my poor, ancient heart to give out."

"Sure, Mom. Don't worry."

"Dr. Abatas?"

"May I help you?" The voice at the other end of the line had a businesslike clip, despite the feminine register.

"Detective Daniel Parks with the Hope Point PD." That was still his official title. He hadn't been fired. Yet. "I have a question about a prescription you wrote for one of your patients."

"You're wasting your time, Detective." The edges of Dr. Abatas's voice hardened further. "Doctor-patient confidentiality."

"I understand, doctor. But this patient is dead."

Even the silence became steely, and he rushed forward to eliminate visions of malpractice suits. "Murdered, Dr. Abatas. Several weeks ago. I was just going over the list of her personal effects taken by the officer at the scene, and our victim had a prescription for Percocet you had written for her. I just wondered what the prescription was for."

"Percocet?" Curiosity eased the annoyance from her voice. "That doesn't seem likely. And I don't recall any of my patients getting murdered lately. I do try to keep on top of those things."

"Ariel Macaro," Daniel said, annoyed in his own turn at doctors who couldn't remember their patients' names. "She was seventeen, a high school senior, long, dark hair, brown eyes—"

"Of course I know Ariel Macaro," Dr. Abatas said. "Or, at least, I know who she was. But she wasn't one of my patients."

"Is there another Dr. Abatas in Jasper County?"

Kermit had been certain, on looking through the phone book, that the name on the prescription had been Dr. Emily Abatas, but his one glance at that prescription had been over two weeks ago . . .

"Just me, as far as I know."

"The prescription came from your office."

"That's not possible," she said, without hesitation. "As I said, Ariel Macaro was not a patient of mine, nor, as far as I know, of anyone in my group."

"Her father thinks it might have been for a sports injury, a pulled hamstring."

"Is this some kind of a joke? Or maybe the joke's on you, Detective. Someone pulling a prank."

"This is no joke, Doctor." Daniel reined in his anger. "A young woman is dead, and I need to follow every possible lead to find out why. Do you think you could go through your records to find out if it's possible if someone else at your office wrote—"

"First of all, Detective, Percocet is serious overmedication for a pulled hamstring. Meds at that level have a potential for abuse and a significant street value. Percocet, Dilaudid, and so on, they all require a triplicate prescription. Only a doctor can write a trip. Each of those prescriptions is numbered, and we keep a record of each one.

"Second, I don't write many triplicates, and I remember the ones I do. Third, I don't treat sports injuries, I treat heart and circulatory system patients. Fourth, if Ariel Macaro had come to me with heart disease, I would not have prescribed Percocet for it."

Dr. Abatas stopped, not winding down, simply finished with her point.

"Heart disease," Daniel repeated, his own heart beating

faster. "You said you work at a medical group? With other doctors?"

"Bay Shore Cardiology. We have offices near Jasper County General."

"I see. Thank you for your time, Doctor. I appreciate your help."

"I did not write a prescription for Ariel Macaro."

"I understand. Thank you, Dr. Abatas."

Daniel was already hanging up the phone, flipping through his telephone book to the yellow pages, a mercifully short process in the Jasper County phone book.

Bay Shore Cardiology had a quarter-page advertisement in the physicians section. Dr. Emily Abatas was first in the alphabetical listing of the five doctor associates. But the headline name at the group stretched across the advertisement in bold type beneath the clinic name: Dr. Royce Preston, MD.

Daniel felt the familiar rush of adrenaline as a puzzle piece suddenly took shape in his hand, solid and defined. And yet, this piece made no sense. Or perhaps it was the puzzle that was muddled.

A high school senior dead, an improbable prescription in her purse. A visiting artist dead, planning to buy a painkiller prescription for a drug addict. A suspected drug dealer missing, another unlikely prescription involved, one he knew carried a street value of fifty to ninety dollars per pill.

Two very separate murders. The prescriptions less than a tenuous connection. Kyle Preston had once dated Ariel Macaro, and he had been seen speaking with Rollie Garcia. Royce Preston, noted heart surgeon, had written Rollie Garcia's prescription, but the indirect link of Dr. Preston's clinic to Ariel was nothing more than intriguing—even if they still had the prescription. Kermit's word was good enough for Daniel, but it would not stand as evidence in a court of law.

Evidence of *what?*

Daniel shook his head. It was impossible that Ariel Macaro and Alain Caine should be murdered by the same person. Besides, the two killings had completely different MO's. One victim stabbed behind a church over a lover's triangle. One shot in the chest execution-style over . . . a drug deal gone bad? They still didn't know.

Although some thought they knew. Daniel had killed Alain in a jealous argument. Much like Tyler Woodridge had killed Ariel Macaro in a jealous rage.

And maybe that was the connection. The continuity of *modus operandi* being not in the method of the death, but in the picture painted for the investigators.

He had assumed his being implicated in Alain's death was coincidence, bad timing. Useful for the real murderer, but not planned.

Yet from the time Tyler Woodridge had been arrested, Daniel had considered the idea that Tyler might have been framed—the bloody knife under his grandparents' trailer, his lack of alibi, his brother's drug connections . . .

If Tyler was innocent, he must have been framed. If Daniel was innocent—

Daniel shook his head, laughing at himself, because there was nothing left to do but laugh when you'd been a detective so long you couldn't even posit your own innocence as fact.

He was innocent. Tyler might be. They might both have been framed. Which meant the person who killed Ariel and the person who killed Alain might be one and the same. Or at least, two individuals in a single criminal conspiracy.

Which meant that person—or persons—might be considerably more creative and clever than the average criminal. And considerably more dangerous.

Tyler Woodridge made a convenient cover for the murder of Ariel Macaro. Daniel less so for Alain—it had taken the gun to cement the connection there. But what if framing Daniel had less to do with providing a suspect for Alain's murder and more to do with halting Daniel's investigation into Ariel's death? He'd made no secret of his doubts about Tyler's guilt. Not something the real murderer would be happy to hear.

What would Kyle Preston's father do to protect him from a murder conviction? And Calvin Macaro? Daniel couldn't imagine him killing his own daughter—and yet, men had done it before. Because she defied him? Or perhaps her death was a message from an angry client. Drug dealers of any level had very little honor.

Daniel sat heavily on a stool at his kitchen counter, the excitement turning to dread in his heart. He felt no closer to an answer, but much, much closer to whoever had killed Ariel and Alain, whoever had brought that horrific violence to his town, his beat, his life.

Whoever had done it knew enough about Daniel to frame him for murder. Knew about his job, his movements, his friends. And had proven capable of great cunning and cruelty to evade discovery. Even now the killer would be watching, listening, aware of any changes in the status quo that kept him—or her—safe. Like a silent spider, attuned to every tug on every strand of its web.

A chill ran down Daniel's spine, despite the fire burning bravely in his fireplace against the cold rain outside. It didn't matter that he had stopped struggling, a caught fly waiting only to be wrapped and stored. Kermit, Destiny, Tom and Garth, Sarah and Serena, Mark Banos and Rollie

Garcia. Every time they tugged against the spider's net, they caught its attention.

And there was no telling what movement might bring it scuttling down the web to entrap them. Maybe Daniel's withdrawal, his reliance on Ben Dillon's and the sheriff's investigations, wasn't protecting them at all.

He remembered asking Kermit what could go wrong. Perhaps the question was, what couldn't?

Chapter 19

Destiny's VW Rabbit rolled to a slow stop in the driveway behind Daniel's truck. Bright sunlight raised steam from the wet roof of Daniel's house, glinted cheerfully in the droplets clinging to the spruce trees at the end of the road. The dazzling light made a dream of the dark rain the day before.

"It's a perfect day for finding a Christmas tree," Sarah said leaning over Destiny's shoulder from the backseat. Fleur's head pushed in beside Sarah's, her happy panting interrupted only by a swipe at Kermit's face with her tongue.

"Perfect," Destiny agreed, sharing a glance with Kermit. They all knew the perfection of their plan would be shattered as soon as they confronted its object. But she had spent most of the night thinking about what Mr. Dyer had said the day before, and about what she herself had said to Daniel outside Mark's shop.

Love isn't about being noble. It's about sticking it out through the hard times.

She had meant it, and yet she had let Daniel pull away, let her own hurt hold her back when he needed her the most. Maybe she couldn't fix the circumstances he found himself in. Maybe her attempts to clear his name had not advanced the investigation in any significant way. Yet she still had something to offer.

Don't forget to share that good heart of yours with your detective.

It didn't feel particularly good. It felt bruised and small and inadequate. But the sunlight streaming down from the sky seemed to be working into her chest, reminding her of the promise of peace and love.

And she was going to share it with Daniel whether he liked it or not.

An explosion of high-pitched yapping burst from the backseat.

Destiny didn't turn her head. "Tell me you didn't let Psyche out of her carrier."

"She's going to have to go pee before we start up into the mountains," Sarah said. The yapping bounced up and down. "I think she saw Edgar running around the side of the house."

"I'll go knock on the door," Kermit offered, managing to release himself from the seat belt without incident.

Destiny gathered her courage. "No, I will."

But by the time they had all piled out of the car, the front door had opened of its own accord and Daniel stepped out onto the walk. Unconstrained by any awkwardness the humans might feel, Fleur bounded over, her entire rear end whipping from side to side as she greeted him. He reached down to scratch her ears.

"We've come to take you Christmas tree hunting," Destiny informed him.

"And you can't turn us down," Sarah added, holding Psyche back as the little dachshund danced at the end of her leash, questing for Edgar.

"Why is that?" Daniel asked, his hand light on Fleur's head, his eyes shades of slate and denim in the bright light, unreadable as they met Destiny's gaze.

"Because you've got the truck!" Sarah and Kermit responded in chorus, almost boisterous from relief at Daniel's neutral tone.

"Besides, it was the only thing Mom would let me out of the house for," Sarah said. In fact, Serena had practically drooled at the prospect of forcing Daniel to spend time with Destiny. She would have joined the expedition, but fortunately for Destiny's sanity, she'd already promised to go Christmas shopping with Jesse.

"Kermit says he's just going to get a potted tree for his apartment," Sarah continued, "but we need one for me and Mom and one for you and Auntie Dess."

"I don't need a tree," Daniel said, matter-of-fact. "And it's too early, anyway. We've still got nearly three weeks until Christmas."

"I want a big one this year," Sarah said, ignoring him. Destiny almost grinned, thinking Sarah was more like her mother than she suspected. "As big as we can get in the house. We'll need your truck to carry it."

"You're not all going to fit in the Toyota."

"We're taking Auntie Dess's car, too," Sarah said. "But we can't carry two trees on it. If you don't go, I guess we just won't get Christmas. And we need some Christmas around here." She heaved an exaggerated sigh.

"I see." Daniel's expression didn't change, but he glanced at his truck, to Kermit and back to Destiny. "I'd hate to be responsible for that. I don't suppose I can refuse in good conscience to save Christmas. I'll see if I can clear my busy morning schedule."

"You better get out your day planner." Destiny dared to smile. "We brought lunch."

"There's snow up there," Sarah added. "The news said

it got down to fifteen hundred feet last night. The afternoon's scheduled for snowmen."

One eyebrow rose up Daniel's forehead. "I'd better get my jacket."

The Toyota rocked as Daniel turned off the highway onto West Ridge Road toward the Forest Service land for which Kermit had obtained their permits for Christmas tree cutting. Daniel glanced in the rearview mirror to see the VW make the turn after him, Kermit neatly avoiding the pothole Daniel had hit.

Destiny shifted beside him. She hadn't said more than two words since Kermit had insisted on driving her car so she could ride with Daniel. But then, Daniel hadn't tried to start a conversation, either.

"There's the fresh snow," he said now, pointing ahead to where white powder dusted the pines alongside the narrow road. Fortunately, the light snow had melted from the asphalt, but older drifts lined the edges of the road, banked by the plows after the snowfall two weeks before.

"It's beautiful."

They rounded a curve, and the trees suddenly fell away to their left, dropping into a steep valley curving through the jumbled Coast Range toward the distant sea. Daniel felt Destiny tense beside him. He wondered if she was reliving nearly skidding over a sheer sea cliff not long ago when a gunman had shot out a tire on her Rabbit.

He slowed around a narrow curve beneath a rocky overhang. Then again, these mountain roads were enough to jump-start anyone's acrophobia.

"I'm sorry."

The words almost startled him into looking up from the road, but he caught himself in time. "For ruining my fun-filled Saturday by dragging me out tree hunting?" The light words hurt his raw throat. "I figure it's my civic duty, keeping the three of you out of trouble for a few hours."

"No. I'm not sorry for that. I should have done this sooner. I had rope in the back of the car, in case you gave us any trouble."

A snort of laughter escaped him. "And here I thought that was for the tree."

"I'm serious."

He laughed again, the dun-grassed hills and forested green valleys that opened along the vistas before him echoing a sudden opening in his heart. "I know."

"I'm sorry for what I said the other night, outside of Mark's shop. You've been doing what you think is right, trying to protect us all. Just because I think it's stupid and delusional doesn't give me the right to call it selfish and cowardly, when I know it's not. When I know it's just your damned code of honor. And you wouldn't be you without it."

The road leveled out, ducking into a stand of trees that hid the drops on either side of the ridge they traveled. Daniel risked a glance at the woman beside him.

Raw honesty sharpened her fine-boned features, cutting him to his soul. He knew what the words had cost her, what she risked, because he, too, had given his heart to love once before and lost it.

"I was afraid," he said.

"I know." She bit her lip. "And I didn't understand that. I thought you were being overprotective because you didn't want me around—until after Sarah got attacked. And then I got mad because you were right."

The steady light in her clear, dark eyes, despite their skeptical tilt, flooded warmth into his chest. But he couldn't let her courage go unanswered.

"I wasn't just afraid for your safety," he said, steering the truck around the next set of curves, well-defined by the snow along the roadside.

"You were afraid of what I'd face from people if you were indicted for murder."

"I was, but I was also afraid—" His fingers clenched on the steering wheel. How much easier this would be if the fear were really in the past, if this drive in the mountains were a new beginning instead of possibly one of his last tastes of freedom. "I knew what would happen if the case went to trial and I were convicted. You'd stick by me. I know your capacity for loyalty."

He glanced quickly at her, then had to look away. Stick to the road. "See, I do trust you. But twenty-five years to life in a state prison, or life without parole, that would be no relationship for you."

"I wouldn't care where you were. I'd still love you."

Her fierceness caught in his throat. "I'd tell you to move on, and when you didn't, I'd feel like I was ruining your life. Your chances for love and a family. You deserve those, Destiny."

His lips curled up in a painful smile. "And if you did move on, then I knew I couldn't bear it. The slow agony of those years was worse to contemplate than the prison food. Better to get it over with."

He slowed the truck and met her gaze. "It would be easier if you stopped loving me now."

Her eyes glinted with tears, but she crossed her arms over her chest and raised an eyebrow at him. "No one ever said life was supposed to be easy."

"Destiny—"

"Mr. Dyer may be right that we can't control the fate of

others, but he's definitely right that that won't keep us from trying. Kermit and I aren't ever going to give up trying to clear your name and find out who really killed Alain. Whether you're sentenced to twenty-five to life or not."

He turned to reply, but she cut him off. "Watch the road! And listen for a minute. I know I'm not on the police force. I know all the arguments for your not talking about cases with me. But that's not going to stop me. You're the detective. It would help us a lot if you'd work with us."

She took a breath. "Kermit told me about that prescription he found with Ariel's body being from Royce Preston's clinic. Did he tell you I saw Dr. Preston at the library yesterday? Preston refused to tell me where he was the night Alain was killed. Flat-out refused."

"Destiny—" He took a breath himself, overwhelmed by how much he loved this woman and how much better it would be for his blood pressure if he didn't. "You saw what happened to Sarah. This case is dangerous. A man is dead. If Mark is right, two men. And if the coincidences are not coincidences, a high school girl, too."

"And if whoever it is isn't stopped, do you think that will be the end of it?"

He gritted his teeth, though he couldn't displace the image of the spider in its web. "It might be."

"Ha."

He banged the steering wheel with a fist. "I don't want it to end with you."

"Then let's end it with the killer."

The road flattened out again, broadening into a long parking area, the last section of plowed road. The rest of the road would be closed to all but four-wheel drive vehicles, snowmobiles, and cross-country skiers for the rest of the winter. Several SUVs and an old station wagon were already parked along the cleared area. Daniel pulled in behind a couple with three children hauling inner tubes out of the back of a Jeep.

"Whoever killed Alain is watching us," he said, the grim reality dimming the excited shouts of the youngest boy as his brother hauled him up the trail on his tube.

"Right now?" Destiny asked, sounding as concerned about his mental health as about the possibility of being spied on.

"That's not what I meant." Daniel shook his head, though the thought made the hairs on the back of his neck prickle. There had been a beige sedan far behind them, behind Kermit, for the entire drive along the highway from the coast . . . But, of course there had been. Highway 299 was the only major highway across the mountains to Interstate 5 for a hundred miles in either direction. Real danger didn't excuse paranoia.

"I mean, whoever killed Alain is keeping tabs on us. Certainly on me and on the sheriff's investigation. Probably on Kermit. Maybe on you." He could almost feel the vibrations across the strands of the web. "I wasn't joking about coming up here to keep you out of trouble. Any move we make might bring the killer down on us."

He could look at her steadily now, and he saw the shadow of fear in her eyes. Yet it didn't dim her determination.

"Are you saying you're going to keep trying to protect us?"

He wanted to laugh at the challenge in her voice. Wanted to reach for her. To hold her. To yell at her. Instead he blew out his breath and ran a hand through his hair.

"Yes," he said. He enjoyed the flash of angry red in her

cheeks, as payback for once more being forced to admit that reluctant logic had brought him to the same place that sheer stubbornness had brought her. "Yes, I'm going to protect you in the only way you've left me. You and Kermit and I are going to figure out who the hell killed Ariel Macaro and Alain Caine, and why, and we're going to nail the SOB."

The stillness in the truck cab stretched for a long moment as she processed his words.

"We'll do it my way," he insisted, as hope sparked in her eyes. "Slow and careful. If there are any risks to be taken, I take them. It's my life this guy's trying to ruin."

"Your way," Destiny agreed, much too fast. But the relief and eagerness dancing in her smile turned up the corners of his own mouth.

"There's no guarantee we'll have any better luck now than we've had before," he warned, distracting himself from the lure of her hope, the desire for her faith, his desire for her. Kissing her would only complicate the situation.

"You've got the experience. Kermit's got the badge. I've got the brains and the charm." She flashed a wicked grin. "Holmes and Watson had nothing on us."

That was it. He was going to have to kiss her. She must have seen it in his gaze, because she stopped laughing, the humor draining from her eyes to be replaced by another warm light. He reached out to touch her cheek. He'd almost forgotten the softness of it. The way the scent of her hair brushed against him as he leaned toward her.

A knock on the window behind him didn't stop him from pressing his lips to hers. Too brief. But he hoped she felt some of what he didn't know how to say.

He turned back to his window, where Kermit was grinning like a . . . like a tall, gangly cop who was getting much too much amusement from his superior's personal life.

Daniel's scowl did nothing to subdue him.

"Hey, Sarah and I'd be happy to leave you two behind, but Destiny's got the lunch."

Daniel turned back to Destiny, and she nodded, digging her daypack out from behind her seat. Daniel pulled his saw from behind his seat and joined Destiny and Kermit around the front of the truck.

Fleur charged over to join them, distributing ecstatic greetings, her thick otter tail pounding against Daniel's leg once or twice before she dashed away, hurling herself into the snow, bounding forward like a gazelle, although with somewhat less grace.

Destiny followed the Lab off the cleared asphalt to scoop up a snowball and toss it toward her. Fleur lunged up to catch it. Snow exploded from her jaws. She shook her head and barked, grinning wide, begging Destiny to do it again.

A burst of frenzied yapping turned Daniel back toward the parking area, where Sarah was hurrying toward them, trying to keep Psyche from leaping out of her arms. She finally gave up, setting the little dachshund puppy down on the road.

Psyche froze, looking down at her cold feet in surprise. But she looked up when Fleur barked again, and seeing her canine idol catch another snowball was more than she could bear. She darted toward Fleur, scrambling dauntlessly up the packed plow drift at the edge of the road. She leaped out into the expanse of white.

And disappeared.

For a brief second there was total silence. Even Fleur froze in surprise.

Then a small, caramel-colored nose poked up out of the snowbank. Fleur trotted over and poked her own nose down to meet it. Psyche barked. Fleur looked up at Destiny hopefully.

"No, we can't leave her there," Destiny said, and Fleur sighed in disappointment as Sarah scrambled over the snow berm to rescue the puppy.

Daniel joined Destiny and Kermit in following Sarah and the two dogs up the snow-covered road into the woods, the packed ruts offering the easiest walking for hiking boots. Snow glistened all around them, smooth, radiant icing across a gingerbread landscape of scattered pines, rock gardens, and burbling mountain streams.

It was little wonder the county sheriff's posse so often got called in to hunt for people lost in the snow up here, Daniel thought. In the bright sunshine, the scents of pine and snow cleansing the lungs, beauty a given, this felt like a place where nothing bad could ever intrude, a sanctuary of light and serenity.

A place where even he could forget about murder and evil for a few hours. A place off the spider's web.

Still, he glanced behind him as they wound into the trees, the chill on the back of his neck more than the cool mountain breeze.

For the most part, Alain's and Ariel's deaths remained distant shadows for the remainder of the morning and early afternoon. Destiny was determined not to allow murder to touch Sarah's enjoyment of the day, and apparently Kermit and Daniel felt the same.

Kermit started a snowball fight, which proved him an admirable tactician, but he had to surrender when he tripped over a hidden rock and fell down an embankment into a drift that swallowed him whole.

Sarah suggested snow angels, but when she dropped

backwards to start one, Fleur and Psyche tried to rescue her. She laughed so hard she couldn't breathe, and Daniel and Kermit had to lift her up out of range of the overeager dog tongues.

Only after peanut butter sandwiches and hot cocoa from Destiny's daypack did they settle into the serious business of choosing a tree.

Destiny tramped with Sarah up hills, through drifts, across creeks, letting Daniel take charge of keeping them in sight of the road, happy to lose herself in the openness of the woods, the startling silences, the physical exertion that counteracted the chill spreading from her mittened fingers and booted toes.

"There it is!" Sarah exclaimed, stopping so suddenly Destiny almost ran into her.

Destiny knew immediately which tree Sarah meant. A perfect fir perched near the top of a small, rocky ravine. Protected by its position on the slope and by the copses of larger trees around it, it grew straight and full, already decked with garlands of snow.

"It's too tall," Daniel said, coming up beside them. "And even if we can cut it on that angle, we're going to have a terrible time wrestling it down the hill to the road."

"But it's the perfect tree," Kermit said, taking the saw and sliding down the small embankment toward the tree.

"You're not going to let him use that saw?" Destiny hissed, holding her breath as Kermit slid to a stop by the tree.

Daniel grunted and followed Kermit down the slope. "You hold the tree while I cut, Kerry. You're taller." He glanced up at Sarah and Destiny. "I don't suppose anyone cares that it's at least a mile back to the truck?"

"Nobody cares," Sarah and Destiny assured him.

Although, halfway back to the truck, Destiny had to admit she cared a little, the sharp fir needles prickling through her mittens, her legs aching from battling the snow. Still, it was worth the momentary agony, struggling along beside Daniel and Kermit, Sarah periodically dropping away to leave a spray of seed for the birds or a handful of dried corn for the squirrels.

Serena had suggested they take the seed to offer in return for the forest's gift of their Christmas tree, and Destiny found she appreciated the small ritual. They hadn't found a tree for her house—just as well, now that she was lugging Sarah's—but she could get one from a lot later in the month, if . . . No. She *would* get one. And she'd set it up in Daniel's house. And they would celebrate Christmas together, no matter what else was happening around them.

As they neared the parking area where they'd left their vehicles, Destiny found the joy of the day slowly dimming. Whether it was the cold seeping into their bones, weariness from tromping through snow, or the simple recognition that they had to return home, back to a reality that hadn't grown any brighter while they were gone, all her companions seemed more introspective and subdued. Even the dogs were quiet, Fleur happy to pad along at Destiny's side, Psyche staring droopily from her cozy spot tucked in Sarah's jacket.

The sun hung not far above the lower ridge to their west, casting long shadows across the snow as they secured Sarah's tree in the bed of Daniel's pickup, the limbs clattering against the shell as they pushed it in. The long tip of the tree poked out over the top of the tailgate, so they had to tie down the shell flap.

"Mom said she'd have a fire going when we got back,"

Sarah said, tying off the last loop of rope. "And some more cocoa."

"And pizza?" Kermit asked. "You and I could stop at the Spicy Sicilian on the way to your house."

"And mulled wine," Destiny suggested, as they all started smiling again, a conspiracy to keep the outside world at bay as long as possible.

"Isn't that cooking?" Sarah asked. "Remember when Auntie Dess offered to make the dough for us to bake our own pizzas?"

Kermit and Daniel groaned. "I think I broke a tooth," Kermit said, poking a finger back into his mouth to check.

"You'd think a woman who can bake chocolate–cream cheese brownies that would tempt a saint to sin would be able to follow a pizza dough recipe." Daniel shook his head.

"Ha, ha." Destiny wrinkled her nose at them. "I make a very fine mulled wine, thank you very much, and if you don't want to try it, that just means more for me."

"Looks like that leaves me to get the tree into the house," Daniel said, groaning again.

Destiny climbed into the truck cab and set all the controls to maximum heat.

"Cold?" Daniel asked, pulling off his gloves to start the ignition.

In answer, she reached across the seat and worked her fingers up under his field coat and flannel shirt.

"Aaagh!" He grabbed her arm before she could pull away, reaching to return the favor.

"Police brutality!" She thrust her free hand over his shoulder and down the back of his shirt.

He jumped again, laughing, and pulled her close, running freezing fingers up her rib cage. She retaliated by burying her nose in the warm crook of his neck just above his collarbone. Daniel's arms tightened around her, and suddenly she was holding him, too, with all her strength, as if to close all the distance that had stretched between them since Alain's death.

She could feel him press his cheek against her hair, his low voice graveled with emotion. "I love you. Don't ever forget that."

She pulled back to meet his eyes, her own gaze steady as she reached up to touch his jaw. "Then keep reminding me."

He wrapped his fingers around hers, squeezing tightly. "I'll try."

She could see his continued fears for the future in his eyes, understood why he had no easy answers to offer. "We do pretty well when we're both trying."

He nodded. "We do."

She pulled back, the loss of his warmth a shock, despite the heat finally pouring from the dash vents. "I guess we'd better get moving before Kermit comes over to shine a flashlight on us."

Daniel grunted, putting the truck in first. "I wouldn't put it past him."

Destiny settled back in her seat, letting the warm air blow over her, her feet and fingers beginning to prickle with the return of blood flow through the outermost capillaries. The roar of the fan was almost soothing, and she stifled a yawn as the truck jolted over several slight ridges of ice, back onto the road.

Every muscle in her legs ached, and would probably ache more tomorrow. Her peanut butter sandwich had worn off long ago, and the thought of Kermit's pizza caused her stomach to growl. Beyond that, she hadn't felt so tired in she didn't know how long. But it was a good tired, a physical tired, not the emotional exhaustion that had drained her for the past two weeks.

The truck followed the road off the level ground of the ridge, and Destiny's stomach swooped at the sudden immediacy of the view as Daniel steered around the first tight curve.

She had to laugh at herself. So much for her newfound bravery facing obnoxious library patrons, death-trap elevators, and winding mountain roads. Apparently that had been depression. A single great afternoon, and suddenly she wished Daniel would take the turns about half-speed.

She hadn't felt this nervous on the way up. Of course, going downhill was always more nerve-wracking. If she closed her eyes and gave in to the warmth seeping through her bones . . .

The cab lurched as they spun around another curve, jerking Destiny's eyes open as she grabbed for the door handle to steady herself.

"Don't you think you should—" she began as she turned to Daniel, but the look on his face cut her off.

She heard the thumping of his foot against the pedal as he wrenched the wheel away from the sheer drop spinning past their bumper.

"Brakes," he said, reaching for the stick shift. "We've lost our brakes."

Chapter 20

Daniel threw the truck into first gear. The transmission screamed in protest, and the wheel bucked against his control, but the gear caught, slowing their acceleration. He jerked up on the emergency brake, shaving enough off their speed to enable him to maneuver the next turn without losing traction. The tight turn slowed them more, but only for a few seconds.

There was no guard rail on this remote mountain road. Daniel remembered all too well the small percentage of road that did not offer a fatal drop to the valleys hundreds of feet below. And there was no rise in elevation in the entire five miles of road back down to the highway.

"Put your hand on the door handle," he ordered, still pumping the brake in the futile hope it might catch. The red brake light on the dash flickered to life. *Now you tell me.* "And grab your seat belt release. Get ready to jump."

She was on the inner side of the road for the moment, the embankment rising high beside her. She'd stay on the road. But hitting the asphalt at their present speed, with the danger of striking her head on the road or the rocks . . . Better than certain death going over the cliff.

"*Daniel,* you won't be able to—"

"If I say it, do it." And confirming his respect for her

courage, she didn't argue, leaving him free to focus his entire concentration on driving.

Or hanging on.

The truck rocked around the next curve, lurching Daniel's stomach, but all four tires reconnected with the asphalt. The road leveled slightly and widened, a ditch opening on the driver's side next to the embankment, a ditch crowded with brush and saplings. And snow.

"Get ready," Daniel ordered, catching a glimpse of Destiny's pale face, hands tense on door and buckle, as he chose his spot. "If we lose traction, bail out. Understand?"

"Yes."

He eased the right wheels off the pavement into the snow. A sudden, wild, heart-lurching skid. Then the tires fell into the shallow ditch, pitching against the drifts.

Sound exploded around them, brush crashing, rocks thudding, saplings thwacking against the grill as the pickup mowed them down. Still the truck lurched forward, toward a curve out into infinity.

"Ready?" Daniel shouted, barely able to hear his own voice over the noise.

"Ready!"

Twenty-five miles per hour. Twenty-two. Seventeen. He clicked his seat belt and reached for the door. Destiny did the same.

"Now!"

He waited the long, terrible seconds it took her to force the door open against the brush. He needed to tell her to jump as far as she could, so the back wheels didn't crush her. But then she was gone. And the truck still rocked toward the curve, the tires ready to bounce back onto the road and across to the drop.

He pushed his door up against the rocking tilt of the tires

in the ditch, nothing but blue sky in his skewed perspective. The door tried to slam shut against him, but he shoved it away. His legs, aching with stress and exhaustion, gave him one last tremendous push, one chance to escape the sudden black-hole gravity of the truck cab.

Even as logic told him he could run faster than the truck was moving now, his boots hit the pavement. His legs crumpled beneath him, and he rolled, his shoulder hitting hard, but not his head.

He rolled, down the slope of the road, his bare hands scraping against the asphalt as he tried to halt his slide toward the cliff edge. He heard the crashing of the truck, but it moved past him, not over him. For a moment, the world was nothing but spinning sky and gray road. And then he stopped.

Silence. Pavement beneath him. Sky above. Waiting for pain. Hands, hip, shoulder. Ankle. He could move fingers and toes.

"Daniel!" Destiny's voice. He sent up a silent prayer of thanks.

"I'm all right." He pushed himself up onto his knees, to see Destiny running toward him across the road. He managed to rise to his feet before she reached him, his ankle screaming, but holding, to take her in his arms.

"I guess you didn't break a leg," he managed, as they pulled apart to check each other's injuries.

"I landed in a snowbank. Your face." She touched his cheek. It must have abraded against the pavement, but when she pulled her hand away, there was no blood.

"Yours, too." She had a scratch across her temple, but no swelling. It must have come from the slash of a branch, not striking a rock.

Car doors slammed, and Daniel looked up to see Kermit

and Sarah trotting toward them, Fleur sending an anxious bark after them from the backseat of the Rabbit.

"Are you two all right?" Kermit demanded as Sarah grabbed Destiny in a fierce hug. "What the hell happened?"

"Brakes went out," Daniel replied, the terse words inadequate to describe that first shock of getting no response from the pedal. He turned to look down the road, and for the first time saw that the pickup had not gone over the cliff after all. The right front tire had popped up out of the ditch onto the curve, but it hadn't had quite enough momentum to bring the back of the truck along with it.

The four of them moved toward the vehicle, almost reluctantly, as if it might suddenly roar back to life and leap past them toward the cliff.

Trying not to hobble, Daniel moved around the front of the truck. The fender and grille had been smashed in, the right door crumpled, the window broken out. Looking back up the ditch, he could see the rock the pickup had struck, denuded of snow by the impact.

"I was going to say we didn't need to jump," Destiny said, her voice remarkably steady. "But maybe it's just as well."

"Plus, another three hundred pounds in the cab might have been enough to give it the momentum to get it out of the ditch," Kermit said.

"Thanks, Kermit," Destiny said, wavering only slightly. "But I don't think I needed to know that."

"What happened to the brakes?" Sarah asked.

"I don't know." Daniel opened the driver's side door, looking down at the pedals. They were worn with age, like the rest of the truck, the faded dash, the broken radio, the frayed seats. All of it was comfortably familiar. Or had been. The black paint of the door felt suddenly unfamiliar under his hand, covering a ton of mindless, grinding metal rather than the dependable, faithful workhorse he'd driven for ten years.

"I had the brakes serviced not that long ago." Though he couldn't remember when, the adrenaline disconnecting cognition in favor of action. "Last spring."

Kermit shrugged. "Let's take a look."

Daniel reached across the seat to the glove box to pull out his flashlight, then followed Kermit around the hood into the ditch to peer under the crumpled front end.

Daniel heard the rustle of tree branches. Looking underneath the truck bed, he could see Sarah's and Destiny's legs as they unloaded Sarah's Christmas tree. He got a sudden image of the four of them stuffed into Destiny's Rabbit with the two dogs, a fir tree as long as the car on the roof, and he almost laughed. Until he shifted his weight and his ankle spasmed.

"Wait. Turn the light over here."

Daniel swept the flashlight around toward Kermit's hands, deep under the right front wheel well of the truck.

"I think I found your problem." Kermit glanced back at Daniel, his face as grim as his tone. Daniel ducked forward to get a better look at the end of the thin, black rubber hose Kermit held.

"Shouldn't that connect to something?" Daniel asked, dry investigative instincts kicking in to override the sudden lurch in his gut.

"Yep." Kermit reached out his other hand, tugged down another free end. "Right here."

"The brake line, I presume."

"Cut clean through. There are two of them, for safety in case of accidental failure. The one on the other side's cut, too."

Their eyes met. Definitely not accidental. They'd have to get a trained mechanic to go over the truck. After they dusted for prints. A formality. He wasn't going to worry about his and Kermit's already having destroyed possible prints. Whoever had done this had worn gloves.

"In my driveway back in Shell Creek?" Though he knew the answer.

"A slow leak, maybe," Kermit said. "Cut through, you'd notice immediately. Not that that's going to do you a heck of a lot of good on a road like this."

They pulled back out from under the truck, the silence of the empty sky around them suddenly thrumming against Daniel's ears. The hairs on his arms stood up.

"I guess we'd better call the sheriff's department," Kermit said.

"Did you bring a phone?"

Kermit's face was answer enough.

"Destiny! Sarah!" He kept his voice calm, practical. "Do either of you have a cell phone with you?" But he knew Destiny didn't have one. He'd been planning to get her a cell phone for Christmas, in case she got into trouble hiking in the woods with Fleur.

Sarah appeared around the back of the truck bed, her hair pulled half out of its ponytail from wrestling with the tree. "Are you kidding? With *my* mom? I'm the only kid in the entire seventh grade without my own phone."

"Get in the car." Still calm, but definitely an order. "You and your Aunt Destiny. We're heading down the mountain."

If it were just him and Kermit, he'd go back up to the parking area, check the ground where his truck had been parked, question the last few die-hard cross-country skiers returning to their vehicles, to discover if they'd seen anything suspicious. Surely whoever had sabotaged his brakes was long gone.

But he was suspended and had no gun. They had no phone, no backup, and two civilians to worry about.

"What's wrong?" Destiny asked, coming up behind Sarah as Daniel and Kermit made their way toward them along the ditch.

"I'll tell you in the car."

She met his eyes, glanced at Sarah, and nodded. "Come on." She wrapped an arm around Sarah's shoulders, turning her toward the car. "You and I get the indescribable joy of sharing the backseat with the dogs."

"What?" Sarah wailed. "It's your car! Aren't you going to drive?"

"I'm going to close my eyes all the rest of the way down the mountain," Destiny said, reaching the car door. "And you're the only one small enough to share your seat with Fleur."

"I'm as tall as you are!"

Daniel suddenly realized why the Rabbit looked strange to him. There was a fir tree precariously strapped to the top. They'd have to remove it; there wasn't time to tie it down correctly. He looked back at Kermit. "You didn't notice anything off about the VW's brakes?"

"No."

"Good. Because I'm planning to close my eyes all the way down the mountain, too." No need to mention he wasn't going to be stomping any brakes anytime soon with a bad ankle. Or that he needed time to think. His mind ran back over the drive up into the mountains, the beige sedan trailing a quarter- to a half-mile behind them on 299. Whether it was that car or another, one he hadn't noticed, someone had followed them.

And while they were out in the woods, playing in the snow, having the best afternoon he could remember in quite some time, that someone had crawled under his truck and cut his brake lines. Not Destiny's. Which indicated a wish to eliminate Daniel in particular, rather than a generalized desire to kill anyone connected with him.

With Daniel dead, the sheriff's investigation into Alain Caine's murder would not need to go any further. There would still be no conclusive proof against Daniel. The case might even officially remain open. But the investigation would be over, and everyone would know it. And there would be no one challenging Tyler Woodridge's guilt.

If Daniel died in a convenient automobile accident, the real murderer would walk away free and clear. Risky, but well-executed. Just like the murders of Ariel and Alain.

This guy was really starting to tick Daniel off.

He grabbed the top of the truck's tailgate to pull himself out of the ditch. The truck shifted under his weight, and he slipped, wrenching his ankle. Something popped, and a sudden pain shot along the outside of his arm.

With a curse, he turned to assess the damage, afraid he'd dislocated his shoulder, though the full pain of it hadn't struck him yet. In the space of a single heartbeat, he had time to see the ragged rip in the sleeve of his field coat, the blood welling through the tear, bright red against the khaki, and the thick, black end of a quivering bolt stuck into the side of his truck.

With the next heartbeat, he was struck from the side, Kermit bowling into him, the young man's gangly height more solid than Daniel would have expected. Kermit's momentum propelled them along the ditch until they sprawled full-length in the snow in the Rabbit's shadow.

"Crossbow!" Kermit gasped. He hunched to his knees.

"They don't have a long range. He can't be far. My gun's in my coat pocket in the car—"

Daniel grabbed his arm, jerking him down as another bolt struck the side of the ditch. "He's close enough."

Kermit blinked up at the bolt. "Oh. Right."

The Rabbit's door swung open over their heads as the car roared to life.

"Get in!" Destiny shouted.

"You first," Daniel ordered, pushing Kermit toward the car.

A bolt struck the door as Kermit climbed in, crawling between the seats into the back with Sarah and the dogs. Destiny ducked out of the way of his knees from her place behind the wheel.

Daniel dragged himself into the front seat, a fir limb grabbing at his head as a crossbow bolt struck the windshield. The shooter's angle was too oblique, and the bolt deflected off over the roof. But the side windows would be excellent targets when he closed the door.

"Stay down, everybody!" Daniel ordered, pulling his legs into the car.

"Psyche!" Sarah shrieked.

Daniel turned to see a caramel-colored snout pop out from behind his seat as Psyche made a break for freedom. He lurched to grab for her, but his angle was wrong. He couldn't reach her, anymore than Sarah could, trapped by Fleur's bulk and Kermit's wildly windmilling legs. He would only be able to grab Sarah to keep her from throwing herself out after the dog.

Yet just as Psyche got her back feet on the edge of the seat well, a blur of cream flashed toward her from behind. Daniel caught a brief glimpse of something fiercely protective in Fleur's warm brown eyes as Psyche's eyes widened with shock. Suddenly the puppy dangled from Fleur's firm grip on the back of her neck, and then the two dogs were in the backseat and Daniel was slamming the passenger door closed.

The car surged forward, too close to the back of his truck, too close to the edge of the curve ahead, too fast around the corner, the rear of the Rabbit nearly fishtailing behind them, the tree scraping across the top of the car. Then they were slamming into the turn of the next curve and down through a stand of pine trees and out of range of the crossbow hunter.

Daniel got his seat belt jammed into the buckle and heard Kermit doing the same behind him.

"Nice driving," Kermit gasped.

"You can slow down now," Daniel added, slitting his eyes around the next curve.

Destiny eased on the brakes, though Daniel could see her knuckles were white from her grip on the steering wheel.

After several more gut-wrenching curves, they hit a level stretch of road through the woods. Destiny briefly lifted her eyes from the road to shoot Daniel a glance.

"This guy," she said, her voice steady despite her rapid breathing, "is really starting to get on my nerves."

Daniel glanced back to catch Kermit's and Sarah's emphatic nods of agreement.

"Right." He dug through Destiny's overflowing glove compartment until he came up with a small first-aid kit. He always thought more clearly when he wasn't bleeding, and he needed to think clearly now. "Somebody's got to stop him. I don't see anybody else volunteering. Let's get started."

Daniel didn't need to add what they were all thinking. They had better stop him as soon as possible. Before he could kill again.

Chapter 21

"Hold still," Destiny ordered, patting Daniel's bare arm dry. Peeling off his makeshift dressing of gauze pads and adhesive bandages had started the blood oozing again, but the crossbow bolt seemed to have merely opened the skin along the fleshy part of his upper arm. "I don't think it did any serious damage, but you ought to get this sewn up at the hospital."

"I'm not wasting three hours in the emergency room over a little cut," Daniel said, stilling on his perch on her bathroom counter at the mention of the hospital. "Just put some cream on it and wrap it, and I'll be fine. Have you checked the expiration date on that antiseptic cream?"

She jerked the tube away from his hand. "It's fine." Antiseptic cream had an expiration date? She checked it surreptitiously. So it had been a while since she had sorted through her medicine cabinet. It was clean. And the antiseptic cream was still good.

"Hold still and let me put this on. I don't think you're going to bleed much more. But if you don't get stitches, you'll have more of a scar."

Daniel gave her a roguish grin as she secured gauze pads over his wound. "Everybody knows women think scars are sexy."

"Maybe if they don't know where they came from." Destiny raised a finger to the faint white slash on his temple that reminded her how close he had come to dying while protecting her from a sociopathic gunman just a few short months before.

Kermit snorted from the bathroom doorway. "He gets all the luck. Gunfights, crossbow attacks. He gets macho scars and I get skinned knees."

"What did the sheriff's department say?" Daniel asked, pulling on the T-shirt Destiny offered him as he pushed away from the counter.

"There was one vehicle parked on West Ridge Road when they got to the scene. A couple who'd been cross-country skiing. They were away from the parking area all afternoon, didn't see anything suspicious. The deputies questioned the landowners on the lower part of the road. They didn't notice anything unusual, either. The parking area was a wash. If there was a puddle of brake fluid, someone covered it with snow."

Skiers and hikers and inner tubers had tramped over the lot all day. There wouldn't be any useful footprints or tire tracks. Destiny knew Kermit and Daniel had expected that, but the disappointment weighed in her stomach. Especially since she knew that if she and Sarah hadn't been there, Kermit and Daniel would have found a way to secure the area, perhaps even chase down the person hunting them.

She glanced down at Daniel's stocking feet. His ankle was the size of a grapefruit. Maybe Daniel wouldn't have been chasing anyone anywhere. Regardless, they had to work from where they were now.

"What about my truck?" Daniel asked, only his wince telling Destiny he was picturing the crumpled front end and the tilted back axle. "Did they get any fingerprints? Anything from the crossbow bolts?"

"Not exactly." Kermit winced, too, his whole face wrinkling.

Daniel paused with his hand on the door frame, prepared to hobble to the living room. "What now? Just tell me they're not planning to arrest me for attempting to murder myself. I've got three witnesses who can swear I didn't fire that crossbow."

"It's more the truck," Kermit said, edging down the hall ahead of them.

Destiny could see he wanted to offer Daniel a hand and that Daniel was equally determined not to take it, though whether from pride or from a fear of bodily harm if Kermit tripped, Destiny wasn't sure.

"When the sheriff's deputies got up to West Ridge Road, the truck was gone."

"Gone?" Destiny repeated, offering Daniel a surreptitious shoulder to grab, enabling him to hop from the hallway to the couch. "There's no way anyone drove that truck anywhere. Especially not without brakes."

The memory of that wild ride shuddered up her spine, and Daniel's hand squeezed her shoulder.

Sarah entered from the kitchen with a tray of hot cocoa, Fleur and Psyche close on her heels. Serena followed with a plate of peanut butter and crackers. Destiny admired her sister's resourcefulness. She hadn't even remembered she had a box of crackers in the pantry.

More, she admired her sister's calm. Getting a call from your daughter saying she'd been involved in a shooting attempt, even a crossbow-shooting attempt, would crack the most laid-back mother's reserves. Yet Serena had not panicked, had not yelled, had not told Destiny she would never be trusted with her niece's safety ever again.

The only sign of the depth of her agitation was the tray

of cocoa Sarah carried instead of mint or ginger tea with honey. Serena never drank prepackaged, sugary cocoa and didn't believe in offering it to others. This cocoa even had miniature marshmallows floating in it.

Kermit grabbed a mug and a cracker before they even hit the coffee table.

"Nobody did drive the truck anywhere," Kermit said, lifting his peanut butter out of reach of Fleur's questing nose. "I think when the deputies found the spot where the truck had crashed into the ditch, but didn't find the truck, they figured we'd exaggerated the damage. Until they looked over the cliff on the other side of the road."

"No," Daniel said, the sudden heartache in his voice touched by resignation. "Not my truck."

"They weren't able to get a deputy to it to dust for fingerprints tonight," Kermit said. He stuffed a cracker in his mouth and spoke around it. "Maybe tomorrow if the weather holds. It's pretty far down there."

"It won't make any difference," Daniel said. "Whoever pushed the truck over the cliff undoubtedly made sure there weren't any fingerprints to be found. Most likely no crossbow bolts, either."

Nothing to encourage the authorities to look past Daniel for Alain's killer. Destiny sucked in a deep breath to settle her frustration. They would simply have to come up with something to make the authorities look. Before the killer found an opportunity to strike again.

"Daring SOB," Kermit noted.

"Stupid," Sarah said. "What if we'd had a cell phone?" She glanced at her mom to see if the remark hit home.

Serena smiled at her, her eyes narrow as a stalking cat's. "What if I hadn't let you off of restriction to go tree hunting with your aunt?"

"He's desperate," Daniel suggested. "He hasn't been able to get me indicted, and the rest of you don't have the sense to give up the search for the truth. Maybe we're getting too close for comfort."

"To *what?*" Destiny demanded, frustrated.

"To who?" Daniel amended.

"To whom?" Sarah corrected, and Daniel mimed flicking a cocoa marshmallow at her.

"The only people I've really upset in the past week are Mark Banos and Royce Preston," Destiny said.

"That you know of," her sister pointed out, a little too smugly for Destiny's liking. "We could pay Mark a visit," Serena added. "I'd be happy to question him." Her eyes shone with grim delight at the thought, but then she shook her head. "Mark knows car and motorcycle engines inside and out, and right at this moment I wouldn't trust him with my shopping list, much less my daughter's life, but I honestly don't think he has the attention span to follow you around just looking for a chance to cut Daniel's brakes."

"You're probably right," Destiny agreed, though she hoped it wasn't simply their fondness—strained fondness—for Mark speaking. "On the other hand, Dr. Preston can't even use a microfiche reader. How would he know how to cut a brake line?"

"What about Calvin Macaro?" Kermit asked. "Plenty of his clients are unsavory characters. I imagine he wouldn't have any trouble finding someone willing to do a little dirty work for him. He sure wasn't happy about Daniel believing Tyler Woodridge might be innocent. He wanted Daniel off that case."

"He's an ex-congressman," Destiny objected.

"That's right," Kermit said. "He's a congressman. A politician. And a lawyer."

"And a father," Daniel put in. "My impression of the man was that Calvin Macaro puts a lot more value on winning than on playing fair, but I don't think his devotion to his daughter or his anger at her death was an act. I can't believe he killed her."

Kermit shrugged. "She was dating the wrong guy. Going behind his back about it. Maybe he caught them together."

"So he dragged her behind a church and stabbed her to death?" Destiny asked. Her derision died as she caught the glance Daniel and Kermit shared. She didn't want to know what they had experienced that made that seem a real possibility.

"What about the other boyfriend?" Kermit asked. "Kyle Preston. I never liked his father being his only alibi."

"Kyle said Ariel told him not to come pick her up for their date at the country club," Daniel told them. "He said he drove by the Macaro house that night, but didn't stop because he saw Tyler's car. Tyler, of course, said Ariel did go out with Kyle while he went to the beach to wait for her call."

"One of them is lying." Serena shrugged at their expressions. "Somebody has to point out the obvious."

"One of the things that bugs me," Daniel said, "is the dog. Ariel's dog hated Kyle Preston. Ariel had to lock the dog in her room whenever he came to pick her up. Her father said the dog was in her room that night."

"To fool her father?" Destiny asked. It felt good to play devil's advocate, to move into the rhythm of deduction they had developed looking to discover who was trying to kill her late that past summer. Only now it was Daniel's life in danger. And it felt as if they were running out of time.

"Ariel had a red dress on," Daniel said, his eyes narrowing as he recalled the scene. "Too sexy for a Baptist youth group, but classy. Matching red pumps, matching purse. Where was Tyler Woodridge going to take her dressed like that? I don't think his mother has a membership to the country club."

"But that doesn't sound good for Tyler," Destiny pointed out. "She might have dressed to go to the country club with Kyle, put the dog up, and then Tyler came by. He must have been jealous. His girlfriend going out with her old boyfriend, dressed to the nines."

"Tyler said Ariel was worried Kyle was getting into drugs."

"That would fit in with the pot we found at the scene," Kermit said.

"Which might just as easily have come from Tyler's drug-dealing brother," Destiny countered.

"Tyler had motive, means, and opportunity to kill Ariel Macaro," Daniel admitted. "But Tyler could not have killed Alain. He was in jail at the time. Do any of you believe the two crimes are unrelated?"

He waited for all of them to shake their heads, Destiny noted, even Sarah, who was scarcely breathing at the opportunity to be involved in the conversation.

Daniel hunched forward on the couch, drawing the rest of them closer with the intensity of his concentration. "And then there are the prescriptions. There's the prescription Kermit found in Ariel's purse, written on the prescription pad of a doctor who worked with Royce Preston, though Dr. Abatas denies ever writing it. Then there's the prescription Sarah found, the one Royce Preston wrote for Rollie Garcia as a 'favor' to a professional acquaintance in the Bay Area. Another strange prescription for the ailment the patient claimed to have. And Sarah's finding that prescription precipitated Garcia's resorting to violent threats and attempted kidnapping."

"Don't forget Mark," Sarah put in, her voice strong, though she had paled at the mention of Rollie Garcia. "He was trying to buy prescription drugs from Mr. Garcia."

"Right," Daniel said. "And he didn't say he was buying the drugs. He said he was buying the prescriptions."

Destiny remembered that night, Mark's insistence that he wasn't after illegal drugs. As if holding a prescription in his hand made the manner of attaining it irrelevant.

"It's almost too bad he didn't get one," Destiny said grimly. "It would be interesting to see whose name was on the prescription pad."

"Dr. Preston?" Kermit asked.

"Or one of his associates," Daniel said. "I'd be willing to bet on it."

"You think Dr. Preston followed us up to the snow, cut your brake lines, and shot at us with a crossbow?" Kermit asked.

Destiny almost laughed at the image of stiff, proper Dr. Preston crouched in winter camo in the snow. Except the thought that was creeping into her head was more tragic than comic.

"Just because the prescriptions came from his office doesn't mean he took them," she said. "Or sold them. He could lose his license over that."

"But if someone stole the prescription pads and forged Dr. Preston's name, why would Dr. Preston back up Rollie Garcia's lie about his prescription for Dilaudid?" Kermit's face reddened. "Oh. Duh."

Daniel nodded. "He was protecting his son."

"Who has a prior conviction," Kermit said, warming to the idea. "Maybe over drugs? Now that he's eighteen, a drug conviction would show up on his record. That wouldn't be too good for his chances to play quarterback at Stanford."

"Mr. Dyer said something about Dr. Preston trying to protect his son, when I saw him at the library," Destiny said, trying to remember the context. "But then, Mr. Dyer was also talking about congressional conspiracies and what our next course of action should be if something untoward should happen to Dr. Preston."

"Would Royce Preston go as far as murder to protect his son?" Kermit asked.

Destiny thought about the man's cold, reserved expression, his dry, passionless voice. And his sudden fire when she mentioned Kyle and his connection to Rollie Garcia. "Maybe."

Silence followed that remark, until Sarah broke into it, uncharacteristically hesitant. "Kyle Preston knows how to use a crossbow."

Daniel almost laughed at the sudden click in his brain Sarah's comment caused. Might have laughed, if he hadn't felt so stupid.

"That's right," Destiny said. "I remember Gemma said something about his bow hunting."

"Garth mentioned it, too," Daniel agreed. "I should have remembered that. It's unusual enough. Very good, Sarah."

Sarah's cheeks colored with pleasure at the praise.

"That's enough." Daniel's pulse quickened with the familiar intensity he felt when the facts of a case began to fall into place. "It's not proof, but it's enough to go looking for proof. If the Prestons aren't in this up to their necks, they'd better have some very good answers ready, because I've got a few questions to ask them."

"Detective?" Kermit said, but it was Destiny who grabbed Daniel's arm before he could rise from the couch.

"You're not chasing any bad guys on that ankle," she said. Her keen eyes met his directly.

"You mean, I'm not doing any questioning without a badge," he said, only a hint of bitterness coloring his voice.

"Don't worry. I'll let Kermit do the questioning, but he's going to need backup."

"I'll call the station, Detective," Kermit said, edging toward the kitchen. "I'm sure with this new incident, Detective Dillon will be more than willing to have a talk with Dr. Preston and his son."

Daniel's jaw tightened, but he said nothing. There was nothing he could say that would not force Kermit to remind him that Ariel's murder was Ben Dillon's case and none of Daniel's official business. It wasn't that he didn't trust Ben's competence . . . Daniel forced his hands to unclench from his knees. The truth was, he *didn't* trust Ben with this. This was his life. He didn't trust anyone to handle it but himself.

These past two weeks, he hadn't trusted anyone to help him, hadn't allowed anyone to help him, and look at what a great job he'd done of helping himself.

His ex-wife, Tessa, had complained of his self-sufficiency. She still called him Robocop when she wanted to needle him. Which was pretty much every time they saw each other. Hadn't Destiny accused him of the same fault? Even before Alain's murder. He hadn't wanted to talk about his job. For good reasons. A cop couldn't discuss sensitive cases with non-cops.

But had he been protecting evidence? Or had he simply been shutting her out, not letting her get any closer to his heart and soul than she already was? What could he have told her about Ariel's murder that night that hadn't been in the papers the next morning? How much faster might he have recognized Kyle Preston or his father as potential suspects in Alain Caine's murder if he and Kermit and Destiny had been working together?

He caught his thoughts up short. None of that had anything to do with Ben Dillon's respectable reputation as a hardworking, thorough investigator. He would sit quietly here on Destiny's couch until they heard from Kermit and Ben.

However long that takes. His jaw ached already.

"I've still got that list of court cases Dr. Preston was reading up on at the library," Destiny said, distracting him from the strain of trying to pick words out of Kermit's murmured telephone conversation in the kitchen. "Mr. Dyer seemed to think it related to Kyle somehow. While Kermit goes to question the Prestons, you and I could look into these cases and see if there's some sort of evidence that could be used against the Prestons."

"Court cases." Daniel raised a skeptical eyebrow at her. Obviously, her mental picture of his waiting impatiently at her house for news was not any prettier than his.

"Mr. Dyer said he was making lists of the attorneys and witnesses for these cases. Mr. Dyer thought they were important."

"Mr. Dyer," Daniel repeated. "And while we're at it, we can check to see if there have been any recent alien abductions in the area. Maybe we're looking in the wrong place for our killer. Maybe he's gone back home to Mars."

"I'll help," Sarah offered. "I'm good at research."

"That's right. Sarah and I could go while you and Serena wait for Maddy to come pick up Psyche."

Daniel's mouth twitched at the blatant threat. "You're a

heartless woman, Destiny Millbrook."

"I try."

"Detective Dillon's out of town this weekend," Kermit announced, returning from the kitchen. "But Vance and Yap are scheduled for duty tonight. They should report in to the station any minute. I'll meet them down there, and we'll take a drive over to the Preston residence."

He grabbed his coat from the rack by the door.

"Vance and Yap?" Daniel asked. This time Destiny wasn't fast enough to catch him before he rose to his feet. "Kermit, Dr. Preston is a noted heart surgeon. This is not an assignment for cowboys."

If Garth Vance punched Royce Preston in the nose, it was not going to look good for the department. Or Daniel's own defense.

"Tom'll be there to keep him under control," Kermit said, shrugging into his coat. "And if anyone in the Preston household starts shooting crossbow bolts at us, Garth's got the best aim in the department."

"Kermit!" Even hobbled by a sprained ankle, Daniel caught him as Kermit reached the door. "The risk is not a joke," he said, all personal hope and anxiety subdued by the reality of the current situation. "Whoever attacked us today isn't just desperate. He's dangerous and resourceful. He's not going to give himself up. If our perp really is Kyle Preston, it could get ugly when you show up on his doorstep."

If he could barely trust Ben Dillon, an experienced investigator, to do his job, how much less could he trust Garth Vance and Tom Yap to protect Kermit's back? Yet, looking into Kermit's clear, steady eyes, he couldn't even voice his fear. Kermit would hear his doubt as doubt of Kermit's abilities. And if he owed anyone on the force his trust, it was Kermit.

"Be careful." It was the most he could say. Any cop would understand the rest.

"I will," Kermit assured him. Then he grinned, echoing Daniel's own words of the day before. "What could possibly go wrong?"

Chapter 22

Destiny didn't know she had been holding her breath until she passed through the glass double doors into the library entrance lobby and breathed freely for the first time in hours.

Daniel must have heard, because he gave her a rueful half-smile as they crossed the open lobby toward the elevator.

"A library is just one of those places," he agreed. "It's hard to imagine anything violent happening here."

"Maybe it's the weight of all that knowledge sitting on the shelves," Destiny said. Then laughed. "Or maybe it's just the automatic dampening of the brain cells thinking of all those students cramming for tests. Either way, I'm glad you sent Serena and Sarah back to their house with the dogs."

She'd left a message on Maddy's machine to pick up Psyche at Serena's. Destiny knew she wouldn't feel safe in her own home again until the killer stalking Daniel was caught. Two men had already broken into her house in the past three months. Admittedly, one had been Alain, but that simply showed how easy it was to do.

"Maybe it's time to get a security system," Daniel said, with that uncanny ability of his to follow her thoughts.

"I've got Fleur." Her automatic response.

The elevator doors shivered open before them, and Charlene Adams walked out, lips tight with some recent frustration.

"The library closes in fifteen minutes," she informed them as they stood aside to let her past.

Possible responses tickled Destiny's tongue, including the fact that she had written the library's most recent informational flyer, which included the open hours for all five branches in the Jasper County Library system. Instead, she nodded. "Thanks for reminding me. We'll hurry."

She registered Charlene's glance of surprise and confused suspicion as she stepped into the elevator.

Daniel hobbled after her. Ice and aspirin had reduced the swelling in his ankle, but Destiny still had no idea how he'd gotten his boot back on. The elevator jerked and shrieked, knocking him off-balance into her shoulder as they heaved upward toward the mezzanine.

Daniel braced himself against the wall and gave Destiny a wide-eyed look. "I never thought it was going to be *your* job that got us killed."

She followed him out onto the mezzanine with a blasé shrug. "If smoke doesn't pour out when the doors open, you haven't even gotten an exciting ride."

The county archives room was empty. Daniel took a seat at the same microfiche reader Royce Preston had chosen, and Destiny realized it was the only one that gave the user an unobstructed view of the door and the glass wall opening out onto the mezzanine and looking down into the library lobby.

Destiny dug Dr. Preston's list of dates and names from her jeans pocket and went to pull the relevant microfiche cards from the files.

"This is newspaper coverage of court cases we're supposed to be looking through?" Daniel asked. Even with her back turned, she could tell he was checking his watch.

"Mr. Dyer said Royce Preston was making a list of the lawyers and witnesses involved."

She double-checked the first date on her list. Flipped through several cards to see if the one she was looking for had been misfiled. It was missing. So was the next one. And the next.

"Someone's already pulled these cards."

"You sure? Maybe they just got mixed up."

She shook her head, still flipping through the cards. "Some of these are for a couple of years ago, from research Dr. Preston must have been doing when Maddy helped him, but the cards I pulled yesterday Mr. Dyer put back for me. Normally, I'd much rather do it myself than let a patron do it, but Mr. Dyer's probably even better at filing than I am."

"Better organized? That's hard to believe."

She shot him a frown at the sarcasm. "More anal-retentive. Should have become a cop."

"Should I be jealous? I know you can't resist us obsessive-compulsive types."

And when he raised one eyebrow like that, she certainly couldn't. She stuck her tongue out at him and turned back to the files.

"I can't believe he'd get this many wrong. All the rest of the ones I pulled seem to be in perfectly good order, and there was quite a pile . . . Wait a minute."

There was a group of cards stuck at the beginning of the drawer, before the first year marker in that drawer. Destiny pulled the handful of cards and flipped through them, checking her sheet.

"Here they are." She brought them over to Daniel and

set them beside the machine. Her arms prickled with unexpected goose bumps. "The whole list."

Daniel's eyebrows scrunched together as they did when something didn't make sense. "Do you think Preston came back today to do more research?"

"Could be," Destiny said. "But he would have asked for help. Any library employee would have put them back correctly."

"Maybe Mr. Dyer wasn't as careful as you thought."

"All the rest of the films I got out for Dr. Preston yesterday were refiled correctly. Only the ones on his list are in that pile. And they include dates from before the ones I pulled yesterday." She lifted the first one, and a tiny flash of color caught in the fluorescent light. An almost invisible spot of green ink. "Mr. Dyer."

She adjusted the film in the reader and spun the dials until she found the headline page of the *Jasper County Register* for the first date on her list, matched with the name Orwell Jones. "Hope Point Oyster Festival a Pearl of a Celebration" was the headline article. A blob of color marked a more prosaic title just below the fold of the first page: "Pot Bust Trial Begins."

"Mr. Dyer pulled these for me," Destiny said. "And marked the stories Dr. Preston was interested in." She smiled wryly as she remembered his parting words of the day before. "He said they'd be in good order when I needed them."

"Mr. Dyer defaced public property?" Daniel asked. "You do hang out with a rebel crowd."

"I bet the ink wipes right off with a tissue," Destiny wagered. She pulled up a chair next to Daniel. "I feel kind of honored that Mr. Dyer would let me in on one of his conspiracies."

"Let's see if we can figure out what he and Preston have come up with," Daniel said, flashing her a smile. "This still isn't going to take my mind off Kermit, Garth, and Tom, but maybe it will be more fun than pacing around your house playing tug-of-war with Fleur."

"And cleaning up after Psyche."

He grimaced. "How can any dog have a bladder that small or need to empty it so often?"

He dug around in his field coat pockets until he found a notebook and a pencil.

"Anal-retentive," Destiny muttered.

He flipped open the notebook, pretending not to hear her, and turned back to the screen. "All right. First case. A property owner and two other men arrested in southern Jasper County for growing large numbers of marijuana plants. This trial is for a Hope Point man accused of financing the operation, providing equipment and helping with the distribution."

Destiny spun the dials to find the rest of the story while Daniel scribbled quick notes.

She scanned through the article. " 'District Attorney Barger says they have a strong case . . . Defendant Orwell Jones'—that's the name Dr. Preston wrote by the first set of dates—'Orwell Jones, owner of Hope Point Salvage, has been out on bond . . . Defense attorney—"

Destiny paused, her pulse jumping. She drew in a slow, steadying breath. "Defense attorney Calvin Macaro says his client, a legitimate businessman, will be proven innocent of all charges."

Sarah sat curled in her mother's cushy recliner, eyes fixed on her well-worn copy of *The Witch of Blackbird Pond*. Psyche slept draped over Sarah's thigh like a Beanie Baby, eyes shut tight, her breathing barely noticeable.

The chime of the doorbell snapped Psyche's nose up fast enough to unbalance her, and Sarah had to catch the puppy to keep her from falling to the floor, though that didn't silence Psyche's startled yapping.

Fleur rose with slightly more dignity from her position guarding Sarah's feet, but she, too, turned toward the door with a low woof rather than her usual exuberant greeting.

"You know something's going on, don't you," Sarah murmured, putting down her book to lean over and stroke Fleur's back. Fleur turned to swipe a lick at her arm, then refocused on the front hall where Serena was greeting their visitor.

They all heard the familiar, exuberant laughter at the same time. Fleur shook out of her stiff, guarded stance and trotted toward the door, tail thumping the chair, the table, the walls. Psyche tried to follow her, but Sarah clutched the little dachshund close, taking in a deep sniff of her freshly shampooed hair.

"You had a good time, then?" Sarah heard her mother's voice as Serena led the visitor toward the living room. "I would love to have a photograph of Chad Geary snowboarding. I just can't picture him doing anything risky."

"Oh, he got more risky than that," Maddy Chance said, her voice giddy with jet lag and laughter. As she entered the living room, her hair bright as flame beside Sarah's cool, dark-haired mother, she held out her right hand with a self-conscious flourish.

Serena whistled, and Sarah leaned forward to get a better look—purely out of scientific, geological interest—at the glittering stone on Maddy's finger.

"Wow," she said, and her mother nodded.

"Wow is right. Congratulations."

"Thanks." Maddy looked down at her engagement ring, and Sarah thought her expression grew uncertain, but when she glanced back up her green eyes flashed as bright as the diamond. "Psyche!"

And then Sarah had to set the puppy on the floor. Psyche's ears flopped madly as she dashed to Maddy. The puppy danced around her mistress's feet, just out of reach of Maddy's hands, barking wildly, her tail whipping in a blur. Maddy finally caught the dog and brought her up to her face, where Psyche proceeded to lick her nose.

"You remember me," Maddy said, her joy at the reunion nearly as ecstatic as Psyche's. "What a smart puppy." She glanced up at Serena and Sarah. "Thanks so much for helping Destiny take care of her. I know she's a handful."

"She's quite a dog," Serena said, glancing at Sarah with something like empathy, though Sarah knew her mother would be glad to be able to put away the carpet cleaner when Psyche left.

"She looks great. You all took great care of her."

"Of course we did," Serena agreed. "She saved Sarah's life."

Maddy widened her eyes, glancing at Sarah, waiting for the punch line.

The telephone rang.

"I'll get it," Sarah offered, jumping up from her chair. She had been looking forward to telling Maddy about Psyche's bravery, but tonight just felt too soon, too close to letting Psyche go. She prayed the call wasn't from Jesse, looking for her mom, sending Sarah back to make small talk with Maddy. For once she got lucky.

"Is that your Aunt Destiny?" Serena called from the living room.

"It's Gemma, Mom."

"Don't stay on the phone too long. I don't want to miss Destiny's call."

Sarah didn't either, but she still grumbled into the phone, "If she'd enter the twenty-first century and get call waiting, we wouldn't have to worry about missing calls."

"Whatcha doin'?" Gemma asked, ignoring the familiar complaint.

"Sending Psyche home," Sarah said bleakly. Then she remembered that for once she had information Gemma didn't. "Your future aunt just came by to pick her up."

"Oh, yeah," Gemma said. "Uncle Chad just called Grandma to tell her about the engagement. Grandma said he was luckier than he deserved and maybe Maddy'd keep him from dying a stick in the mud like Grandpa."

Sarah rolled her eyes. "Couldn't you once pretend to be surprised when I tell you something?"

At least she'd had one adventure that day that Gemma couldn't possibly know about. She couldn't tell her friend everything, not until Kermit arrested the bad guys, but Daniel's brakes being cut wasn't a secret. "You'll never guess what happened today."

"You went to get a Christmas tree," Gemma said. "You told me you were going to do that when I called last night. But you'll never guess what happened at the game. Brian Tilson came over to talk to me and Grandma, and he asked if you were coming to the game, and Jennifer Bright was walking by, and she heard him, and she goes, 'What do you care what those geeks do,' and Brian goes, 'What's your problem, Jennifer?' and she—"

"The game?" Sarah said, her brain stuttering back to the beginning of Gemma's monologue. Something fluttered in her stomach, something much less pleasant than Brian defending her in front of Jennifer.

"Yeah. You know. Hope Point played Garfield? We should've won them big time, but we just barely squeaked by. But you haven't heard the best part. Jennifer goes, 'What's *your* problem? What, do you *like* that geek Davis or something?' and Brian goes—"

"A football game?" Sarah asked. She leaned against the kitchen counter, her breath suddenly tight.

"Well, duh." Gemma paused. "What's wrong with you?"

"Was Kyle Preston playing?"

"Sarah, he's just like the star quarterback. Of course he was playing. Not as good as usual. He had two interceptions in the first quarter. But then he started getting on track."

"What time did the game start?"

She could almost hear Gemma shrug. "Like around one?"

And lasted a couple of hours. There was no way Kyle Preston could have left the game, driven up to West Ridge Road, cut Daniel's brakes and shot at them with a crossbow.

"Was his father at the game?"

"I don't know. I wasn't looking for him."

"Gemma, I've gotta go."

"*What?* Sarah, what's going on?"

"It's Daniel's case. They might be arresting the wrong person. I'll call you back as soon as I can and tell you all about it."

"Okay." Gemma was the kind of friend who let you do what you needed to do. Sarah appreciated that about her. "I'll have my cell phone on all night."

"I'll call," Sarah promised again. She moved the receiver

toward the handset, then jerked it back to her ear. "What did Brian say?"

"He said, 'Yeah, Jennifer, I do like her. What's it to you?' "

Sarah hung up the phone, her ears burning, a crazy, dizzy smile on her lips. But she couldn't think about Brian. First she had to tell her mother about the football game and they had to get the information to Daniel and Auntie Dess.

Chapter 23

"Calvin Macaro?" Daniel asked sharply.

Destiny nodded, checking the date again. "This must have been one of his first cases after leaving Congress."

As Daniel leaned in beside her to read the rest of the article, Destiny caught the scent of snow and pine.

"Interesting." He drew the word out. "Let's look at the follow-up articles associated with that case. I didn't work on it, but now that my memory's jogged I seem to remember something about it. I think Macaro's legitimate businessman, Mr. Jones, got off free and clear. There was some problem with a warrant or something."

Destiny scrolled through the film for the next several days' papers. The *Register* followed the case closely. Daniel wrote down the names of the witnesses in his notebook, though the only one either of them recognized was Officer Garth Vance, who testified for the police. No mention was made of a botched warrant, but from the limited testimony given by the prosecution witnesses, even Destiny could see that there must have been evidence the D.A. was not allowed to introduce. Mr. Jones was, indeed, acquitted.

"Poor showing by the department," Daniel muttered, as Destiny switched the microfiche card for the next one Mr. Dyer had marked. "But that happens. Why would Royce Preston find it interesting?"

"Mr. Dyer said something about him protecting his son," Destiny said. "But this doesn't seem to have anything to do with Kyle. There aren't any high school students involved."

"What's the next case?"

"Timothy and Candace Blackwell."

The article announcing the Blackwells' trial also began on the paper's front page: "Accused in Hot Water."

" 'Tim and Candee Blackwell are accused of laundering methamphetamine profits through their hot tub sales business in Deepwater,' " Destiny read. "D.A. Barger prosecuted this case, too."

"Defense attorney?"

Destiny scanned to the next page. They repeated it together. "Calvin Macaro."

Though the alleged crime occurred across the bay in Deepwater, the county's Drug Task Force made the bust, and once again, Garth Vance was listed as a witness, along with Tom Yap and several other officers Daniel knew.

Following the course of the trial through the paper, Destiny thought the circumstantial evidence against the Blackwells appeared incriminating, but the jury apparently decided the D.A.'s case was not strong enough and acquitted them.

"I'll make you a bet," Daniel said, glancing at Destiny's list. "I bet that William P. Crockett II also hired ex-Congressman Macaro as his defense attorney."

"I'm not taking that bet." What had Mr. Dyer said about a congressman's involvement giving you a heads up there might be a conspiracy? Destiny scanned through the first page of the first article about the trial. "Another drug case. There he is. Calvin Macaro. So, we know what Royce

Preston was hunting through the paper for. He's interested in Calvin Macaro's court cases."

Intensity darkened Daniel's eyes to midnight-blue, and she knew he was as intrigued as she was, but his voice remained calm. "The question is, why?"

"The library is closing."

They both started, glancing guiltily toward the door to the archives room where Charlene stood frowning sourly at them, her clear complexion sallowed by the lighting and her pumpkin-colored blazer.

"Ms. Adams." Daniel pushed back his chair and stood, the simple gesture turning the full force of his professional charisma on the library supervisor. He strode the few steps to her, barely limping, and offered his hand. "Detective Daniel Parks, Hope Point Police Department."

"Can I help you?" Charlene asked automatically, thinking better of it a fraction too late.

"I hope so," he said, with that combination of sincerity and humor that Destiny found irresistible.

Charlene Adams was a harder sell. "The front doors are already locked. You have time to check out any materials you've already collected, and then even library employees have to leave." She shot Destiny a look. "We open again Monday morning at nine."

"I understand," Daniel said, with a complete lack of compliance. "And I would hate to inconvenience you. However, Ms. Millbrook has been helping me with some important research for an ongoing police investigation. I will probably have all the information I require within the next fifteen minutes."

"I still have Maddy's key," Destiny spoke up, moving to join them at the door. "I'd be happy to lock up for you and set the alarm if you're ready to go home, Charlene."

To her surprise, Charlene's expression wavered. Daniel pounced.

"I'm investigating a murder, Ms. Adams," he told her gravely, glancing out the door to make sure no one could overhear him. "I'm afraid the killer is still free. This information might help us to put him behind bars where he belongs. I would be grateful for your help."

Pink blossomed on Charlene's cheekbones, though her voice remained clipped. "Of course, Detective. I have to clear the rest of the library and then I have some invoices to go over upstairs. I will come and check on you in half an hour. Ms. Millbrook is competent to assist you with anything you need to find."

"Thank you," Daniel said. "We'll be out of your way as soon as we can."

He returned to their microfiche reader, Destiny a step behind, trying to decide if Charlene had meant to compliment her or not.

"I don't know how you do that," Destiny said, setting up the next card of film on the reader. "Charlene wouldn't bend the rules for her own mother."

"She seemed perfectly reasonable to me."

"Wait until you try to weasel past your allotted thirty minutes."

"We'll just have to work fast."

They did, scanning through the newspaper articles on the rest of the cases Royce Preston had listed.

"All cases in which Calvin Macaro served as defense attorney," Daniel said when they reached the final name on the list. "Most drug-related. All acquittals or mistrials."

"All clients with money to pay for their defense," Destiny noted. "All fairly high-profile cases."

"Good for Macaro's career," Daniel agreed. "The more

he wins these cases, the more he'll get hired to defend. And if he does have his sights set on the Senate or the governorship, it can't hurt to show he wins his cases."

"But he's getting criminals off," Destiny objected.

"He'd probably claim he's protecting innocent citizens from unfair accusations by police informants and drug dealers." Daniel tapped her list of names. "These aren't drifters and pushers. They're not violent offenders. He's picked his clients carefully. And if an opponent accuses him of being soft on crime, he's got his record in Congress to show. He spoke out against legalization of drugs, for the death penalty, in favor of more funding for police and prisons."

"So he's a good lawyer," Destiny said, removing the latest card from the reader. "And a skilled politician. Why does Royce Preston care? None of it is linked to Kyle Preston in any way."

"What if Royce Preston thought Calvin Macaro was the one getting his son into trouble with drugs again?" Daniel suggested.

"And he was looking for evidence that Calvin Macaro was dirty?" It made a certain kind of sense. "That still doesn't give us a motive for Ariel Macaro's murder."

"What's the last case?"

Destiny checked her list. "That's it. We're out of clues." But there was one last card in Mr. Dyer's pile. She held it up to the light, saw the tell-tale green ink.

"Maybe that's the tie-in to the little green men," Daniel suggested.

She stuck it in the reader, searching for the mark. "Another thing those cases have in common, they don't look good for the police."

"Those are, what, seven—" He counted. "—eight cases.

We do lose occasionally. I've had a couple of acquittals on cases I've investigated. A lot depends on the jury, the judge, the attorneys. Things the police have no control over."

"Problems with warrants," Destiny commented, tapping the list. "Missing evidence. Witnesses recanting their stories, accusing the police of harassment. How often has that happened with cases you've investigated?"

He didn't answer. She glanced over to see him frowning down at his notebook, his pencil checking a name here, another there as he went down his list of witnesses. His eyebrows began creeping closer together.

Destiny glanced back at the microfiche reader. A smear of green circled part of a page. It marked a calendar of community events, a list of groups meeting that day or the next.

She checked the date at the top of the page. "Daniel, this is the paper for the day that Alain died."

He didn't answer as she scrolled down the page. The headline story for the inner section of the paper described a new Native American exhibit at Pacific Coast Community College, and a blurb below the fold mentioned the time and place for the arts and crafts fair, but she saw nothing significant in either article.

She fiddled the knobs to return to the green mark. Perhaps Mr. Dyer's pen had slipped and he'd indicated the wrong page. She couldn't believe his inclusion of that day's paper was an accident. But how a list of pancake breakfasts, lodge meetings, and self-help groups related to Alain's murder . . .

Her hand froze on the knob as her eye caught the last item on the list.

"Destiny." Daniel's voice sounded tight beside her, but she didn't look up.

Beating the Addiction, the item read in bold type. *A sup-*

337

port group for teens in trouble and their parents. Meets tonight from 7:00 p.m. to 9:00 p.m. at the Calgary Bible Church. Call Edward Dyer at 555-3064 for more information.

"Destiny, all these cases that Macaro won, most of them involved the Drug Task Force."

"Mr. Dyer said he knew where Dr. Preston was the night that Alain was murdered, but that he couldn't tell me."

She had half-suspected that Mr. Dyer knew Dr. Preston had gone to the fairgrounds that night. After Kyle, probably.

"And the ones that don't involve the task force, most of them identify Garth Vance as one of the investigating officers."

In the back of her mind, she'd thought that Mr. Dyer suspected Royce Preston of killing Alain out of some crazy idea that Alain meant to sell drugs to his son.

"Two of these cases Vance's name doesn't come up as a witness, but on both of those Tom Yap's does. They were partners. If Yap worked the case, it's a good bet Vance did, too, and vice versa. Missing evidence. Just like the Ariel Macaro case. Browbeating witnesses. Just like the Alain Caine case."

But it wasn't a desire to protect his friend from prosecution that had kept Mr. Dyer silent. It was confidentiality. And it wasn't supposition. He knew for certain where both Royce and Kyle Preston were at the time Alain Caine was murdered, because they were both with him. He couldn't tell her directly, but she had no doubt that's what he meant her to learn from this paper.

"Daniel, neither of the Prestons could have killed Alain. They were at a drug addiction support group at the time he was killed."

She glanced over at him, a sick feeling pooling in her

gut. When they'd worked it out in her living room an hour ago it had made perfect sense. A reckless kid, a drug seller, maybe a killer. A father who would do anything to protect him. A trail of forged prescriptions to connect the crimes.

"Damn." She closed her eyes and shook her head as if that would change the truth. She tried a half-smile at Daniel. "At least we know Kermit isn't walking into a crossbow ambush." Another thought chased away the smile. "I hope Officer Vance keeps his temper under control. Punching a murderer isn't good, but punching an innocent heart surgeon would be really, really bad."

"Not as bad as shooting him." Daniel pushed back his chair and struggled to his feet, grabbing his notebook.

"He wouldn't shoot an unarmed man." Destiny stood, too, an unpleasant chill running down her back at the grim anguish sharpening Daniel's face.

"He almost shot Tyler Woodridge," Daniel said. He grabbed her hand to pull her from the microfiche reader toward the door. "And a dead suspect in that case might have made all the rest of this completely unnecessary. No one would have looked any further for Ariel's killer."

"What are you talking about? Wait, the cards—"

"Take care of it Monday morning."

"Daniel!" Charlene was going to kill her.

"We've got to get to Kermit. I can't trust anyone from the station to understand—"

They'd reached the door to the mezzanine and Daniel hobbled to the stairs, faster than the elevator, if more painful. His anxiety caught in Destiny's throat as she grabbed his arm to help him down.

"Understand what?" she demanded.

"All those cases that Macaro won, all that police incompetence, Garth Vance was involved. What if Macaro was paying someone to help swing the cases his way? What if Ariel Macaro found out?"

He grabbed the stair railing, steadying himself, and glanced over at her, eyes dark with anger. "Then again, Garth Vance did programs at the local high schools with Tom Yap. Who better to know about the high school drug scene? Who better to get to know Kyle Preston, help him distribute phony prescriptions, put him in contact with drug-selling drifters like Rollie Garcia? Ariel Macaro heard rumors about Kyle's drug involvement. What if she got too close to someone whose entire career could be destroyed if she discovered his drug connection?"

"Officer Vance?" The question came out on a gasp of air, as if someone had knocked the wind from her. "Daniel, that's crazy."

"Royce Preston thought something suspicious was going on with those court cases. He obviously knew his son's drug troubles were not over. Maybe he suspected Vance's involvement and was trying to collect evidence against him."

"But why would Garth Vance kill Alain?" They'd reached the bottom of the stairs. If the library had seemed a place of calm, inviting sanctuary half an hour earlier, now, empty of patrons and staff, the lighting dimmed to overnight gloom, it felt strange, shadowy, ominous.

"You're a police officer," Daniel said. "You're taking kickbacks from a drug dealer. You go to his trailer to get a payment. Instead of the drug dealer, you find a smart-ass painter with more sarcastic curiosity than good sense who not only realizes something's up, but who met you the day before and recognizes you as a police officer up to no good."

"If it was Vance, he could just say he was working undercover or something." That would cover him even if he'd already said something incriminating before he recognized Alain. Except that it was Alain. Alain, who would keep needling and teasing, even if he believed the excuse. Especially if he believed it.

He'd keep prodding and making comments until the bad cop, already on a knife's edge of nerves, considered him too much of a danger to let him live.

Destiny shut her eyes against the vivid scene, but the darkness didn't block out the pillow, the shot, the look of utter surprise on Alain's face.

"And he'd shoot him with a gun stolen from the police evidence locker," she said, her voice small and sick.

Daniel's hand squeezed her arm. "Something easy to dispose of. Or easy to leave in a field for investigators to find if he got lucky enough to turn the suspicion onto another cop."

"He'd broken up the fight between you and Alain," Destiny said.

"And he knew I was going home alone from the arts and crafts fair."

"Sarah saw him bullying witnesses at the fairgrounds."

"And he had access to the evidence in the Ariel Macaro case. He could have removed that suspicious prescription from her purse."

Destiny's skin felt cold, her breath short, as though she'd been suddenly plunged into the sea. And a shark was circling somewhere out of sight.

"Not the front doors," she said automatically as Daniel headed that direction. "No, never mind. Charlene's still here, so the security system won't be engaged. I'll just lock them up again behind us."

Hopping and using the sweeping length of the circulation desk as a crutch, Daniel set a fast pace toward the doors. Destiny stumbled after him, digging through her pockets. Doggie doo bags. Hair clip. As if a single barrette was even going to be visible, much less useful in her disastrous hair.

"Aha!" Key chain. She flipped through it, the keys rattling in her jittery hands. The library key resembled her house key, but it was the one closest to the flat brass Labrador charm near the key to the VW . . .

"Uph." She thudded solidly into Daniel's back. He'd stopped in the darkest portion of the lobby five steps from the door.

"Daniel, I can't see the keys."

She moved around him to head for the brighter light shining above the glass front doors. A light which cast an orange pallor on a nearly shaved head floating in optical disembodiment above a night-dark uniform.

Destiny suspected Garth Vance's face showed nearly as much surprise as hers did.

She could hear his voice through the glass, but the sudden buzzing in her ears muffled the words. She could read his lips clearly enough, however.

"Open the door!"

Chapter 24

Open the door. A perfectly reasonable request. A perfectly reasonable action, to unlock the doors for a police officer who had just gone out to arrest a suspected double murderer on Detective Daniel Parks's say-so.

He couldn't possibly know that Detective Parks had just convinced her that he, Garth Vance, was a cold-blooded killer and the double murderer they were looking for.

Except. Except he had come looking for them. And he didn't look happy about it.

"Damn it, open this door!"

She heard the words this time, as he reached for his belt. She couldn't seem to open her mouth to reply or to move her feet, but they suddenly moved for her, helped along by Daniel. Her arm jerked backward, and her feet followed, sending her stumbling after Daniel into the dark depths of the lobby.

Glass shattered behind them. A nightstick cracking open a man-sized hole in the doors.

Wildly, Destiny pictured Charlene's reaction to the destruction—the convulsions, the ambulance crew. "Get back, give her air!"

Then she was stumbling back behind the reference desk and into the nonfiction stacks. The bookcases ran straight back toward the wall, but there was an aisle halfway down.

She and Daniel slipped around the end of a case, out of sight of the main lobby.

"Keep your head down." Daniel's fierce whisper brought her back to herself, the sound of their breathing, the smell of dust and books, the glint of light catching the edges of the shelves.

"Come out where I can see you!" Anger frayed the edges of Garth Vance's voice. "Damn it, Parks, come out and give yourself up. You don't want to get your girlfriend hurt."

Daniel shifted, and for half a second Destiny feared he had some crazy idea that surrendering himself to Vance might actually protect her from harm. But instead he leaned in to whisper in her ear. "Fire exit?"

She gestured down the aisle between the cases, running toward the far side of the library. "Past the reference section," she breathed. "By the encyclopedias. But the door is in clear sight from the center of the lobby."

There was another door through the circulation office. If she'd been thinking, they could have darted out that way. But from their current position they'd have to pass across the open lobby to reach the circulation desk.

"What I want to know is, why'd you do it, Parks?" Vance's voice came closer now. He knew they were in the stacks somewhere. He'd move slowly, listening for their movements, but he could take all the time he needed to check each row of shelves. "A detective's salary isn't enough for you? You needed drug money, too? Mr. Law and Order himself. Isn't that perfect irony?"

"Head for the door." Daniel's whisper startled her, and Destiny realized she'd fallen into the trap of Vance's voice. "You have a phone at your desk?"

She nodded. She quashed the inner voice screaming against splitting up. If she let Daniel go, she might never see him alive again. But he was a cop. Stopping murderers was his job. And Garth Vance wasn't going to allow them to run out that fire door together. He'd follow her, and she would have to trust Daniel to stop him.

"Weapon?"

She ran a quick mental inventory of her work space. "Scissors. Metal ruler. A three-hole punch?"

She felt the whisper of his silent laughter, though she hadn't intended to be funny. His fingers tangled in her hair, and his lips brushed against her ear. *I love you.*

She reached up and gripped his hand. *Be careful.* Strange how with an armed killer stalking them they could say so much without a word, and all the words they'd said for two weeks had only kept them apart.

Daniel held her shoulder while he glanced down the aisle behind them. He squeezed. All clear. Slowly, they eased across the open aisle to the back of the next bookcase. Down the next aisle, Daniel would have a straight shot to the reference desk. Destiny would continue between the rows toward the reference section.

They could hear the creak of Vance's footsteps as he paused near the stacks. She wondered why he moved so slowly. Surely he couldn't be afraid. He was the one with the gun.

She met Daniel's eyes in the gloom. He nodded. She tensed.

"Dr. Preston spelled it all out in his suicide note."

Daniel's hand clutched her shoulder, and she barely suppressed the exclamation that rose in her throat. *Dr. Preston dead? Suicide?* Mr. Dyer's words rang in her head: *It might be good for someone else to have a list of those cases, if anything happens to Royce.*

She'd nearly laughed. Mr. Dyer and his conspiracy theories. *Just because you're paranoid doesn't mean somebody isn't out to get you.*

"He admitted to passing you prescriptions and prescription drugs to sell. Told how you distributed them through Rollie Garcia and even to high school kids. How you stole drugs from police evidence. How Ariel Macaro found out and you killed her."

Destiny shuddered at the anger in Vance's voice, the voice of a man who could kill a bright, compassionate high school student because she threatened his petty little crime kingdom.

Daniel brushed a kiss across her hair and started down the aisle toward the lobby. The reference desk lurked ten feet from the end of the stacks, a dark island in the dim illumination of the lobby. Destiny watched him ease to the end of the row of shelves.

She would have to create some kind of distraction to allow him to slip across the empty floor to the semicircular desk. She grabbed a sturdy book from the shelf beside her. She couldn't read the title on the dark cover, but she knew the layout of the stacks even in the dark. Gardening. Or maybe pets.

"His note told how he helped you shoot that artist at the fair and what you did to Rollie Garcia. Even told us where to look for Rollie's body. Not that the D.A. will need another corpse for a capital conviction. But it will be nice to have all the loose ends tied up."

Destiny heaved the book over the cases, toward the sound of his voice. It spun in the air, flapping open several cases down. It offered no danger to Vance, but made a satisfying clatter as it flopped and crashed to the floor.

She heard Vance's grunt of surprise as she scrambled back another three feet to the end of the next case, but he didn't fire. She glanced down the next aisle to catch the last dark brush of movement as Daniel rolled through the opening between the reference desk and the low work shelves behind it.

He was in. But if Vance heard him dialing the telephone, he would be a sitting duck.

"What makes you think you're going to get away with this?" Destiny demanded, her voice ringing loud in the closeness of the stacks beneath the mezzanine, then fading to nothing as it wavered out into the high-ceilinged lobby.

She turned her head as she spoke, changing the direction of her voice, hoping it would confuse Vance enough to slow him down. "Too many people are dead. There's too much evidence, even if you kill me and Daniel. We've already passed your connection with Macaro along to Chief Thomas. He'll know you killed Preston after forcing him to write that note."

An entire section of books burst off a low shelf the next row down from hers, tumbling to the floor in a great clap of noise. Vance had effectively cleared a space where he could see through the case without exposing himself. Destiny desperately scrambled back another row and darted around the end of the case, her heart pounding against her chest.

"Preston's not dead!" Vance's voice rang out, strung as tightly as her own. "He took enough Elavil and Valium to kill a horse, but he was still breathing when we got to him. He'll live. I'll make sure he lives long enough to testify against you, Parks. Damn it, I will. I don't know if you're involved or not, miss, but if you don't give yourself up, you're aiding and abetting. You'll go to jail if you don't get shot."

Destiny opened her mouth wide, trying to keep her panting breath silent. He was close enough he might hear her very heart beating.

It had been so easy to forget Vance wasn't the simple, straight-ahead redneck he pretended to be. He had her trapped. He could go to the end of his bookcase now with no fear of being ambushed. If she darted back out of her aisle into the one between the bookcases, he would have her in his sights. She could go down to the other end of the aisle, the lobby end, but he might anticipate that, might be waiting at that end for her.

But she couldn't stay where she was. He'd be on her in seconds. She had to go one way or the other. But if he was already in the aisle next to hers, if she moved, he might see the movement between the gaps in the books . . . She suddenly knew exactly how a rabbit feels when he knows the bobcat is nearby. On hands and knees, trying not to sob, trying not to breathe, she broke in the direction of the reference desk.

"Police!" The voice that rang out through the lobby sounded familiar, though Destiny could not place it immediately. "Garth! Where are you? What the hell is going on in here?"

Risking a quick glance, low, around the end of the bookcase, she saw Officer Tom Yap standing in the open space between the reference desk and the circulation desk, gun in his right hand.

She nearly cried out in relief. The cavalry! But though the library wasn't far from the police station, had Daniel even had time to complete his call? And surely the cavalry would bring more than one horseman? Where was Kermit?

The truth struck her. Officer Yap had come looking for his partner, thinking Vance would be arresting Daniel, having no idea that Vance was a killer, now a very desperate one. Vance had already killed three, maybe four, and was working on two more. Why should he balk at killing a fellow officer, even a friend?

"Tom!" Daniel's voice ricocheted from the reference desk. "Get down! Take cover! Vance killed Ariel Macaro and Alain Caine and probably Royce Preston."

"What?" Yap turned slowly toward the desk, his detached irony swept away by an expression of confusion.

Move, Destiny wanted to shout, but her voice wasn't working.

"He knows we know enough to dig up the evidence against him," Daniel said. "He can't let us out of here alive. Get out. Call for backup."

Yap took a step toward the reference desk, gun half-raised. "We're supposed to arrest you."

"He was throwing cases for Calvin Macaro, stealing evidence, selling drugs." Daniel's voice sounded as desperate as Destiny felt. "Preston found out, and Vance had to kill him, too. We can prove it. Vance said Preston's suicide note said Preston helped me kill Alain Caine, right? But Preston couldn't have done that. We can produce a witness that he was somewhere else at the time."

"What the hell is this bullshit!" Garth Vance's voice bellowed from the other side of Destiny's bookcase, flattening her to the ground. He knocked against the case as he stepped away from it. She watched his boots as they strode a yard into the lobby. If he turned back, he would see her.

"We've got him trapped now, Tom. I don't think he's armed, after all. But the SOB's nuts. I don't know what the hell he's talking about."

Destiny saw Tom Yap turn toward his partner, the cool irony firmly back in his expression, though his voice was almost gentle. "I know, Garth. I know you don't."

He raised his gun and fired.

Chapter 25

"The library looks pretty dark." Serena peered out her side window for a better view. "I think it's closed."

Sarah sat in the Subaru's backseat, one arm across Fleur's back as the big Lab pointed her nose between the two front headrests, watching where Serena was driving. Which was more than Sarah could say for her mother.

"There's Destiny's car, though," Serena continued, scanning the parking lot.

"You turn here, Mom."

Her mother glanced forward and spun the steering wheel toward the lot entrance. The car's right tires bounced across the curb.

"Auntie Dess had Maddy's key," Sarah reminded her mother as Serena pulled up beside the Rabbit. "And there's two squad cars over there. One of them's Kermit's. I guess he's already back from the Prestons'." The knowledge deflated her sense of having important information, but not her urgent interest in what had happened. "I'd still better tell them about Kyle's game today."

She opened the door, and Fleur pushed past her, stepping on her feet. Sarah grabbed the leash as it trailed by her and followed Fleur out onto the asphalt.

She heard her mother's door close behind her.

"Come on Fleur, back in the car," Sarah said. "You're

just along for the ride. No dogs in the library, even after hours. Hop in."

Fleur's tail wagged briefly, but she didn't even turn her head in Sarah's direction. She leaned forward into the leash, toward the library, and Sarah leaned back.

"We might as well take her with us to check the doors," Serena suggested. "They're probably locked, anyway. We can take her for a walk up the street while we wait for everybody to come out."

Serena started for the library entrance, and Fleur happily charged along after her, giving Sarah little choice but to follow.

The orange glow of the streetlights at the edge of the parking lot did little to chase away the shadows thrown by the bulk of the three-story library building. Sarah could see dim night lighting through the tinted windows rising up the front to the second story, but she couldn't make out anything beyond them.

As she followed her mother around the edge of the building into the entranceway, she saw that a muted light glowed above the front doors. Fleur tugged her toward the doors, and Sarah saw that the right one looked strange, not reflecting the light as the left one did. But it took her another few steps to process the difference.

"The glass is gone," she said, at the same instant her mother stopped and grabbed her arm.

"Someone's smashed it in," Serena said, leaning a step closer to look at the damage. "A break-in. I guess that explains the two squad cars out front. Come on. Back to the car. They're not going to want us messing with the evidence."

Her mother sounded as calm as her name. If Sarah hadn't glanced up, she would never have seen the flash of apprehension behind Serena's matter-of-fact tone.

"Do you think somebody went in there after Auntie Dess and Detective Parks?" The thought sucked the breath from Sarah's lungs. Someone had tried to kill them just that afternoon. What if he'd followed them to the library? What if he'd broken in and—

"Destiny and Daniel are fine," Serena said, though she pitched her voice low and pulled Sarah back a step. "Of course they're fine. They called the police. Now let's get back to the car."

"Fleur," Sarah hissed, her nerves still on edge, though relieved by her mother's logic. "Fleur, come. Let's go."

Fleur looked back at her, disappointment wrinkling the dog's face. But she shifted to follow Sarah.

Shouts rang out from the interior of the library, freezing them all. Sarah couldn't make out the words, but the anger and fear in the voices sent dread shooting up the backs of her legs. She tugged back on Fleur's leash. She didn't want those voices to find them out here. But Fleur's ears swiveled toward the library doors, and Sarah realized that one of the voices was Daniel's.

"Sarah." Serena pulled her backward, and Sarah stumbled just as Fleur jerked forward. The leash flew from her hand.

Sarah lunged after Fleur, breaking free of her mother's grasp and scrambling after the end of the leash as it whipped through the smashed door. She stepped on it, lost it, skidded on broken glass as she desperately stomped on it again.

Fleur jerked to a stop. Sarah grabbed the end of the leash before the dog could yank it out from under her foot. She glanced up past Fleur to see two figures standing in the library lobby, both more shadow than man in their dark police uniforms.

One was speaking. He raised his hand, almost in slow motion. There was a flash, illuminating the barrel of his gun, before the noise hit her, knocking her back a step. The other man toppled to the carpet.

From his position, crouched on the floor beneath the curving desk holding the reference computers, a dead telephone receiver dangling beside his head, Daniel could not see Tom Yap. However, the gap at the back of the reference desk, between the desk and the shelves of forms and supplies and interlibrary loans that formed the back of the reference librarians' work space, allowed him a view of Garth Vance's legs.

With the gunshot reverberating in his skull, Daniel watched the legs crumple, watched Vance fall backwards, heard his head strike the floor.

Daniel's first concern, before the shock, the confusion, the disbelief, was the distance to Vance's gun. Too open. Too far. His second concern was that Yap knew exactly where he was, and that Yap was less than fifteen feet away.

The plastic-handled scissors he held were not going to do him a whole lot of good.

Daniel's third concern was the only bright spot in a very dark hole. Tom Yap didn't have a clue where Destiny was. Daniel prayed she was headed straight for the fire exit.

With one part of his brain still repeating, not Tom Yap, not Tom, there's some mistake, he dropped the scissors and reached over to the shelves to heft the three-hole punch. If he could heave it at Tom from an unexpected angle, it might give him just enough time to dive back toward the stacks before Tom could get a shot—

The burst of sound that struck his aching eardrums was not the firing of Officer Yap's 9mm. It was a dog barking. A big, upset dog. Not nearly big enough. And undoubtedly not alone.

He heard Destiny's shout at the same time he rose from behind the desk, heaving the three-hole punch at the symbol of law and order standing in the center of the lobby. Despite Daniel's complete lack of skill at throwing long, awkward objects, the punch nearly struck Tom's hip as Tom spun at the sound of Destiny's voice. He stumbled sideways at the attack, even as he lifted his gun toward Daniel.

In the interminable second it took Daniel to drop back below the desk, he saw Serena tackle Sarah, driving them both through the swinging half-door through the circulation desk. Freed from restraint, Fleur dashed across the lobby, completely ignoring the homicidal psychopath with the gun to rush crying and tail-thumping into Destiny's arms.

Daniel reflected that there might be valid reasons for the dearth of Labrador retrievers being used as police dogs.

Despite the canine's distracting charge, Tom's bullet exploded through the computer monitor just to the left of Daniel's head.

"Forget it, Tom!" He shouted to hear himself over the ringing in his ears. "It's over. I've called for backup. They'll be here any second."

"You can do better than that, Detective. I disabled the phone lines."

Another bullet smashed through the plywood-thin front of the reference desk.

"It's over," Daniel repeated, despite the fact that his voice located him for Tom's aim. He could still hear Fleur's tail whacking against the bookshelves. Eventually Tom would notice it, too. "You can't kill us all. Even if you could, there's no story that would cover it. Your only hope is to run."

"No story?" There was real amusement mixed into the snapping tension in Tom's voice, a wild, edgy laughter that told Daniel all he needed to know about the likelihood of Tom's backing down. "Bad cop suspected of murder shoots and kills the heroic officer who tries to bring him in single-handed. Knowing he can't escape, he kills his family, turns his gun on himself. Everyone's heard that one before."

"That doesn't leave much room for you to play hero." Daniel ducked to the side, but Tom waited to fire.

"Hero?" Loathing warped the sarcasm in Tom's voice. "What makes you think I'd care about that? Acclaim in the department? Respect from my fellow officers? Come on, Detective. Let Vance get the glory. I don't need recognition from a bunch of self-satisfied losers. I've been laughing at you all for years. Your petty departmental politics, your petty triumphs over petty crime, your petty righteousness."

"What do you care about then?" Daniel didn't hide his scorn. He'd obviously struck a sore spot, and it might keep Tom talking. "Not honor, not respect, not loyalty. It's not like you need the money."

Tom laughed again. "That's the great thing about rich parents. No one questions a fast car or a hot tub. No one's even thought to find out if I even really have parents, much less rich ones. There is no way I'm going to end up like my father, Detective, dying poor after a lifetime of hard, honest work because the American Dream has become a joke. Hey, if CEOs can steal their way to the good life, why not Tom Yap?"

He was walking as he spoke, circling toward the entrance to the reference desk. Once he reached it, he'd only have to step forward a few feet to get a clear shot at Daniel.

"The thing is, it was all so easy. Stealing drugs at the scene of the bust, selling them back to the dealers. Getting in on the teen drug scene. They're creative little bastards. Like Kyle Preston and his father's prescriptions. That was all his own idea. I just helped him make the connections. Sabotaging cases for Calvin Macaro. I explained what a sleeze he was to the daughter, you know, the dumb bitch, to convince her to keep her mouth shut about Kyle's extracurricular activities, stupid SOB couldn't handle it himself, but she was so holier-than-thou it was enough to make you sick."

Daniel had two choices. Charge Tom from the reference desk entrance or dive over the top of the desk in the opposite direction. Neither of them gave him good odds. But the frontal attack at least sent him in the direction of Garth Vance's body—and Garth Vance's gun.

"Killing was easy, too. Easier than you'd expect. And so easy to get away with. The hardest part was aiming that damn crossbow I borrowed from Kyle. Poor kid had no idea I was using it to frame him. I should have stuck to my gun instead of getting fancy."

"You botched Royce Preston's suicide." Destiny's voice rang defiantly from the stacks, still too faraway from the emergency door. "Officer Vance said he found him alive."

Daniel cursed silently at her bravado, but Tom only laughed, apparently content to save killing her until after he finished with Daniel. "That unfortunate state of affairs can be easily remedied at the hospital."

Daniel crouched at the very end of the desk counter, calves and thighs tense. Another couple of steps . . .

A sudden screech of metal rent the open silence of the lobby. It took Daniel a long second to identify the rattling, shaking rumble from the end of the nonfiction stacks nearest the circulation desk. The elevator.

"Charlene!" Destiny cried out.

He'd completely forgotten about the library supervisor, working on her invoices on the second floor. He heard Tom's footsteps change, moving back toward the elevator.

Without giving himself time to think, he propelled himself forward, out into the open space between the reference desk and the stacks. But Garth Vance's body wasn't where he'd expected. It was five feet farther toward Tom and the elevator.

Tom caught the movement of Daniel's desperate lunge and turned. Daniel had no choice but to let his momentum carry him forward into the stacks, one, two, four bullets smacking into books and ricocheting off the metal shelves above his head.

Easy enough for Tom to reload when necessary, since he had the only weapon.

Rolling forward, Daniel got his feet under him, gasping at the pain in his injured ankle, and pushed ahead to the gap between the stacks running parallel to the back wall. Destiny and Fleur hit the same gap from two rows down at the same time he did.

He gestured. She nodded, turned, and ran, Fleur on her heels like the hounds of hell, for the reference books and the exit. He turned and ran the other direction, toward the elevator, though with his jerking, awkward stride there was no way he would reach it in time to do anything for poor Charlene Adams.

A bullet blew past in front of him. Tom was running parallel to him at the other end of the row of shelves, firing down the aisles.

As they neared the elevator, Daniel stopped his headlong rush. Letting Tom charge ahead of him, he spun down the nearest aisle, coming out five yards behind Tom just as the elevator doors shrieked open.

They both had barely a moment to register that the elevator car was empty before Tom spun around to face Daniel's charge.

A loud crash beside them caused Tom's aim to hesitate, Daniel just catching a glimpse of a shattered microfiche machine below the mezzanine as he ran. A gunshot exploded in his ears an instant before his lowered shoulder struck Tom's midsection.

Destiny hit the emergency exit bar with both hands, the sudden jangling rattle of the alarm drowned by the gunshot that rang out at the same instant.

With her back exposed against the expanse of door, she waited for the pain, but none came. She turned. At the other end of the lobby, she saw two forms struggling on the ground in front of the elevator.

She couldn't tell which was on top. Couldn't tell if the shot she'd heard had struck Daniel.

She hesitated only a second. Daniel wanted her to go for help, but the alarm would bring the fire department and the police. And surely Serena and Sarah had escaped out the employee entrance to the circulation office by now and were running for reinforcements.

Her legs betrayed her momentarily, wobbling as she started back toward the elevator, but Fleur knew where she was headed and pulled her forward into a steady run.

The distance seemed endless, time stretching out as dark and untouchable as the two-story rise to the lobby ceiling. She had a moment of astonishment at seeing Garth Vance struggling to his feet, swaying like a zombie from a B horror movie, and then she was past him, Fleur lunging toward Daniel and Officer Yap.

Destiny saw that Daniel sat on top of Yap, both hands

wrapped around the wrist of the hand that held Yap's gun, leveraging it down to the ground while Yap pounded at Daniel's face with his left fist.

Fleur took one side and Destiny the other. She stomped down on the fingers wrapped around the gun. But she thought it was Fleur's 150-decibel bark in his ear that caused Yap to release his grip on the weapon.

Destiny snatched it up from the floor, the gun's grip strange against her palm, the rubber still warm from Yap's hand. A wave of revulsion swept through her, unexpected, as if she held a poisonous serpent in her hand, death itself.

She looked down at Officer Yap, both his arms now pinned beneath Daniel's. Fear and hate glared up at her, bright even in the dim shadows. He had killed Alain. Taken someone she had once loved out of the world. Taken an artist and a young woman with a glowing future. All for . . . What? Money? A sense of power? To prove his cleverness?

He had tried to kill Daniel. Would have killed her. And still she didn't feel the hatred that burned in his eyes. All she felt was exhaustion and disgust.

She pointed the gun at his head. The barrel twitched, the serpent alive in her hand. Maybe she was deluding herself about the hatred she didn't feel. She didn't much care.

"Are you all right?" she asked Daniel, though her eyes remained locked on Yap's, promising him that if he moved, she would pull the trigger. From the corner of her eye, she could see Fleur giving him the same look from Yap's other side. "Did he hit you?"

"No. You?"

"No. That last shot. I thought he must have . . . ." Her voice shook, but her hand never wavered.

"He never got off that final shot," Daniel told her.

"It hit my leg," Yap ground out, his voice so coiled with

fury it was unrecognizable. "If you don't get the hell off me, I'm going to bleed to death."

"Sounds good to me."

Destiny's finger nearly jerked on the trigger in surprise at the voice coming from behind her shoulder. She lowered the gun, shaking, even as she turned to see Garth Vance beside her, definitely standing, though he leaned with his hands on his thighs.

"Nice shot, Garth," Daniel commented.

"Sorry it took so long to get it off. I didn't want him to notice me moving."

"Grab his police piece, would you?"

As Vance bent down, Destiny saw why Daniel had not yet allowed Yap to move. Yap still wore his police weapon in his belt holster. The gun she held must be a throw-down weapon, unregistered perhaps, or stolen from the police evidence locker. A gun he'd meant to put in Daniel's hands after killing her and Vance.

"He shot you," she reminded Vance, as Daniel rolled Yap to his stomach, wrenching the man's arms behind him to cuff him with his own handcuffs.

"When he sent me to arrest Detective Parks, he warned me over and over again that Parks'd be armed and dangerous."

Probably hoping Vance would get trigger-happy and save Yap the trouble of cleaning up his own mess, Destiny thought.

Maybe Vance figured that, too, because his lip curled in anger and disgust. "Detective Parks isn't as good at the range as me, but he's been in a firefight before. I never have. I put on my vest. I think the impact bruised a rib, but the damn thing works."

"You put on a vest for me?" Daniel asked, wincing as he

got to his feet. "I'm honored, Garth."

"My leg," Yap reminded them, face turned sideways from the carpet.

"Go ahead and bleed to death." Vance lifted his boot, thought better of it and kicked the floor. "You bastard. We were *partners*."

Yap laughed, an unpleasant sound that shook his torso as he rolled to his side. He quit moving when a low rumble began in Fleur's throat. "Why do you think I agreed to work with you, Vance, when everybody else thought you were a loose cannon, a loser? So I'd have an idiot for a fall guy if I ever got caught."

Vance's face reddened, and Destiny saw his hand clutch Yap's gun. But then he shrugged, managing a bark of laughter himself. "I guess being a loser isn't so bad. Better than being so clever you're lying on the floor with a bullet wound in your leg and looking at a death sentence."

Daniel bent back down and grabbed Yap's left leg. Destiny could see the dark stain spreading across the officer's lower thigh. Daniel pulled a utility knife from his pocket and cut open Yap's uniform slacks.

"I don't think Vance hit an artery," he said. "I guess you'll make it to trial, after all."

"Is it safe to . . ." The tentative voice from the staircase paused, tried again with a thin attempt at authority. "It's all right to come down now?"

Charlene stood with her hand on the stair rail, her face white enough to glow in the dim light, but her back was ramrod straight, her chin firm.

"You can come down, Ms. Adams," Daniel told her, voice equally authoritative and professional, respectfully ignoring her fear. "You sent down the empty elevator?"

"I came down the back stairs to see if you were finished

in the archives room." She descended to the bottom step, but stopped with a hand still on the rail for support. "I heard shots and shouting. I tried to call 911, but the phones were out. I could see what was happening down here from the mezzanine. I thought the elevator might provide a distraction."

"It did," Daniel assured her. "And the microfiche machine was perfectly timed. I may owe my life to your bravery. We all may."

"Oh." The color returned abruptly to Charlene's face. She lifted her hand from the rail, thought better of it, and sat abruptly on the stairs. But her face beamed.

Daniel looked up, toward a noise at the front doors. "Ah. It looks like the cavalry has finally arrived. Late, as usual."

Destiny turned to see Kermit striding across the entrance lobby, Officer Grace Martinez close on his heels. Fleur saw Kermit, too, and before Destiny could prevent it, the Lab leaped over Yap's head and charged over to her soul mate, nearly knocking him to the floor.

"You never save any of the fun for me," Kermit complained, wrestling Fleur back down to her own feet. She must have seen the professional look in his eye, because she sat obediently at his heel. "Even the dog gets more busts than me."

But there was no echo of his lighthearted comments in his eyes as they took in Yap's prone form.

"He took my patrol car," Kermit said, voice cold. "When we found Preston and the suicide note, I knew something was off, but I didn't know what. Tom wouldn't let me come with Garth to tell you what had happened. He told Garth my friendship with you would be a liability. He called for another unit to come with the EMTs, and then had them 'escort' me back to the station. Hinted I might be your accomplice. No one would listen to a word I had to say until Serena and Sarah arrived to get help."

"I listened," Grace told him.

"Lieutenant Marcy didn't."

"Lieutenant Marcy's an—" Grace swallowed her comment. "The perp's bleeding."

Destiny saw the flash in Yap's eye, knew he'd recognized Grace's pejorative term for the deliberate thrust it was. Yap was no longer a police officer in his colleagues' eyes. He was just another low-life suspect.

"We need to patch him up before we move him," Daniel agreed.

"I'll get a kit from the car," Grace said. "But there's an ambulance on the way. They can transport him. You want me and Kermit to ride with him, Detective?"

"Yes. Stay with him until he's safely incarcerated. He's dangerous."

"Got it."

Destiny almost smiled. And Daniel was a detective again. Not that Kermit or Grace had ever thought he wasn't. But Daniel had.

He met her gaze, clear-eyed, controlled, confident. She glanced away so he wouldn't see the tears in hers. But she heard the stiff, trying-not-to-limp stride as he moved to her side.

"Why don't you give me the gun, Millbrook," he suggested, taking it from her fingers, cramped around the stock. He handed the gun to Kermit, grabbed Fleur's leash and, putting an arm around Destiny's shoulders, turned her toward the door.

"Where are you going?" Kermit demanded.

"To the station to give our statements," Daniel said.

"And then we're going home."

"We've got work to do!" Vance gestured around the library. "Evidence to collect. Witnesses to question."

"Get to it," Daniel recommended with an almost beatific smile. "And call Ben Dillon back from his vacation. I'm still on administrative leave."

Epilogue

"What do you think?" Destiny climbed down the stepladder and shifted it out of the way of the tree. The star she'd just fixed on top still tilted forward, despite the extra rigging of twist-ties she'd used, but it shone brightly, echoing the cheery fire in Daniel's fireplace.

Daniel gave the thickly decorated fir an appraising look from his seat in his recliner, eggnog in hand, his ankle raised high on a pack of ice cubes, though Destiny thought that was more to get out of tree decorating than because the ankle was still swollen. She'd finally gotten him into the emergency room after their stop at the police station the night before, and the X rays had shown nothing broken.

"Well?" she asked, gesturing at the tree.

"It looks like someone tied it the wrong way to the top of a VW Rabbit and punched the accelerator up to seventy."

Destiny grabbed her own mug of eggnog off the coffee table and stepped back, careful to avoid Fleur and Edgar stretched side by side in front of the fire. She paused by Daniel's chair for a better look at the tree. "Besides that."

Daniel's hand grabbed her elbow, pulling her down to sit on the arm of his chair. He wrapped an arm around her waist. "I remember saying I didn't want a tree."

"It was too tall for Serena's living room." Not that they'd tried to set it up there. Serena had only needed one look at the poor, beat-up tree to be sure it wouldn't fit—even with trimming.

"It's had time to recover a little," Destiny observed. In fact, to her eyes, the tiny colored lights shining through the bare spots and reflecting in Daniel's tall windows created the effect of a galaxy of stars, close enough to touch. And the sap from the broken branches they'd removed filled the room with the fragrance of snow-filled woods. "I think it's beautiful."

"Me, too."

She glanced behind her to see Daniel's eyes on hers, reflecting the firelight.

His expression was thoughtful. "I was wrong about not wanting a tree. I'm going to need it."

She took his cup and set their eggnog down on the table before leaning back into his lap. "I'm sorry about Tom Yap."

His arms tightened around her. His voice was low, but hard. "I'm sorry about Ariel Macaro, Alain Caine, and even Rollie Garcia."

Destiny shuddered. The Jasper County Sheriff's Posse had found Garcia's body in a shallow grave off a logging road where Royce Preston's "suicide note" had indicated it would be. Dr. Preston was still in serious condition at County General, but he had been lucid enough to confirm to police that Tom Yap had forced him to write the note and take the overdose of pills by threatening to have his son, Kyle, indicted for Ariel Macaro's murder.

Kyle had admitted to taking Ariel out the night of her murder. Unnerved by her suspicions of his drug-selling activity and wanting to impress her with a story of working undercover for the police, he had arranged for her to meet Officer Yap. Unfortunately for Ariel, she had asked too many questions and Yap's exposure of her own father's courtroom machinations had only increased her determination to learn the truth of the situation.

Yap had decided she was a liability. He had also rightly assumed that witnessing her murder would shut Kyle's mouth and keep him too frightened to back out of their arrangement.

Destiny could not turn herself back into the person she had been, upset about Daniel's refusal to discuss the Macaro case. Since then she had nearly lost him to a car crash, a crossbow attack, and a gunfight in the library.

As long as he was alive, she could keep working on his other quirks. Life gave her the opportunity for patience and forgiveness, for herself as well as for Daniel. Something she had never truly been able to give Alain.

"I'm sorry," Daniel said, brushing the hair back from her cheek. "I'm sorry the last memory you'll have of Alain is me threatening to kill him." When she turned her head to meet his gaze, he gave her an apologetic grimace. "Even if he did deserve it."

She shook her head, caught by the tears threatening her eyes. "I feel guilty. I've been so worried about everything else, I've hardly thought of him."

"You haven't had time to grieve."

Laughter choked on the sorrow in her throat. "What are the stages of grief again? I've gotten as far as anger. He could be such a pain in the ass in life. And he was even more trouble dead."

Daniel's smile held a reflection of her own pain. "I think Alain would have liked that."

Destiny turned in the chair to wrap her arms around his shoulders, burying her head in his neck. She could have lost him, as easily as Alain. Could still lose him, to death, to fear, to pride, or even simple careless neglect. "Daniel—"

"I'm not Alain." He whispered it fiercely against her hair. He had to stop reading her mind like that. "I'm not going to leave you."

She leaned back to meet his gaze with her own fierce emotion. "Even if I'm inconvenient? Even if I bug you about your cases? Even if Fleur chases your cat?"

Fleur lifted her head from the fireplace rug, glanced at Edgar and thumped her tail before sighing back into sleep.

"Fleur helped you save my butt. She's got a free pass for the next week or so. And as for you—" His blue eyes drew her in with their dark intensity. "I knew you were going to be inconvenient from the moment I met you."

Considering that the first time they'd met she'd walked into his police station saying she'd been murdered, she could hardly argue with him.

"If you weren't inconvenient, I'd probably be out of a job right now, even if I wasn't in prison, and Tom Yap would still be on the loose. I guess I can learn how to share my day with you without passing along confidential information."

His fingers brushed her temple as he repeated, "I'm not Alain Caine. I'm not going to run away from you because you're independent, intelligent, incorrigible or inconvenient. Those are the reasons I fell in love with you. Your inconvenience is not going to frighten me now."

Destiny tried out his raised eyebrow trick. "That almost sounds like a dare."

His own eyebrow danced. "Try me."

She pushed herself off from the back of the chair, but he grabbed her arm before she could get up.

"Where are you going?"

"I'm going to go get a toothbrush out of my bag and put it in your bathroom."

He tugged on her arm, pulling her back down into his lap. "Oh, no, you're not."

"No?"

His eyes widened in mock horror. "Let you unpack your bath bag in my bathroom? I'll never find my sink again under all that stuff. No. *I* will unpack your bag while you call your sister to thank her for our tree. You'll find your toothbrush in the toothbrush holder, and that's where I expect it to stay."

She met his gaze, letting the warmth flow through her, easing away the doubts and fears and terror of the past two weeks. In Daniel's eyes she could see reflected the fire, the starlike dance of the Christmas tree lights, and the deeper, warmer, truer light of her love shared with his.

"That's all right," she told him. "It can wait until after."

"After what?"

She let the warmth ease her into his lap as she melted her lips across his.

"Oh." And he kissed her back.

About the Author

Tess Pendergrass grew up in a small town on the northern California coast where she spent countless hours enjoying long walks in the woods in the rain with her dog.

Tess and her menagerie, including Fleur's inspiration, Amsel, currently reside with Tess's own hero in Alabama where they are learning all about exotic entities like sunshine and wild turtles.